PRAISE FOR
THE GIRL FROM WIDOW HILLS

"A hauntingly atmospheric and gorgeously written page-turner, *The Girl from Widow Hills* is a deeply thought-provoking, riveting mystery about the complex weight of history and the dangerous power of the lies we tell ourselves."

—Kimberly McCreight, *New York Times* bestselling author of *Reconstructing Amelia* and *A Good Marriage*

"Sleepwalking is creepy. You're asleep, but you're walking through the night—like the living dead. I knew when I started *The Girl from Widow Hills* I was in for some shivers. But I had no idea the terrors that were in store."

—R. L. Stine, bestselling author of Goosebumps and Fear Street

"With Hitchcockian flair, Megan Miranda shrewdly examines what becomes of the people at the center of those rare, sensational news stories that capture the nation's attention. *The Girl from Widow Hills* gave me the creeps in the best way possible."

—Chandler Baker, *New York Times* bestselling author of *Whisper Network*

"Miranda flaunt[s] her considerable talent for jaw-dropping, yet believable, twists. Even jaded readers might not see this one coming. An unusual heroine anchors this creepy, fast-paced chiller. This is Miranda's best book yet."

—*Kirkus Reviews*

"Miranda, a best-selling author of thrillers for both adults and YAs, sprinkles the present-day narrative with transcripts and reports from Olivia's past, building suspense with startling plot twists that lead to a stunning climax. Another compulsive page-turner from an accomplished author."

—*Booklist*

"This is a great whodunnit, done well. Olivia/Arden narrates, but Miranda (*The Last House Guest*) creatively uses media transcripts, newspaper reports, book excerpts, and voicemails to piece together her fragmented story that ends with a chilling twist."

—*Library Journal*

"Psychological thriller fans will enjoy the ride."

—*Publishers Weekly*

"*The Girl from Widow Hills* is a creepy, compelling portrait of a life forever warped by unwanted fame, a timely theme in this era of internet celebrity and the fall from grace that often follows. . . . It's a shivery kind of fun to wonder along with Olivia whether those close to her should be trusted or feared, and to urge her on as she races to unravel the past without unraveling her sanity."

—*Bookpage*

"The small-town cast is drawn in shrewd, suspicion-arousing detail; you'll point fingers at someone new every few pages."

—*Martha Stewart Living*

"With chilling twists and turns, this book will keep you captivated in the sand."

—*BookBub*

"If you can relate to your past coming back to haunt you, then this book is for you."

—*PopSugar*

MEGAN MIRANDA

THE GIRL FROM WIDOW HILLS

POCKET BOOKS

New York   London   Toronto   Sydney   New Delhi

Pocket Books
An Imprint of Simon & Schuster, LLC
1230 Avenue of the Americas
New York, NY 10020

This book is a work of fiction. Any references to historical events, real people, or real places are used fictitiously. Other names, characters, places, and events are products of the author's imagination, and any resemblance to actual events or places or persons, living or dead, is entirely coincidental.

This Pocket Books paperback edition February 2024

POCKET and colophon are registered trademarks of Simon & Schuster, LLC

Simon & Schuster: Celebrating 100 Years of Publishing in 2024

For information about special discounts for bulk purchases, please contact Simon & Schuster Special Sales at 1-866-506-1949 or business@simonandschuster.com.

The Simon & Schuster Speakers Bureau can bring authors to your live event. For more information or to book an event, contact the Simon & Schuster Speakers Bureau at 1-866-248-3049 or visit our website at www.simonspeakers.com.

Manufactured in the United States of America

10 9 8 7 6 5 4 3 2 1

ISBN 978-1-6680-3508-5
ISBN 978-1-5011-6544-3 (ebook)

For my family

PROLOGUE

I WAS THE GIRL WHO survived.

The girl who held on. The girl you prayed for, or at least pretended to pray for—thankful most of all that it wasn't your own child lost down there, in the dark.

And after: I was the miracle. The sensation. The story.

The story was what people wanted, and oh, it was a good one. Proof of humanity, and hope, and the power of the human spirit. After coming so close to tragedy, the public reaction bordered on rapturous, when it wasn't. Whether from joy or pure shock, the result was the same.

I was famous for a little while. The subject of articles, interviews, a book. It became a news story revisited after a year, then five, then ten.

I knew, now, what happened when you turned your story over to someone else. How you became something different, twisted to fit the confines of the page. Something to be consumed instead.

That girl is frozen in time, with her beginning, middle, and end: victim, endurance, triumph.

It was a good story. A good feeling. A good ending.

Fade to black.

As if, when the daily news moved on, and the articles ended, and the conversations turned, it was all over. As if it weren't just beginning.

THERE WAS A TIME when I knew what they were after. Reaching back to that cultural touchpoint, whenever someone would say: *The girl from Widow Hills, remember?*

That sudden rush of fear and hope and relief, all at once.

A good feeling.

I HAVEN'T BEEN THAT girl in a long time.

CHAPTER 1

Wednesday, 7 p.m.

THE BOX SAT AT the foot of the porch steps, in a small clearing of dirt where grass still refused to grow. Cardboard sides left exposed to the elements, my full name written in black marker, the edge of my address just starting to bleed. It fit on my hip, like a child.

I knew she was gone before I woke.

The first line of my mother's book, the same thing she allegedly told the police when they first arrived. A sentiment repeated in every media interview in the months after the accident, her words transmitted directly into millions of living rooms across the country.

Nearly twenty years later, and this was the refrain now echoing in my head as I carried the box up the wooden porch stairs. The catch in her voice. That familiar cadence.

I shut and locked the front door behind me, took the delivery down the arched hall to the kitchen table. The contents shifted inside, nearly weightless.

It clattered against the table when I set it down, more noise than substance. I went straight for the drawer beside the sink, didn't prolong the moment to let it gather any more significance.

Box cutter through the triple-layer tape. Corners softened from the moisture still clinging to the ground from yesterday's rain. The lid wedged tight over the top. A chilled darkness within.

I knew she was gone—

Her words were cliché at best, an untruth at worst—a story crafted in hindsight.

Maybe she truly believed it. I rarely did, unless I was feeling generous—which, at the moment, staring into the sad contents of this half-empty box, I was. Right then, I wanted to believe—believe that, at one point, there had been a tether between my soul and hers, and she could feel something in the absence: a prickle at her neck, her call down the dim hallway that always felt humid, even in winter; my name—*Arden?*—echoing off the walls, even though she knew—*she just knew*—there would be no answer; the front door already ajar—the first true sign—and the screen door banging shut behind her as she ran barefoot into the wet grass, still in flannel pajama pants and a fraying, faded T-shirt, screaming my name until her throat went raw. Until the neighbors came. The police. The media.

It was pure intuition. The second line of her book. She knew I was gone. Of course she knew.

Now I wish I could've said the same.

Instead of the truth: that my mother had been gone for seven months before I knew it. Knew that she hadn't just disappeared on a binge, or had her phone disconnected for nonpayment, or found some guy and slipped into his life instead, shedding the skin of her previous one, while I'd just been grateful I hadn't heard from her in so long.

There was always this lingering fear that, no matter how far I went, no matter how many layers I put between us, she would appear one day like an apparition: that I'd step outside on my way to work one morning, and there she would be, looming on the front porch despite her size, with a too-wide smile and too-skinny arms. Throwing her bony arms around my neck and laughing as if I'd summoned her.

In reality, it took seven months for the truth to reach me, a slow grind of paperwork, and her, always, slipping to the bottom of the pile. An overdose in a county overrun with overdoses, in a state in the middle of flyover country, buried under a growing epidemic. No license in her possession, no address. Unidentified, until somehow they uncovered her name.

Maybe someone came looking for her—a man, face interchangeable with any other man's. Maybe her prints hit on something new in the system. I didn't know, and it didn't matter.

However it happened, they eventually matched her name: Laurel Maynor. And then she waited some more. Until someone looked twice, dug deeper. Maybe she'd been at a hospital sometime in the preceding years; maybe she'd written my name as a contact.

Or perhaps there was no tangible connection at all but a tug at their memory: *Wasn't she that girl's mother? The girl from Widow Hills?* Remembering the story, the headlines. Pulling out my name, tracing it across time and distance through the faintest trail of paperwork.

When the phone rang and they asked for me by my previous name, the one I never used anymore and hadn't since high school, it still hadn't sunk in. I hadn't even had the foresight in the moment before they said it. *Is this Arden Maynor, daughter of Laurel Maynor?*

Ms. Maynor, I'm afraid we have some bad news.

Even then I thought of something else. My mother, locked up inside a cell, asking me to come bail her out. I had been preparing myself for the wrong emotion, gritting my jaw, steeling my conviction—

She had been dead for seven months, they said. The logistics already taken care of on the county's dime, after remaining unclaimed for so long. She would no longer need me for anything. There was just the small matter of her personal effects left behind to collect. It was a relief, I was sure, for them to be able to cross her off their list when they scrawled my address over the top of all that was left, triple-sealing it with packing tape, and shipping it halfway across the country, to me.

There was an envelope resting inside the box, an impersonal tally of the contents held within: *Clothing; canvas bag; phone; jewelry.* But the only item of clothing inside was a green sweater, tattered, with holes at the ends of the sleeves, which I assumed she must've been wearing. I didn't want to imagine how bad a state the rest of her clothes must have been in, if this was the only thing worth sending. Then: an empty bag that was more like a tote, the teeth of the zipper in place but missing the clasp. There once were words printed on the outside, but everything was a gray-blue smudge now, faded and illegible. Under that, the phone. I turned it over in my hand: a flip phone, old and scratched. Probably from ten years earlier, a pay-as-you-go setup.

And at the bottom, inside a plastic bag, a bracelet. I held it in my palm, let the charm fall over the side of my hand so that it swung from its chain that once had been gold but had since oxidized in sections to a greenish-black. The charm, a tiny ballet slipper, was dotted with the smallest glimmer of stone at the center of the bow.

I held my breath, the charm swinging like a metronome, keeping time even as the world went still. A piece of our past that somehow remained, that she'd never sold.

Even the dead could surprise you.

In that moment, holding the fine bracelet, I felt something snap tight in my chest, bridging the gap, the divide. Something between this world and the next.

The bracelet slipped from my palm onto the table, coiling up like a snake. I reached my hands into the bottom of the box again, stretched my fingers into the corners, searching for more.

There was nothing left. The light in the room shifted, as if the curtains had moved. Maybe it was just the trees outside, casting shadows. My own field of vision darkening in a spell of dizziness. I tried to focus, grabbing the edge of the table to hold myself steady. But I heard a rushing sound, as if the room were hollowing itself out.

And I felt it then, just like she said—an emptiness, an absence. The darkness, opening up.

All that remained inside the box was a scent, like earth. I pictured cold rocks and stagnant water—four walls closing in—and took an unconscious step toward the door.

Twenty years ago, I was the girl who had been swept away in the middle of the night during a storm: into the system of pipes under the wooded terrain of Widow Hills.

But I'd survived, against all odds, enduring the violence of the surge, keeping my head above water until the flooding mercilessly receded, eventually making my way toward the daylight, grabbing on to a grate—where I was ultimately found. It had taken nearly three days to find me, but the memory of that time was long gone. Lost to youth, or to trauma, or to self-preservation. My mind protecting me, until I couldn't pull the memory to the surface, even if I wanted to. All that remained was the fear. Of closed walls, of an endless dark, of no way out. An instinct in place of a memory.

My mother used to call us both survivors. For a long time, I believed her.

The scent was probably nothing but the cardboard itself, left exposed to the damp earth and chilled evening. The outside of my own home, brought in.

But for a second, I remembered, like I hadn't back then or ever since. I remembered the darkness and the cold and my small hand gripped tight on a rusted metal grate. I remembered my own ragged breathing in the silence, and something else, far away. An almost sound. Like I could hear the echo of a yell, my name carried on the wind into the unfathomable darkness—across the miles, under the earth, where I waited to be found.

**TRANSCRIPT FROM PRESS
CONFERENCE**

OCTOBER 17, 2000

We are asking for the public's assistance in locating six-year-old Arden Maynor, who has been missing since either late last night or early this morning. Brown hair, brown eyes, three feet six inches, and approximately thirty-eight pounds. She was last seen in her bedroom on Warren Street outside the town center of Widow Hills, wearing blue pajamas. Anyone with information is urged to call the number posted on the screen.

CAPTAIN MORGAN HOWARD

Widow Hills Police Department

CHAPTER 2

Friday, 3 a.m.

HEARD MY NAME AGAIN, coming from far away, cutting through the darkness.

"Liv. Hey, Liv." Coming closer. "*Olivia*." The scene sharpened, the voice softened. I blinked twice, my vision focusing on the row of hedges in front of me, the low-hanging branches, the light of a front porch glowing an eerie yellow through the leaves.

And then Rick's face, the white of his shirt as he turned his body sideways and angled himself through the line of vegetation dividing our properties. "Okay," he said as he approached, hands held out like I might spook. "You okay?"

"What?" I couldn't orient myself. The chill of the night wind, the dark, Rick standing before me in a T-shirt and gray sweatpants, the skin wrinkled around his eyes, callused hands on my arms near my elbows—then off.

I took a step back and winced from a sting on the sole

of my right foot, the pain jolting through the fog. I was outside. Outside in the middle of the night and—

No. Not this. Not again.

My reflexes were too slow to panic yet, but I understood the facts: I'd come to in the wide-open air, bare feet and dry, itchy throat. I took a quick tally of myself: a sharp pain between two of my toes; the hems of my pajama pants damp from the ground; palms coated with grit and dirt.

"All right, I got you." Hands on my shoulders, turning me back toward my house. Like an animal that needed to be led back inside. "It's okay. My son, he used to sleepwalk sometimes. Never found him outside, though."

I tried to focus on his mouth, on the words he was saying, but something was slipping from me. His voice was still too far away, the scene too dreamy. Like I wasn't entirely sure I was back from wherever I'd been.

"No, I don't," I said, the words scratching at my throat. I was suddenly parched, desperately thirsty. "It doesn't happen anymore," I said, my feet rising up the front porch steps, a tingle in my limbs, like the feeling was returning after too long.

"Mm," he said.

It was true, what I'd told him. The lingering night terrors, yes—especially around the anniversary, when everything felt so close to the surface. When every knock at the door, every unknown caller, made my stomach plummet. But the sleepwalking, no, it didn't happen anymore. Hadn't since I was a child. When I was younger, I'd taken medicine, and by the time I'd stopped—a forgotten dose, then two, then a prescription that had not been renewed—I'd outgrown the episodes. It was a thing that had happened in the past. A thing, like everything that came before, that was left behind in another life, to another girl.

"Well," he said, standing beside me on my front porch, "seems like it does, my dear." The porch light cast long shadows across the yard.

Rick put his hand on the doorknob, but it wouldn't turn. He jostled it again, then sighed. "How'd you manage that one?" He looked at my empty hands, like I might have a key lodged in my fist, then narrowed his eyes at the dirt under my nails, his gaze drifting down to the blood on my toes.

I wanted to tell him something—about the things my subconscious was capable of. About survival, and instinct. But the evening chill finally registered on a gust of cool wind, goose bumps rising in a rush. North Carolina summer nights, the altitude could still do that. Rick shivered, looking away as if he'd be able to see the cold coming next time.

"Do you still have a key?" I asked, crossing my arms over my stomach, balling up my hands. He was the original owner of both his lot and mine, and I'd bought this house directly from him. Rick had designed it himself. At one time, it had been occupied by his son, but he'd left town a few years back.

Rick's face tightened, the corners of his lips pulling down. "I told you to change the locks."

"I'm getting to it. It's on my list. So do you?"

He shook his head, almost smiling. "I gave you everything I had."

I pulled at the door myself, imagining this other version of me. The one who must've walked out the entrance but managed to lock the handle behind her before pulling it shut. Muscle memory. Safety first.

The porch beams squeaked as I walked to the living room window. I tried lifting the base, but it, too, was locked.

"Liv," Rick said, watching me peer in the darkened window, hands cupped to my eyes. I hadn't flipped a single light switch inside. "Please get the locks done. Listen, my son's friends, they weren't all good, not all good people, and—"

"Rick," I said, turning to face him. He was always seeing another version of this place, from years ago, flushed out long before I'd arrived. Before the hospital came through, and the construction, and the shiny new pavement and chain restaurants and people. "If someone was going to rob me, they probably wouldn't wait over a year to do it." He opened his mouth, but I held out my hand. "I'll change them, okay? Doesn't help with the situation right now, though."

He sighed, and his breath escaped in a cloud of fog. "Maybe you got out some other way?"

I followed him down the porch stairs and stepped carefully through the grass and weeds as we paced the perimeter together, as if we were following the ghost of me. My bedroom window was too high to reach from the slope of the side yard, but it appeared secure. We tried the back door, then the office and kitchen windows—anything within reach.

Nothing was disturbed, nothing gave an inch. Rick looked up at the set of beveled glass windows from the unfinished attic space on the second floor, frowning. The windows were partly ajar, leading to a small balcony that was purely decorative.

I fought back a chill. "I think that's a stretch," I said. The upstairs was mostly unused, empty space, anyway, except for the single wooden rocking chair left behind, which was too large to maneuver down the stairs—as if it had been built in that very spot and was now trapped. A single bulb hung from the center of the exposed-beam ceiling, the only place you could stand fully upright between the slanting eaves.

There was one narrow stairway up, tucked behind a door in the hallway. The space was too enclosed, too dark, every one of my senses elevated. From up there, you could hear the inner workings of the house: water moving through the pipes, the gas heater catching, the whir of the exhaust fan. I rarely went up there, other than to keep it clean. But any time I did, I'd gotten into the habit of opening those windows immediately after climbing the stairs, just to get through the task.

I'd heard if you were ever trapped underwater and didn't know which way was up, you could orient yourself by blowing out air and following the bubbles—a trail to safety. The open window worked much the same. If I ever needed it, I'd feel the air moving and know which way was out.

I must've forgotten to close them after the last time.

But a jump from up there would've done a lot more damage than dirt on my hands and a scratch on my foot.

Rick shuffled his feet, and it was only then that I noticed he was barefoot, too. That he'd heard me or seen me in the night and rushed out to help before grabbing his own shoes, or a coat. He circled to the back entrance of the house, and I followed.

"My son, he used to keep a key . . ." He bent down to

the bottom rail of the wooden steps. Fished his fingers into the splintered hollow. Pulled out something coated in mud. He placed a hand on his knee as he straightened again, then handed me the metal with a crooked grin. "Still here, I'll be."

I slid the key into the back door, and it turned. "Hallelujah," I said. I handed the key back to him, but he didn't take it.

"Just in case," I said. "Please. I'll feel better knowing you have a copy."

He was frowning when I placed it in his open palm, but he slid it into the pocket of his sweatpants. He looked like a different person in the night, without his jeans and flannel shirt and his beige work boots laced tight, regardless of the fact that he had long since retired from his job as a general contractor. He had just turned seventy earlier this year, his hair a shock of gray over a deeply lined face—all proof that he'd spent decades out in the sun, building his own life by hand. He still tinkered around in his shed, still told me if I ever wanted to finish the upstairs space, we could do it together. But apart from his typical attire, he seemed smaller now. Frailer. The contrast was unnerving.

Rick entered the house first and flipped the light to the kitchen, peering around the room. The wineglass had been left in the sink. I felt the urge to straighten up, prove I was taking care of this place. That I was worth it. He was soft-spoken but perceptive, and his gaze kept moving, to the arched entrance, to the dark hall.

Rick was the one I'd gone to when I'd found a baby bat hanging from my front porch in mid-daylight; when there'd been a snake at the foot of the wooden steps; when I'd heard something in the bushes. He'd said the bat had probably gotten lost, then he'd used a broom to urge it along; he'd declared the snake harmless; he'd told me to stomp my feet and make noise and act bigger than I was to scare whatever might be watching. Most of the wildlife had been driven farther back with the development over the past couple of years, but not all of it. Things got lost. Things staked their claim. Things stood their ground.

He was looking over the house now as if he could see its past remaining. Different people inside, with a different history. He twisted the gold band on his ring finger with his other hand.

"I heard you yelling," he said. "I heard you."

I closed my eyes, searching for the dream. Wondered what I'd been calling into the night. Whether it was a noise or a name—the word on my tongue, in my memory, as my eyes drifted over the bare kitchen table. The box of her things tucked out of sight in my bedroom closet now, where it had been stored since it had arrived two days earlier.

"I'm sorry," I said.

"No, no, don't be." His hands started to faintly shake, as they seemed to be doing more and more now. The tremors, either from the start of illness or from craving his next drink. I didn't ask, out of politeness. Same way he didn't ask about the marks on my arm even though his gaze would often linger on the long scar, eyes sharp before cutting away each time.

He raised his trembling fingers to my hair now, pulling a dead leaf from a spot above my ear. It must've gotten caught as I walked through the lower-hanging branches between our properties. "Glad I found you," he said.

I shook my head, stepping back. "I used to. I used to

sleepwalk. I don't anymore," I repeated, like a child who didn't want it to be true.

He nodded once. The clock on the microwave said it was 3:16. "Get some sleep," he said, pulling the back door open.

I had to be up in less than three hours. It was pointless. "You, too."

"And lock up," he called as the door latched shut behind him, the silverware drawer rattling. His bare feet made hardly any sound as he walked down the back steps.

Now I peered around the house like Rick had done, like I was looking for signs of an intruder. Holding my breath, listening for something else that might be here. Even though it was just me.

I trailed my fingers down the wall of the dark hallway as I headed for the bedroom door, gaping open at the other end. I flicked the switch just inside. The sheets were violently kicked back, pulled from the corners of the mattress. A chill ran through me. The scene looked familiar—the aftermath of a night terror. Though I hadn't had one in years. My childhood doctors had attributed the episodes to PTSD, a result of the horrors of those three days trapped underground.

It was the box on the shelf of my closet, I decided. My subconscious, triggered by that almost-memory—of the cold and the dark—that may have been real, but maybe not. That same nightmare I used to have as a child in the years after the accident:

Rocks, all around, everywhere my hands could touch. Cold and damp. An endless darkness.

I used to wake from the nightmare feeling that even the walls were too close—kicking off the sheets, throwing out my limbs, pushing back against something that was no longer there. The fear lingering in place of the memory.

I remembered what my mom used to do back then. Hot chocolate, to calm me. The pills, to protect me. A hook and eye on the top of my door, for night. A rattle, the first line of defense, so she would wake. So she would stop me this time.

I turned back for the hall, and the glow from the bedroom lit up the wood floor. A few drops of blood trailing down the hall. I couldn't tell whether that had happened before I left the house or just now. I followed the trail, but it stopped at the entrance to the kitchen again. On the left, the hall forked off to the kitchen and another bedroom, which I used as my home office; on the right, the arched entrance to the living room led straight to the front door. There was no sign of blood anywhere else. Just this hall.

I sat on the living room sofa, examining the cut on my left foot. Something was wedged between my first two toes. A splinter, I thought at first. But it was too shiny. A small piece of metal. No, it was glass. I pulled it out with my nails and held it to the light, narrowing my eyes, to be sure.

It was small and sharp, coated in dirt and blood, impossible to tell the original color. I looked around the room, searching for something that had been broken. A vase on the coffee table; a glass mirror over the couch; a lamp on my bedside table. But nothing appeared damaged or disturbed.

I kept going, room by room. Checking upstairs, even, though I kept nothing fragile there. The stairway didn't have a light switch, and I felt my way through the dark, trailing my hands along the narrowed walls. The moonlight slanted through the open windows, and the shadow of the rocking chair came into focus. I reached up for the chain to turn on the light, but when I pulled it, nothing happened. I felt around the space above my head, but there was no bulb attached to the base. Now I couldn't remember if there ever had been.

A chill ran through me from the gust of cold air funneling into the room. I pulled the window doors shut, latching the hook between them—there was no screen, a bird could've gotten in.

When I looked out into the night from this height, my stomach dropped. I backed away quickly, heading downstairs before the panic set in, resuming my search. Checking the shelves, the windows, counting the cups in the cabinets, peering into the garbage can. Growing restless and increasingly panicked as the minutes ticked by.

Searching for signs of what I had done in the dark.

She's a tiny little thing. Well, you've all seen her picture by now. Big brown eyes and all that hair. She was just standing there in the middle of the street, in the dead of night, outside my kitchen window. This was before she went missing. Maybe a month or two back. My daughter was sick, so I was getting her a glass of water. Spooked me at first, seeing someone standing out there, watching back. Until I turned on the porch light and saw it was her. I called out to her from the front door, but she didn't answer. I knew who she was, knew her mother. Knew where they lived. It's not that far, not even a mile, probably. But she must've walked all that way barefoot, in the dark. Had to cross three or four streets between her house and mine—I'm just grateful there aren't many cars out that time of night.

I walked up to her and said her name again,

but she just stared right through me. There was nothing behind her eyes.

MARY LONG
Resident of Widow Hills

CHAPTER 3

Friday, 6 a.m.

HADN'T GONE BACK TO sleep, too high on the adrenaline, trying to understand what had happened during the blank spots of my mind.

But everything seemed calmer in the daylight. The sliver of glass could've come from anywhere. Outside, maybe, from any time in the past. A forgotten shard rising up from the dirt in the rain; the earth turning over.

The disorientation and panic, a side effect of waking up outside with no understanding of how I'd gotten there. A biological reaction. I had to keep busy, keep occupied. Keep my mind from drifting back to the contents of the box in my closet. The sweater. The phone. The bag. The bracelet.

I took a long shower, focusing instead on the pressing matters of work: the quarterly report for the hospital and the unyielding budget that required department cuts to be made—and it would be up to me to give an opinion on the matter. Two years in, and I was still proving myself.

My alarm went off while I was getting dressed, and when I silenced it, I noticed a text that had come through late the night before, just after midnight.

A quick drop of my stomach at Jonah Lowell's name. Even now. Every time. *Thinking of you.*

Of course. Unprompted, after months of silence, waiting until I'd successfully excised him from my thoughts. Of course, in the middle of the night, when I could picture him in his living room, hair disheveled, feet propped up, bourbon beside his laptop.

Last I'd heard from him was three months earlier, in May, when he'd texted: *Will you be in town for graduation?*

A slippery slope with him.

Back in May, I'd responded on impulse, had slid into an ongoing conversation, an endless flirtation. I'd been talked into a visit. I knew better now.

With the distance, it had been easy to forget why it hadn't worked.

To be fair, I was here in Central Valley, with my current job, because of Jonah. He'd been my grad school professor in health care management initially, was coming here on a temporary consulting assignment, and there would be a spot for me in the group if I wanted it. I was in even before I knew the details: It was a newer hospital in a rural area, necessary to the surrounding communities but still looking to find its footing—and its funding. It had been having trouble getting doctors and nurses to come and then stay.

Central Valley really was halfway from one place to the next, but not close enough to either extreme to commute. The college was too far to the east, and no one but the skiers heading west came out this far. On the map, this town

was a pit stop. A bathroom break between the outer edge
of a larger town and the mountain lodges.

I'd come because I thought I was in love with Jonah
back then. But I'd stayed because I was fully in love with
the place instead.

When the hospital offered me a full-time role, I accepted. It was good for my résumé, a higher position with
more autonomy than I'd land at a larger facility, and I'd
already recruited a lot of the staff.

Most of the doctors and nurses were young. Not en-
trenched in a community with their families but free of
the roots that held them in place, willing and hungry for
an opportunity.

Central Valley was a town that had transformed itself
around the hospital, that existed in its current form because of it. All shiny new and built over a rural stretch of
land, with the best of both worlds. It was a young town,
and I was young.

The town center was self-contained and self-
sufficient. It provided and fueled itself in a closed
loop. The old Victorians getting fresh coats of paint,
renovated porches, new landscaping. On the outer
arch: apartment complexes with glass-walled gyms and
mostly empty playgrounds. I'd lived in one such building myself when I first arrived, in housing provided by
the school.

It was so different from where I was from, seven hours
to the west. Widow Hills, Kentucky, was perfectly nice,
with tree-lined streets and cookie-cutter houses that
backed to the woods, but nothing new had come to the
area in at least two generations. It seemed no one wanted
to put a business in a place called Widow Hills.

Nothing bad had happened in Widow Hills to give it the name. It was, up until my accident, a very safe place to live. At least that's what the articles all said.

Living in Central Valley required more of an active process. It attracted a certain type of person, outdoorsy and weatherproof. Who would trade convenience for adventure. Stability for curiosity.

But *here*. *Here*, I told the potential hires, you could ski and hike and tube down the river. *Here*, you could discover something—about this place and yourself. *Here*, you could be the person you always imagined you might be.

Say it enough, and you might convince yourself, too.

Every day on my way in to work, I'd pass a house with a for-sale sign in the yard. Every day I caught sight of something new as the leaves changed and fell. A bird feeder. A balcony from a second-floor window. A set of slate stepping stones through the open grass field.

Something about it called out to me. Reminded me of the ghost of that first house, with my mom and me. Before the cameras and the money. Before the move to a generic suburb with a white picket fence—the first in a series of steps that would bring us several states north but eventually circle us back to nowhere.

When the consulting assignment was finished, and I accepted the job but lost the subsidized housing, the first place I thought to call was the number on that sign.

Jonah had seen it once when I'd first moved in, laughed under his breath, and declared I'd gone full-country. I said I was only a handful of miles from the town center, as the crow flies. He said the fact that I now used the term *as the crow flies* only proved his point.

I'd spent enough of my time unraveling the things he

said and meant. Trying to decide whether it was a critique of me or of him. Whether his words meant anything at all other than a way to pass the time.

I dressed early for the day. Slipped on my shoes. Tied my hair in a quick bun. Cleaned the blood from the crevices of my wood floor on my way out.

I decided to ignore the text.

THERE WAS A TWENTY-FOUR-HOUR grocery-slash-convenience store three blocks from the hospital, where my road intersected with the rest of civilization—one of the few places native to the town. It was called Grocery and More, and there was no name more fitting. Here, you could get dinner and packing tape; a magazine and a box of nails; Advil and wine. The owners understood the importance of a twenty-four-hour one-stop shop when servicing hospital personnel with nontraditional hours.

It was just barely before seven a.m. when I pulled into the lot. There were a couple of cars scattered throughout, but nothing like the afternoon crowd.

Inside, there was faint classical music playing. It was a time warp not only in that you could never tell what time of day it was in the bright fluorescent-lit interior, but also because of the layout. There was a spinning rack of chips beside an aisle of unfinished lumber and hardware. Fruit and ice cream in refrigerated bins around the corner. A coffee station next to the checkout area. One clerk working the early shift, watching a TV behind the counter, which was tuned to an old black-and-white western with the sound off. He tipped his head to me when the door soundlessly swished closed, sealing us back inside.

I picked up a basket beside the entrance and went straight for the hardware aisle. The sleepwalking was probably a one-time thing, but it wouldn't hurt to add a lock.

Everything was a balance: A few extra seconds spent unhooking this lock in a fire could be deadly. But so could turning on the stove in my sleep. Walking into the road. Getting hit. Getting lost. Falling.

The hook-and-eye latches were buried under a mismatched assortment of locks and hinges, but I finally got one in my basket. I'd just turned out of the aisle when I collided with another shopper.

"Oh—"

"Shit, sorry," the other woman said.

Our baskets had caught, and we set them on the ground to disentangle them.

She hadn't looked up yet, but I recognized her. Almost-white-blond hair pulled back in a ponytail, sharp angled cheekbones. Someone from the hospital, but she was out of uniform, and it always took my mind another second to catch up. Scrolling through a list of faces, removing the stethoscopes, the name tags, the scrubs. This was Dr. Britton in the emergency department. Sydney. "Hey. Hi, Sydney. Sorry about this."

She stood slowly, her basket hooked on her arm, indentation already forming in her pale skin, weighed down by the microwave lasagna and the bottle of red. "Liv? God, I'm sorry. I didn't even notice it was you." She raised her arm slightly, the basket swaying. "Just getting off work. I make no excuses."

She eyed my basket—empty except for the hook-and-eye latch—and then rubbed her eyes with her free hand. "Sorry, if I don't get out of here soon, I'll crash before the

microwave finishes. And I've got a marathon of *Law &
Order* waiting for me."

"Enjoy," I said. Then I turned down the next aisle,
spent a few moments trying to remember the type of liquor in Rick's cabinet. Settled on a bottle of dark rum that
looked the same shape and shade—as a thank-you, and as
an apology.

I stopped for a coffee before paying.

"Quite the eclectic basket you've got here," the checkout clerk said. He was cheerful and soft and of indetermi-
nate age, somewhere between twenty-five and forty. But
his smile was contagious, even this early in the morning.

He scanned the hook-and-eye lock, rang up the coffee
I'd just poured myself beside the counter.

"Hey, it's your store," I said. I, too, made no excuses.

He laughed once, loud and sharp, then paused at the
liquor, looked from the bottle label to me, then back.
"ID?"

I pulled it from my wallet, and he took it from my
hand, squinting.

Something fell in the aisle behind me. The sound of
boxes tumbling off their stack. I turned, smiling, expecting to see Sydney, clumsy with fatigue. How you can get
with lack of sleep. Disoriented. Slow to react. But instead
I saw a man in jeans and a short-sleeved button-down,
ball cap on, tuck himself away behind the spinning rack
of chips.

My smile fell, my shoulders tensed.

I thought, from the way he seemed to be watching,
that maybe it was someone I knew. But there was something else. A long-cultivated instinct.

It was the way he was standing—half-hidden—that

made my skin prickle. The way he turned back to the chips, spinning the rack but looking at nothing. A feeling I hadn't gotten in a long time: a feeling that meant they were looking for me.

It made sense: On the ten-year anniversary a decade earlier, the journalists had come out of the woodwork. In supermarket aisles, outside the high school entrance, resting against the side of our neighbor's house. Manifesting from structures all over town like something out of a horror movie.

I'd been sixteen, a junior in high school. I saw my English teacher interviewed on the news, saying I was a good kid, a solid student, a little quiet, but who could blame me. My mom went on a talk show—it was an offer we couldn't turn down, she said, though I refused to join her. They showed our new house on the news. Blurred out the numbers, as if that mattered. Used my picture from the yearbook.

I received letters of every type, from every sort of person, for the next six months.

We were praying for you—

Wow, you grew up nice—

Think you can just ignore the people who helped you, ungrateful bitch—

It was part of the reason we'd moved again—this time to Ohio. Part of the reason I'd changed my name. So I could start fresh as an adult. Enter college as someone new. The gift of being a person with no history.

The twenty-year anniversary was less than two months away. Would there be more media coverage, regardless of whether they tracked me down? Was it still of public interest, all these years later?

"Have a good day, Olivia," the clerk said, pulling my attention. My ID was in his outstretched hand. I slid it back into my wallet, then peered over my shoulder again, but the man was gone.

"Thanks," I said to the clerk, keeping my head down as I strode for the automatic-exit doors.

He was there. Outside, waiting. Leaning against a blue car parked next to mine. Unwrapping, on the hood of his car, a breakfast sandwich that didn't seem like it had come from the store. "Hey," he said, all nonchalant, taking a bite. Taking his time.

The lot was otherwise empty. I unlocked the door, but kept the keys in my hand, an old instinct rising.

He chewed and swallowed, pointing his sandwich at me. "I know you," he said.

"Don't think so," I said. He had the air of a journalist, if not the look. Not the clothes and not the car, from what I was accustomed to. But the way of casually lingering, pretending he hadn't been waiting just for me.

"Olivia, right?"

I was already shutting the driver's-side door. Mentally working through the moves to escape, tallying the seconds to get away. The time to start my car and accelerate out of the lot versus the time it would take him to do the same—and follow. I didn't second-guess myself. I'd been born with a healthy dose of self-preservation, and I'd learned to trust my gut.

In my rush to leave, I didn't give him another glance. Couldn't say what he looked like if asked, other than: guy, white, average height and build. Perhaps he'd known my name to start, or perhaps he'd just overheard the clerk inside.

Whatever he was after, I didn't have to speak—I knew that by now.

But how easily he could topple everything I'd built. The comfort of anonymity. All that I'd run from in Widow Hills. Here, the scars just scars—*surgery after an accident*, I always said, and that wasn't a lie. My name was my legal name now. I stuck to the truth: *Moved here from Ohio for college; fell out of touch with my family; came into some money when I was younger.*

None of these things were lies.

People tended to fill in the blanks however they wanted. It was not my job to correct them.

Yes, I found her on my porch once. I worked the six a.m. shift that day, had to leave just after five. My dog was barking, and it was still dark when I opened the door, but there she was. I remember I said, "Honey? Is your mom okay?" Because I couldn't remember her name.

She turned around and walked back home. I didn't realize she was sleeping.

I wish I'd told someone, but I didn't know.

STUART GOSS

Resident of Widow Hills

CHAPTER 4

Friday, 8 a.m.

THERE WERE MANY BENEFITS to working in a hospital, in theory. Access to doctors and nurses, a behind-the-scenes look at how things worked, personal connections to book an appointment last-minute.

But what you gained in accessibility, you lost in privacy. Since I'd been with Central Valley Hospital, I visited doctors less, not more. The times I'd been sick, I'd stopped at the Minute Clinic instead. The doctors and nurses were people I saw every day. And I'd have to give a medical history, a personal history. I shuddered at the possibility of old details somehow making it into their system. Where they might notice that my arm had to be reconstructed and then fixed again as I grew, that there was a lack of full mobility due to the buildup of scar tissue around my shoulder. Where they might wonder why.

After the story ended, after the fade to black, these were the things that didn't fit onto their carefully constructed page: the trauma of surgeries; the long process of recovery; the questions from the curious; the feeling of always, always being watched.

All I needed was a sleeping aid, possibly, to keep me in deep sleep. An easy remedy. Harmless.

The entrance to the hospital looked like a rich but rustic hotel, with log-cabin beams crisscrossing the walkway to the entrance. In the front, there was a greenway with a walking path and benches for employees and visitors to take lunch breaks.

I always parked in the back lot, partly to avoid the ER entrance and the corresponding waiting area. Bennett called me a germaphobe, but I had good cause: When I first started working here, I promptly got sick—a virulent virus I was sure would kill me. Or, at the very least, force me to never eat again.

Everyone said I'd build up immunity over time, but it hadn't happened. That first winter, I'd come down with bronchitis, with a cough so vicious I'd bruised a rib. Since then: strep, something viral, a rash with no origin.

I still kept hand sanitizer in my bottom drawer. Stayed three feet away from visitors to avoid a handshake.

Bennett said I made people nervous, but I hadn't gotten sick since.

That's because you've built up immunity, he'd said. But I wasn't willing to risk it.

Mostly, though, I came in through the back to be closer to the stairs and bypass the elevator, my least favorite technological advancement. Sliding doors, one way out, a steel box. I avoided the opportunity to take an elevator whenever possible, steering clear of small spaces for the obvious reasons.

From the back entrance, the only signs of life at this time of day were from the gift shop, a family of three clustered near the glass entrance, balloon in a child's hand. I could smell breakfast coming from the cafeteria down the hall, but it was quiet before the breakfast rush.

When I unlocked the door from the third-floor stairwell, my hall appeared vacant. The wing was closed to patients, accessible only through a keypad beside a swinging set of doors at one end, or a key from the back stairs. This was less because of the offices and more because of the nurses' lounge and medicine room.

It was early enough that most of the administration hadn't yet checked in for the day, but still, it was hard to tell. People moved quietly. Everyone wore rubber-soled sneakers or clogs, and I'd adopted the same—because I was the only one you could hear coming, and I found my own presence unnerving.

My office was halfway down the hall, but turn the corner and you'd hit the nurses' lounge and the central medicine room placed strategically across the way. I could see shadows passing quickly underneath the double doors at the other end of the hall, where the patients were.

I stopped just outside the lounge, peering through the small rectangular window, listening to the silence. A woman with curly auburn hair, her back to me, was reading something on her phone. The lounge was open to nurses in every department, but she was not someone I recognized; not someone who would know me.

Then I stepped backward across the hall to the medicine room. I held my breath as I eased my elbow down on the handle, feeling it give.

We didn't have the tightest security, and I should know. I was on the original committee that helped determine need versus cost effectiveness, and we didn't have a whole lot of cash coming in. A new security system was low on the list. We had guards in the ER and police on call. But we were a lot more lax upstairs, especially because of the keypads sealing off the restricted areas. People weren't consistent about locking the outside door to the medicine room because the drawers themselves were locked and accessible only by code, and it was a pain to do both. Part of my role was uncovering and slashing areas of redundancy.

I kept the lights off now, checking out the boxes in the cabinets that lined the walls. While the pharmacy kept strict regulations on the inventory, I knew that the boxes of samples from pharma reps ended up scattered haphazardly in the cabinets above, alongside the non-drug-related equipment—tubes and gauze and needles.

Anyway, if the medicine wasn't locked up, I assumed, it wasn't a danger. There must be some sort of generic sleep aid in the mix. Something to knock me out and keep me that way. Reset my internal clock and my sense of stability.

The first cabinet seemed to contain mostly topical ointments and creams. I opened the second, moving boxes around, looking for something that sounded relevant. The labels I could discern highlighted acid reflux, generic painkillers, and allergy treatments. The words were hard to read in the dark, and I leaned closer to see the containers hidden at the back of the cabinet.

The door swung open behind me with no warning, and I pulled back so fast that I scraped the side of my hand against the wooden frame of the cabinet.

It was my reaction that gave me away. My heart racing, my feet frozen. Bennett stood in the doorway; he let the door swing shut, flipping the light. He blinked twice, and I looked down, trying to adjust to the sudden glare.

"What are you doing here, Liv?"

Bennett Shaw was my closest friend at the hospital. Though I didn't have many long-term friendships throughout my past to compare it to, after more than two years of working on the same hall, of regular lunches and semi-regular dinners, I thought he probably considered me the same. He'd even invited me back to his childhood home in Charlotte for Thanksgiving last year, had said he had a big family, that they wouldn't even notice the extra seat taken.

He was also a stickler for rules, a man bound by ethics. In medicine, you have to be. There are consequences for missing something, for forgetting, for being late. There are lives in the balance. Concerned more with the logistics of keeping the hospital staffed and the money flowing in the right direction, I had the luxury of removal. If I fell behind, I could catch up. If I sent the wrong information, I could apologize and resend. No mistake was permanent.

Usually, I loved how Bennett adhered to the rules. When you grow up with a lack of predictability, structure feels like a blessing. I knew what to expect of him and what he expected of me.

"Please tell me this isn't what it looks like." He took a step closer. I could tell by his voice—deeper, quieter—that he was upset, and I needed to head it off.

"I'm not sleeping," I said. It was something I thought he would understand.

His volume only grew. "Melatonin. A glass of wine. A hot bath. Take your pick. Just get the fuck out of here."

I shook my head. "It's more than that. They're just samples, right?" A play on naïveté, but he wasn't having it.

He stepped to the side, arms crossed. Waiting for me to leave. "So talk to Cal," he said as I pushed through the door.

"Who the fuck is Cal?" I asked, but he'd already pulled the door shut between us, leaving me in a shaky haze, wondering what I had just done.

I'D BEEN STUCK IN meetings all morning, but I kept peeking into the nurses' lounge every time I passed by. I hadn't seen Bennett since he'd found me in the medicine room. Each time I replayed the scene in my head, it grew worse.

The dread in my gut was stewing—what would he think; what would he say; what would he do? He was the nurses' shift supervisor, and I was the wing administrator, comparable roles in different chains of authority. We ended up collaborating frequently, but we reported up separate ladders. Bennett had started working here just a few months after the hospital opened, four years back. He'd seen it develop from the ground up and had a strong investment in its success.

He could report me. That was his job.

I busied myself at my desk by looking up this "Cal" on the personnel database, trying to see where Bennett was directing me. I eventually landed on a name that made sense: Dr. Calvin Royce, specializing in sleep disorders. His bio and credentials were listed beside a directory photo.

"Jesus," I said out loud. I was glad I'd seen his face before running into him somewhere, so I could desensitize myself first. He was almost unnaturally good-looking.

There was a faint knock on my door. "Come on in," I called.

The first thing I saw was a cup of coffee, then an arm extended through the doorway. "I come in peace," he said before pushing the door fully ajar.

My shoulders relaxed for the first time all morning. Bennett set the coffee on my desk and fell onto the sofa against the wall. He'd helped me move it in here in exchange for his unlimited usage. He said he preferred the quiet of my office to the lounge. I rarely locked my office—there was enough security at either end of the wing as it was—so I'd often find him sleeping here, his long legs hanging over the armrest, one arm folded over his eyes, until his watch faintly beeped and he sat straight up like a vampire rising from the dead.

I swiveled the monitor in his direction, my own act of contrition.

He raised one eyebrow. "You're really not sleeping."

"I'm sorry," I said. "I didn't think it was a big deal."

He rubbed his palm down his narrow face. Sharp cheekbones, sloped chin, light brown hair, and hazel eyes. When he was clean-shaven, he always got carded when we were out. Patients sometimes complained and requested an adult, though I knew he was almost thirty.

Looking at Bennett, it wasn't hard to picture the child he once was. It was right there, close to the surface, and

he embraced it. Didn't try to dress it up in suits and facial hair. He was the youngest of five siblings and was accustomed to being viewed that way. I knew, even though
I'd declined the Thanksgiving visit. He talked about his
family constantly, whereas I tried at each opportunity to
distance myself from the child I'd once been.

The most distinct feature, in the photos, on the news,
had been that head of wavy brown hair, disproportionate on my small frame. So I'd highlighted the color to
almost-blond ever since college, had blown it straight
each morning. Every year older was another layer of removal between me and that girl. Until this morning, I'd
thought she was unrecognizable. I'd thought I had made
it, that my real life was now beginning.

"Me, too," he said. "I overreacted. But things have
been going missing from there, and . . ." A gesture of his
hand. "Sorry I jumped to conclusions." An accusation di-
rected at someone else now.

"I get it, it looked bad."

"Obviously, if you were trying to take something
worth anything, you'd be in the locked drawers. Not the
free shit."

"I'll make a note," I said, then pointed at the screen.
"But this? Is this a joke?"

He smirked. "Dr. Cal. That's what he likes to be
called, FYI. Or at least that's what everyone calls him in
the lounge. Just don't make direct eye contact, and you'll
be fine."

I wasn't sure exactly where Bennett's sexual attraction
lay, only that it wasn't with me. He was remarkably close-
lipped about his personal life, which was part of the allure
of a place like this. We could bring our history with us

in the diplomas on the walls, or choose to keep our pasts to ourselves. We existed in the present. We looked to the future.

"What sort of deal with the devil does it take to be a doctor *and* look like this? And why have I never heard of him before?" I asked.

"Because you're not in the lounge," he said. "Trust me. He was all anyone could talk about for weeks. Just started last month."

Which was probably why I hadn't heard of him yet; he hadn't shown up in any reports. A new hire also meant a decent chance of me getting in with a quick appointment.

"So, I'll see you out tonight, right?" he asked, standing to leave.

I looked at him head-on. Bennett worked Saturdays, and he typically passed on the Friday-evening activities. Or refused to commit, occasionally dropped by for a quick drink before claiming he had to head home. Though from the way he checked his phone throughout the night, I sometimes assumed he was heading somewhere better. If I teased him about it—*Hot date? Better offer?*—he'd only smile. He basked in the mystery—and in my fury—like it was a game.

By this point, it sort of was.

"You planning to stay for more than one drink this time?" I asked.

"Just found out my ex is in town, I could use the rein-forcements."

And with that—the spark of curiosity making my back straighten, a grin of his own at my reaction—he knew he had me.

"An ex, huh?" I said, looking down at my computer.

"I'll be there if I can." An echo of his usual answer. But I was serious. "I'm wiped."

"Please don't leave me alone with Elyse," he said.

Elyse was new, and she leaned extra close when she spoke, hand on my arm and eyes wide, even just to say something benign, like *The drinks are half-price*. I had liked her immediately. She reminded me of those girls I watched in high school and college, asking each other *Are we going out?* and *What do we want for lunch?*, automatically including herself—and therefore me—in a partnership.

She'd started at the hospital back in the spring, had established this Friday-night meetup between us in her very first week—a routine I'd unsuccessfully attempted to loop Bennett into as well. Until, apparently, tonight.

I took a sip of Bennett's coffee, dark and bitter. "This is terrible. Are you sure it isn't a punishment?"

He took the cup from my hand, removed the lid, took a sip himself before wincing. "Okay, so, the coffeemaker in the lounge was empty, and I don't actually know how to make it."

"You're going to start a revolt. People have quit over less."

Just a few months ago, a bleary-eyed woman I barely knew had come into my office and quit out of nowhere. When I asked why, she said, *It's the scent, like something's burning. But no one else seems to notice.*

I'd asked her to show me. Hospital safety fell under my jurisdiction, after all.

No, no. At Mapleview.

The same apartment complex I'd once lived in myself. As soon as she said it, a whiff of a memory—singed plastic; the burned remnants in a toaster—and then it was gone.

I got it. There was always something about the apartment buildings that felt slightly off. Luxury amenities but sterile and void of personality. Everything was temporary there.

The Mapleview apartments were occupied mostly by nurses and doctors testing out the location, so everyone was respectful of the long working hours, the round-the-clock shifts. We'd grown accustomed to speaking in whispers. To catching doors with our feet before they slammed shut behind us. To standing too close when we spoke.

Working in health care consulting meant we were acutely aware that the state of our health and survival depended on the ability of the care providers to rest between shifts.

But the silence, and the constant schedule changes, they did something to our circadian rhythm. Some people adapted, and some didn't.

Can't you try a different building? I'd asked.

But she'd simply frowned like it was all too late. *I gave it a shot*, she'd said. *But it's time to go back.* Looking around my office like she could sense it even there. Waiting for it to reemerge. Like a thought that had taken over everything else, impossible to escape.

All for the best, really. Elyse had been her replacement.

But it reminded me that all of us were really only one degree from the start of a slide. Something that worms its way inside and refuses to release you. A simple thing at first, that you can't ignore and can't shake. Until it permeates everything. Until you can think only in terms of this one simple thing—its presence or its absence—driving you slowly mad.

What we had here was a perfect combination of factors.

The ground has been saturated from the record-breaking rainfall in September. The ground is like a sponge, to an extent. But at some point, it just won't absorb any more.

Monday night into the early hours of Tuesday, we had a very slow-moving storm, and the system just sat on top of us for hours. We had more than two inches of rain come down between two and four a.m. It doesn't sound like much, but six inches of rushing water can lift a car. How much do you think it would take for a small child?

CHAPTER 5

Friday, 5:30 p.m.

DR. CAL'S RECEPTIONIST LEFT a message that he would stick around after hours to fit me in. This was after she'd first tried to schedule me in two weeks' time and I'd told her it was urgent. The magic word, especially from a colleague at the hospital.

By the time I left my office, the administrative wing was as empty as it had been when I'd arrived that morning.

Dr. Cal's office was two floors up, on the fifth floor, and I took the stairs. The hallway lights were off. Only a strip of light filtered from under one doorway—the rest of the offices appeared closed up for the day.

I knocked before turning the handle, poked my head in. The receptionist was in the process of gathering up her things, eyes on the clock behind her.

She spun at my entrance. "Oh," she said, hand to heart. "Olivia?" Her red lips pulled into a practiced smile.

"We've been waiting for you. Go on in, he's expecting you." Her purse was already packed, sitting on top of the desk, a pair of heels sticking out.

"Thanks for squeezing me in," I said, heading toward the door.

Dr. Cal was facing away when I pushed the door to his office open, though I assumed he'd heard us chatting—there wasn't much distance between us.

But maybe I was wrong. Because he turned around with an expression that went from neutral to beaming smile within the span of a second, like I'd really surprised him. I guessed he was one of those people who lost contact with reality as they sank deeper into their work.

He rose to a full six feet, hand extended, as I shut the door behind me. And then there was just a steady hum of white noise, like a ceiling fan, dulling everything, and faint classical music.

I almost smiled. *That's it, that's his trick*, I decided. *Lull you to sleep in his office. You're cured.*

"Olivia Meyer, so nice to meet you," he said as his hand met mine. "Seems we have some friends in common."

I didn't know Bennett considered him a friend, or whether Dr. Cal had asked around before agreeing to see me. I looked away first, scanning the room for a place to sit. I took the only other spot, a cushioned love seat across from his office chair. There were three pillows in varying shades of blue softening any possible edge. Even his furniture was designed to inspire sleep.

He settled back into his chair, rolling a little closer, hands clasped together over a pad of paper in his lap.

"Now," he said, "why don't you tell me what's brought you to my office today."

He tilted his head, eyes focused on me. I cleared my throat, looking anywhere but directly at him, as Bennett had jokingly suggested. The degrees on the wall, the certification, the articles printed out and framed—they were too small to read closely. I couldn't tell whether he was displaying general advice or showcasing his own work.

Probably the latter.

Everything about this room, and him, was deliberate. To judge from the way he was sitting, body angled and waiting, Dr. Calvin Royce was someone who knew exactly what he looked like. He had probably perfected the angle and smile in the mirror. Slept with a teeth-whitening tray, or an eye mask, at the very least. When he crossed his leg over his knee, the bottom of his pants rose up to reveal a quirky neon green sock with dog bones, probably designed for disarming. A conversation starting point. A way in.

I decided point-blank he was a sociopath.

It was easier to avoid someone's charm when you could see behind it from the start.

"Last night, I was sleepwalking," I said. The truth, then. The reason I was here. *An urgent sleep issue* was what I'd told his receptionist, after all.

A slow nod, his face giving away nothing. He didn't blink. "Has this happened before?"

"Not since I was a kid. Almost twenty years ago. I thought I outgrew it. Or it was fixed. Either way, it stopped happening."

Another nod. "Were you seen by a doctor back then?"

Everything about that time was a blur. There had been so many doctors. Checkups and follow-ups; pre-ops and post-ops and physical therapy, before my mother decided they were doing more harm than good, perpetuating the trauma.

"Yes, I was given medicine, and the sleepwalking stopped," I said, so he would know that I was aware of my own history and how best to address the issue at hand. All I needed was his signature.

"You were given medication as a child?" he asked, head tilted slightly in the other direction now. A better angle of the jawline.

"Yes," I said.

"What kind?" He twirled his pen in his fingers, ready to make some notes.

A rattle in an amber bottle. The scent of hot chocolate. "I'm not sure."

The pen stilled. He looked unsure, like maybe I was pulling this out of thin air. "That would be unusual," he said.

But I didn't want to tell him—it wasn't a usual case. I had wandered away from home while asleep, without regard to the storm that was raging through. Gotten swept away by the flash flood that came through the valley with a vengeance.

This was why I trusted myself and my instincts. More even than my conscious thoughts. Because I knew, underneath, there was something stronger. Something that understood how to survive. That there was a person I could not remember who had endured something unimaginable for three full days before someone found me.

It was how I knew I was right to change my name. To break it off with Jonah. To stay here.

It was why I had picked that house but hadn't changed

the locks yet. And why I had bought that hook and eye at
the store. Why I was sitting here right now.

The less I actively dissected a situation, the clearer the
answer became.

"Are you on any medications currently?" he asked, pen
hovering over the yellow notepad once more. "Sleepwalking can, unfortunately, be a side effect of other sleep aids.
Even over-the-counter ones."

"No. Though I guess there goes my hope for a sleep
aid."

He gave me a small smile. "Walk me through the
night," he said. "Before you went to sleep."

It had been a night like so many others. I had run into
Bennett heading out at the same time, and we'd grabbed a
burger at the grill across the street before going our separate ways. "Nothing out of the ordinary," I said. "I ate dinner out with a friend, finished some paperwork at home,
watched TV, had a drink, went to bed." I shrugged. It all
sounded so mundane when reduced to a sentence.

"What was the drink?" he asked.

"A glass of wine." The bottle had partially turned, but
it unwound me at the end of the day.

"Alcohol can contribute to sleepwalking," he said.

"It hasn't in the past," I said. "And it was only half a
glass." I never drank a lot at once. I'd gone out with my
roommates in college at the end of sophomore year, let
myself get to the point where the night had leaps and gaps,
and then I'd never done it again.

We had been at a party in another dorm, and from what
I could gather, a senior I liked had pulled me into the storage area under the stairs. I couldn't be certain how long I'd
been in there, but the story ended with me barging out in

a fury, the guy following a moment later, bent over, hands held to his bloody nose.

By the next day, the story had taken on a life of its own: my roommates high-fiving me, announcing to anyone who would hear, *Don't fuck with the girls in 423!* But I couldn't say for sure. Couldn't say whether I was protecting myself or reacting to the small, dark space—needing, above all, to escape.

They couldn't really know the girl in 423.

I knew better now—fearing, most of all, that disconnect between my mind and body, when I was no longer the one in control.

The therapist I had to see briefly in high school was the one who explained that my need to always know my exits, to calculate my steps, was probably a symptom of the PTSD that manifested alongside my primal need to escape—a coping mechanism to feel in control.

This was just routine: that half-glass at the end of the day while I watched television; a bottle of wine that usually managed to turn before I could finish it. There had been nothing unusual about last night.

Dr. Cal tilted his head back, assessing me. "Tell me about yourself," he said.

"Excuse me?"

Then he shook his foot, like maybe I hadn't noticed the dog bones. Waiting for me to make conversation, give something away. Eventually, he gave up and put his feet solidly on the floor.

"Anything stressful in your life?"

"Yes." I didn't elaborate. He wasn't a therapist.

"I know how it is here," he said with a tight smile. "After hours is when the work really begins, am I right?"

"Partly." But I had managed to keep up just fine to this point. That was the work culture at a place like this. Each of us putting in the extra hours, here and at home—a shared exhaustion that bound us together. Even though I was in a different department, it permeated everything. They had their patient appointments, I had the administrative meetings; and after, we did the paperwork or the research or the list of obligations that had to be fulfilled one way or another. We were in it together, and it kept us all afloat.

"The older I get, the harder it is to sustain," he added, though I was guessing he was somewhere in his thirties, and he seemed to be holding everything together just fine. "You've got to make sure you're putting yourself first. Carve out rest. Stick to healthy patterns. Eat well. Exercise."

I let out a small laugh, and he genuinely smiled, like he was pleased with himself for successfully cracking through my surface. But the truth was, I hadn't noticed the creeping exhaustion, the lack of nutrition or energy, until he started tallying it off. I felt the inadequacies all rising to the surface under his gaze. All the things I wasn't doing to keep myself healthy. The caffeine in place of calcium, potential weak spots in my bones. The quick meals on the go. The bags of chips I grabbed from the cafeteria instead of the apple. Layers of stress piling on top of one another, my body rebelling. The simplest things.

Still. "I was hoping for something a little more concrete and attainable," I said. Not a *change yourself, change your life* mantra.

He sighed, leaning back in the chair, getting comfortable. "Usually, I'd like to run some tests before prescribing

something. Especially since you're not sure of your medical history. We could try to track down your old records to
get a better idea of a previous diagnosis, but even then . . ."

I was already shaking my head, and he stopped talking.
"It was so long ago," I said. Twenty years since the sleepwalking; ten years since the last therapist.

He blinked slowly. "Well," he continued, "either way,
it's not as simple as taking a pill. We'd want to get to the
root of things, the underlying cause. Find any stressors,
make lifestyle adjustments. See if we can't manage this
without pharmaceutical intervention, which can have its
own list of side effects. Make sure you really are sleepwalking and not, say, having a seizure." He scanned the
paper in his lap, as if looking for answers hidden under
my words.

"I woke up outside," I snapped. "My neighbor found
me."

He looked up from the pad of paper on his lap, eyes
wide and jaw tensed. The first true sign of emotion. Of
excitement. A peek behind the curtain.

"You live alone?" he asked.

This was more information than I generally liked to
disclose to a sociopath. "Would that change the diagnosis?"

"It's important to educate the people around you." He
clicked the top of his pen, once, twice. "I'd like to do a
sleep study."

"You want to watch me sleep."

"Not just me."

"That's not better."

"You're funny." He didn't laugh.

"Thing is, I don't really have time for that," I said,

deflecting. "As I'm sure you can relate." I also worried I would be a guinea pig. Something to pad his bottom line. Prove his worth at a new place.

He leaned forward again, clasped his hands together, then placed them on his knees. "All right," he said. "Let's talk again after the weekend." Then he pushed himself to standing, strode past me, cracked the door. The receptionist looked up from her desk, where she'd been waiting for us to finish so she could finally leave for the day. "Jessie?" he called. "Let's get Olivia on the schedule for later next week."

I stood, effectively being dismissed. "And in the meantime?"

"In the meantime, I want you to document your sleep. When you go to bed each night, when you wake. Any incidents. And if so, what you were doing in the lead-up to them. What time of night they're occurring. Don't worry," he said, "we'll figure it out."

He put a hand on my shoulder, caught my eye, smiled reassuringly.

Up close, I noticed a nick on the underside of his jaw. A crumb on his collar. I started a tally, smiling back.

TRANSCRIPT FROM SPECIAL REPORT WITH SALLY HOLMES AND GUEST LOU JORDAN, CIVIL ENGINEER

OCTOBER 19, 2000

SALLY HOLMES: Tell us about the drainage pipes that everyone's been talking about.

LOU JORDAN: Right. Well, the county drainage system all flows south. If she entered, as they believe, where there was a missing grate at the northern access point below the town center, there are four different forks farther south, depending on the water flow.

SH: It's my understanding that they found her shoe near the access point. If she got swept down into the pipes, would there be any air down there?

LJ: During the surge, no. The pipes were likely flowing at full capacity. All water, no air. But there are access points above. Twenty-three different input locations, and if the water was high enough, it could hypothetically bring you close.

SH: So you're saying she could have made it to one of these locations?

LJ: [Pause.] There's always a possibility. But then what? The access points should all be sealed iron grates. And when the water recedes, she would drop back down with the water level.

SH: And it's going to rain again.

LJ: Yes, it's going to rain again tonight.

SH: Is there a chance she's still alive in those pipes?

LJ: That's not for me to say. I'm just an engineer.

SH: Well, as an engineer who designs these systems, what would you be doing right now? Would you be draining them?

LJ: There's no way to do that in time for the next rain. Me? I would be searching. I would pray to God I found her before nightfall.

CHAPTER 6

Friday, 7:30 p.m.

ELYSE AND BENNETT WERE already at the bar, though at first I could only see Elyse.

She was leaning half across the bar top, in a green shirt that somehow caught the dim light, gesturing to the bartender, who was already smiling and walking toward her.

She had that effect on people. Even Bennett. Even though he found her *too happy*, or *too loud*, too herself. Impossible to embarrass, or entirely unself-aware. I knew he enjoyed her company, despite himself. She had dark hair that was halfway between wavy and curly, and the only time she wasn't waging battle with it, pushing it out of her face or tucking it behind her ears, was when it was tied up in a messy ponytail on top of her head. She never seemed quite put together, and there was a certain charm in that.

"See?" Elyse said, turning to Bennett. "I told you. She always comes."

Bennett pressed his lips together and looked away, as if embarrassed to be caught talking about me. Elyse technically reported to him, since he scheduled the nurses' shifts, and he seemed to always be trying to maintain some semblance of a professional distance with her.

"I was just saying," he said, picking up his half-empty beer. "What? You *were* late."

Elyse stood, fast hug, air kiss on my cheek, which was how she always greeted us when we met up outside of work, like we hadn't seen each other hours earlier. Hands on my arms, a whiff of her coconut hair product. I caught Bennett smirking. The first time he'd swung by for a quick drink, we'd been standing at the bar, and this was how she'd greeted him. After, he'd given me that same look, the same half-smile, as he leaned in, repeating the gesture on me—his laughter in my ear: *Is this what we do now?* A joke we were both in on.

But sometimes, when I looked at Elyse, I saw another version of me: of what might've been possible, the person I might've grown into. Maybe it was just the hair—I imagined that would be what mine would look like now if I left it natural, grew it out. Or maybe it was just how she moved through her world—like everyone was an ally, a friend—how casually and easily she could make a connection. Sometimes, watching her, I got a flash of nostalgia for something that didn't even exist.

"I had an appointment," I said to Bennett as Elyse slid back onto her seat. "There was direct eye contact. I forgot myself."

He laughed over a sip of his drink, then coughed, smiling. "I did warn you." Then, turning serious: "How'd it go?"

I sat down on the empty stool beside him. It was more crowded than I was used to, probably because of the band setting up in the corner. "Underwhelming," I said. But I knew I'd earned his forgiveness. Going through the proper channels.

Elyse looked between the two of us, as if trying to keep up. I hated that feeling myself, of knowing you were on the outside of a joke, peering in.

I waved my hand dismissively. "Had to see a doctor to get a new prescription," I said.

"Ah," she said, still not getting it but losing interest.

"Thank you," I said, picking up the third beer on the bar top, practically brimming over. Friendship was having someone who ordered your drink the second they saw you walk in.

"Oh, someone was looking for you earlier," Elyse said. Bennett gave her a quizzical look, but she shook her head. "Before you got here. Hey, Trevor," she called, gesturing the bartender closer once more. "Who was looking for Liv?"

Trevor held up one finger to the customer he was currently serving, backing toward us. He had hooded eyes, olive skin, dark hair, a falcon tattooed on his forearm—the cultivated look of bartenders everywhere. But he was smitten with Elyse. And he didn't do brooding very well, under her attention. He came whenever she beckoned, smiled easily, laughed easily. "Older guy. Salt-and-pepper hair," he said.

"Cute?" she asked, gently teasing.

He smirked. "I guess, if that's your thing."

"Oh, it sure is Olivia's thing," Bennett mumbled.

Elyse widened her eyes, and even Trevor looked down, busying himself with a water ring on the counter.

"Sorry but," Bennett said, hands out, not sorry at all. My relationship with Jonah had been a terribly kept secret when we'd started at the hospital together, but it was still supposed to be off the radar. Bennett was the only one I'd confided in when I'd broken it off. We'd been in line for breakfast, sliding our trays across the metal, and he'd briefly paused, briefly looked up. *Finally, she's come to her senses,* he'd said, grabbing a banana. Which was a shitty way to find out the person you considered your closest friend had thought you were a fool the entire time you'd known each other.

I closed my eyes now, ignoring him. "What did he want?" I asked Trevor.

Trevor leaned over the bar, lowered his voice so it didn't carry. Like a promise that he was on my side and not Bennett's. "Didn't say. Just asked if Olivia Meyer was here."

I blinked. Until that moment, it hadn't occurred to me that Trevor knew my last name. Then again, he'd asked for my ID the first time I came in. And I left my credit card for him every Friday night.

"I said I hadn't seen you," he continued. "The guy said he had plans to meet up with you." He shrugged, looking around the crowd. "Haven't seen him since, though."

I shook my head. Goddamn Jonah. I checked my phone, but he hadn't texted again. Of course, the reason he was thinking about me was because he was coming to town. I was a convenience, nothing more. He probably had a follow-up study planned at the hospital. Or worse, a new contract to pitch. And he knew where I'd be after work on a Friday.

"Did you know he was coming?" Bennett asked.

"No," I said through gritted teeth.

"Who?" Elyse asked, leaning closer.

"Liv's last boyfriend. The professor," Bennett said in this pretentious tone. So that I could imagine him saying it before, saying it all the time to others, whenever I left the room.

"I should go," I said.

Bennett grabbed my wrist as I reached for my purse. "Liv, come on. You just got here," he said, letting go. *Sorry*, he mouthed, so only I could see.

"I'm just really tired," I said. Another truth.

"I didn't know," Elyse said, fumbling with her hair, tying it into a high ponytail as she spoke. "I didn't realize it was an old boyfriend." She hadn't been working with us back then. She'd never met him, and I sure hadn't brought him up.

"He's not even an old boyfriend," I said. Which was sort of the problem. Jonah wouldn't commit until I found my backbone and called it off. It wasn't an ultimatum. I'd just grown sick of it.

There was always some excuse:

I shouldn't—

If people knew—

What would the school say—

My reputation—

Except he did. And people already knew. As far as I knew, the school said nothing. And his reputation seemed to be getting on just fine, which now included *slept with former grad student.*

Mine, on the other hand . . .

Bennett was right, though, whether he knew it or not. Generally speaking, my type was older. I found myself drawn to men more when they were no longer covering up their insecurities with bravado. The ones who told me: *This is what I like. This is what I want of you. This is what I will give you in return.* With a confidence that meant they'd already come to terms with who they were.

Jonah was probably drawn to me for the inverse.

My glass was still mostly full, and it tasted bland, watered down somehow. "One drink," I said. "And then I'm going to bed."

Bennett relaxed in his seat again, eyes scanning the room. "Speaking of exes," he said, gesturing toward the entrance. His apologies always came like this, in tiny appeasements. In pieces of himself that he gave away, knowing full well he'd held on to them for far too long.

I followed his gaze. A woman in a casual black dress, long legs and long blond hair that fell in waves over her shoulders. She was stunning. I was stunned.

"Damn, Bennett," Elyse said. She nudged his shoulder, but he remained stoic. Sometimes, like now, Elyse got it wrong, aiming for levity.

"Why don't I know her?" I asked.

"Because," he said slowly, "you never asked." I must've physically jolted, because he put his hand up, shifting direction. "It was before your time, Liv. She worked in the ER for less than a year, left a month or two before you started. We were together for maybe six months."

Yet several years later, she was still the ex in town for whom he needed reinforcements. Must've been one hell of a six months.

"What's her name?" Elyse asked, eyes still focused on the woman across the bar.

Bennett looked from me to Elyse before answering. "Keira," he said.

I'd made a mistake. These were things I should've asked. Back then. Right now. Jonah was probably the main reason we'd never discussed relationships. I avoided the topic; it was supposed to be a secret.

I'd thought I knew enough about Bennett's life to matter: that he was single; that he was the youngest of five and had grown up in south Charlotte and moved away because, in his words, his siblings cast a long shadow; that he became a different person when he wasn't working.

But these were all surface things. Not: *Did she hurt you, do you miss her, why are you out with me tonight—for this?*

That was the danger. If you didn't want someone to pry into your past, you had to keep out of theirs.

"Is she coming back?" I asked.

He shook his head once, never taking his eyes off her. "She's visiting her old roommates. She's getting *married*. They're going to be her *bridesmaids*."

I could hear it then, the pain in his voice. All the things she must've been for him.

I felt just like I had in Cal's office, sitting across from him as a collection of flaws. Of course Bennett's attraction did not extend my way. Of course not. Not after her.

He'd broken up with her right before I'd arrived. There must've been gossip—I knew what the hospital could get like. It must've been awkward. Maybe he was looking for a new group; people who didn't know them as a couple, who wouldn't pick sides in the aftermath. Maybe that was why he sought *me* out—a friendship of convenience.

He turned on his stool, facing me, knees bumping

mine. "Is it more awkward if I go say hi or pretend I don't see them?"

"You should go say hi," I said. I took a long drink, swallowing too fast, feeling like something was lodged in my throat.

He gave me a small smile, took his beer, didn't look back. She smiled at him as he approached, gave him a one-armed hug. Her friends opened their circle, and he stepped inside. And after, he didn't leave. Joining their conversation. Laughing. Doing a really excellent job pretending to be happy for her, if she'd truly hurt him that badly.

I turned to Elyse, but she was whispering something across the bar to Trevor. He shook his head, laughing. Then he took her hand and wrote something on her palm in black pen as she smiled.

The laughter behind me was too loud. The band started playing, and I couldn't even hear myself think. Someone nearby was smoking, or had smoked outside and their clothes now reeked of it.

"I'm gonna go," I called, leaning toward Elyse's shoulder.

She looked me over slowly, frowning. "What's wrong?"

"I don't feel good." I left cash on the bar top, more than enough to cover my drink.

Everything was off. The light, the sound, the taste of my drink—lemon-tinted, like something had soured. I felt ungrounded in the moment, caught off guard by all the things I'd gotten wrong. Elyse looked to Trevor, then back to me, as if weighing her choices.

"Stay, I'm fine. But I should probably head home."

"Call me tomorrow?" she said, hand on my arm, but if

I hadn't been reading her lips, I would've missed it. Even her skin felt too hot, and I had to stop myself from pulling away too fast before leaving.

I'D HAD TO PARK on the grassy embankment outside of the lot, due to the overflow of cars. The parking lot and the surrounding streets were well lit. But when I took the turn forking off from the town center, the roads became darker, and there were glimpses of the town that existed before. The winding streets where the pavement faded and crumbled; and an old gas station, abandoned, the tall grass growing wild, cracks in the lot, the single pump rising like a husk—the first sign of the apocalypse.

I had to take my street slow as it meandered through the woods, unlit but for the houses set farther back from the road. There could be deer around any curve. I'd seen the damage that could do, and not just to a car.

The entrance to my driveway was hard to make out in the night—just the shadow of my mailbox beside Rick's. As I turned in, I could see the lantern from Rick's front porch through the trees. Mine remained dark. I'd either forgotten it in my rush to leave, or the bulb had finally burned out, like Rick had been warning. He was always telling me to replace the lights, the smoke detector batteries, before they went out on their own. When I cut the headlights in my drive, I wished I'd listened sooner.

Seventeen steps to the front porch. A faint glow through the bushes, from Rick's place. I used the light from my phone to guide the path. Walking up the porch steps, I heard something scurrying in the bushes.

Three steps to the front door. I stomped my feet, like

Rick had taught me, to let them know I was here. Let the animals know I'm not small, I'm not prey, but something to fear.

Key in the lock; door shutting behind me. When I stepped inside and flicked the porch light, meaning to scare whatever nocturnal animal might be lurking, it remained dead. Instead, I turned on every light inside, until all I could hear was the electrical buzz of an overhead bulb.

It was the solitude that made me do it. The quiet hum inside after the noise of the bar. The fact that Bennett was still hung up on his ex-girlfriend, probably laughing with her even now; and Elyse had the bartender, Trevor, just starting something new; and Cal was so good-looking he was probably a sociopath; and Rick wore a wedding ring but lived all alone.

It was my head, and the way it was making me feel, disconnected, circling some darkness.

I went to the fridge, poured the last of the wine bottle into my glass. Then I opened up my messages and sent Jonah a text—*Thinking of you, too*—because it was the truth, and that had to count for something.

THE SOUND OF A chime jolted me from sleep. I reached out an arm on instinct, in the direction of my bedside table. But my knuckles hit on something rough, too close.

A chill, my eyes adjusting to a dim light, trying to orient myself. And then I heard the rest: the crickets, the leaves rustling overhead.

That dim light between the bushes, coming from Rick's house.

Something chimed again, and I followed the noise, looking down. It was the noise of an alert on my phone—a missed call. I must've brought my phone with me and dropped it.

It was buried in shadow now. Hand at the tree again—the rough bark of the trunk—but something felt sticky, like tar. I held my hands close to my face. My palms were too dark, like they were coated in dirt. I rubbed my fingers together, and they caught.

This time the phone started ringing, and I moved closer, hands held in front of me to block the jagged branches, tripping over a log before I reached the sound. Knees in the hard dirt, my palms stinging. I placed my hand on the log to right myself, but it was too soft.

A snake, my first instinct. I scrambled away before my mind even had time to process.

But the shadow hadn't moved. The phone kept ringing. I pushed myself to standing, stepping closer. I nudged the shadow with my bare foot, feeling the familiar roughness of denim this time.

And then silence.

My head swam in a sudden rush of understanding. I moved the branches of the bushes aside to be sure: the shape of a torso; arms; the back of a head.

A man.

A sound escaped my throat. I stepped back. Closed my eyes. Took a breath.

Sometimes, when I wake, the two worlds combine—the dream and reality. An echo of one in the other. And so it's possible the body is a figment, and I can walk it back, retrace my steps, climb backward into bed, and in the morning there will be nothing here, just a lingering sense of doom. A shudder as I walk to my car; the ghost of a memory.

But it's the wind that made me sure. Moving the blades of grass in a symphony over my toes, something greater than my imagination. A chaos beyond the reach of my mind.

My eyes shot open, burning in the night wind.

How long had I been standing here? How long ago had this happened?

I looked down at my hands again, understanding without seeing—they were red.

Behind me, the front door gaped open across my yard, a darkness inside.

But when I started running, I instinctively headed the other way. Passing the body in the yard. Through the tree line. Tripping over the hedges as I ran. For Rick's.

Because when I'd gone to him about the snake last year, before he'd declared it harmless, he'd come over with a shotgun. Tried to give it to me after, with his shaking hand. Said he was too slow to get to it should he need it now, inside the locked case, and anyway, he had another. I couldn't take it; didn't know how to use it.

But Rick's house was safety. He would know what to do.

And when he opened the door, he did, right away. He took one look at me, and I peered over my shoulder to try to get him to understand. "There's a man—outside—"

I held up my palms; the red was so bright in the open doorway. His eyes scanned over me quickly, and he looked at my hands again, at my mouth—"Rick, help"—and he seemed to understand then that it wasn't me who was hurt. He took me by the sleeve and pulled me across the threshold, and he closed and locked the door, and it was too warm inside, but I was safe.

I was shaken and dirty, and Rick looked out the front window. Looked hard into the darkness, his fingers trembling against the window frame, his breath fogging up the glass. He stared for a long time, not going for the gun, not going for the phone, and I waited, because he would know what to do.

Rick turned around, eyes glazed. But he seemed to be looking beyond me, somewhere.

And he said, in a voice I'd never heard before, "Wash your hands."

It's a common occurrence in children. Most will outgrow it. For parents, if you witness or suspect that your child is sleepwalking, there are some things you can do to protect them.

Put a bell on their door, something to wake you. Try to limit the amount of furniture or fragile items in the room with them, so they won't accidentally get hurt.

What happened to the Maynor girl was an accident. A tragic accident. And sometimes, despite our best intentions, accidents happen anyway.

Most times an episode passes with no incident. There are, of course, other disorders to be aware of. Episodes that veer more actively and dangerously than merely walking in your sleep. True sleepwalking mostly tends to mimic basic things you have already done.

But if your child seems to be acting out their dreams, running, fighting . . . that's not sleepwalking. That's evidence of another type of disorder.

That's when you should be concerned. That's when they could be a danger to themselves or others.

CHAPTER 7

Saturday, 2 a.m.

RICK LEFT WITH A yellow flashlight and nothing else. No knife, no gun, no means of protection. Just a look over his shoulder and a glance toward my hands: "Now," he said.

I stumbled toward the hall bathroom, which I had used only once before.

There was peeling yellow wallpaper behind the mirror, the green stems of the flowers gone gray from humidity. The shower faucet behind the curtain was dripping, and the second door connecting the bathroom to the bedroom was slightly ajar.

In the silence, I tallied the ways out: the door I'd just come through; the door leading to his bedroom, the windows beyond the bed—which was made. Insomnia, I was guessing. The pale light always shining from his house, even in the dead of night.

In the garish bathroom light, my hands looked almost

comical. Theatrical. And I had to use my elbow to turn on the faucet. My hands were shaking, even though the water was on hot, the red swirling down. I couldn't feel the temperature until it was already scalding, and I yanked my hands back—a baby pink.

As the water circled, I imagined the shadow again. The shape of the body. The stillness. What Rick might see.

The beam of the flashlight sweeping the earth. His footsteps approaching—

I closed my eyes. Maybe I was wrong, the scene too dark and fractured. Maybe whoever lay out there was just injured, bleeding. Passed out drunk.

I waited as the water ran cooler, rubbed soap up my arms to my elbows, scraped my fingernails against one another. Until there was no more visible blood, just the scent of vanilla, so thick it was almost cloying.

I scanned the rest of my body for signs; my hands were clean. Turning them over: a small nick near my wrist, barely visible. Clean shirt. Dark pants. A tear at the knee; stiffness settling in. I sat on the edge of the tub, rolling up the leg of my loose pajama pants. A gash running down the kneecap.

I pressed a stack of toilet paper against the cut, trying to stop the blood, then opened the cabinet under the sink, looking for a bandage. An amber prescription bottle, a pair of nail clippers, a pile of towels. A small trash can and something wedged beside it, in the corner. Something black and metal—

I leaned closer, nudging the garbage can aside.

The metal fell with a clunk, and I jumped back, pulse racing.

A gun.

A gun, hidden. Not one of his shotguns, locked up in a safe down the hall. But kept here. Four steps from his bedroom. Three steps from his living room. So he could get to it fast, should he need it.

I heard Rick's footsteps coming up the porch again, slow and steady. Behind the trash can, there was a roll of black electrical tape. I tore off a piece with my teeth, wrapped it over my knee, pulled the fabric back down my leg.

I looked fine. Everything was fine.

The sound of the front door opening and closing, footsteps pausing for a moment at the entrance. Like the danger had passed.

Had he nudged the man with his toe, gotten him to wake, gotten him back on his feet, walking him to his car—

Had there been a car?

I hadn't noticed. Had I even looked?

I remembered the light from Rick's, the darkness of my own house. The open doorway. I didn't remember a car . . .

Footsteps again, and then a tap at the bathroom door.

"Liv? You okay?"

"Just a minute," I said. I eased the cabinet door closed, holding my breath.

"Liv. I'm going to have to call the police now."

A pause. And then: "Okay," I said, speaking to my own reflection. Not a call for help. The police, he said.

He was dead.

Everything slowed. My breathing, my thoughts, my movements.

His steps retreating. Images flashing and lingering— the phone, the body, the blood. The feeling of pins and needles in my fingertips. A sour taste in my mouth—the walls were too close, and the drip of the faucet behind me grew louder, more insistent. I couldn't get a deep breath.

I pulled the door open, desperate for air.

I HEARD RICK ON the phone from where I waited in the living room. He was pacing in the kitchen as he talked. "Yes, there's the body of a man at the edge of my property. Deceased, yes. No, I don't know. I'm not sure. I don't know."

He spent a while in the kitchen, even after the conversation stopped. And he didn't look my way at first when he came back to the living room. Stared, instead, out the front windows. Eyes slightly narrowed, a twitch at the corner.

"It takes so long," he said, "for help to get here. For the police to make it out this far."

"Rick, did you see? Who it was, I mean?"

He turned in my direction, blinking slowly. "Never saw him before, that I could tell. There was a lot of blood, though." Eyes drifting away again. Drifting straight to the cabinet beside the television, to the bottle of liquor sitting on top. Then he turned back to me, glancing at my hands, my pants, my bare feet. "Sit down, Liv. Sit down and take a breath."

I walked to the couch, though the stiffness in my left leg, and the electrical-tape bandage, turned my walk to a slight limp.

"What's the matter?"

"My knee," I said, sitting on the edge of his sofa. "I cut it. On a root, I think."

He frowned at the tear in the fabric. "You tripped out there," he said, but he said it like a statement, not a question.

"Yes," I said, and he nodded once. And I realized he was saying it like it was a story, my story, something I had to cover up. "Rick, I tripped over the . . . over the body." I couldn't say the name. Who I imagined might be out there. Couldn't even think it.

"Okay," he said. And then, "They're here." Even before a flash of light cut through the front curtains. "Stay in here. I'll show them."

A man was dead, and how many men could it be, lurking outside my house? That phone I'd heard must've belonged to whoever was out there. My mind kept drifting back to Jonah, to the text I had sent him—*Thinking of you, too*—and the one he had sent back, seconds later:

What are you thinking?

Because that was Jonah, always digging deeper, to find the heart of the meaning. Always asking it of others but not himself. The dynamic of his classroom carrying over, seeming like a natural extension—though it wasn't.

What I was really thinking: That I knew it was a mistake as soon as he responded. That I was smart enough this time to see him clearly, not as Professor Lowell, the thrill of his extra interest, but as a forty-one-year-old man trapped in a perpetual state of late adolescence, in danger of trapping me there, too.

When I didn't respond, falling into my bed instead, into a sleep I couldn't find the beginning of—a haze of wine and adrenaline and exhaustion—had he driven out this way?

Or had I texted him to come? Had I responded in my sleep?

The blackout I'd had from drinking during that episode at the end of sophomore year in college was the closest I'd ever felt to sleepwalking. Knowing, after, that something had happened, seeing the evidence, hearing others talk about it, but never able to get there myself. Another thing forever lost to me.

The night and the rain; the drainage pipe. The cold earth and stagnant water.

It had been only one glass of wine last night, but Dr. Cal's words echoed in my head, faintly accusing.

The voices of several people out front carried through the thin window, and the sound of footsteps made me sit upright, unsure what to do with my hands. I folded them awkwardly in my lap until my fingers felt numb, hooked together unnaturally.

A woman followed Rick inside. "Liv, this is Nina," he said. He introduced her so casually, I couldn't tell at first what her role was. Whether this was someone he had called to the house personally; whether this was someone on our side.

Nina stepped inside carefully, her gaze roaming the room—she was smaller than I was, wearing gray slacks and a black windbreaker. Boots that seemed in contrast to her dress pants. She had light brown skin and sleek dark hair pulled back in a low ponytail.

Her face gave away nothing. "Nina Rigby," she said. "I'm with the police department. Mr. Aimes said you're the one who found the body?"

Her face was completely delicate, as if made of glass—tiny upturned nose, gently sloping cheekbones, rounded chin, like I could fit her entire face in my hand. But it was unlined and expressionless, even now, when discussing a body just steps away. And when her brown eyes set on me, I changed my mind: stone, not glass.

"Yes. Do you know who it is?" I asked, the words scraping against my throat, wondering if she could hear my heartbeat from there. I concentrated on slowing my breaths, counting the seconds, in and out.

She paused, sat beside me on the couch, barely making an indentation. "We're not sure just yet. But what I'd like to do right now is get your statement while it's all still fresh. Why don't you tell me what happened. How you found him."

I took a second deciding what to say; I had spent my life telling lies by omission. Excising the irrelevant, the past, becoming someone with a different history or none at all. And so it was instinct. To tell the truth without all the facts. The details coming in an odd, detached way, in response to each question. *I heard a noise. I found him out-side. Yes, I touched him. I'm sure, I touched him. No, I can't remember how. I can't remember.*

"What did you hear?" she asked, homing in on specific details.

"A phone." The truth. It had woken me from the haze. Let her think it had carried across the yard.

"Who did you think it was out there?"

Jonah, at his desk, reading my text. Feet up, in his worn jeans, bourbon in a glass—

"I didn't. I didn't know. I just heard the ringing, and it was coming from the direction of Rick's house, and—"

"Liv keeps an eye on me, Nina. She checks in," Rick said. This, too, was not a lie. In the last few months, I'd started to notice that tremor in his hand—I worried about him. I worried about him driving. So I picked up groceries

if I was going to the store, and I knocked on his door if I
hadn't seen him out all day.

Nina Rigby looked at him closely, like she was reading
between the lines: Did I head outside because I thought
it was Rick needing help? A good story that emerged between the details, whether it was true or not. Couldn't it
be true? Couldn't Rick believe that, too?

Except Rick knew I had been sleepwalking outside yesterday. He knew, and he was covering now.

"Did you know he was dead?" she asked.

"I, I shook him." *Hands out in front of me, pushing at some-
thing that was no longer there.* "I put my hands on his body.
It was dark. I just shook him, and . . . he didn't feel right.
He was in the bushes. There was blood. Even in the dark,
I could feel it." Sticky, viscous, as I leaned against the tree.
"I touched a tree out there, too."

Her eyes drifted to my hands. I could smell the soap
from here. "I washed my hands. I didn't want to get it on
Rick's things." The truth.

She nodded once, barely perceptible. "Did you feel for
a pulse?"

"I don't remember. I don't think so. I just started running."

"For here?"

"Yes."

"Why'd you run here?"

The open door behind me, in the dark. Instinct carrying me forward—"Something happened to that man, and
I was scared."

"There've been animals," Rick said. "We've seen them.
Heard them."

Nina's head turned swiftly, the first crack in the demeanor. "That was no animal, Mr. Aimes."

In the silence of the room, I could hear the crackle of a walkie-talkie in the distance; the low hum of voices outside; a car door closing. Nina inhaled sharply, turning to face me. "I'd like you to walk me through exactly how you found him."

I looked to the window. Didn't understand what she was asking. Hadn't I just done that?

"From your house," she added, standing. "Mr. Aimes, I'm going to have someone else come take your full statement. Ms. Meyer, I'd like you to walk me through where you were when you heard the phone. It could help us. Would be good to know whether he was closer to your house at first, or whether he was already incapacitated when you heard it."

I pushed myself to standing, unable to stop the wince as my leg bent.

A tiny indentation formed in Nina's forehead. "Are you okay?"

"My knee," I said. "I cut it."

"She tripped," Rick said, and we both stared in his direction.

"Cut it on a root, I think. It's fine, though. I'm fine."

EVEN THOUGH OUR HOMES were close, Nina and I were prevented from walking through the border of the property line. "We're not sure how far the crime scene extends right now," Nina explained. She turned on her flashlight as we started walking down the long drive to the main road, where we could then cut back to my driveway.

But she immediately turned back, frowning at the way I was walking. "Let's take my car," she said. "These driveways are so dark, anyway."

She led me to her unmarked car, held the passenger door open for me before walking around to the driver's side.

Up close, Nina Rigby was captivating in her contradictions. Upturned nose and downturned mouth, giving her the simultaneous look of both aloofness and gravity. No makeup, as far as I could tell, but with her hands on the wheel, I saw that her short nails were painted a subtle pink.

Out on the main road, I couldn't see any other cars—no sign of how another person had arrived. We made a sharp turn into my driveway. Our mailboxes were positioned side by side, the individual driveways diverging from there.

Just as we pulled in past my mailbox, bright lights lit up the space around the crime scene, white and unnatural. I could see gnats swarming in the glare.

There was no car in the driveway but my own.

She turned the car off, and without the headlights, the only glow was from the crime scene, the bushes lit up in an eerie glow between the properties. Shadows of men falling outward, stretching toward us.

"Your house is completely dark," she said.

"Sorry, I need to get a new bulb for the porch light."

The car door slammed shut behind her, and by the time I climbed out, she was standing in front of my porch, looking straight ahead.

But she wasn't waiting for me to enter, I realized. She was staring at the open doorway. The darkness beckoning. She flicked on her flashlight, shining the beam over the front porch, lighting our way. "Did you leave the door that way?"

"I think so," I said.

She led the way, and I gripped the banister, not wanting to bend my knee more than necessary.

Nina looked back once, frowning at my steps. "You sure you're okay?"

"Fine. I just don't want to make it any worse." But my entire body was on edge, practically thrumming. She could probably hear it in my voice.

Nina stepped to the side at the entrance, like she was waiting for me. But she pushed the door farther open with her foot, shining the flashlight inside. Her shoulders were tense, and for a moment I flashed to all the things that could be waiting here, in the dark.

My hand brushed against the light switches inside, until the living room lit up in an eerie glow. I breathed slowly, taking it in. The couch and the cushions, just as I'd left them. No evidence of someone else who had been here with me. But the air was cooler, from the front door left open. "Okay if I take a quick look around first?" she asked, and I nodded. Maybe she'd come back with me to make sure no one was hiding out here. To make sure it was safe.

Nina walked slowly around me, her footsteps echoing on the hardwood. I followed behind to each room, still barefoot and dirty, my toes curling on the cool floor. She flicked another light in the hallway. Then the kitchen light, with the faucet left dripping. Next, the office, messy and barely used.

The only place she didn't search was upstairs, the steps hidden away behind the door in the hall that looked like a coat closet.

She stopped at the entrance to my bedroom, flicking on the last light. "You heard the phone from here? From inside?"

It was colder in here, and I felt a gust before I saw the reason: The window beside the bed was ajar, the sheer shades billowing in. Nina strode across the room, pushing apart the shades—ignoring the unmade bed next to the window, and my phone, faceup on the bedside table.

I didn't remember opening the window. But I didn't remember making it out of the house, either. Maybe it was that familiar dream, pushing back against the four walls . . . maybe I wanted to see a way out.

She leaned closer, her head to the place where a screen should be. "I can hear them talking," she said, half to herself.

Now that she mentioned it, I could hear it, too, the voices at the crime scene carrying in the wind. I could've heard a phone.

My own phone buzzed on the nightstand. Nina saw it first and frowned. "Kind of late for a text," she said.

And then, just as she reached for it, it started ringing. She picked it up, held it out for me, and I knew from the photo lighting up the display—the call was coming from Jonah's cell.

I froze, and it rang a second time. Was it one of the officers outside, calling back the last-known number? Would I have to face it right now, with Nina watching?

"Gonna take it?" she asked, practically placing it in my hand. The skin around my knee pulled as I sat on the edge of the bed.

I fumbled the buttons twice before answering, and held the phone to my ear. "Hello?" I held my breath, could hear my heartbeat inside my head.

"Liv, I know it's late and you were probably sleeping, but I have to say this—"

My breath escaped in a rush, everything unspooling inside me. "Jonah?" I looked up at Nina, who was frowning. His name was on the display. Of course it was Jonah. "Where are you?"

"That's what I'm trying to say, if you would give me a minute." His voice was slurred, the words tripping over one another. "In my office, trying to make sense of this shit schedule I've been given. Trying to see how I could make it work."

"Make what work?"

"You. Us. I was stupid to let you go, so stupid, and—"

"Jonah, don't do this. It was a mistake. I have to go." I ended the call, my fingers faintly trembling.

I looked to the window again. It wasn't Jonah out there in the bushes. This had absolutely nothing to do with me.

It was entirely plausible that I heard the phone, and it woke me. It was entirely plausible that I heard it in my sleep, and that was what brought me out there.

I decided something right then. The story was true, and I could believe it. It was as true a story as any: I heard the phone, I woke up, I saw the man, I ran.

The truest stories are the simplest ones.

Nina was still watching me. "What was a mistake?" she asked.

"Responding to a message from my ex last night."

She nodded, then took in the room again, slowly tallying things one by one. The open window. The bed. The hallway. Back to me, eyes roaming over my clothes, my exposed skin. I followed her gaze to my knee, to the tear in the fabric, the red seeping through the makeshift bandage.

"Let's get you to the hospital," she said. "We should really get that checked out."

I wasn't sure whether this step was optional. Whether this was a suggestion or a requirement. What the rules were when you found yourself inside the orbit of a dead body. But I didn't object.

This house would tell a story if she knew what to look for, and I didn't want her to see some other possibility hidden underneath. I wanted her out of the house.

I wanted us both out, and far away from all of this, as soon as humanly possible.

TRANSCRIPT OF INTERVIEWS COMPILED AT SEARCH HEADQUARTERS

OCTOBER 19, 2000

PAMELA CROUCH: They weren't doing enough. It was obvious. We know the difference between a rescue and a recovery.

CHARLIE MENDOZA: If we don't do it, who will? That girl's mother is watching. That girl is still out there somewhere.

WILLIAM HARRIS: It's math. Get enough people and divide the area up. We've got enough people now. They're coming in from everywhere.

ANITA LAFAYETTE: I heard there are divers coming.

CHARLIE: Heard they're gonna drill down in some areas where they think there might be air.

PAMELA: I heard there are even more people coming. Volunteers from other states.

ANITA: The high schools are bringing some of their portable field lights. We'll keep searching. We'll keep at it until she's found.

WILLIAM: They're using infrared now. Got those from a hunting club, a group of concerned citizens. Like I said, it's math. Get enough people, enough gear, and it's just a matter of time.

CHAPTER 8

Saturday, 4 a.m.

I WASN'T ACCUSTOMED TO THE night shift at the hospital—the flip side to my day. There was extra security; a staff I wasn't completely familiar with. Nina Rigby led me through the ER entrance, not realizing I was an employee.

I filled out the paperwork with the least amount of information possible. My insurance, my name, my date of birth—the usual. Nothing that required a medical professional to dig any deeper into my personal history: I was always aware of where that could lead. I wasn't sure how much information was tied to my new name, how much had transferred, how much each system was connected— but the less I provided, the less likely anything would be questioned.

It was a cut on my leg. That's all. Nothing else was relevant.

Except I knew what *would* be available and easily

accessed right now, shared on this very system: my recent visit with Dr. Calvin Royce.

Even without the details, the visit itself would imply something.

I hoped no one saw it and mentioned it. Not in front of the police.

The waiting room was full, with some noticeably sick children ahead of me, including one with an audible wheeze who, thankfully, got called back first. But having the police escort must have bumped me up the list. After I'd checked in, Nina Rigby went up to the reception desk, showed her ID, and said something to the woman that I couldn't understand—but the woman peered up at me for a split second, and we didn't have to wait long to be called back, vitals taken by a nurse I vaguely recognized. She must've filled in for someone on the day shift in the past.

I was glad for the loose pajama pants, and pulled the material up to my thigh, so the wound could be cleaned and assessed.

The nurse spoke with a soothing smile, and I couldn't tell whether she recognized me, either—or at least recognized my name. Eventually, she left us in the semi-private curtained area, me in the single bed, Nina sitting in the single visitor chair against the wall.

Nina Rigby was practiced in stillness, it seemed, and it was making me anxious, and restless. All I could do was stare at the gap between the curtains, keeping watch for the doctor and trying not to think of the events that had led us here.

The buzz of Nina's phone made us both jump, and she distracted herself for a while texting someone on the other end. Her face gave away nothing.

"The body was found on Mr. Aimes's property," she said. "That's the primary crime scene, though they may have to expand it once we get a better look in the daylight. Okay if they need to check over the property line, in your yard?"

She was looking at her phone when she said it, and when I didn't respond at first, her eyes cut sharply to mine.

"Sure," I said.

She continued typing, then slid the phone into her bag.

"How long have you known Mr. Aimes?" Nina asked. I wasn't sure if this was related to her phone conversation or just her personal curiosity. But I erred on the side of caution, assuming they had taken Rick's statement back at his house already. I needed to be careful to match his story.

"I bought the house from him. Over a year ago. He keeps an eye out for me, and I try to do the same. I don't think he has any family in town."

"No," she said, "he doesn't."

I looked her over, with her clean pressed slacks, the boots, the windbreaker. I didn't know her role in this; Rick had introduced her as Nina, and she'd never clarified whether she was an officer, an investigator, a liaison. She didn't look old enough to be in charge, but she had the air of authority. Such was the benefit of small towns. Same way I had my position in the hospital so young. "You've known him awhile?"

She crossed one leg over the other before answering. "I grew up here. I knew his son."

I had opened my mouth to ask another question when the doctor pulled back the curtain in one swift movement.

She said hello absently, eyes to Nina, then to my bare leg, then down to the paperwork in front of her. "Good news is this doesn't seem to be anything but a surface injury. Bad news, cuts like this over a joint still generally require stitches to heal correctly. And, unrelated, I'm a little concerned about your blood pressure." She stood closer, sliding on a pair of gloves. "Let's take a look."

"Dr. Britton?" I asked. Even though of course it was her. Sydney, with her trademark sleek blond hair and sharp cheekbones, now dressed up in a white lab coat, glasses perched on top of her head. Hadn't it been just yesterday when she'd been checking out of work, tired and in need of sleep, picking up wine and a microwave meal from the G&M? Yet here she was, fresh-eyed and sharp, with no recognition on her face.

She blinked twice, like she was trying to slide me into context. "Liv?"

"You two know each other?" Nina asked, suddenly standing.

"I work here," I said, and the tiniest of lines formed in Nina's forehead. "Not as a doctor . . ." I pointed to the ceiling. "Upstairs. Administration."

Nina looked at me closely, as if she could see the potential for all the other things stored inside that I had not offered up. "Nina Rigby," she said, directing her words to the doctor. "Detective with the police department."

Detective. The word chilled. Turned this visit into something else. Was I still being questioned here? Was I a suspect? I was cooperating, and I didn't want to ask. Didn't want to make the wrong move, drag things out that should remain buried.

"Sydney Britton," the doctor replied. She was looking

carefully between the detective and me. Categorizing everything that was not right—from my dirty feet, slipped into flip-flops, to the worn pajama pants. I felt the night, wild and clinging to me.

"What happened to you?" Sydney asked, voice different—not as a doctor but as an acquaintance.

"I hurt my knee outside. I tripped."

"Well," Detective Rigby added, letting the word hang in the air. "She tripped over a body she discovered outside. Which probably explains the blood pressure."

Sydney's head jerked to the side, taking in what the detective was saying. She slowly turned back to me. "A body, huh? That must've given you quite the scare." But her tone was flat, and I wondered if the detective could hear it, too. We'd all seen bodies here, in various states. Maybe, in her opinion, it was a disconnect I should have perfected by now. How desensitized she must be to trauma and death. Even to me, they were rows on a spreadsheet. Tallies in the day.

But not in the yard. Not around our homes. Not in the middle of the night, when we woke up with no idea how we'd gotten there. I was betting Sydney's blood pressure would be through the roof, too, if a body were the first thing she saw upon waking.

Sydney took a steady breath, then placed her gloved hands around my kneecap.

Detective Rigby leaned forward and cleared her throat. "The knee, it's from an impact injury?" she asked.

The doctor's hands stilled as the two shared a prolonged look, and I suddenly understood. It was the reason she'd brought me here, and why she was *still* here—to figure out what had happened out there. Whether I had tripped. Whether I had omitted some other details in the lead-up. She might not be questioning me in an official capacity now, but she was gathering information. She was checking out my story—seeing if it held.

The question she never asked that was lingering under the surface: Was there something else I'd neglected to share? Some measure of violence that led to another?

Sydney turned around and pulled the curtain abruptly shut, blocking the view of the nurse who had been standing nearby. Not that it would stop her from hearing.

"You tell me, Liv," Sydney said, gloved fingers gently pressing into my knee again. "Is that how it happened?"

Three women in the room, understanding what else could've been possible out there. The dirt on my clothes. The blood. The fear.

I winced, leaning back on my elbows. "I didn't know it was a body at first. I heard the phone, and I tripped over it." A shudder. "Over him."

Sydney looked into my eyes for a moment before turning to the detective. "Yeah, this sure looks like a hard, uneven impact. A root or a rock, I'm guessing?"

I shook my head. "I think so. It was dark. It all happened so fast."

I watched as the doctor quickly scanned the rest of my body—the clean shirt, the exposed skin. I'd assessed myself in Rick's bathroom, and Detective Rigby had done the same when we were in my bedroom. There was nothing to see. No reason to suspect a different version of events.

Detective Rigby went back to her chair, sending messages on her phone, and Sydney got set up to treat the wound.

After numbing the area, she cleaned and stitched me up,

her hands fast and practiced. A pattern that was hypnotiz-
ing to watch. When she finished, she tore her gloves off
quickly, the sound like a snap cutting through the room.
"All right. We'll need to see you back in about ten days to
have the stitches taken out. It looks worse than it is, with
the localized swelling. Let's get you an anti-inflammatory.
Maybe with something to take the edge off the nerves,
yeah?"

"Yes, okay," I said.

"Any drug allergies or adverse reactions we need to be
aware of?"

"None," I said. One time, when I was a teenager, I was
given a medication to calm me before what the doctors
claimed was a routine procedure to fix an outstanding
issue in my arm, and I had no recollection of anything
until hours after the surgery, when the nurse beside my
bed finally said, *Welcome back, Arden*. I wasn't sure if that
counted as an adverse reaction, but at the moment, I wel-
comed the idea. Of taking a pill and disconnecting.

"Is there someone at home with you?" Sydney asked,
eyes on the chart she was filling out.

I couldn't tell why she was asking, just like with Dr.
Cal. Whether she had access to other information that she
wasn't disclosing.

When I didn't answer, she paused and looked up. "This
medicine I'm prescribing is also a pretty decent sedative.
Just making sure someone will be around to check in on
you."

I was about to answer that my neighbor would cer-
tainly check in when the curtain peeled back, and a wide-
eyed Elyse stood on the other side. "Well, shit," she said.
"Hey. You okay?"

Her face was completely clean of makeup, her hair tied up on top of her head. Loose T-shirt, leggings, sneakers. I tried to see the signs of Trevor on her.

"What are you doing here?" I asked.

But I knew. The look from the woman behind the desk when I checked in. Or the nurse who had taken my blood pressure. Or the one with her back turned when the curtain was pulled shut. The way information swirled through back channels in a place like this.

"You didn't call," Elyse said. Then she looked at the detective, confused. Stuck out her hand. "I'm Elyse, a nurse here." Waiting for an explanation.

"Nina Rigby. I'm the detective who got the call to-night." She reached out to shake Elyse's hand.

Elyse's handshake paused almost comically. Then she turned to me again. "Are you okay? What happened?"

"It's not me," I said. "There was a body, and I tripped."

The corner of her mouth twitched, and I couldn't tell whether the unintentional humor was in my delivery, or whether there was something darkly comic at the core of the entire situation.

"Well, if you need a ride home, I've got you," Elyse said. She turned to the detective. "I can take it from here."

Detective Rigby smiled tightly. Sydney grinned at Elyse. "She's just about all set," the doctor said. Then she turned to me. "I can also probably get the paperwork sped up, seeing as none of the departments want to look bad in front of you." She patted the edge of the bed before leav-ing. "Glad you have someone here with you."

Detective Rigby stood and handed me her card. "There's going to be some activity around your house," she said. "A team will be at the scene for most of today, at least. And there will probably be some follow-up visits. Some paperwork."

"Thanks," I said. It was a relief that she was leaving. A sign that she had gotten what she'd come for. That the story held.

The detective paused at the exit. "I've got your initial statement, but it might help if you write down everything you can remember as soon as possible when you're back at the house, for when the time comes. See if being back home triggers anything else. You're a witness, and memories have a way of . . . slipping after too much time." She stared at me before stepping through the gap in the curtains.

Elyse made an overexaggerated grimace when the detective was out of sight. "Yikes," she said. "She's very intense. I didn't expect that when I first saw her."

"She is investigating a death. That's probably the required demeanor," I said.

But Elyse was right. There was something about Detective Rigby that made you focus on the wrong thing. I'd spent the last hours beside her trying to unravel the surface of her and missing what she was actually doing here. I wondered if this was how she worked—letting people underestimate her and seeing what they gave away in the process.

I'd let her into my house, let her look around. Let her sit beside me while the doctor gave an opinion on my injury. It had probably worked out for the best. She'd seen inside both Rick's home and my own and must've realized no crime had taken place inside.

But I'd let her in, not even realizing what she was doing. I'd let her in before I'd had a chance to see it for myself. That could have been a huge mistake. I had to be more careful.

"I'm gonna go check on the paperwork," Elyse said, squeezing my leg. "Sit tight, okay?"

Separated from me by the curtain, the bustle on the other side fell away—a reality happening somewhere else. A shadow rushing by. A beeping from somewhere down the hall.

A phone started endlessly ringing, and my mind was back in the darkness, struggling for context. I closed my eyes, trying to find it—the memories, before they slipped. Searching, like Detective Rigby had suggested:

Texting Jonah, wineglass in hand. Realizing it was a mistake. Walking to the bedroom . . . Somewhere in the following hour, I'd gotten changed, climbed into bed, placed the phone beside me on the nightstand. But I couldn't pull those details to the surface. They were mundane, the minutiae of each day, a subconscious routine. I could picture it but couldn't be sure the memory was from last night specifically, above any other typical night. Instead, I heard the ringing. Felt the impact of the hard earth. Saw the shadow beside it, and the dirt and blood and—

"Liv?" Elyse was standing in the gap of the curtains but now rushed to my side, hand to my wrist. "You're breathing too fast. Your pulse is racing."

She looked to the hall like she was going to call for a doctor, but I gripped her hand. "I just want to get out of here. Please. I want to go home."

Her large brown eyes searched mine, and she nodded. She placed a hand at my elbow as I stood. "Yeah, we're getting out of here."

———

EVEN EXPEDITED, IT WAS nearly an hour after Dr. Britton had finished up by the time I had the discharge papers and the prescription from the pharmacy in hand.

Elyse yawned as we walked across the lot for her car. The sky in the distance was lightening with a purple glow. I eased myself carefully into the passenger seat of her white sedan, and I dropped my purse on the floor behind me. She had a small overnight bag, which could've been from changing out of her scrubs after work last night, but also could've been because of the evening plans that I'd just interrupted.

"Were you with Trevor?" I asked as she slid into the driver's seat.

"No, no. I didn't stay out much longer. The music, blah. And Bennett turned all sulky after talking to his ex. What a trip. No offense, I know he's your good friend, but he can be kind of a mood killer." She drummed her hands on the wheel. "Did he call you? Last night, I mean."

I took out my phone, scrolled through, but there had been nothing other than Jonah's call. Everyone had gone home to a typical night, it seemed. "Nope."

"He was not too pleased that you left without saying goodbye. I told him you weren't feeling well, but . . ." She shrugged. "When he left, I figured he was calling you." She looked my way, and I shook my head. "I texted him when I found out you were in the hospital," Elyse continued, "but it didn't seem to go through. I called and left a message, but it went straight to voicemail. I think his phone was off." A cut of her eyes in my direction. "Sorry, I didn't know how else to reach him."

"No, that's all right, he's like that." The rule follower, silencing his cell for all sleeping hours when he wasn't on call. Often turned off, for good measure, so people wouldn't expect a response.

"I'm sorry," Elyse said, taking a deep breath. "I'm talking too much because I'm nervous. Because I don't know what to say. Are you okay? You're obviously not okay. I mean, other than your knee. There was a detective. And a *body*. I wouldn't be okay."

"I'll be okay," I said, hoping it was true.

Her grip tightened on the steering wheel. "And he was just . . . there?"

Looking at her, I thought briefly that she might still be drunk. How many hours had it been since she'd left the bar? She'd had at least two drinks before I went home, and she hadn't seemed in a rush to leave. "Just lying there."

"And you found him? In the middle of the night?"

The darkness and the ringing and then the shadow— "I heard a phone." Trying the story on for size. Getting used to the way it felt, until I could see it myself, what had happened during the gap of my memories.

"I heard it was a box cutter," she said, voice lowered.

The air kicked in through the vents, a sudden icy blast.

I cracked my knuckles on the side of my leg. Hadn't thought much about the logistics of what had caused the blood.

"Sorry, I'm doing it again," she said. "Talking too much."

"No, it's okay." I cleared my throat. "Where'd you hear that?"

"The nurses. Some of us have a group chat. You know, for . . . keeping the next shift in the loop on things."

She had stopped herself before she confessed to violating HIPAA privacy rules, for saying that the nurses might share patient information or stories via texts. A fine line, with or without names. The gray area between legality and morality.

But I knew my name must've been mentioned. That someone told her a cop had brought me in to the hospital. I guessed it wasn't technically confidential, as long as my medical history wasn't shared.

And now, on another floor, a man had likely been brought to the morgue. Another examination happening elsewhere, trying to unspool the story from a different angle.

I knew Central Valley didn't get a lot of murders. I'd checked what I was getting into before I moved here. Not as quiet as Widow Hills, but the deaths we documented and tallied were mostly illness, or accidental, or expected. It was worse in the winter, with the icy, winding roads and the mountainous terrain. Even then, there weren't typically police investigations surrounding them.

"What else did you hear?" I asked as she turned onto my street. "Do you know who it is?"

She eased her foot off the gas, seeing the police cars still parked on the side of the road. "No. Not that anyone's saying. Just that. A man brought to the morgue. And that you were there, too." Her eyes cut to the side again. "This is scary, Liv."

One more honest thing, then: "I know."

ALANA COX: We're going live to Tiffany Lu, who's joining us from the volunteer headquarters in Widow Hills, Kentucky. Tiffany, can you tell us what it's like there right now?

TIFFANY LU: Good morning, Alana. The search for six-year-old Arden Maynor is now entering the third day in Widow Hills, Kentucky. What had first been driven by a majority-volunteer outpouring of resources and support has now turned into a massive undertaking on a national level.

At the most recent press conference last night, Captain Morgan Howard was pressed for his thoughts on the status of the search. He said that, quote, "We will find her. That's what we're here to do, and we're going to do it."

He was then pressed on what the chances were of finding her alive. Captain Howard's answer was evasive yet firm. He responded, quote, "A child is not a statistic."

Alana, we've been interviewing various residents in the area over the last few days who have told us that locals themselves have organized searches through the easier terrain. But there's now an experienced rescue operation combing the treacherous terrain in the valley. Helicopters are scanning the area from above with infrared, looking for heat signatures that could match a child's. And there are teams preparing to explore the system of drainage tunnels wherever they are accessible.

It's a race against time, and they're using every hour and every person at their disposal. It may be three days since there's been any clue or hint to her whereabouts, but the people surrounding the search are undeterred.

For all of us at the volunteer headquarters, it's becoming easier to believe Captain Howard's promise. The general feeling on the ground is that they will not stop until the child is found.

ALANA COX: Thank you, Tiffany. And thank you to everyone on the scene for all you're doing to find her. For the rest of us, we can only watch—and hope.

CHAPTER 9

Saturday, 7:30 a.m.

ELYSE TYPICALLY BRIGHTENED A room or a mood. But there was no helping the situation of my house. It was the crime tape we could see to the left when we pulled up my drive. The voices carrying across the yard as she helped me up the steps, one leg awkwardly following behind, stiff from the stitches. And it was something else when we stepped inside, a scent I couldn't place—not quite sweat but something that made me imagine a person. A whiff of product. A reminder that a detective had been in here with me, looking around.

I wondered if anyone else had been in while I was away. If Rick had let them in using the key I'd given him. There were probably guidelines against that, but these were all people who knew one another, with a shared history that meant more than protocol. Rick had even introduced the detective as Nina.

The lights had all been left on from the night before, but the house suddenly felt like a stranger. A creak in the hall where I didn't remember one. An empty nail hole in the wall over the kitchen table. A tear in the window screen over the sink.

Elyse stood beside me, unfolding the directions that came with the prescription. "You're supposed to take this one with food." She placed the page faceup on the table. "Sit tight, I'll get some breakfast going."

I picked up the paper, reading over the details as Elyse took a carton of eggs from the fridge. I read the description of the medicine to myself, then bit back a laugh.

"You okay over there?"

A sleeping aid. The prescription was for a pain reliever that was also used, at times, as a sleeping aid. "Just realizing how much easier it is to get a prescription for something on the surface. The cut wasn't even that bad, really." I shook the amber bottle, tipped a pill into my hand, took it with a sip of water from the sink.

"I think it's also about how you got it, Liv."

I plopped down in the chair at the kitchen table, resting my leg on the spare one to keep it straight and elevated, per Dr. Britton's written suggestions. Elyse cracked an egg over a bowl, then reached for another.

"What's the worst thing you've seen?" I asked.

She froze, the yolk running. "In this hospital?" she asked, staring at the bowl. She shook her head. "I don't work in the ER, so I don't see the worst of it, you know? Some of the other nurses, they talk, though. They see a lot more . . ." She was staring out the window with the torn screen, but her eyes seemed unfocused. "Anyway, it's best to leave that at work. It's really the only way."

"I know, I just, with the texts you mentioned sharing, I thought maybe it helped to talk about it . . ."

"My job . . . it's not what I expected. I don't know what I expected, really, but I need to shut it off at the end of the day."

"I get it," I said. I thought of Sydney and the bottle of wine, the promise of *Law & Order* reruns waiting for her at home. Me with my glass of wine. We all had our routines.

Elyse crossed to the fridge, pulled out the milk and butter, kept talking as she moved around in my kitchen. "I was in a really bad car accident when I was seventeen. So much of my memory of the recovery was just . . . pain. The nurses kept me sane, kept me positive and focused. They're who I remember, those same faces, day after day. I just wanted to be one of those people."

"I didn't know that," I said, my voice softer. I was always surprised by the things I didn't know about other people, like I was the only one with an unknown past. I'd never been good with sharing, nervous about the past creeping in, giving too much of myself away—so people rarely shared in response. It had kept me guarded, closed off.

I wanted to tell her something now, to cross that divide. Something about last night that I didn't have to keep hidden—

She stepped back from the stove abruptly, eyes fixed straight ahead. "Liv, someone's out there."

I stood, the chair scratching against the floor. "The police?"

"Definitely not. Some old guy in flannel."

"Oh," I said, my heart rate slowing. "It's just my

neighbor, Rick." Elyse must've heard me talk about him in the past, but they'd never met.

I opened the back door, Elyse just over my shoulder. Rick was walking through the trees just beyond the edge of the yard, but he didn't seem like he was heading this way. There wasn't any place else he could be going, really, not without his truck.

"Rick?" I called.

He changed direction, ambling toward me, and when he came closer, he was normal Rick, in his flannel and work boots—a comforting sight, even now. "Glad to see you're back home. I had to get out and clear my head." He peered over his shoulder, like he was checking for someone, then lowered his voice. "They said it's fine if I come and go as long as I keep off the marked area, but every time I step out front, I feel like I'm being watched."

I nodded. After my night with Detective Rigby, I understood. I had felt like every word and action was being filed away and assessed. I thought then of the gun under Rick's sink. The electrical tape. The things he had hidden away. Also: the light on at his house, the bed that was still made when I showed up. All the things the police could've found or noticed.

But he had gone to check on the body. He had made sure my hands were clean before the detective showed up. I felt partially guilty—I was the one who had pulled Rick into the nightmare, who had gone straight to him instead of to the police.

"I just got home. This is my friend Elyse."

"Hi there," he said, taking one step back. "I see you're in good hands, then. You just holler if you need anything."

"Thanks, you know I will."

He turned back but stopped halfway. "Everything go okay with Nina?"

"Nina?" Elyse cut in. "Wasn't that the detective?"

I knew Rick had given a statement, just as I had—and I wanted to ask. Wanted to make sure they matched up, wanted to know whether there was anything else the police had mentioned to Rick. But not with Elyse here. Not with the police just on the other side of the walls.

"Yes," I said, answering them both. "It was fine. She brought me to the hospital for my knee." I gestured down. "I needed stitches."

"Oh, good. Good," Rick said. "I know her family. She was always a good kid." Then he turned away.

None of us were kids anymore, but I wondered if Rick could only see us that way, so far removed from his own past. "Call if you need anything, Rick," I said to his back.

I closed the back door, and the silverware drawer rattled, a quirk of the house.

He raised his hand in acknowledgment as he walked away. I watched from the window, standing beside Elyse, as he turned back for his own house, satisfied that I was home and safe.

"That was odd," Elyse said, the moment between us long gone.

"No. That's just Rick. He keeps an eye on me."

"Mm," she said, turning back to the eggs. "Where do you keep the whisk?"

I pulled out the middle drawer, handed it to her, and as she turned away, beating the eggs over the countertop, I stared at the top drawer.

A box cutter, she'd said. Something sharp and short and efficient. I'd used mine just a few days earlier to open the box of my mother's things. I held my breath, eased the top drawer open slightly. Pens and scissors and a pad of paper. I moved a few things around with shaking hands, but I didn't have to. I could already tell: It was gone.

"I should've asked," Elyse said. "You good with scrambled?"

I eased the drawer shut, feeling untethered, a balloon floating away.

"Liv?" she asked. "That pill isn't working already, is it?"

"Sorry," I said, shaking my head. "Yes, scrambled is great." I heard the click of the gas before the flame caught, the sizzle of butter in the pan on the stovetop.

I didn't like enclosed places, which was part of the allure of the house: the openness around it; the multiple windows and exits; the rooms that flowed from one straight into another. But now I felt bound by the perimeter, like people were watching; like I shouldn't leave without reason.

The box cutter wasn't where it was supposed to be. Something breaking open inside me. All the possibilities of where it might be.

The box had arrived on Wednesday, and I'd used the box cutter to slice through the tape. I'd pulled out the contents, gotten swept away in the moment . . . I must've slid it into a different drawer afterward, my mind unfocused. Or left it inside the box by accident, as I replaced each item.

"Sit," she said, pointing the whisk at me. What I really wanted to do was ask her to leave so I could go through the drawers one by one. Search the house top to bottom until I found it, and be sure. Because that was the problem: I could never be sure. Not until I had it in my hand.

Elyse slid the dish in front of me, and I continued to surprise myself, scooping up the eggs like I hadn't eaten in days, practically ravenous. Even after all this.

"You might want to slow down a bit . . ."

I put the fork down, a memory surfacing.

Eggs on the tray in front of me. My mom beside the bed, arms crossed. The doctor at the foot of the bed. The sound of the fork against the tray, nothing satisfying, an endless bottom. "Slow down, Arden—"

The days after the rescue. Scenes flickering into focus—though incidents that might not be real.

It had been happening like that ever since I opened the box—this blurring of time.

I'd passed a group of nurses gossiping in the lobby the morning after the box arrived, and thought I'd heard my mother's laughter—the unrestrained, high-pitched giggle that used to make people expect a child or a teen instead of a full-grown adult woman with a child of her own.

The same thing had happened around the ten-year anniversary. Flashes of memories that could not be mine:

Walk down the porch steps, and I'd see a little girl in a nightgown doing the same, the scene in sepia tones, like an old photograph. Ride the bus to school down the tree-lined street, and see a cluster of volunteers trudging through the thick foliage, searching for me. Close my eyes at night and see my mother with her hand to her neck as she called my name into the emptiness.

These memories did not belong to me. They were images from the news. Stories from the articles. From my mother's book.

This was another truth I discovered back then: A story about you doesn't necessarily belong to you. It belongs to the writer. To the witness. To the teller.

When they say: *The girl from Widow Hills, remember?* What they were reaching back for weren't your memories—they were their own.

I was too young to really remember, and too much time had passed anyway, the trauma buried under so many layers that it existed only in the physiological reactions: the flutter of my pulse as the doors slid shut in an elevator; a ringing in my ears in the darkness of a movie theater before the first trailer kicked in; the cold sweat that came over me when someone stood between me and an exit—the need, the compulsion, to act.

It had happened the first time in the high school locker room, right after the ten-year anniversary: a girl standing between me and the only way out.

I thought it had probably happened again that time I was drunk in college.

Six years had passed since that last episode.

Now that box had kicked everything closer to the surface again, as if the past and the present could coexist on the same plane.

"I missed dinner last night," I said, explaining.

"You've been through a lot. Adrenaline like that takes a toll. But it'll make you sick if you eat too fast. And you want that painkiller to stick." Elyse ate standing up at the counter, barely touching her food, gazing out the kitchen window, as if watching for something.

Like whatever she'd heard about was made real by her standing there—the fear transferring to her by mere proximity.

"What do you think happened out there?" I asked.

She stopped moving the food around her plate. "I don't know. It's pretty deserted out here, though."

"It's not deserted," I said.

"You know what I mean. Look, I love your house. I'm jealous of it, really. I'll probably be living in that same shitty apartment until I'm fifty by the time I pay off all my debt. But come on, Liv. It's so dark at night. A reason people might want to come out here. Meeting in the middle of nowhere for a drug deal. Or, I don't know, someone could've driven out this way and dumped the body, less chance of witnesses." She shook her head, like she was clearing the image.

I could understand her point of view. She lived in the apartments where most of the newer hires moved at first, before deciding whether they were going to stay. The younger people tended to live there anyway, with the gym and the pool and the on-site laundry. It was convenient in more ways than one. My area was just as close to work but not as traveled. The lots had been cut wider, from before the industrialization. I'd gotten a good deal, when all was said and done.

Still, I thought the chance of random crime was higher near her, as the population density increased. Where people and walls abutted one another.

This, out here in the openness, had always felt safe. My primary fear was not of other people, of what they might do. I was afraid of being trapped, and even then, of people not knowing where I was. I kept my phone beside me at all times. And I liked having Rick close by; I liked that he noticed when I was gone. I liked being sure that, should I not return one day, there was someone who would know. I thought it was easier to be overlooked where Elyse lived, with the rush of bodies and activity.

We finished eating in silence. I tried to help clean the

dishes, but she took the plate from me, gestured with her free hand down the hall. "Go get some sleep. I'll stick around in case you need anything."

I was grateful that I didn't have to ask. My limbs had turned sluggish, and my walk was slow and deliberate.

Elyse followed me down the hall to my bedroom, eased a pillow under my leg to keep it elevated. Her gaze drifted to the window, and I could see the activity reflected in her eyes.

"Are they allowed to be on your property?" she asked, edges of her mouth pulling down.

"The body was close . . . just over the property line." My voice was slurring, a lightness settling in my head. Every worry becoming smaller.

So they were still out there. And coming closer. I felt I should care more—something in Elyse's expression said I should. But I was already drifting. The sleep, dark and heavy, pulling me under.

TRANSCRIPT OF EMMA LYONS'S LIVE INTERVIEW WITH LAUREL MAYNOR

OCTOBER 19, 2000, 7:03 P.M.

EMMA LYONS: I'm here in front of the site of the volunteer center with Laurel Maynor, Arden's mother. Laurel, thank you so much for sharing your time with us today. We want you to know that all our viewers have been hoping and praying for Arden.

LAUREL MAYNOR: Thank you. That means a lot.

EL: You were telling me earlier how strong your daughter is.

LM: She is. She's only six, but she takes ballet. She runs outside, she rides her bike. She's always moving. She knows how to swim. I know she can survive this.

EL: We believe it, too. And everyone who has gathered here from as far off as Michigan believes it. That's why they're here. We heard at first that concerned citizens weren't happy with the search effort. Do you believe that's changed with all the attention Arden's case has gotten?

LM: Yes. People keep coming, keep finding new ways to help. It's given us all more hope. I'm so grateful.

EL: Is there anything else you'd like our viewers to know about your daughter?

LM: I just want her back. I want to go back in time to a few nights ago and wake up sooner—

EL: Hold on, just a moment— Yes? What? Please repeat?

LM: I want—

EL: No, sorry. Not you. Hold on. Say once more? Oh my God.

LM: What is it? What happened?

EL: Please pardon the interruption, but we're reporting here live with the news that someone believes they've located Arden Maynor.

LM: What?

EL: Ms. Maynor, they think they've found your daughter.

CHAPTER 10

Saturday, 3 p.m.

I WOKE DISORIENTED.

The open bedroom door. The rattle of a bottle down the hall. An image of my mother in the kitchen, the amber container in her hand. That blurring of time.

But I was also in my bed, my leg elevated, arms lying still at my sides. Like I hadn't moved an inch. I couldn't tell whether I'd been asleep for a minute or an hour.

I reached for the phone on my bedside table to check the time, but it wasn't there. I couldn't remember whether I'd brought it in with me when I went to bed.

"Elyse?" I called, pushing myself up on my elbows. My throat was dry, my voice raspy, and I tried again. "Hello?"

A shadow filled the hallway, and my eyes struggled to focus. "Look who's up."

I knew the voice before his face clarified, and I fell back on the pillow, wondering if I should be mortified that Bennett was seeing me like this. "When did you get here?" I asked.

"About an hour ago. Sorry it wasn't sooner, I couldn't find someone to cover my shift on short notice until after lunch." He stepped into the doorway, leaned against the wall. "Elyse swapped with someone's night shift. I sent her home to get some sleep."

I couldn't tell if that was Bennett being generously friendly or being aware of his role as the head-of-shift nurse. In addition to setting the schedule and handling any issues that came up during the shift, he also had the unenviable job of documenting and reporting infractions. So he'd never send anyone to work who he thought wasn't up to the task.

I bent my leg slightly; the stitches ran vertically on the outside of my kneecap, and the swelling seemed to have gone down enough to allow for a little more motion. "How long have I been asleep?"

"It's just after three. You've been sleeping like the dead." And then, with a glance to the window, he winced. "Can I come in?" he asked as I pushed myself to sitting.

"Yes, but I can get up just fine." Sitting upright, I felt better. Not just the leg—I felt vindicated that what I'd really needed all along was a sleeping aid. I'd have to ask Sydney for a refill.

"I'm sure you can. But just in case." He stepped closer to the side of the bed. He'd been in my house plenty of times, but never in my room.

"I'm not going to sue you if I fall, Bennett."

He grinned tightly. Hospital protocol. Step one, never allow any further damage. He held out his hand, and I took it, his other hand at my elbow as I stood, steadying me. But I wasn't about to let him help me around the house.

"What's next," he said, stepping back, his eyes roaming slowly over me. He wrinkled his nose and suddenly seemed five years younger. "Shower, maybe?"

I hadn't changed from the night before, and the remnants of mud at the bottom of my pajama pants had caked and hardened. Maybe that was the source of disorientation when I woke—the scent of fear and adrenaline clinging to my clothes.

"You're always full of good ideas," I said. Standing closer to him, I could tell he was assessing me in a medical way. Could I walk straight? How was my sense of balance? Were my eyes focused? Pupils normal and reactive? "Are you going to check my pulse next?" I asked.

He smiled for real then. "Would you let me?"

"No," I said.

"All right, well, good luck, then." He gestured toward the bathroom. "Don't get the stitches wet," he called as I closed the door behind me.

"I know," I called back, rolling my eyes. But I also knew there was no way he would send me on my way if he thought I wasn't able to handle myself. There was something reassuring about knowing Bennett's assessment. That I was fine and would be fine. That the danger had passed.

This was how he handled patients, prodding them out of bed, convincing them to circle the floor. A firm push toward getting better even as they resisted. A detached, clinical kindness.

I wanted to run the wash immediately, destroy all

remnants of the night before. But that would look suspicious with Bennett here. And he'd probably insist on doing it himself.

My feet turned the water in the tub a dull brown, dirt lingering from last night. Circling the drain was a piece of a leaf, which had probably been tangled up somewhere in my hair. I scrubbed under my nails, but they had already been cleaned in Rick's bathroom.

After, I slipped on a pair of loose sweatpants and an oversize shirt—no use pretending at this point. My bedroom door was open, but there was no sound coming from the rest of the house. "Bennett?" I called, stepping carefully into the hall.

Bennett had obviously made his mark on the house. He was an organizer in both times of stress and times of boredom, and I couldn't tell which was the source right now. He'd stacked the magazines I'd occasionally bought at the G&M, by date. It looked like he'd also fluffed and redistributed the throw pillows on the couch. The living room smelled faintly like glass cleaner. I wouldn't have been surprised if he'd wiped down the windows and the furniture while waiting for me to wake up.

And now he seemed to be tackling the porch. The front door was ajar, and he was on the small stepstool I usually kept beside the fridge, replacing the light bulb.

I knew the surface of Bennett well. Could see something of myself reflected in his way of interacting with his surroundings, how deliberate he was with what he chose to do or say. There was always a familiar comfort with him.

But when Elyse started at the hospital and latched herself on to our twosome, it recalibrated the dynamics of our friendship—like I could see it now only from the out-side in, with all the things he kept hidden from me. Ben-nett was harder to read, with a layered exterior I couldn't always see beneath. Elyse was a little more on the surface, and there was a different kind of comfort in that.

Right now Bennett's cool focus on his task was giving me my first moments alone since the police arrived.

I used the alone time to open the rest of the drawers in the kitchen, searching for the box cutter. Rick had given it to me when I'd first moved in, to help unpack the boxes. It had a black handle and a shock of blue paint on the edge, something that once reminded me of a child's room. It should be easy to spot, easy to find. But it wasn't in the drawer with the pot holders, or the coupons and receipts, or the Pyrex containers.

I had just closed the last utensil drawer when Bennett's voice cut through the room. "I picked up some things, if you're looking for something to eat. Didn't know what you had to work with here."

I turned, hand to heart, noticed the brown G&M bag beside the fridge. There was a half-drunk glass of orange juice resting on a square of paper towel beside it.

"I do own food, Bennett."

He dropped the old light bulb into my trash, care-fully tied up inside another plastic bag, then grinned as he poured me a second glass of juice. And I trusted that he knew what would be best for me. It was so easy to let someone care for you. How long it had been since it wasn't the other way around—searching for my mother when she didn't come home at night; searching the house for pills; searching for a place to wait out her mood swings between care and anger and paranoia.

When I moved away, every time the phone rang, it suggested that something had happened to her. I'd realized I couldn't save her. None of us could. The only people we could save were ourselves.

"You look like you're feeling at least two hundred percent better," Bennett said.

"I was starting from a pretty low place."

I placed the glass on the counter, feeling the cold work its way slowly down my esophagus, like everything had become paralyzed while I'd been sleeping.

"You should keep off the leg when you can," he said.

We relocated to the living room, where the remotes were lined up on the coffee table. He'd found coasters in some side table drawer, and we used them now for our glasses of juice. They were only ever out when Bennett was over. Bennett lived in a new townhome community closer to the hospital—whenever I stepped inside, it was so clean that I questioned whether he actually lived there.

We could hear the investigators calling to one another from somewhere in the distance, and Bennett turned the television on, volume low, the dull hum of the weather report drowning out their voices.

"So. Want to tell me about last night?" he asked.

"You first," I said. The steady rhythm of his voice was a comfort, even amid all this chaos. It calmed me, seeped into me. I sometimes thought I was a chameleon, quietly changing shades to blend in with the environment. I didn't know whether this was an inherent part of myself or a coping mechanism from all the attention. This pull toward camouflage. The need to not draw extra notice.

He grimaced. "You were gone by the time I got back to my seat."

I remembered Elyse telling me that Bennett had been irritated when I'd left without saying goodbye. Flashes of early in the evening came back to me. Elyse flirting with Trevor. Bennett talking to his ex. It still prickled.

"I wasn't feeling good, I told you."

His knee bounced beside me. "Liv, why didn't you call me? When you got to the hospital? I had a message from Elyse, but I didn't know whether you were okay until I got to work in the morning."

"Oh. I'm sorry."

His expression darkened, and he looked off to the side. "You should know you can call. Even though my phone was off, leave me a message. Let me know you're okay. Don't let me wake up to this again." He took out his phone and played Elyse's message, her voice high and tight, cutting through the silence: "Goddammit, Bennett, pick up the goddamn phone. Listen, I just heard there was some incident at Liv's place. She's at the hospital now. Thought you'd want to know."

Then dead air.

"An incident," Bennett repeated. He shook his head. "That's the first thing I heard this morning. Nothing else. Nothing from you, nothing about whether you were okay. By the time I got to the hospital, you'd been released. By the time I reached Elyse, you were asleep."

My stomach sank. The truth is, I didn't know why I hadn't called him. Hadn't even thought to do so. Maybe I just wasn't used to having that person to depend on. I was unaccustomed to the expectations of longer-term relationships. My friendships in the past had existed by proximity and hadn't bridged the gap of time from high school to college, from college to grad school, from grad school to here. I maintained a comfortable, casual distance and relied on myself.

"I think I was in shock," I said. "And then Elyse was there. She said she called you."

He looked at my cell, which had been placed on the table, from wherever he'd found it during his organization spree. "Did you call Jonah?" There was a cutting tone in his voice.

"No, I didn't." I hated that Bennett still brought him up, but the truth was, I *had* texted Jonah last night after the bar.

"Well, he's been calling you."

I sighed, leaning back. "He drunk-texted me a couple of nights ago. I may have texted him back last night in a bad moment. When you were all . . ." I moved my hands around uselessly. "He wanted to see if we could *make it work*, but I don't want that, and I told him that." Or at least I thought I did. I couldn't remember. He had called when Detective Rigby and I were in the house, and I'd been too shocked to see his name; to realize he wasn't dead in my yard.

"I see," he said. Short, to the point. Bennett flipped the channel from the local news to a baseball game, and I could almost pretend this was normal. Like we were drinking beers and watching a game, instead.

"Your ex is very pretty," I said.

"She is," he said, staring at the television.

"Sorry it didn't work out."

He shook his head. "I'm not. The whole time we were together, I got the feeling she was always looking around for something else. That I was a way to pass the time until something better came along. I called her on it, and she balked." He shifted so he was facing me. "But sure looks like it was true, that she found what she was looking for pretty damn quick after that. Then of course it became a chicken-or-egg argument—that I had pushed her away with my lack of confidence in our relationship and not the other way around."

I sighed, head resting on the back of the couch. "Jonah didn't want anyone to know about us until I broke it off." I raised my glass of orange juice toward him in a mock toast to our own relationship shortcomings.

"If it makes you feel any better, it was obvious anyway. I knew the second I met you. To watch the two of you together, well. You don't have the best poker face, kid."

"It's embarrassing, in hindsight." I'd fallen for Jonah because he took an interest in me, because he didn't know anything about me other than what he'd learned in his classroom. It was a thrill when he smiled at a comment I'd made, his face lighting up, surprised. It was a thrill when he'd sent me a text that night, telling me, *I've been thinking about what you said in class all day*. It was thrilling to imagine myself as that person.

"Well, we learn, I guess. I learned I don't want to get involved with anyone hung up on anyone else, even if it's just the idea of someone," Bennett said. "Also made me think twice about ever dating a colleague again."

He was holding his breath, and I knew he was saying something more.

"To be perfectly honest, I thought you weren't interested in women, maybe."

He laughed, surprisingly loud. "Do you think anyone who doesn't hit on you is gay?"

"Yes," I said, and he laughed again. "That's the medicine talking." It wasn't just anyone. It was someone who spent as much time with me as he did. But who still kept his distance, kept a part of him closed off. Or maybe we were just too alike.

"Am I a colleague?" I asked, because the rules on this were fuzzy.

"Ish," he said, grinning. "To be clear, I have not been waiting around for you to get over yourself. I like this." He gestured to the space between us on the couch. The distance. Or the comfort.

"Maybe we shouldn't be having this conversation when there's a crime scene outside my house and I'm hopped up on painkillers."

"No, this is exactly the right time to do it, so that if it turns out I've read the whole thing wrong, we can both chalk it up to a medicine haze, and you'll forget about it in the chaos of everything else happening."

Even now, I was comfortable, and I didn't know whether it was the buzz of the pills or him. I wasn't good at this, at knowing how to build a long-term connection. But he leaned closer, like he was going to tell me a secret, and then he did: "I was fucking terrified," he said, his hand shaking in the space between us. I grabbed it, just to get it to stop—because it scared me, the intensity of the reaction. But I understood how a trauma could alter your frame of reference. How, when tragedy was averted, the reaction might swing to the other extreme.

"I'm okay," I said.

He squeezed my hand once, let it drop between us. "I'm really glad."

My phone chimed again.

Bennett pulled away, rolled his eyes. "You better get back to him so we don't have to listen to this all day."

I picked the phone up, scrolled through Jonah's string of messages, feeling nothing. Bennett stood, and I caught him staring out the window. I wrote back to Jonah: *This is a really bad time. Please stop calling.*

"What do you think happened out there?" I asked. Elyse had provided a safe theory, but I knew Bennett's would cut closer to the truth.

"I think we're about to find out," he said.

I craned my neck, even though of course I knew. Detective Rigby was on her way.

We interrupt the scheduled programming with some breaking news. Arden Maynor, the little girl who was swept away during a storm in Widow Hills, Kentucky, has been found. We repeat, Arden Maynor has been located.

Early reports indicate that she is alive but trapped. After nearly three days of searching, a cheer erupted outside the volunteer headquarters.

We're trying to get to the scene, and as soon as we do, we will bring you right there. Until then, stay tuned.

CHAPTER 11

Saturday, 4:30 p.m.

BENNETT LET DETECTIVE RIGBY inside. He introduced himself, shaking her hand.

Her gaze slid from Bennett to me, sitting on the couch, leg elevated on the coffee table. "I'm glad you've got people checking in on you, Olivia," she said. "How are you feeling?"

"Better," I said, and it was true. It was a terrible thing that had happened, but terrible things happened everywhere—I saw them come in every day at work.

My friends had come to help. It didn't have to be how it was in the past.

She sat in the armchair beside the couch, and Bennett took our empty glasses to the kitchen, giving us the illusion of privacy.

"Did you take my advice and write down your memories of yesterday evening? I'd like to revisit a few points."

I shook my head. "No, sorry, the medicine made me

fall asleep pretty much as soon as we got back. I just got up." I gestured to my wet hair as evidence.

"May I, then?" she asked, motioning to the notebook on her lap, the folder underneath.

"Sure."

"I want to start here. I was wondering, did you run to Mr. Aimes's house because you saw him awake in the house somehow?"

I blinked twice, trying to find my bearings. This was a trait I generally liked in people, when they were no-nonsense, straight to the point—telling me what they wanted of me, so there was no confusion. But I felt caught on my heels, and I was careful not to say something before I'd had a second to think things through.

"No, it was just instinct." I hoped she didn't ask why. It was the same question I'd been asking myself. Why there instead of my own home, where my phone had been left behind? Whether I thought there was still something out there; whether the thing I feared was myself.

"And what was he doing when you arrived?" she asked.

I couldn't remember. There were parts that stood out in my mind: the phone, the body, the running, the bathroom, the gun. But there were already gaps forming, mundane details that I'd failed to hold on to.

Anyway, she was asking the wrong questions, focusing on the wrong element. I'd been prepared for questions about the sound I'd heard, the body I'd found. My own actions. Not about Rick.

I stopped talking, didn't want to say something to incriminate him when he'd done so much to cover for me.

"Rick is a friend," I said. "I went there because it's where I felt safest."

She continued staring, clicked her pen once. "Walk me through what he did after you arrived."

I closed my eyes, trying to see. "He went to check outside. I don't know. I was in the bathroom."

"He checked before calling 911. Any reason why?"

Yes: for me. To make sure we knew what he was calling in.

"Neither of us thought to call 911. I wasn't thinking at all. It's not like we've dealt with dead bodies before."

"That's not entirely true," she said, her calm face belying the subtle accusation.

"I work in hospital administration. I don't deal with patients," I snapped back.

I heard dishes in the sink, and her eyes cut to the side before sliding back my way. "You know about Mr. Aimes's wife, right?"

"I know she died, that he lives all alone." Had he seen her body back then, too? Had he needed to call it in himself? Had she taken her last breath at their home and not at the hospital?

"Do you know how his wife died?"

I shook my head, not wanting to say: *I never asked.* I didn't want to pry. Neither of us dug too far in the other's life, and it was there that I found comfort and safety.

She took a slow breath, dropped her voice. "I was just a kid. A senior in high school. Gunshot." She punctuated the word with her hand, thumb and pointer finger in the shape of a gun. "One of those guns he keeps in his house. I'm sure you've seen them, just sitting there in a case in their hall. Officially ruled suicide, but I've heard things."

"What sort of things?"

She shrugged. "Like I said, I knew his son, Jared. I was

a couple of years younger, but my brother was friends with him, used to hang out up here a bunch. Mr. Aimes built this house for him, to keep him here. Expected his son to stay right here, can you imagine? My brother said it was oppressive. Mr. Aimes liked to control things, it seems."

She kept talking, but I was picturing the gun under the sink. The cabinet down the hall full of shotguns. The one he tried to give me for protection. Maybe Elyse was wrong; maybe it was a gunshot and not a box cutter. Maybe that was the sound that drew me outside to begin with—

"His son took off soon after. I think, until then, it was his mother that kept him here. But after?" She shook her head. "I think it's telling that he couldn't look at his father after. That he couldn't live here anymore. Mr. Aimes held on to this place for years, hoping he'd come back. Jared got married, has a kid. Tell me, Olivia, have you seen his son visit in all the time you've been here?" She let that sink in as she made herself more comfortable, settling back in the chair. She didn't even need me to answer.

I used to believe most people were good, or at least had good intentions. They mobilized to save you. They rallied in a crisis. The people of Widow Hills demanded more action, and they got it.

I believed that firmly until the ten-year anniversary, when I realized that some of those same good people felt they were owed something. That there was a scorecard, always, being kept. And I had not reciprocated what had been owed. By then I was firmly in the negative.

"How long ago?" I asked, because I was living in his house. A house I'd once thought was a happy place, a place built with two hands and good intentions.

"Would be about a decade now," she said. And the place had sat empty all this time. "No one wanted to live so close to a man who was a suspect in his wife's death, unofficial or not." She shook her head. "He shouldn't be keeping all those guns there. Not at his age."

I didn't know what to say, because I agreed. But I also wondered if I'd run there last night because I knew he had them. Because there was safety in that illusion.

"Just be careful here," she continued. "Be careful who you trust. You're walking into something with history, and you don't know the whole story."

I thought of Rick in my backyard early this morning. Rick asking me about my conversation with the detective. Had he been concerned that she'd already told me and was there to do damage control?

But. He'd covered for me. He could've easily said: *I found Liv asleep outside the night before.* And as far as I knew, he hadn't.

Detective Rigby pulled the folder from under her notebook. "Okay, I've got something to show you." Like she'd accomplished what she'd set out to do. A part one to guide the story, shake something loose in me. Change the framework of the context. "He's not from here, the man you found." I could feel Bennett standing just on the other side of the kitchen entrance. Detective Rigby's story had worked its way inside, changing my perspective.

Maybe it was an intruder.

Maybe Rick had seen him first.

It would explain why he was awake when I showed up, why he didn't take out the gun for protection—because he already knew what had happened.

The detective had a photo in her hand, and she laid it

on the coffee table. I held my breath, thinking it would be a photo from the scene. Eyes closed, life drained from him.

But it wasn't. In the photo, the man was alive. He had salt-and-pepper close-cropped hair, deep-set eyes, and a completely neutral expression. The white of the background made me think license or passport.

"Oh," I said. Those eyes. Under the ball cap. A tip of the head. The way his mouth moved when he said my name. *Olivia, right?*

"Do you know this man?" Detective Rigby asked, leaning closer, like she could read something in my expression.

"No," I said. "Yes. I don't know him, but I saw him once. I don't know who it is."

"Where did you see him?"

"Outside the G and M yesterday morning. He said my name like he knew me." I'd thought he was a journalist, watching me, waiting for me. Maybe he was. But then this was about me. Still, maybe Rick saw him, watching me.

A little overprotective.

A little fast with the trigger.

"Was he following you?" the detective asked, her voice growing faster, tighter. Giving away her excitement. "What did he want?"

How desperately I wanted to keep the past where it belonged. I could feel the stirring of panic—if he was a journalist, they'd want to know why. The sinking of my stomach, the numbness in my limbs, the room too hot, muscles suddenly wound tight with the urge to *move*—my body fighting back.

"I don't know. I only saw him the once. I didn't like

the way he was watching me, so I left. He said he knew me, I said he didn't. That was pretty much it." It was instinct, how I answered with the bare minimum required to craft a scene. Giving the necessary facts while leaving out the context. "Who is he?" I asked. There were other possibilities. A man asking for directions. Someone who liked what he saw and followed me home.

"Name's Sean Coleman. His license says he's from Kentucky. We're still in the process of tracking down his next of kin, so we need to keep this between us for the moment." ·

The porch light flickered in my peripheral vision, but she didn't seem to notice.

"What?" I said, though I wasn't sure if any noise escaped at all. My throat felt dry, and the air turned cold and empty.

The detective's eyes latched on to mine.

"His name," I said. "What did you say?" I had to make sure I was hearing it right. That I was exactly where I thought I was, in the present. That the dream or the nightmare wasn't rising up and overlapping.

"Sean Coleman. Fifty-two years old. You know the name?"

My ears started ringing. It was a name forever tied to mine. In every article, every news story. Too common a name to turn up on its own in a search, but add Sean Coleman and Arden Maynor, and there he would be. His hand reaching into the grate. Circling my wrist. I'd heard the story a thousand times.

His photo beside mine in the news broadcast. The hero, looking off to the side. He looked so young then.

The moment I'd been found was played over and over

again. That woman reporter, interviewing my mother as the news came in.

In that moment, she was every mother, and I was every child. It aired again on the five-year anniversary in every special broadcast, and again on the ten-year. It played to emotions; it was the video that people remembered the most.

But there was another clip, one that hadn't endured quite as long. It was a little grainy, a little disorganized; you couldn't see our faces. But it was the moment that counted.

Sean Coleman, the man who had found me.

Bennett was there now, standing just inside the living room, listening.

Four walls closing in, and nowhere to go, no way to escape.

The past had found me. It was here. It was time.

"Yes," I said. "I know the name."

DON MULLER: Welcome to the viewers who are just tuning in. We've got Emma Lyons on the scene, and what you're about to see is some pretty dramatic imagery. Emma, can you tell us what we're looking at?

EMMA LYONS: Don, right now we're just beyond the perimeter set up by the rescue operation. We've got a pretty clear shot through the trees to that clearing, where the activity is happening. Fred, if you zoom in there . . . Don, let me know if you can see that all right? Can you see the man near the ground?

DM: Yes, we can see him.

EL: The man in the green shirt, with his back to us—he's the one, we believe, who found Arden Maynor. Look closely. Over his shoulder, there's a hand holding on to the fabric of his shirt. That, we believe, is the hand of six-year-old Arden Maynor, trapped under the grate. Her hand is gripping the back of his shirt. She's alive. And not only that—it seems she's conscious.

DM: Incredible. Absolutely incredible.

EL: I almost can't believe it myself, Don. It's miraculous.

DM: What's the scene like there, Emma?

EL: You can absolutely feel the excitement in the air. There's an energy in the crowd. But they still have to find a way to get her out.

DM: Can you fill us in a little on anything you've heard about the ongoing rescue operation?

EL: Of course. They're being very careful. They don't want to do anything to disturb her. The lid to the drainage pipe there is sealed pretty good. We hear the man who found her fastened a belt around her to hold her close. They're reinforcing those safety measures right now, so that she remains safe, first of all. They're going to have to stay like this for a while, until they figure it out—the best way forward. This access point is actually not one that's mapped on the city system, but something older, from the original system, back when this area was a mining community. So there's a bit of confusion over how best to reach her. They're about to begin drilling through the surrounding earth, to see what they're dealing with.

DM: Do they know who it is, Emma? The man who's holding her up?

EL: We haven't gotten official word, but several of the local folks we've been interviewing tell us he's from the adjoining town. A thirty-two-year-old by the name of Sean Coleman.

CHAPTER 12

Saturday, 5 p.m.

THERE WAS A VISCERAL reaction to speaking about the past. Something I'd long gone out of the way to contain. A shaking that started in my fingers, a tremor that worked its way through my body, though no one seemed to notice but me. The precursor to panic; something that seized my mind and body alike. This biological desire to keep the past contained, in a different part of the world—a different person, with a different name.

I'd thought maybe the detective was too young to remember. That enough time had passed. It was our parents' generation that really experienced the case so immediately, who felt that terror and relief deep in their bones. So I started at the beginning. Assuming she knew nothing.

"I was born Arden Olivia Maynor," I said. "There was a terrible accident when I was little. I was lost, trapped, for days. And it felt like the entire country was watching my rescue. I changed my name before college, to escape the media attention. It was just . . . so much."

As soon as I said that name, I could see recognition settling in, sharp and surprising.

"The girl who was swept away in a storm," Detective Rigby said, something close to awe in her voice. "The girl who held on to a grate for three days." She didn't mention the sleepwalking, but she must've known it. That fact must've been there, lodged somewhere in the back of her mind.

"Well, no. Not exactly," I said. That was the story my mother seemed to want to believe—something beyond miraculous. The story, hyperbolized in memoriam. "But yes, I was swept away in the flash flood and trapped somewhere in the pipes for three days before making my way to that grate. I was found clinging to it, three days later. Sean Coleman. He was the man who found me. That's his name."

The detective didn't blink, didn't even seem to be breathing, when I told her what the name Sean Coleman meant to me. I could sense everything shifting as I spoke. The investigation resettling from Rick's house to right here.

Because it had to be about me.

He had to be heading for my property, my house.

Sean Coleman had to be coming here.

Or he was watching. At least that much was clear.

Detective Rigby said she'd be back, but I stood as she walked toward the door, trying desperately to convey something—twenty years' worth of meaning—into a pointless request. "Is there any way—" I began.

She turned at the door, her mind already halfway across the yard, or on the phone, to the next person she would tell. A chain that had just kicked off, and here I was attempting to ask her if there was any way to stop it. To leave me to my life, when the man who saved me was dead. I knew it wasn't fair. And yet I asked. "What if none of this is relevant?"

She did me the benefit of acting like I had a chance, even though we both knew that wasn't a fair thing to ask. "I don't know yet," she said. "But what I can do is let you know first, okay? I'll let you know what we find out. Sit tight, and don't talk to the media."

Of course I wouldn't. But I could already see the headline. The hook. The man who saved me had come back looking for me twenty years later. And now he was dead outside my house. I could already see the fingers flying across the keyboard, matching the speed of the rumors. The Girl from Widow Hills. Moving backward in time, from the ten-year anniversary, to the five-year, to the original event.

A part two: *Where are they now?* From hero to victim. From victim to witness. A reshuffling of roles. As if, all along, we were in a tragedy—it had just taken us a few extra decades to get there.

The detective left, and I was still staring at the closed door when Bennett shifted behind me.

He was holding his phone out in front of him, like he was following a map. Though he'd obviously just performed a quick Google search, seen all he needed to know. As his hand dropped to the side, I saw my photo from years earlier, smiling at me from upside down.

I couldn't read his expression. "I wasn't trying to hide it,"

I said. "I just tried to move on. The things people say, Bennett. The letters they would send. It's a thing that happened to me, and I don't even remember it. I mean something to them. I can't be who they want me to be. I don't want to."

"I'm not judging you," he said. And yet something had closed off. A door we'd just pushed through swinging back. "It's just, I've known you for over two years. We know each other *pretty well*, Liv. Were you ever planning on telling me?"

All I could feel now was the space between us. A rift opening up.

"We don't really know that much about each other," I said, and his face shifted, like I'd hurt him. I'd been wrong about him—there was plenty on the surface that was easy to read if I watched closely.

Maybe it wasn't for his lack of trying—he'd invited me to his family home, after all. Maybe he'd been able to read into me more than I'd thought, and understood that he had to move slowly, handle with care. But he wasn't being honest here, either. "Come on, I didn't even know about your girlfriend until yesterday."

"It's a little different, not bringing up the ex who dumped you. And, like, not telling someone you were famous and changed your name. Seems like something pretty important."

The truth was, I hadn't considered telling him. Or anyone. It was a thing I had fought to keep behind me for so long, it had never occurred to me to let it out voluntarily.

"I guess that's my answer, then," he said.

"I've never told *anyone*, Bennett." Couldn't he understand? It wasn't a lack of trust in him specifically. It was everyone. It was survival.

"No one? No boyfriend? No college roommate?"

I shook my head. Nothing had ever lasted long enough that it would need to come up. And that was probably why I didn't go to Charlotte with Bennett for Thanksgiving last year, volunteering instead to remain as the hospital's on-call contact throughout the holidays. Preferring a makeshift dinner with a group of people who had stayed behind. Joining the open-to-all potluck organized by Sydney Britton; having pie with Rick after, watching a football game on his couch.

"No one," I reiterated.

He frowned. "Don't you think that's a little messed up?"

Oh, didn't I. As if I needed him to say it; to see it. Of course, I couldn't really escape the fallout. Change your name, change your address—none of it could ever change what had happened. It had screwed up my life back then. And it was screwing it up now, just in a different way: twisting myself to fit the confines of a safe and quiet life.

"You have no idea," I said, my teeth gritted together. "You have no idea what it's like. We had to move from Kentucky to Ohio in the middle of high school after the ten-year anniversary, it got so bad. You should see what it did to my mom, the things it pushed her to." I shook my head. There was a faint tremor in my fingers, but my voice kept dropping, going steady somehow, even as I was falling apart. "I moved away from her, all alone, to start over here." How to explain the feeling of panic, deep in my gut; waking up in the middle of the night in a cold sweat, my heart racing, sheets thrown back—like I was still trying to escape. Wondering if I ever would.

"Okay," he said, eyes closed. "I get it. I'm sorry." He

looked around the room, out the window, back at me. "We don't have to do this right now."

But I wanted to tell him something on my own, something he wouldn't just read on his phone later. "I have a scar," I told him. I lifted my left arm out to the side. "Can't move my shoulder above this."

His eyes settled on my upper arm. I knew he'd seen it before. "I thought it was from an accident."

"It *was* an accident," I said. "Dislocated shoulder. Fractured humerus. I needed surgery to get things back in place. Nails and wires to hold it together."

"Broken and dislocated?" He winced. "That's rare in a kid. Must've been incredibly painful."

"I don't remember it," I said, shrugging it off. "I also don't like enclosed spaces."

He scratched the back of his head, looking off to the side. "And here I thought you were a germaphobe."

"I mean, I am. But the space is the primary culprit."

He smiled then, eyes lighting up in that familiar way, so I knew I was amusing him, whether he wanted to admit it or not. Maybe I could do this. I could be both Olivia and Arden, and Bennett could accept past and present as one.

But then his face darkened, jaw tipped toward the window, to the invisible place where someone had just died. "You didn't recognize him? At the store?" A tone of incredulity. Bennett, sifting through the facts, like the police would be doing somewhere else.

I shook my head. "It's been twenty years." To me, he remained that ageless photo in the papers. That single clip from his lone interview. He'd faded into the background after, an ancillary piece to the story. I could see the similarities, now that I was looking for them, underneath the passage of time. The deep-set eyes. The shape of his mouth. But in my mind, he was still so young.

Sean Coleman. To think he wasn't much older than we were now when the media first shone its light on him. That he was thrust into the camera with the same speed at which he'd grabbed my wrist. What I'd remembered from his interview was that he was soft-spoken and tentative. Nothing like I'd remembered of the man in the store: *Hey, I know you.* So sure. So different from the soft-edged, shell-shocked face after the rescue.

Bennett paced the room slowly, scanning the surfaces he'd seen dozens of times before, like he was looking for something new. Something that might clue him in to a different person—one he'd never met.

"What were you seeing Dr. Cal for?" He wasn't looking at me when he asked it, and the entire room suddenly changed.

My jaw tensed. "I told you," I said, words even and measured. "I couldn't sleep."

I knew why he was asking. The information at his fingertips, tucked away in his palm. The girl from Widow Hills had been sleepwalking. That's what made it such a compelling story. She'd been swept away at night, and she hadn't even seen it coming.

He turned to face me, no longer acting nonchalant. "I'm just saying, you know how the hospital can get." And didn't I? How long had it taken for Elyse to show up in the ER after I'd been brought in? How long before everyone knew the details of the case? About the body and the method of death?

"There are HIPAA laws, and like I said, I'd been having trouble sleeping."

I could imagine the detective asking it instead, the implied meaning underneath. I was glad she had left. But Bennett was doing the same, seeing the present through the filter of something that had happened long ago.

Bennett had his eyes closed, one hand held out in front of him in defense. "I'm just saying. Someone must've seen you walk into his office. That's it. The rest is conjecture, nothing more."

Bennett was probably filing everything away in his mind. Deciding, right then, which side of the line I fell on. "Seriously, Bennett? It's *your* conjecture."

He cringed, then took a step closer. "No, I wasn't saying . . . I'm sorry. I'm having kind of a hard time with this. It's just a lot of information all at once."

"I didn't even know who he *was*," I said, hands balling up. My nails dug into my palms. "Or do you think I'm lying?"

"No, I believe you. Of course I do. Anyway, you have the world's worst poker face. But that detective . . . have you talked to a lawyer about this?"

I shook my head. I had been worried when I realized my story was being tested at the hospital, but it had stood up to scrutiny. And now I was cooperating, sharing the past I'd fought to keep hidden for so long. I didn't want to give Detective Rigby any reason to take a closer look. "I didn't do anything," I said.

"I know, it's just . . . You know my sister Mackenzie is a lawyer. I can ask her what she thinks."

"Bennett . . ."

"Just as a hypothetical. She won't do anything with it." And then, at my pause, "It can't hurt."

Though I wasn't sure if that was true. In the past,

people who came under the guise of help also wanted something in return. I may have been born with a healthy dose of self-preservation, but I developed the lack of trust legitimately.

"Please don't."

"Okay," he said. "Just—" He took out his phone. "I'm sending you her contact, in case you change your mind. She's technically on maternity leave, but knowing my sister, I'm sure she checks in at the office. Just tell her I sent you."

"All right," I said. "Thank you."

Bennett's expression softened, eyes to the window again. "I don't like you living so close to that guy. What's his name? Mr. Aimes? I heard what the detective said about him."

As if we could go back. Somehow center the story around Rick instead. As if he could unsay it all.

"Rick," I said. "He's always been good to me, Bennett."

He sighed. "I wish I didn't have to go right now, but I do, unfortunately. Elyse said she'd be back tonight."

"It's fine," I said. I didn't need a babysitter. The cops were still out there; I felt safe knowing they were probably keeping a close eye on both Rick and me.

I knew the irony was that the increased media attention probably saved my life when I was lost. A lot of people were watching the search, so they couldn't stop looking, even though most people thought—even if they wouldn't say—that I had probably been killed immediately, in the initial flood. And if I hadn't been, the chance of finding an air pocket, of making it to safety, was small. The chance of reaching that grate and holding on where I'd be found? Even smaller. The chance that Sean Coleman was walking by that very spot? Borderline miraculous. That's what made it a story that prevailed.

But I also knew what the story could demand of you, after.

This was what people wanted: They wanted it all. They wanted to fit you in a box. Hold you in the palm of one hand. Sum you up in one sentence. The shorter, the better. So they could understand who you were and the role you were intended to play for their benefit.

Right now the police interest would keep me safe. I was sure of it. I just didn't know what would happen next. There was a line, and you had to stay on the right side of it.

"There's food in the fridge," Bennett said. "And I found the remote between your couch cushions. If you're looking for hair ties, there were about twenty there, too."

"Ha."

"And that bracelet." He pointed to the ceramic bowl on the side table. "It needs to be fixed, though."

"What bracelet?" I didn't wear much jewelry; it got in the way at work. Maybe it was Elyse's, but she rarely wore any unless we were going out.

"Looks like a dance charm? Never took you for a ballerina, but I'm learning a lot this afternoon."

I was already shaking my head. That bracelet was in the box, in the corner of my bedroom closet. Hidden away with the rest of my mother's things.

"Is it not yours?" He picked it up, the whole thing dangling from his thumb and pointer finger. So dainty and fragile. Two of the chain links had torn apart in the middle.

"It is. Well, it was my mom's." I hadn't been a dancer

since I was a small child. Even then, I didn't think a five-year-old in a tutu qualified.

He dropped it in my palm, and I gripped it tight to keep my hand from shaking. The scratch on my wrist glared back at me. I imagined the bracelet there. "It was in the living room?" I asked.

"Under the back pillows of the couch," he said. "Look, I should probably get some sleep before my shift tomorrow. Will you be okay?"

"Yes." I needed to get back to my bedroom to check the box. Figure out what had happened. Despite what I'd told Bennett, I no longer thought of Rick's proximity as a comfort, either. I no longer knew what had happened in this house.

"Elyse said she'd swing by before heading in to her shift tonight. But I'm also going to leave my phone on. You can call me," he said. He raised his arm like he might pull me into a hug. He did, but it was awkward, and stiff. Like we were pretending at something now. Arden Maynor was a stranger to him.

As she was to me.

AFTER BENNETT LEFT, I looped the bracelet over my wrist, trying to line it up with the scratch. Trying to trigger a memory. Searching deep into the recesses of my mind, trying to shake the night into focus.

Had I walked to the closet, clasped this on my wrist? Listened as the charm jangled when I moved? The sound I remembered close to my ear as my mother braided my hair.

She'd worn it for as long as I could remember, even

though, after the accident, that part of me drifted. The damage to my shoulder meant I'd lost the flexibility: a buildup of scar tissue from the dislocation, and the bone below that took too long to set. Still, after everything, she enrolled me in classes. As if to prove that I could go on.

She showed those pictures to the press six months later, sold others for publication. The long scar, exposed and on display. I wondered what they'd paid for them; I wondered what I was worth.

I hated being watched. By the five-year anniversary, old enough to make my own decisions, I wanted nothing more to do with it. By the ten-year anniversary, I suspected that I was, and continued to be, a commodity for her.

Looking back after so much time, Arden Maynor felt like a role I'd played once. A character I'd read about—her backstory in a book. *Describe her in three words: brave; capable; survivor.* Play the role until you believe it. Until you become it.

But I was no longer that girl. I'd shaken her off, piece by piece.

In high school, I'd found my own skill: running. One that required mental strength more than physical skill, though no one seemed to believe me when I said that. I wasn't built like a runner. My legs were shorter than the average runner's, but I could cut through the air, and if I went out fast, no one could catch me. It defied logic, because I couldn't catch someone else. Never seemed to gain on them. But I knew something no one else did. I'd learned long ago that endurance was a feat of the mind and not the body, so I gave over to that someone else. A brief disconnect. The switch flipped. Another voice in my head, and all it ever said was *Hold on*—as if my life depended on it.

But for years after, my mother wore that bracelet. It didn't matter that I was no longer that girl. She held on to that image with a fierceness I'd never understood.

I'd stopped noticing it only after the ten-year anniversary, when things started disappearing from the house: things she sold, things she lost. By the time I left home, I thought it had long been traded for something else.

And now it was here. Here, out of the box, in my living room. Had I been wearing it—had I lost it—before the body of Sean Coleman was discovered outside my house?

Finally, I was alone. No Bennett, no Elyse, no Detective Rigby, no Rick stopping by. Just this house and its secrets—waiting for me to uncover them.

EMMA LYONS: Mr. Coleman, will you walk us through how you found her? How it happened?

SEAN COLEMAN: It was luck, I found her. That's all. I was walking home from the search, a shortcut back to where I'd parked my truck. The streets in Widow Hills have been lined with cars for days, you know? So I was just walking back. And that's when I saw.

EL: What did you see?

SC: I saw her hand, and I knew. I knew it was her.

EMMA: What did you do?

SEAN: I called for help. I grabbed her wrist and I called for help but no one heard me. So I took my belt and secured it around her waist, to hold her closer. And I called for help over and over until someone came. I didn't want to leave her there. It felt like forever before someone finally heard me and showed up.

EMMA: Did you say anything to her?

SEAN: Yeah, I just kept repeating myself. I told her: *I've got you. I've got you. It's okay now, Arden. Open your eyes.*

CHAPTER 13

Sunday, 6:30 a.m.

THE PROBLEM WITH SLEEPING all day, I learned, was that I would be up all night. The events of the last few days and nights had recalibrated my circadian rhythm, and it was doing something to my head.

The first thing I'd done after Bennett left yesterday was check my mother's things. I'd gone to the closet to find the box that I'd left on a shelf in the upper corner, bringing the stepstool from the kitchen to reach. But the box was on the floor—in a back corner, on the bare wooden floor.

Everything else was as I'd left it inside: the sweater, the canvas tote bag, the phone. Even the plastic bag that had contained the bracelet.

No box cutter, though.

The bracelet sat on my bedside table, and I brushed it into the drawer below—a compulsion to keep it close and hidden at the same time.

The rest of the house seemed both strange and familiar. Signs of Bennett's organizing or Elyse's curiosity. Things that had been used or moved, but not by me. The further I searched, the more I wondered: Had someone been through my desk drawers? My bedroom closet? For what purpose? But on second glance, I couldn't be sure. Couldn't tell whether everything was exactly the same as I'd left it, after all. If I was remembering some other time.

It could get like this at the hospital, too, with the same daily routines, the same visitors in the gift shop and faces in the cafeteria. Until a month had passed and a new group had cycled through, but I couldn't tell when the shift had happened.

I'd thought about taking one of the remaining few pills in that vial from Dr. Britton to reset my internal clock, but I didn't like the thought of being in such a deep state when I was alone over here. Not now. Not when someone had been watching and I hadn't realized it. Not when Rick had a past I hadn't understood. Not when someone had ended up dead.

As the sun was rising, things appeared to be getting back to normal outside. The police had finished processing the scene, and the cars had left sometime in the night. All that remained from the scene of the crime was a flutter of yellow tape in the distance.

My kitchen still smelled like yesterday's dinner, and I took the trash bag to the outside bin, tucked against the side of the house, facing away from Rick's place. It was the first time I'd stepped outside that I hadn't felt like I was being watched.

Outside, I tipped the large bin to the side so I could swing the bag over the edge, but something clattered at the bottom first. I stood on my toes, peering in—and saw the remnants of a glass light bulb.

Bennett? I was pretty sure he'd brought it in yesterday wrapped inside a bag, dropped it in the kitchen trash.

The only place missing a bulb was upstairs, in the attic space.

A chill ran up my spine, across my neck, down my arms. That opened window, that sliver of glass between my toes—

I dumped the trash and headed back inside, down the hall, behind the door that looked like a coat closet. I was glad for the daylight when I climbed the stairs. The attic space felt too warm, too enclosed, but the light slanted through the beveled glass windows, casting shadows across the exposed hardwood.

Standing in the spot beneath the empty bulb socket, I bent down, looking closer at the hardwood. The sunlight caught on a tiny piece of glass between the floorboards. My eyes scanned the surrounding area: another piece to the right, catching the light—both so small they had become wedged between the wood beams.

Behind me, closer to the steps: a droplet of blood that I hadn't noticed in the dark.

I looked up at the empty socket, realizing what must've happened. Somehow, before Rick found me outside that first night, I'd been up here. I'd broken a light bulb. I'd stepped in it. I'd cleaned it up.

The disorientation felt nauseating. Or maybe it was being in this room—the inability to take a deep breath, to imagine the open air, a way out.

I backed to the stairwell, unable to imagine what had drawn me up here in the first place.

Had I opened the window that night?

At least now I knew why I'd been outside that evening. I'd cleaned up the broken glass, brought it outside, dumped it in the bin. Maybe I'd tried to get back inside before realizing I'd locked myself out.

The details were slippery, impossible to get a firm grip on. I felt like I was creating a story from scratch. It was a story that made sense, based on the pieces left behind.

But Thursday night felt like an entirely different lifetime.

It was getting harder and harder to pull the events surrounding Friday night into focus, even. Like, as with twenty years ago, something too large to process had happened, and the connection in my memory had snapped and twisted, and nothing looked the same anymore.

I was living clearly in the after, now. After Sean's body had been found at the edge of my property. After the past had found me again.

These were the facts: Bennett had bought enough food for two but left abruptly the previous afternoon; and Elyse had never stopped at my house on her way in to work, like she'd told Bennett she would.

This was how it started.

Ten years ago, when the old interviews aired, there were the classmates and teachers who got closer, who wanted me to confide; who wanted to be part of the story, always willing to spin a new piece of gossip after. People who saw me as a conquest. Like something to be dissected and studied.

There was the other side, too. People who didn't like that they'd missed something, who wanted to be the center of their own story; people who left, either abruptly or slowly. But the result was the same, and I could see the signs coming this time.

The facts made things bad enough; media attention would make it worse.

I blamed the media attention of ten years earlier for pushing my mother into a perilous descent. During the first handful of years after the accident, she was able to feign normalcy. Even though she wasn't sleeping, not when she was supposed to. The lingering effects of trauma, in hindsight: how she'd check in on me every hour, every thirty minutes, every ten. Overinvolved in every activity, every interaction. Unable to still her mind from the worry of whether it might happen again.

The case made all of us, and then it unmade us.

My mother was tragic until she was neglectful. Tossed to the media with no training. Given money for her story and then torn apart for the very same tale years later. She was dissected, piece by piece, in articles and interviews and think pieces. And she dulled it with the most readily available remedy.

The only people who showed up for her were the ones who wanted something from her in return: a piece of the story or the money. An old boyfriend named Nick Valdene, who'd been in and out of our life since before the accident, and who, from the way they talked, may or may not have been my father. I hoped not, but it didn't matter. He was gone again by the time she'd written a check to pay off his debts. And then new boyfriends, new friends, the wrong type; the very wrong type.

After the ten-year anniversary, and her talk-show appearance, the renewed attention, people started making contact of every kind. The calls began. The letters started coming. Every single kind, and you didn't know which until you opened it. Messages on the answering machine, wanting to know how we'd put the money to use. The real question, implied underneath, was of course this: How had we put my miraculous survival to use? Was I worth it?

They wanted to see it, the physical manifestations of their generosity and hope.

They came from far away and close to home. High school was a minefield.

Around that time, I became something else: the girl who got attention. Who wouldn't give interviews. Who wasn't grateful enough. Who forgot where she had come from.

Who was still, years later, trying to escape.

We had to leave. My mother didn't like it, either. Didn't like the version of her reflected in their questions. In the things they would see in her answers. It was happening to both of us, this dismantling of our lives.

When we moved to Ohio and I registered at the new school, I started going by my middle name. Some people knew, but few people cared. It was a thing my new classmates couldn't really remember, either. By the time I enrolled in college, I'd made it official, changing my last name as well. Believing that the only way to escape was to become someone new.

By this point, Arden Maynor was as much a mystery to me as she was to anyone else.

Luckily, most of the original donated funds were tied up in a trust to be accessed for college. Though my mother bled through the money from her appearances and book advance, she couldn't touch that. The fund paid for my education, including my master's, and supported me while I was in school. And the fund financed a big chunk of this very house.

I didn't know whether it was an act of supreme cruelty or bravery that I turned her down when the trust transferred to my possession. It was the last I saw of my mother, the last I heard of her. And I hated that this was the image that remained: that too-skinny person, fidgeting, biting the side of her thumb, looking nervously over her shoulder. Another possible version of me.

Maybe I did feel like I needed to earn it, for all the people who helped us.

I thought I had made good choices with the money: anonymity and a fresh start, and that wasn't nothing.

But now that was in danger. I could see it coming, that slide, threatening to bring me back to the start.

I CALLED ELYSE. I had made a mistake in keeping this from Bennett. I might not have known her as well, or for as long, but she had made herself a part of my daily life; she had confided in me about her accident, what had brought her to this field. I had to be the one to share the news, not let her find out like Bennett had, tainted with the feeling of betrayal. I wanted her to understand, and to understand the need to keep it quiet.

I hoped Bennett hadn't called her to warn her, in a sudden shifting of allegiance.

That was the problem with the start of any story. You had to get ahead of it.

Her phone kept ringing until voicemail picked up, with her trademark perky tone: *You've reached Elyse! Leave a message!* Every statement Elyse made seemed to be punctuated by an exclamation point, or a comma, or an ellipsis as she left her thoughts midsentence, drifting, waiting for you to pick them up and continue.

"Hey, it's Liv. Please give me a call when you get a chance."

I checked the time. I could catch her in person before she left the hospital if I hurried.

I HEARD SOMEONE COMING before I reached my car, and I gripped my keys in my hand—how I used to prepare myself in college, the first time away from home, the points jutting out between the fingers of my fist, like there was danger lurking around every potential corner.

People following, people watching and waiting until I was alone.

But when I spun, it was just Rick, hands in the air, fingers faintly trembling. "It's me. It's just me." He didn't move any closer. My eyes drifted to the yellow tape caught in the bushes between our yards.

"Sorry," I said, lowering my hand.

"Well, I was just coming to catch up, to talk about . . . You've had company, and then I figured you were sleeping, so I didn't want to call and wake you."

He was watching for me, though. How easily could he see what went on here from his house? There were trees and bushes between us, but I could see the glow of a window when he was awake. Rick fidgeted on his feet. And I wasn't sure whether the thing that was stressing him was the body in his yard or what the detective might've told me. What he might've done.

"I have to run out. Do you need anything?" I asked. I often brought him what he needed. Like he'd told Detective Rigby, we looked out for each other.

"No, Liv. I'm all set. I'm just worried about you. About what they were saying . . ."

I flinched. "What were they saying?"

He frowned. "That you needed stitches. That you'd gotten hurt. And I didn't know, I didn't ask you then . . ." His throat moved before he continued. "I didn't ask if you'd been hurt out there."

I shook my head. "I tripped. Running to your house." I heard the flutter of tape caught in the wind. I tried to reconcile the Rick I knew with the one Detective Rigby knew. Yes, he had a key. He knew where the spare had been. His light was on when I ran to his house that night.

I gritted my teeth. This was the detective, this was how it worked—the story planted by someone else, growing into its own thing, its own mess.

And I had to get ahead of it. "Listen, Rick, did they say anything about the man's car? Was it nearby?"

"No. They showed me his picture, that's all. No one's telling me anything. Not who he is, not what he was doing here. Not how he got here. Though I'd imagine it'd be pretty hard to tell, what with all the animals, to know which way he came from. Whether he came in from the front road or somewhere in the back."

The back. Our houses backed to trees, but the property eventually sloped down to a creek. I'd been that far only once. After the creek, the land crept upward toward someone else's property, someone else's home.

"I'm fine, Rick," I said. "Call if you need anything, okay? I'll be out for a bit."

"The man who was here last night," he said, stepping closer. "That your boyfriend?"

"Just a friend." I unlocked the car, not needing to get into the specifics.

"Well, he was arguing with that other girl. Out front. I could hear it all the way from my house. I was working in the yard, cleaning up the mess from the police."

Suddenly, I pictured Rick in my backyard when Elyse was here, just beyond the tree line. How close he had been. And how he'd noticed me walking to my car just now. Detective Rigby's words about his relationship with his own son—that his attention was stifling. There could be an element of truth in that.

I opened the car door. "They're very different personalities," I said. I could picture it, Bennett telling Elyse she had to get home, get some sleep. Work protocol, and he was the one in charge. "But they're both good people. Good friends." God, how I needed that to be true.

I KNEW, AS SOON as I pulled into the hospital lot, that I'd missed her. She always parked her white car near the lot exit when she was working—for a fast escape, she joked. This was something else I had liked about her—this feeling that maybe she was always tallying the steps to her escape as well, but she had the confidence to joke about it. I wondered if I'd ever reach that point, if I weren't so busy trying to hide it.

After circling the lot twice to be sure, I idled in an empty spot, called her cell once more, but hung up as soon as I got her voicemail again. Chances were, she went straight home after the night shift and fell asleep. She usually had Sunday off, and she probably needed the day to catch up. At least I hoped that was why she hadn't gotten back to me yet.

THE G&M ON A Sunday morning looked about the same as any other morning. A scattering of cars, a vague sense of déjà vu, so I could almost picture the blue car, Sean Coleman's forearms leaning on the hood, the rustle of the wrapper of his breakfast sandwich.

I know you.

I parked close to the entrance and walked through the automatic doors, feeling ungrounded. Inside, the same man sat behind the register, the same silent show on in the background. He was helping someone at the register.

Dr. Sydney Britton, like a repeat of Friday. "Hi, good morning," I said as she headed toward the exit.

She stopped dead in her tracks when she noticed me. "Liv. How are you feeling? You're not on your way in to work already, are you?"

"No, I just came for a coffee."

"The leg?" she asked, nodding at my knee.

"Seems a lot better already." I still held it out straight when I sat down, and I still took the stairs slowly, but I thought that was more out of caution than necessity.

"Good, that's good. Take care, and we'll see you for a follow-up next week, okay?" She hitched her purse on her shoulder, turning to go. The bottle in the white plastic bag clanked against something else. I could see the outline of the frozen meal.

"Sydney, wait," I said. "Do you remember the other day when I ran into you here?"

She blinked slowly. "Sure."

"Do you remember someone else in here with us?"

She smiled tightly. "The ends of shifts all sort of blend together after a while, Liv." I wondered if this was her daily routine. Dazed after a night shift, bottle of wine and a microwave dinner. Repeat. "Harvey might know better," she said, tipping her head to the register.

By the time I turned to thank her, she was already striding out the door.

I walked up to the coffee stand beside the register. "Harvey?" I asked, turning his attention from the television as I filled my cup.

"Can I help you?"

"I was in here a few mornings ago. Friday. I wanted to ask you something."

His eyes searched my face, but he didn't respond.

"You said I had an eclectic basket. You asked for my ID."

He nodded slowly, tentatively.

"Do you remember another man in the store?"

His face changed then, eyes closing. He shook his head. "The police already talked to me. I can't possibly remember everyone. And as I told them, the recordings don't save past a day." He pointed to the camera in the corner, over the television set. "No point, if there's been no crime. Not worth paying for the storage service. I heard he died. I'm sorry, did you know him?"

"He tried to talk to me," I said. Wanting desperately to hear what Sean Coleman had to say. What he was there for. Not a journalist. But still coming out of the woodwork twenty years later for a reason.

"I even went through the receipts with the police," Harvey said, ringing me up. "But I don't think he bought anything. I sort of remember him browsing. Maybe. I work this shift most mornings, though, and it's hard to tell them all apart after a while. Same routine, different day," he said, sharing Sydney's view.

"Thanks anyway," I said, paying for the coffee, my fingers shaking.

I SAT IN MY car drinking the coffee, not wanting to go home just yet. Searching the news on my phone to see how far the story had gotten.

The police had been here—in the time since I'd told Detective Rigby about seeing Sean Coleman at the G&M, they'd been here and talked to Harvey. They'd asked for the footage. They'd looked through the receipts. I could picture them pausing at mine, looking closer—*A hook-and-eye latch? A bottle of dark rum?*

With shaking hands, I typed in Sean's full name, then held my breath while the results loaded.

There was nothing recent. Social media profiles and job titles. It was a common name. I checked under the News category, but all that came up was some high school kid's track times. I felt my shoulders relax slightly, then took another sip of coffee.

This time I typed *Rick Aimes* into the search bar. Another common name, another broad net. I added Central Valley, and the first thing that popped up was the obituary for his wife, Marie. There were scant details. Just the survived-by names—Rick and his son, Jared—and the date of the service.

My phone rang as I was scrolling for any more details, and I jumped, almost dropping it in my lap. Bennett.

Probably making sure I was okay, now that he was up. I was glad he was calling; it made me think I was overreacting—about all of it.

"Good morning," I said.

"Hey, is Elyse there with you?" He sounded slightly out of breath, like he was in a rush.

"No, no. I'm out at the store."

A pause. "When did she leave your place last night?"

"She didn't," I said. "She didn't stop by."

Bennett cursed under his breath. "She fucking quit. Left an email and her badge and fucking quit. Didn't come to her shift, didn't ask someone to cover. Completely irresponsible, left them short-handed. Couldn't even be bothered to call it in. And she's not answering my calls now."

"That's not . . ." I began, about to say *That's not like her.* But what did I know? As much as I'd come to depend on the routines of our friendship, she'd been here only a handful of months; she'd slid into my life so fast, she could probably extract herself just as quickly.

"What did you say to her?" I asked, accusing.

"Excuse me?"

"I heard you were arguing. My neighbor heard."

He lowered his voice. "I was angry about her voicemail. Angry at the lack of information. I was riled up and . . . I took it out on her, but it had nothing to do with *her.*"

I knew how he could be, though, how he could find the one thing that really struck deep, and twist. "Bennett," I said. "She *quit.*"

"God, it wasn't that bad, I swear. Not something to fucking quit over." But he said it tentatively, because what did we know? What did we know about the things that could push another person to extremes?

"She's not answering my calls, either," I said. "But I'll swing by her place. I'm nearby." Which wasn't entirely true. The Mapleview apartment complex was in the other direction, heading out of town, but it kept me from going back home, sitting with my thoughts, chasing them down the rabbit hole. And I wanted to see her anyway, talk to her face-to-face.

"Tell her . . ." He trailed off, and I heard the crackle of the hospital intercom. "Jesus, just tell her to call me back."

I SPOTTED ELYSE'S WHITE car right away. I parked in the spot beside hers, then noticed that the inside light was on. It would drain her battery, if it hadn't already. Circling the car, I realized it was the driver's-side door, just slightly unlatched. I could picture her last night, pissed off, riled up herself. Her mind half-focused as she exited the car. I leaned my hip into it, nudging the door fully shut, and the light turned off.

I pressed her apartment number on the intercom, but it was still chiming when a man exited the front security door, holding it open for me. It happened every time; I looked the part of a resident here—same age as the man, same determined stride. He might've even recognized me from when I lived here myself. He nodded once as we briefly passed.

I continued to the door at the end of the hall. There was a woven doormat, a wreath of dried, fake flowers, a pink sticky note that said: *Package in the mailroom*.

I knocked, then leaned in closer, calling her name as I knocked again. "Elyse? It's Liv. Can we talk for a second?"

Nothing. I pressed my ear to the door. Silence.

I knocked again. "Bennett called me. Elyse, open up."

Silence.

"Elyse!" I called again, more urgent.

This time a door did open—the neighbor across the hall. His eyes were bloodshot, and he wore gym shorts and nothing else. "Can you please keep it down?"

"Have you seen Elyse?" I asked.

He shook his head as he closed the door.

I listened again, for water in the pipes or movement inside. Her car was here. She hadn't turned up for her shift. She'd abruptly quit, and that worried me. I thought of Elyse, showing up for me at the hospital and then staying while I slept—knowing it was what I needed without having to ask.

"Dammit, Elyse," I mumbled, then stepped back, looking for where she might leave a key. Knowing Elyse, there would be a spare in case she forgot her set. She wouldn't worry about someone else finding it. She would say, *No big deal.* She would say, *Have you seen this place? What's someone gonna take, anyway?*

There was nothing under her mat, though. And very few options over where else a key might be. I ran my hand over the doorframe and came back with nothing but dust. I checked behind the flower wreath, coming up empty again.

Maybe I was wrong. Maybe she left one with a neighbor instead.

I knocked on her door once more; then, on second thought, pressed down on the handle.

It gave.

I pushed the door open. "Elyse?" I called. "It's me. It's Liv." I eased the door shut behind me quietly. "I just want to make sure you're okay."

Something felt off. It wasn't the disorder; that was normal Elyse. The purse on the sofa of the living room, contents falling out. The phone on the floor, facedown. The drawer hanging open in her bedroom, clothes spilling over, visible through the open doorway from down the hall.

It was the way I'd missed her at work; the way I'd frantically knocked on her door—like I'd known somehow that she was slipping through my fingers.

I checked anyway, room by room, calling her name. Kitchen, bathroom, bedroom. But I'd known it as soon as I stepped inside. I'd known it even sooner, in some instinctive way, when I turned the unlocked handle.

Elyse wasn't here, and something was wrong.

Looking Back on the Rescue That Gripped a Nation

By Miles Truman

It's hard to believe it's been nearly a full decade since the search for Arden Maynor—the six-year-old girl from Widow Hills, Kentucky, who was swept away into the storm drain system while sleepwalking. But we will mark the ten-year anniversary in a matter of weeks.

If you were to visit Widow Hills now, you wouldn't see much evidence of what happened over the three-day search-and-rescue operation. Before the rescue, the town wasn't known for much other than its name: Widow Hills was so named because of the solitary cluster of mountains in the distance, where the clouds settled regardless of the surrounding weather, like three heads huddled together—a pocket of rain you could see across a clear sky.

But in the span of hours, Widow Hills went from a small town fading into obscurity to a place on the map.

Town and state officials never anticipated a storm like that. There were locally provided maps of the unmarked drains, the unofficial creeks. What would a six-year-old do while sleepwalking?

The community demanded attention, and they got it. The people of Widow Hills saved their own, and it's still a source of pride and respect, as evidenced by the plaque that remains at the spot where Arden Maynor was found, commemorating the rescue.

Business was never so good as in the days during and following the search. But after the search-and-rescue teams, the volunteers, and the surrounding media left, a fog akin to depression settled over the town.

Ten years later, and the town of Widow Hills appears much as it always has in the days before Arden's disappearance—with the exception of some of the faces. Laurel and Arden Maynor left soon after, but ask anyone who grew up here, and they remember.

And so do we.

Why did this case grip a nation? What makes a story like this take off?

Was it the initial event? The fact that she was sleepwalking—and suddenly, every parent could imagine this happening, something beyond all logical control?

Was it the photo plastered across the local news in that first press conference: the large brown eyes, her haunted expression, so serious for a child of six years old?

The picture of that tiny shoe stuck in the grate beside the open drainage pipe?

Did the media just like the name Widow Hills, deciding it would reach more viewers?

Or maybe we were all desperate for something to hope for, something bigger than ourselves.

More likely, it was a combination of all these things—an idea catching and spreading, capturing us all.

Whatever the reason for its initial reach, it was a story that could bond people together. They would celebrate together or they would grieve together.

That was the one sure thing: Whatever happened, we would be in it together.

Is it any surprise that people want to know what's become of Arden Maynor, no longer a child but a teenager? This person they prayed for and hoped for?

They bore witness to it all, felt what her mother must have felt, kept vigil through the night beside Laurel. They witnessed the moment she was found; they followed every moment of her rescue.

If you watched, if you helped, if you prayed and hoped and cheered, you already know the truth: We were a part of something good. Something that mattered. Arden Maynor is alive today and living her life because of the actions of so many. And that still matters a decade later.

That is something that will always matter.

CHAPTER 14

Sunday, 12 p.m.

MY HEAD WASN'T RIGHT.

It was the lack of sleep. It was my fear of going home. It was the way I partly expected everyone to start disappearing from my life.

And so I wasn't sure whether I was seeing things that shouldn't be there—everything through the filter of a dead body near my house, the investigation, the lack of sleep. Whether I was seeing danger in places it didn't exist.

I knew Bennett would have the most logical assessment. And I was right.

Bennett had talked me down from the ledge when I called him from Elyse's vacant apartment in a panic, explaining that she wasn't there, that her car was still in the lot, that her purse and her phone were left behind. Bennett walked through each step, carefully and logically: *Picked up by that guy, the bartender—Trevor? Went out*

*drinking. Using a different purse. The forgotten phone would ex-
plain why she hadn't answered our calls . . .*

His tone made me put down her cell, stop scrolling
through the notifications—me, Bennett, work, repeat—
and feel like an intruder. Which, at the moment, I was.

She quit, she was pissed, she went out. It made sense.
But I couldn't shake the other vision: of her running,
taken, trapped—waiting for someone to find her.

Which was why I'd been waiting until noon for the
bar to open.

I needed to be sure either way. And I didn't want to call
the police over nothing but a person blowing off steam—
bringing extra attention to myself.

Now I was drumming my fingers on the wheel,
watching for when the light inside Bill's Tavern turned
on. This was where we'd been on Friday evening. The
last moment of normalcy before everything spiraled out
of my control.

The lot was mostly empty now, the opposite of Friday
night, when the cars had overflowed from the lot onto the
grassy embankment on the side of the road—the promise
of cheap drinks and live music.

At 12:06, I gave up on waiting. The front door was
locked, but I cupped my hands to the smudged glass,
peering inside the dimly lit interior. I could just make out
the shadow of a person in the distance, behind the bar—a
faint light illuminating the space from deep within.

Eventually, the man behind the bar came around and
turned the lock, but he only partially opened the door.
"We've got about five minutes before the kitchen is
up and running," he said. He looked about as far from
Trevor as possible. Older, unapproachable, irritated by

my presence. There was something slightly familiar about him, but I'd been feeling that about everyone recently: the people at the hospital, the residents of Elyse's apartment building. Like I might've seen them all before, in passing. But maybe not. Maybe I was searching for it now, knowing what I'd missed in Sean Coleman.

"Sorry, I'm looking for Trevor?" I said.

The man shook his head. "He doesn't work today." Then he let the glass door swing shut.

I moved my foot into the doorway to catch it, then followed him inside as he strode across the restaurant floor. "Do you know where I can find him?"

He paused at the bar before easing himself behind the counter. He looked me over like he was assessing the threat of a person who had barged into a closed establishment. This was when it paid to be small and unassuming.

"I'm not in the habit of giving out employee information," he said, his words carrying through the empty space. I'd never been in here on a Sunday afternoon, and it seemed so much larger without the crowd and the noise. I could hear dishes from the kitchen, low laughter.

"It's really important," I said, standing on the other side of the counter. Then, at the condescending look he gave me, I added, "It's about a mutual friend. I work at the hospital." Letting him fill in the gaps. Letting him wonder at the implication, true or not.

Eventually, he took his phone from the back pocket of his baggy jeans. "I can call him myself," he said, "though I can't guarantee he'll answer. He works late hours, as you might guess."

He dialed from the other side of the bar, looked right at me as he spoke. His face was round and aged, his eyes small and dark. We stared at each other in silence for so long that I was worried the call had gone to voicemail, when he finally broke the silence. "Trevor, sorry to bother you, I've got a woman at the restaurant by the name of . . ."

"Olivia Meyer," I said.

"Olivia Meyer," he repeated. "She was asking for your contact. She says it's about a friend . . ."

"Elyse," I said. This was ridiculous. Couldn't he just hand me the phone and let me talk to Trevor?

"Elyse," he repeated, and then, based on whatever Trevor must've told him, he did slowly hand me the phone.

"Liv? What's going on?"

I backed away from the bar, though I was sure this guy could hear. There was nowhere to go for privacy. "Is Elyse with you?" I asked.

"What? No, why would you think . . ." Trevor's voice was both tense and gravelly, like we'd woken him and he was still trying to get his bearings.

"I can't find her, and she didn't show up for work. And her car is at her place, but she's not there. I just want to make sure she's okay." Like I knew Rick would do for me. I wasn't sure who else would notice if something was wrong in Elyse's life.

A pause. "I'm not sure what you expect me to say. She's not here."

"You weren't seeing her? You weren't with her? Any time in the last few days?"

"No, I wasn't seeing her. I haven't seen her. Look, I barely know her, really."

Which was a protest too far. He knew her, and he liked

her hanging around, and we all knew it. "Listen, she just up and quit, out of the blue, totally out of character . . ."

"She quit? Well, none of my business." His words were coming out clipped, irritated.

"When did you last see her?"

A sharp exhale. "I guess Friday night. With you. Listen, if that's all . . ."

"Just, can I give you my number? So you can let me know if she calls you?"

He sniffed. "She wouldn't. I mean, she doesn't even have my number. Sorry, but I gotta go."

The call disconnected, and I stared at the man behind the bar. He hadn't moved during the entire conversation.

Hadn't Trevor written his number on her hand just a few nights earlier? Or did he think I hadn't noticed?

The man walked around the bar, hand extended for his phone. "I recognize you," he said, and my shoulders tensed on instinct. "You come in with that girl sometimes, the one with the dark hair?"

"Elyse," I said. "That's Elyse." How had I never noticed this man? Maybe that was why he seemed vaguely familiar. I wondered if this was the owner or the manager, maybe even the source of the establishment's name.

He nodded once, ran his hand back through his thinning hair, laced with a healthy dose of gray. "Can't say I'm surprised she quit. The amount of time she's here, I'm surprised she hasn't been fired by now."

I didn't respond, started walking for the door. This was no time for his judgmental tone. The nights we came out, we were blowing off steam. It was how people functioned.

There were other logical possibilities, I knew, about

where Elyse might be. She could've still been in her building, in another apartment down the hall. Or maybe when I'd arrived, she'd been at the glass-walled gym, which I hadn't even thought to check.

And that was why her door had been left unlocked.

I was jumping to conclusions, seeing this place like Rick might now, with a different history, with its hidden dangers lurking under the surface. Operating like a detective, digging into the life of someone who probably just wanted to be left alone, threatening to turn her life into chaos for no reason.

A body in the yard could do that to you.

"Hey," the man called, snapping his fingers. "I know where I've heard your name."

I'd just reached the glass doors, but I stopped walking, turned slowly. Held my breath.

"Olivia Meyer. Right. That guy ever find you?"

I blinked twice. I knew someone had asked for me on Friday night, and I'd assumed it was Jonah. I wasn't sure how this man knew about that. "Which guy?"

"Don't know. He came in a few times last week. Each time, he'd ask for you by name. I didn't know who you were until just now."

I scrolled through the old photos on my phone until I pulled up one of me and Jonah. It took a while to find; all the photos I had of us had been taken alone, in the confines of our own privacy. Jonah hated any pictures at all but occasionally indulged me. How secretive we thought we had been.

I turned the photo the man's way now. In it, Jonah was sitting on the sofa in my old apartment, watching television; I'd slouched across him to get the shot of us both.

Jonah looked like he was smiling, but really, he'd been saying, *What are you doing?*

"Is this him?" I asked.

The man leaned forward, narrowing his eyes. "No, not that one, dear." His face stretched into a smile for the first time, and it was unnerving.

My stomach lurched. "Do you remember what he looked like? What he said?"

"Not really. Maybe a little older than this one," he said, pointing to my phone. "When you work at a place like this, you get to know pretty quickly what someone is after, though. Just like your friend Elyse."

His eyes were twinkling, and I knew he was enjoying this. That he got his kicks out of knowing more than everyone else, seeing everything.

If it wasn't Jonah, and it was an older man, I could place my bet. Most likely, Sean Coleman had come to the bar Friday evening, looking for me. He'd been in the bar hours before me. Asking for me by name. And I'd missed him, or he'd missed me. And then he ended up outside my house. I didn't think the police had gotten this far—to the bar. They'd worked fast, interviewing the people at the G&M, where I'd seen him last.

"He was in here more than once, the guy asking for me?" I asked, ignoring his tone. How long had Sean Coleman been here, looking for me? Following me?

"He definitely had a vested interest," he said, not answering my question directly.

"What day?" I asked.

"Does it matter? I don't remember the day, but I can guess what he wanted." He took a few steps closer. "You seem like a nice girl, and I have a daughter about your age, so I'll tell you the same thing I told her. Men that much older—"

"I'm all set with advice, thanks. Unless you've seen Elyse." I raised an eyebrow, gripped the handle of the glass door. I could be outside in two seconds, to my car in ten. The keys were in my purse; I could grab them on the way.

He rocked back on his heels, not coming any closer. "In that case . . ." He trailed off, gesturing toward the door.

I SWUNG BY ELYSE'S apartment building once more before heading home. I'd convinced myself that the disorder inside was just typical Elyse, home late, home drunk, dropping her bag, pulling out her clothes, falling into bed.

Had I not seen a room like this before? Hadn't I lived with that myself? Which was why the memory prickled: I was projecting.

My mother worked nontraditional hours, too, as a health care aide, before she completely imploded. She was contracted by several different clients for home care, with a rotating schedule. If she was asleep in the middle of the day, I'd worry, shaking her awake, only to learn she'd just gotten back and didn't have to return until the next day. It was impossible to know whether she was keeping up with her job until she was home for good.

Chaos always nagged at me, worried me, like a precursor to some danger that only I could see coming.

When I returned, Elyse's car was no longer in the lot. I again waited for someone to open the front door, walked down that same hallway, knocked on her apartment door, which now had the sticky note removed.

Of course Elyse had been back. She was fine, and I was

overreacting—the panic and disorientation over one thing coloring everything else.

When she didn't answer my knocking, I checked the knob, and this time it was locked. I knocked again, but there was no response. I called her as I walked outside, but her phone by now was off. The call went straight to voicemail.

She'd quit, and now she was avoiding me.

I CALLED BENNETT ON the drive back home. "Elyse went totally off the grid," I said. I was surprised he even picked up; he was usually a stickler for the rules of leaving his phone in his locker while he was working.

"What do you mean by *totally off the grid*?"

"I mean her car is gone and the phone is off. Trevor hadn't seen her. She'd been back to her apartment, and she knew I was looking for her, and she took off anyway."

"I'm sure she'll be back, Liv. Maybe she went home for the weekend."

It always caught me off guard when Bennett talked like this, about going home. He'd lived here four years, and yet there was a childhood house several hours away that he referred to as home.

Still, I couldn't remember Elyse ever talking about home the way Bennett did.

"You're sure?" I asked. "She *quit*, Bennett. Does that sound like someone who's planning to stick around?"

"She wouldn't just . . . She's your friend . . ." He let the thought trail.

"Right, you're right," I said before ending the call. But I knew how fast someone could make an impulsive decision and change their entire life.

My mother had quit her job in Widow Hills after I was found. Thought we could live off generosity and the book contract alone—and we did for a time. She didn't want to go back to work when we needed her to. Had developed a deep distrust of the medical establishment after the surgeries and the rehab and the medicine. She said no one was interested in fixing me, just wanted to pry deeper and find more things in need of fixing, bleeding us dry.

It was why, I think, I felt a pull to health care from the other side. I wanted to fix things from the top down, establishing an order to the chaos.

IT WAS MIDAFTERNOON BY the time I turned onto my street. I needed to do that now—apply an order to the chaos. Establish a routine, a simplicity to my life. I would go home and clean, do the laundry—erase all remnants of the earlier evenings. I'd spot the blue paint of the box cutter and return it to the kitchen drawer. I'd install the hook-and-eye latch over the doorjamb, which would've saved me so much of the trouble from the start: leaving someone else to find the body. I'd have an early dinner and set my alarm and get back to the weekly routine, in a show of normalcy.

There was a single unmarked car parked along the short stretch of road between Rick's driveway and my own. I'd thought the police were finished up, but I could see two figures emerging from the car—Detective Rigby and a much taller man. Detective Rigby was in a suit, but this man did not appear to be a member of law enforcement. He wore jeans, a brown bomber jacket, aviator sunglasses covering his eyes.

Detective Rigby raised her hand as I pulled into my drive, and the man's head turned slowly, watching me go. I nodded back but kept glancing in my rearview mirror. They were both still standing there, at the edge of the property, near the car.

The detective was gesturing as she spoke, but the man barely moved in acknowledgment. My stomach twisted, imagining who it might be. The press, digging up property records, asking questions. And here she was, giving him a personal tour, when she'd promised to give me a heads-up first.

They disappeared from view as I pulled in front of my house, but I couldn't shake it from my mind. I had to know what they were doing here.

My steps along the drive made enough noise that, once I got close enough to hear the detective's voice, their conversation stopped abruptly.

"Everything okay?" I asked, shading my eyes as they came into sight.

The detective's gaze trailed after me, but her expression gave nothing away. With the sunglasses, I couldn't tell whether the man was looking my way at all.

"Olivia, this is Nathan Coleman," Detective Rigby said, and my stomach dropped. *Still in the process of tracking down his next of kin*, she'd told me. "He requested to see where we found his father."

"Oh," I said. It hadn't occurred to me that it would be his son. That he would be someone my age. Here, on my property.

Something in his jaw twitched, and he stepped forward, extended his hand.

"I'm sorry," I said, my hand sliding into his rough grip.

"I'm sorry for your loss." He reminded me of someone I knew, but that kept happening. Everyone here seemed like a figment of someone else. I couldn't see his eyes, but there was something in his build that was similar to his father's. His grip, capable of holding me up.

"This is Olivia," Detective Rigby said. "She's the one who found your father." His handshake paused. I imagined the inverse: *Your father found her.*

But she said none of those things; her face gave away nothing. Nathan Coleman didn't know.

"Well, then," he said, a faint drawl under his clipped words, "I'm sorry, too."

We both turned at a sound from the other direction. A door swinging shut at Rick's house. "That's Mr. Aimes. He's lived here for years," Detective Rigby said. We could just see him on the porch with a broom, looking this way.

Nathan Coleman turned his head from Rick back to me, like he was trying to determine which one of us his father had been here for.

"I'm sorry, I have to go," I said, the apologies multiplying. I needed to extricate myself from the situation. There was no good place for this conversation to go. Information was a thing that could chase you, and it was now right on the cusp of catching me—tainting everything to come.

The girl from Widow Hills, remember? Of course they would. Thinking they could find the answers there. Reaching back, this time, for anything they might've missed.

I wanted my own answers first.

CENTRAL CAROLINA UNIVERSITY—
OFFICE OF ADMISSIONS

APPLICATION FILE—Olivia Meyer

CONTENTS: Guidance Counselor Letter Re:
Permanent Record

FEBRUARY 5, 2012

To Whom It May Concern,

Per your request for further information,
I'm writing today about a senior of ours who had
applied to your institution, by the name of Olivia
Meyer. The incident in question about which you
are inquiring occurred while she was enrolled in
a previous school, so we can't speak directly to
the nature of the infraction. Though my hope is to
provide some potential context.

Olivia recently turned eighteen and legally
changed her name. Before that, her legal name was
Arden Olivia Maynor.

Attached please find an article from the year
2000 (you may well remember the Widow Hills
case yourself). There was a flurry of new press last

year surrounding the ten-year anniversary (second article attached, from 2010). It's my understanding that her family had to leave town over some form of harassment. They came to us at the start of this school year.

I'm writing in confidence, as she has never spoken of these things directly. This information was provided by her mother. Her mother mentioned an incident at the previous school, related to PTSD from her childhood ordeal, and asked us to keep watch for any troubling behavior. All I can say is, since attending our school, Olivia has been nothing but a model student.

When I first received her transcript last year, I knew right away who she was. I remembered that case. I remembered watching. I'm sure you'll agree it's a miracle she's here at all—a few minor infractions notwithstanding.

Regards,

Thomas Woods

Norfolk County Schools, Ohio

Director of Counseling

cc: Norfolk County Office, copy for file

CHAPTER 15

Sunday, 8:15 p.m.

THE DAY'S ADRENALINE WAS wearing off, and I stood in the kitchen toying with the prescription bottle of pills made out in my name, weighing which was the bigger concern: what I might do while sleeping; or being unable to wake in a true emergency.

There was a killer out there. Someone who had been within sight of my house. Who had been so close, while I was sleeping.

Bennett had said I'd slept like the dead. When I'd woken, hours after taking the pill, I hadn't moved an inch. But if the smoke detector went off, if someone broke in . . . would I be able to regain consciousness? Would I be able to run or fight?

I slid the vial beside the microwave and got to work installing the hook-and-eye latch.

I found a power screwdriver in my office, in one of my

plastic bins of batteries, nails, and random tools. I checked each bin, just in case—no box cutter. I carried the step-stool from the kitchen and installed the hook-and-eye latch on my bedroom door, fully out of reach. To unhook it in the night, I'd need to pull the ladder from the closet, climb the steps, reach my hand up. So many extra steps, like I was trying to outsmart my subconscious.

There was always the window in case of emergency—if I couldn't get the door open in time. No screen to slow me down. A drop onto patchy grass and packed dirt, a far-ther fall than from the living room window in the front, due to the sloping ground and the crawl space. But not far enough to hurt me.

The sound of the screwdriver must've blocked out the signs of the car approaching, or the footsteps on my porch, because I'd just dragged the ladder back into the closet when the doorbell rang. My heart was in my throat as I walked quietly into the living room, trying not to make a sound—though of course my car was out front; it was obvious I was home.

I peered around the living room curtain, caught sight of a car I didn't recognize.

I couldn't see an unfamiliar car or hear a phone ring anymore without remembering how it used to be. The press tried the friendly approach first, hoping for a quote or a photo, but got increasingly invasive. At the least: *The person inside did not answer the door*—with an accompanying picture of my property.

I remained perfectly still, tallying the layers of pro-tection and options. Phone in my back pocket, with De-tective Rigby's number programmed; screwdriver in my hand; back door; windows.

The person on the porch took a step back, now in view of the living room window. I could see only his profile, but it was the man from earlier. Nathan Coleman.

I opened the door just as he turned away, hands deep in the pockets of his jeans.

"Hi, sorry," I called to his back. Apparently, I was only capable of apologizing to him.

He shifted slowly, and in the twilight, he looked like a different person. Now that his glasses were off, I could see the hollows around his eyes, like his father's. The lack of sleep, or the grief. What he'd been hiding earlier. It changed the angles of his face, made him seem open, more vulnerable.

"Hey," he said, eyes lightly skimming over me, then lingering on my hand with the screwdriver. "Didn't mean to make you nervous. I just . . ." He gestured to his car. "I tried your neighbor first, but he didn't answer, either."

"I didn't hear you." I held up the screwdriver, then placed it on the entryway table. "I was just fixing something."

His eyes changed, almost like he was trying to smile. He shifted on his feet, standing on the other side of the doorway. "When I was here earlier, Detective Rigby, she said we'd need to get permission to get closer, that the . . . the material from the scene had all been gathered already, and that's private property. I said no, I didn't want to bother anyone. But here I am again, and I don't know why. Why I keep driving past, why I stopped this time . . . It's not like he's still here, like it means anything . . . I don't even know where it happened, exactly, and I'm trying not to trespass, I'm just trying to feel something."

It took until he was halfway through his rambling for

me to realize he was asking for permission. That I was the one who could grant it, allowing him onto my property. I thought about calling Detective Rigby, asking if she needed to be here, but I wanted to keep things light and unofficial, make myself a tangential component—in on the information but out of the picture.

"I can show you," I said. "If you want to see?"

He tipped his head once, then started following me down the porch steps. We walked in silence toward the edge of the property, my stride somehow matching his, though he was solidly over six feet tall, and I was only a few inches over five feet.

The crime scene tape was gone, the police done collecting the evidence, but the spot where Sean Coleman had been found had a pull to it, like a black hole. Some of the dirt had been dug out around the body. What remained was a slight dip, upturned earth patted back down unnaturally. I stopped a few yards short, and Nathan did the same.

He was staring at it like he could see something in the emptiness. Something below this level. But all I noticed was the proximity to my house behind us: the bedroom window in sight; the light inside, and a straight view down the hall.

I didn't belong out here, sharing in the grief of this man I'd never met and didn't know existed until mere hours ago. "Take all the time you need . . ." I said, stepping back.

He turned to face me then. "We weren't close," he said, rooting me in my spot. Because I understood how sometimes that makes it worse. How you're trying to feel a connection across the absence. I'd searched for it myself inside that sad box delivered to my front porch. Would I have felt more if I'd found the spot where she had died? I didn't even know whether it had happened in a hospital, or a hotel room, or a house. Whether she was found alone on a street somewhere—or worse.

Maybe it was the uncertainty that kept pulling me back. The guilt about all the things I didn't know and hadn't asked.

"My mother died earlier this year, and I didn't even know it," I said.

He nodded once, never breaking eye contact.

"She was cremated before I could even claim her." The guilt, coexisting with the knowledge that it wasn't my fault, that it was for the best that I'd cut off contact.

I knew then why I was out here with him. Why he'd seemed familiar in a way I couldn't quite put my finger on. It was something I recognized in myself. A separate exterior that presented as a hardness in him. But I could recognize its presence, something similar to my own. A shell formed out of necessity, of loss, of survival. And in that moment, it felt like we were two surfaces reflecting, an endless hall of mirrors.

"Do you feel safe here?" he asked, talking so low I had to lean in to hear the deep timbre of his voice.

But there was too much to sift through in the question. "I used to," I said. Now there had been someone killed within sight of my bedroom window. Now I knew a woman had died from a gunshot wound in the house next door. Now I could hear the echo of crime scene tape fluttering in the place it used to be.

A cold dread seeped into my bones. I shivered, deciding whether to ask about the investigation—nervous about where that conversation could lead. But I had to get information. It was the only way to keep on top of the story, not let it take you over and consume you. I looked back toward the main road. "Did they find his car?" I asked.

He shifted his jaw slightly, mulling over either the question or me. "On a different road nearby. The police have it now."

So he'd driven here. Not dumped here, like Elyse had thought. He'd driven, and kept his car hidden, and walked . . .

"You're scared," he said.

I nodded, because it was the truth. But also because I didn't know what had happened out here. Worried that it could've happened to me just as easily. That anyone could've gotten into my home.

He took in the scene once more, gaze moving from the spot in the yard, to Rick's house, to my own. "I won't take any more of your time, Olivia. Thank you for this."

We walked back toward his car in my driveway. He lingered in the spot between his car and my front porch, like he wanted to say something more.

"Do you want to come in?" I asked on impulse. Because, despite my misgivings, I was always trying to undo someone else's damage. Or maybe it was something baser than that. Maybe because, like he said, I was scared. "I could get you something to drink. Or eat. Before you head back." I wasn't sure which hotel he was staying at, but none of the hotels in the area was particularly inviting.

He looked at my front door for a long moment. It seemed like he very much wanted to come in. But he shook his head. "I should be getting back, get some sleep, get my head on straight."

"Right. Okay. Me, too."

He took out his wallet and slipped a card from a pocket. "My cell is on the back. In case you want to talk. I'll be in town at least a few more days."

I was standing on my porch while he backed out of my drive. When he was out of sight, I saw, through the trees, Rick's porch light switch on.

MY PHONE WAS RINGING when I stepped inside— and my stomach dropped, my mind always flashing back to the body in the yard. Then I was overwhelmed with the hope that it was Elyse, finally returning my calls. But instead it was a video call from Jonah.

Better to be done with this once and for all than have him calling weekly until he got the message. I answered with a curt "Yes?"

Jonah didn't seem to get the tone. He smiled widely, sitting in his favorite chair in the living room. I could picture the crystal tumbler just out of frame. "Finally caught you," he said. "Is now a better time, Liv?"

"Not really," I said. "Jonah, listen, I shouldn't have texted you back. I don't want to go back to the way things were—"

"Neither do I. I was a fool, Liv, can you give me a second for an apology?"

I closed my eyes. A year too late, a year smarter, and Jonah just one more thing that was best left in the past. God, why was everything resurfacing all at once? How could you become someone new when everyone kept pulling you back to the person you once were? How could you fight that sort of gravity?

"I accept any and all apologies, Jonah. But I've moved on, and it's absolute chaos here. So, no, this is not actually a better time."

"Is it the hospital?" he asked, sitting upright. "Did something happen?" Because that was his project, a way he could claw his way back to essential.

"No. There's a literal crime scene outside my house, okay? Someone died."

Jonah's face was a blank sheet. He was not good at the unexpected, never was. Liked to be in control, in the classroom and out. He'd seen this conversation going one way, but it had suddenly veered, and he was slow to recover.

The phone wobbled as he switched hands, brought himself too close to the frame, his features losing proportion. "Who? Who died?"

I lifted one shoulder in an exaggerated shrug. "No one you know. No one who worked at the hospital. It doesn't involve you."

"I should be there," he said. "You shouldn't be alone there right now. God, I'm so sorry, I didn't know."

"No, you shouldn't. I'm not alone, Jonah. Drop it."

His eyes narrowed now, like a different path was presenting itself. "You're seeing someone?" A condescending tilt to his head. "Tell me, is it Bennett? Of course you are. You always did like being taken care of." He lowered his voice, his entire demeanor shifting. "This isn't the right move, Liv."

"You don't know me as well as you think. You're wrong about all of it."

He raised one eyebrow. "Am I, now?"

I shifted my jaw; I hated getting drawn into his circular discussions, which would inevitably lead exactly where he intended them to end.

"Both options can't exist at once, Liv." Like he could apply his logic to life. Twist the data to fuel his own argument. "Are you seeing someone, or are you alone?"

"It's none of your business."

I could hear the ice in his glass. He took a sip before speaking. "Well, it's after nine p.m., and you're home, and no one else is there. So it seems to me we both know the answer."

This was how Jonah worked, talking me in circles, doing the same in a meeting, in his class. So he always came out on top. And he was right—I did like being taken care of. Where he was wrong was in assuming he was ever the one to provide that stability.

Something had changed, in either him or me. But I could finally see him clearly for everything he was. A leech. Needing attention to thrive. Needing to feel superior and knowing he could get that only from someone younger, less established, less sure of herself.

I hadn't formed strong connections with my classmates, didn't like their questions about parent weekends, or visiting home, or summer plans. I dove into my studies, and took internships and jobs, and Jonah liked my drive, my maturity. The exterior shell I presented as a defense. An interior he could mold at his will.

Three seconds to escape. One step to extricate myself from this conversation.

"Jonah? Don't call me again."

And then I did what I should've done months ago, a year ago, before that, even—the first time he texted me personally: *I've been thinking about what you said in class all day. Would love to discuss further.* The thrill was the same, then and now, as I blocked his number.

I DIDN'T TAKE THE pill, and slept lightly. Later at night, I heard a car driving by, and I pictured Nathan Coleman, not sleeping, drawn back to the scene of his father's death, over and over. How we were all being drawn back together. And how I could see myself clearly, finally, reflected in someone else. How grief and survival could coexist. How, despite what Jonah believed, you could hold two versions of the truth—and yourself—in your hand at the same time, and both could be completely real.

FINDING ARDEN

Copyright: Laurel Maynor, 2002

Excerpt, p.1

I knew she was gone before I woke. It was
pure intuition.

I knew my daughter better than any other
living being.

When Arden was little, I could tell if she'd
be sick the next day. When she'd run down the
hill out back, I could tell in the moment before
when she was about to fall.

I woke up on the morning of October 17
earlier than usual. Something had woken me.
There was a sinking feeling in the pit of my
stomach. I started calling her name before I
even got to her room.

My heart was racing before I got there, even
though I couldn't explain why.

And then I saw her empty bed. And I knew for
sure. It was my worst nightmare.

People often ask me if I believed that Arden
would be found alive, especially as one day
turned to two, and two days turned to three.
The answer is always yes, and that's the truth.
Because there were other things I knew about my
daughter besides the fact that she was missing:

I knew she was a fighter. She came into this world kicking and screaming. I swear she could be heard clear across the county the day she was born.

I knew she wouldn't go out of this world without a fight, either.

CHAPTER 16

Monday, 8 a.m.

WAS RELIEVED TO WAKE and find my room exactly as I'd left it. Ladder tucked away in the closet, hook and eye securely latched, phone facedown beside me. I'd even locked the window, just to add a few extra steps. I hadn't even known how to lock it until last night, when I ran my fingers along the border, feeling for the latch. The window was unreachable from the ground outside, anyway.

Elyse still hadn't contacted me, and I couldn't help but swing by her apartment once more on the way in to work. It stung that she was avoiding me—more than I thought it would, given my history. But whatever had happened between her and Bennett was partly my fault. I'd thought, if I could just talk to her, I could convince her to come back.

It took a little longer to get inside the apartment building this time; apparently, I'd missed the morning rush, both in and out.

This time it was her neighbor across the way who held the door. He didn't seem to recognize me in his rush, barreling through the doorway in his slacks and button-down.

"Hey, excuse me, have you seen Elyse?"

He did a double take, then leaned against the door as he slid me into context. "She moved out."

My stomach dropped. "Are you sure?"

He shrugged. "Her apartment's vacant. That's all I know. Maybe the lady next door, in 121—Erin, I think?—she might know more. They hung out a lot. I think they worked at the hospital together. She might already be gone for the day, though. We all usually leave around the same time." He checked his watch, then let the door swing shut behind him.

I couldn't think of any Erin I knew who worked with us, but if she wasn't in our department, that wasn't saying much.

I walked down the hall to Elyse's apartment. Even the wreath and the doormat were gone. I knocked once just in case, pressed down on the handle, but it was locked.

A door clicked open somewhere down the hall, then closed again. Apartment 121, I thought, but no one was out in the hall. Maybe just a trick of the acoustics, and it was a door around the corner, out of sight.

But I paused in front of apartment 121 on my way out. The doorway was bare, with no personal touches. I knocked twice and swore I could hear movement inside. A presence on the other side of the door. A shadow at the peephole, looking out.

"Hi, I'm looking for Elyse?" I said, in case anyone was there.

But if they were, they didn't move again. I started to doubt myself, what I'd heard, what I'd felt.

I remembered suddenly how spooked Elyse had been at my house—looking out the window, the fear transferring to her by proximity. And Nathan, asking if I felt safe there. Even he could sense the danger radiating from my place. Could I really blame her for leaving? Wouldn't I have done the same if I'd had some other place I considered home?

EVERYONE TRIED TO ACT normal when I arrived at the hospital. Faces that were either too friendly, or people who averted their gaze entirely, pretending to be absorbed in their phones.

I had found a dead body outside my house, and everyone knew it. Everyone knew I'd been brought in with the detective. I could only imagine the type of gossip swirling through the back channels, whispered between shifts in the lounge.

I stopped in the cafeteria for breakfast and coffee, which wasn't my normal routine. But I needed the caffeine to focus; I felt slow, a step behind.

This early in the day, there was just a scattering of people around the tables. But I felt their eyes on me, their voices falling to whispers. On my way out of the cafeteria, I passed a nurse from the ER. She did a stutter step in the hall, called out a too-loud "Good morning!" as I passed. As if surprised to see me back at work.

Or maybe I was just projecting. Maybe she didn't know me at all, was surprised to see anyone in her path. Maybe I was just vaguely familiar to her, as she was to me.

I took the back stairwell again, my steps echoing in the silence. The distance between the click of one door latching and the other opening on the third floor was something I could count in my head. Thirty-two steps. Half a minute.

Inside my wing, the hall was strangely empty. Since I'd stopped for breakfast, I wasn't as early as I'd been on Friday, before the shift began. By now, the morning rounds were usually in full swing, and the administrative meetings were getting started.

Bennett was typically off on Mondays, but I walked by the nurses' lounge, just in case his schedule had shifted to accommodate the past weekend. The only person inside was the woman with auburn hair, on her phone again. Same as last week, when I'd backed into the medicine room.

I was overcome with a vague sense of déjà vu. I knew the nurses who worked up here best. Though everyone could use the lounge, they were the ones who'd usually be resting on the couch.

A door opened behind me, a man in scrubs leaving the medicine room. He saw me standing there and smiled. "Morning," he said. But he took a minute turning the lock to the medicine room behind him, even as I walked away.

My stomach churned, imagining the stories. It was the same feeling I had gotten ten years earlier, people watching and talking, before the panic attack that I didn't know was a panic attack. The slow buildup, and the rapid unraveling, before I recognized it for what it was and could put a name to the physical reaction.

Would it escalate, as it had back then? The comments?

The attention? Until I found myself trapped—at the mercy of something else beyond my control?

Ten years earlier, everything had boiled over with an incident in the gym locker room.

Their voices still echoed a decade later.

Living off other people's hard-earned money—

My parents said they donated, probably paid for your house—

A group of girls scattered around me. One in particular standing between me and the exit of the gym locker room, the walls narrowing as the voices grew. Until I had to move. Had to get out.

The school counselor attributed the incident to PTSD, but it didn't change the reaction. I was sent home for a week. I was just lucky it hadn't made it on the news.

But it was a good story. *Describe her in three words: angry, unpredictable, dangerous.*

My mother stressed the need to stay offline, to keep random people on the Internet from contacting me on social media, and private messages, and lesser-known chat rooms. I had quickly learned never to search for my own name. But I still saw it, heard about it. Kids bartered information, discovered the power of it. At that age, it was what we had.

Ten years later, we hadn't much changed. We all just had more access to the truth and the lies.

IN MY OFFICE BETWEEN meetings, I pulled up Elyse's employment file. I hadn't been involved in the hiring process, not since I'd taken on my full-time role.

But this was all information at my disposal. If she'd gone home, as Bennett suggested, I might find another contact number in her file—to put my mind at ease. To stop seeing the image of her staring out my window, frowning.

If my mother could see me now, I was sure she'd laugh. Call me, in an offhand way, *the powers that be*. That unseen, unnamed force that determined her fate each time she was removed from a position or reassigned. The powers that gave her shit hours, or denied her employment, or ignored her situation. *The powers that be* were unwavering and unsympathetic. *Robotic assholes*, I think was her preferred term. And now here I was.

But I was nothing like she'd imagined us to be. I wanted to make a difference. Fix a broken system from the top down.

The small thumbnail photo with Elyse's ID badge was up on the screen, grainy to the degree of blurry, along with her original application. Elyse Ferano was twenty-five and had three different places of employment before landing here, including a few months' gap in between, noted as a medical leave. I remembered she'd mentioned a bad accident, and I wondered if she had follow-up issues. It had been the same for my arm.

But still. She had moved around a lot in the time allotted. I wondered who had hired her, how she'd gotten through the referral calls. She'd listed previous jobs from all over the state. Her most recent referral was from a rehab facility near the coast, at least four hours away. I couldn't tell which place she might consider home.

On impulse, I called the most recent contact name.

"Henry Masters," he answered on the first ring.

"Hi, my name is Olivia, and I'm calling in regard to a referral for a previous employee of yours." I'd opted against giving away my information unless specifically asked.

"Hold on," he said. Then, "Go ahead," like he was pulling up the files on his own end, waiting for a name.

"A nurse by the name of Elyse Ferano."

"We are not able to comment at this time," he said without even a moment's pause. Those were the types of lines we gave instead of putting a name on blast. There were repercussions for that, for saying the wrong thing and keeping someone from getting a job. What some called honesty, others called slander. So we stuck to the neutral comments, speaking in code, but we all knew what it meant.

"Oh, I'm surprised, I was under the impression that you referred her in the past?" Unless the hiring committee had failed to follow up, which was really unacceptable.

"Yes, sorry, we're in the midst of an internal investigation, which has put all referrals on hold."

So it may not have had anything to do with her at all. Except he'd asked me for her name first. He'd acted like he would answer. He'd made a mistake.

"Can you share the specifics?" I was grasping at straws here, and I knew it.

"I cannot, as it's ongoing." I could hear his chair squeaking in the background, like he was twisting his seat back and forth.

"What sort of investigation?"

A sigh. "A previous issue that's just recently come to light during an inventory audit."

Dammit, Elyse. "Thank you for your time," I said, my voice sounding small even to me. I placed the phone gently in the cradle.

Bennett had mentioned things going missing from the medicine room. I thought back to when he'd caught me in there, laying in to me, borderline accusing me, before apologizing after for the overreaction. Someone had been taking things. He'd mentioned it casually; maybe he wasn't sure. But he was keeping an eye out. Had he been suspicious of her?

I wondered if this was what had sent Elyse on the road so quickly. The police lingering around my house? Seeing Detective Rigby in the hospital?

Sean Coleman's death had nothing to do with her, but she'd spooked when she saw the detective at the hospital after she showed up in the middle of the night; she'd seemed uncomfortable with the police activity outside my house, watching out my window.

And then she'd gotten into a fight with Bennett.

Even now I didn't want to believe it, didn't want to see the worst in people. Especially someone I'd really cared for. But people were like that—often you only got to see the shell. The surface calm. The charm.

Even the manager at the bar had hinted at it—that she'd hung around a lot. Maybe he was referring to things I wasn't aware of, a crowd of people other than my own. Maybe that was what she and Trevor had been discussing and why he'd been so cagey on the phone.

She'd been skimming from our inventory. Possibly to use or possibly to sell.

And now she was gone. Not returning to a safer haven. But off to the next place, no forwarding address, no notice, no goodbye. Like she could feel the net closing in on her and had to escape it first. How many of us were outrunning something?

I stared at my computer screen, unsure what to do next. Protocol said I should report this to Bennett, but it could wait. There was no urgency any longer. And I still felt some allegiance to her. I didn't want to be so wrong about people—again.

I looked to the empty couch and debated checking out, attempting a nap. It was lunchtime, but without Bennett or Elyse, I didn't want to brave the whispers in the cafeteria. I leaned my head back and closed my eyes, settling on something close to meditation instead.

A few moments later, there was a shuffling of fabric from out in the hall. I opened my eyes, thought I saw a shadow under the door. I stared at it, wondering if it was someone pausing in the hall, checking their phone, when the doorknob began to faintly turn. It barely made a sound, and I held my breath, watching it move.

My heartbeat grew louder, and I looked for a way out: the windows behind me that I could crank open, but I was three floors up, over the parking lot; the phone on my desk, though I didn't know whom to call.

I pretended to make a call, hand on the receiver, just in case. "Hello, this is Olivia Meyer," I said loudly. The door handle dropped. The shadow left.

I waited, listening, before leaving the phone and walking around my desk. I opened my office door, peered down the hall. Expecting maybe someone lingering, waiting to talk to me. But it was empty from the stairwell entrance on the left to the locked double doors on the right. Whoever had been out there was gone.

My ringing office phone drew me back inside.

"This is Olivia," I answered, heart still racing.

"Olivia, it's Dr. Cal. Can you please swing by my office this evening before you head out?"

I was caught off guard, wondering why he was calling, whether I'd gotten my schedule wrong. "Oh, um, I didn't think we had an appointment this soon . . ." I pulled up my calendar, didn't see anything in there.

"It's important. A few items we need to discuss. Some paperwork I forgot to take care of. So. Five-thirty?"

"Sure," I said.

This time I locked my office door behind me on the way out.

POSTMARKED: LEXINGTON, KY
MAY 21, 2011

How much did they give you for that
new brick house, for that white picket
fence, for that nice black car? What's
the going rate for that fake life you're
living?

How much do you owe the people who
made this life for you?

How much do you have left?

I know the answer to that one. More
than you deserve.

If you're not careful, you'll get what
you really deserve.

CHAPTER 17

Monday, 5:30 p.m.

HELLO?" I CALLED, STEPPING into Dr. Cal's outer office. His secretary seemed to have left for the day already. Maybe there'd been some wires crossed. Maybe I wasn't on the final calendar. Maybe the mistake with the appointment was his and not mine.

"Come on in!" Dr. Cal's smooth voice called from his inner office, door partly ajar once more. "Sit, sit," he said, with his too-wide smile and too-white teeth. He crossed his ankle over his leg, in that same chair, and I checked his socks. Orange. Pumpkins, maybe? It was still August.

"I know it's a little early for the season," he said, shaking his foot, "but fall is always my favorite time of year."

I had no idea what I was doing here, and he wasn't giving me any hints. "Um, I wasn't sure why you needed to see me, and I'm on my way out, have to be somewhere soon . . ."

"Right," he said, planting both feet firmly on the

ground. He grabbed a folder beside him, opened it up, twisted it my way.

He held himself very still. His demeanor was making me nervous.

The form appeared to be a disclaimer, with my name and birth date already filled in. Something about a sleep study, best practice recommendations, a release of liability—

He cleared his throat. "I forgot to have you sign this when you were here, when you opted out of doing a sleep study."

I tilted my head. Had I? He'd mentioned one, and I'd put it off, saying I didn't have the time right then—I wouldn't have said my response was official in any way.

"It's standard," he said, handing me a pen.

"Sure," I said, adding my signature. He'd left the date open, and I hastily scribbled it in. I wasn't sure why he was calling me in so urgently over this.

He flipped the folder closed, took a slow breath, shoulders relaxing. "Have you been keeping that journal, like we discussed?" he asked.

"Not yet. I've had a few rough nights."

His face darkened, and then I knew for sure he'd heard. "My secretary told me there was an emergency the other night. Are you okay?"

"I'm okay," I said.

He looked down at my knee, at the way I held my leg out straight to keep the stitches from pulling. I could walk without a limp, but I was being cautious—not wanting to pull anything apart before it had fully healed.

"Is that from . . ." He let the thought trail.

"I tripped," I said.

He drummed his pointer finger against his knee, the pace increasing. "Were you—did you—was it like you mentioned last time? That you woke up outside?"

"No," I said firmly. "I tripped because I found a body in the dark."

His face was impossible to read, no emotion behind it. "That must've been terrible," he finally said, like he was trying on empathy for the first time.

"It was," I said.

He sat back in his chair, the folder still in his lap. "Olivia, these things we were discussing, it's hard to determine what the diagnosis is without a sleep study. Whether you could be a danger to yourself or those around you."

I stared at him blankly until he cracked first, looking down, making some useless note.

The twenty-year anniversary approaching, the panic of being found and put on display for others to pick apart. The night terrors becoming something more . . . Anything I said now would indeed end up in some medical file. If it got to that, a detective asking for the records, subpoenaing them somehow, I wanted there to be a record of this, too.

"Must've been extra stress, like you said," I offered.

He let out a slow sigh, like he was relieved. "Good, good." He put the folder on his desk, patting it once.

I could've laughed. It was the first time I'd found him truly funny.

That paperwork was to cover his own ass. Dr. Cal had called me in here, worried about his liability. He'd heard the rumors, and he knew I'd been to see him beforehand, and, like Bennett, he'd made that leap. I'd come to him for help, and he'd brushed me off, and now he was scrambling.

Here Bennett had been worried about word getting out that I'd been seeing someone for sleepwalking and everyone would know—HIPAA laws be damned. When really Dr. Cal was terrified. Maybe not a sociopath after all. He was too nervous, too unnatural.

A narcissist, though, yes.

It wasn't good for business if your patient woke standing over a dead body. Not a five-star recommendation. Not the type of press he'd want, either.

"I'm sorry to hear about . . . everything going on. It must be very stressful. How have you been coping?"

"It is," I said. "You know Sydney Britton in the ER?"

"Yes, I'm familiar with the name," he said.

"She gave me this pain pill/sleeping aid combo. Knocked me right out. I didn't move all night."

He blinked at me slowly. "Well, that's good news, knowing you didn't have an adverse reaction to it. Why don't you email that name to me and I'll get you a refill, should you need it."

"Perfect," I told him. Fucking perfect.

He'd feared he had made a mistake, and now he was swinging to the other extreme. Everyone wanted to save their own ass, present the perfect image. At the end of the day, we were all products to be consumed by the public, at their will.

"I'd like to keep working with you," he said. "I think you're a very interesting case."

I almost didn't respond, because he was, even now, trying to see how he could use this story for himself. So many careers had been made from the original event: the reporters who were there, watching it live; the doctors who looked over my case until my mom realized they were using me for their own case studies, something to help their public image and pad their résumés; the friends who had shared photos and anecdotes, inserting themselves into the story for their own momentary taste of fame.

But I had to keep him on my side. "I think I have an appointment with you on Thursday. Guess I'll see you then?"

"Great, yes. And just so you know, you can talk to me, Olivia. I take privacy very seriously. I spoke with my secretary, too. She understands the sensitive nature."

As evidenced by the fact that I was here after hours, that he'd called instead of emailing to set this up, that there was absolutely no record of my presence today.

Only Bennett knew the full truth—knew about my visit here and how it might connect to the case. And I had to believe he was on my side.

THE HALLWAY OUTSIDE DR. Cal's office was mostly empty already. I'd checked my phone, looking for any contact from Elyse or Bennett. But I had no new messages.

It was late enough in the day that I knew Bennett shouldn't be sleeping, especially if he hadn't had a shift here today. I needed to ask him if he had suspected Elyse. I had called his cell, leaning against the wall, when the door to Dr. Cal's office swung open again.

"Didn't mean to spook you," he said, looking at his watch, "but I'm heading out, too."

The call switched over to voicemail, and there was nothing to do but fall into stride beside him, heading toward the elevators.

I didn't want to mention that I wasn't planning to take the elevator but was heading toward the fire stairwell instead—would take the five flights down, like I always did. With the doctor beside me, it was hard to break away without getting into all the reasons why a steel trap was not my ideal means of travel.

The elevator doors dinged and slid open, but no one was inside. "After you," he said.

I hesitated for a moment, thinking I could tell him I needed to swing by my office first, except I had my canvas bag with me, and I'd already claimed I was in a rush, on my way out.

I stepped inside, closed my eyes as the doors slid shut, pressed my back into the cold metal wall. Listened to the hum of the gears kicking in as the elevator lurched downward.

My stomach dropped as it started to move.

I counted the floors with each ding. Four—"It's a real tragedy, about that man . . ."

Three—"My secretary said he wasn't from here. Drugs, maybe? We've all seen the statistics rising. No place is immune . . ."

Two—"Are you going to stay out there still? With everything that's happened?"

The elevator jolted to a stop just before the chime for the first floor. "Excuse me?" I said, stoic.

"Jessie said, well, it's kind of in the middle of nowhere. And you live all alone."

Jessie sure had a lot of information for someone I'd met once for twenty seconds.

"I'm not all alone out there," I said, because at the end

of the day, no matter what had happened in Rick's previous life, I realized that was absolutely true.

ON THE WAY HOME, I paused my car at the entrance to my driveway. I hadn't checked the mail in a few days. Not Friday night, when I'd stumbled in from the bar, and not Saturday, when I'd been brought back home by Elyse, watched over by both her and Bennett.

Now there were several days' worth of envelopes and magazines stacked inside. I usually tossed half of it as junk. As I sorted through the stack, I found a handwritten envelope at the bottom of the pile.

There was no stamp, no return address. The only words on the front were my name. No street address, town, or state. Someone had dropped this here in person. I didn't recognize the handwriting, though there wasn't much to go on.

I tore the envelope open, pulled out a rectangle of unlined paper.

My hands started shaking before I even finished skimming the first sentence.

> *Olivia,*
>
> *You may not remember me, and even if you do, you may want to forget.*
>
> *Maybe you do remember and just don't want to talk to me, and I understand that, too.*
>
> *My name is Sean Coleman, and we were connected many years ago. I was involved in your rescue in Widow Hills.*

I understand if you want to leave this all behind you,
but I feel some responsibility toward you. I've come a long
way to see you. I don't want to scare you, but I need you
to contact me.

Please, you can call me at the number below anytime.
I'll be staying at the Highland Inn through the end of the
week.

Fuck.

I read it again. A third time. Trying to see something new each time.

Had Sean Coleman come here on Friday night to leave me this letter? Had it been sitting here, waiting for me to find it, ever since?

For one terrible second, I debated tucking it away with the pile of junk mail, slipping it into the trash can, pretending it never existed.

But he'd come here for a reason. He'd come here for me.

And it sounded like he'd come here to warn me about something.

RETURN TO SENDER

No Forwarding Address

POSTMARKED: LEXINGTON, KY

MAY 26, 2011

It's time to tell the truth. You know what to do. And you know what will happen if you don't.

CHAPTER 18

Monday, 7:15 p.m.

HAD TO CALL DETECTIVE Rigby. Sean's son, Nathan, deserved to know.

They both deserved to know, for different reasons.

I knew what that phone call out of the blue had been like—that your parent was dead. The way information could hurt, just from the fact that it caught you off guard, like whiplash. I pulled out his card. I hadn't looked at it closely the first time: Nathan Coleman, Security Systems.

He looked the part. I could see him assessing the door-frames and windows. Determining how best to protect a property. It occurred to me now that I might need this type of service going forward.

I took a deep breath. I'd call Detective Rigby first; then I'd tell Nathan directly.

This letter . . . this letter meant there was no keeping it a secret anymore. This letter meant Nathan would know exactly who I was and why his father had come.

Everyone would.

Rick's truck turned the corner, heading from the direction of town. As he approached, I slid Nathan's card back into my purse. Rick idled beside me, window down. "Everything okay, Liv?"

There was a heap of plastic grocery bags in the back of his truck.

"Just getting the mail," I said, tucking the stack of envelopes under my arm. "I'll be over in a sec to help you with that."

"There's no need . . ." he said before driving away, but that was what he always said. The two of us, we were alone out here, and we depended on each other. He, too, was going to find out the truth about who I was. Better from me than someone else. I knew from experience that no one liked to learn they'd been friends with a liar. I'd already witnessed Bennett's reaction, felt the cooling, the distance; listened as he worked through his theories of what I might be capable of. And Rick had already seen me sleepwalking.

After taking my car up the drive, I dropped the pile of mail on the entryway table. Then I left through the back door behind the kitchen, heading for Rick's. I avoided the crime scene that I'd shown Nathan yesterday, instead cutting through our backyards.

There was a small garden in Rick's yard, mostly overgrown at this stage. I imagined vegetables and a flower bed, what might have existed before. At the edge of his yard was a shed, and the door was open. I heard movement inside as I walked by.

"Rick?" I called, peering in.

He was facing away, hunched over a wooden countertop.

"Just putting away some tools. Had to fix something in the kitchen earlier," he said, glancing over his shoulder. I waited just outside the doorway, watching him drop a screwdriver into a bin on a shelf. Everything smelled like sawdust and paint.

"The groceries in the truck?" I asked.

He waved his hand. "I already got them inside, Liv. But thanks for always checking in." He turned back to his workbench.

"Sure thing," I said.

The back door to his house was slightly ajar, the plastic bags visible on the kitchen table. I let myself in, deciding to wait for him here. I'd done this before, emptying his groceries. In the past, I'd even picked them up for him at the G&M.

He'd cleaned recently, everything shiny, the scent of dish soap lingering. Which explained the contents of his bags. In addition to the milk and cold cuts, bread and frozen meats—still waiting to be unloaded—there was a bag of fresh cleaning supplies: paper towels, a packet of sponges, rubbing alcohol, bleach.

I started stacking away his food in the fridge and freezer, an outlet for my nervous energy. I'd come to tell Rick about my past, to explain things in a way that wouldn't make it seem like I'd been lying about who I'd been for the last few years. That he hadn't made a mistake by selling that house to me, with or without the large cash payment.

The last bag contained the cleaning supplies, and I wasn't sure where he stored them. I thought, like me, he might keep his supplies in the cabinet under the sink. I opened both cabinet doors at once, but there was nothing inside except a stack of rags, like from a ripped-up shirt. The scent inside was sharp and astringent.

This was where the cleaning supplies had been, I was guessing. I pushed the rags aside to make room for his new containers—and a shock of blue caught my eye.

There were moments I could see coming.

Moments, like my mother claimed in her book, that felt instinctive. Otherworldly.

Heard it was a box cutter, Elyse had told me.

And here it was, under Rick's sink. That box cutter I'd last used on Wednesday to open my mother's box. That box cutter that was usually in my kitchen drawer.

Of course it would be here. I'd been searching and couldn't find it anywhere.

Now it was in my hand.

"I told you, I got it," Rick said.

I spun around quickly, though I was low to the ground, sitting on Rick's tile, with him looming over me. It was the first time I'd heard him speak that way. Sharp and ir-ritated. Not even when I'd shown up Friday night, hands covered in blood. Not even when he'd called the police. I saw him suddenly as Detective Rigby did: overbearing and capable of violence.

It occurred to me that I should be afraid.

But I had the box cutter in my hand, holding it up to him now. The blade tucked safely away, a scent coming off it, like bleach. The bright blue paint on the bottom of the handle.

"Why do you have this?" I asked, pushing myself up off the floor.

He staggered back a step, then two, feeling for the chair behind him. He eased himself down gently, just as

I reached full standing. Then he shook his head, looking down.

"You know why," he said.

"No," I said, all my senses heightening, "I really don't."

I tried to picture this in his hand, in the night, in the dark. Seeing a man outside, watching my house. Sneaking up behind him—

"I found it that night." His eyes rose to meet mine, and they were dark and glazed. There was a twitch at the corner of his left eye.

"Where?" I said. Because that was the hole in the story. How it got from my house to his hand.

"When I went out there. To check." In the silence, I heard a grandfather clock ticking from somewhere down the hall. "It was there, in the bushes." And then lower: "I recognized it."

Yes, because he had given it to me.

"No," I said.

It hadn't been there. There'd been a body, and the blood, and then I ran—I shook my head, clearing the thoughts that were circling. "Then why is it *still here*. Under your sink?"

"You showed up in the middle of the night, and you asked me for help. I was trying to help."

My entire body was thrumming, the images shifting. "No."

"I cleaned it, but," he continued, "I don't know if they'll search my garbage. You can't just throw stuff out. You can't just . . . disappear things." Then he looked at the back door, partially open. He lowered his voice. "They're watching, Liv. They're watching the both of us. Wanting to know how some stranger ended up dead on the line between our properties."

I closed my eyes, clinging to the facts. Something beyond panic was setting in. "You keep a gun in your bathroom. I've seen it."

"I told you, Liv, not everyone here is . . . I'm getting old, I'm not fast enough."

Like the danger was somewhere else and not in this very house.

But I kept going, needing there to be another possibility. "Detective Rigby said . . . she said there were rumors after your wife's death, and I shouldn't trust you . . . that it wasn't a suicide."

He froze then, looking so small, so sad. He exhaled, his body folding over itself. "Nina Rigby was a good kid. Her brother, though. He was part of the problem. That group, they got my boy into some things and . . . Liv, they were not good people." He ran his hands down his face, a shudder working through his body, and then it was gone. "I was out in the shed when the gunshot sounded, I promise you."

"The detective said—"

"Nina was eighteen," he said, voice rising. "And I'll tell you what people said. People said my story had holes. That I was close enough to hear the shot, and I waited too long to call it in, and that was true."

"She said your son knows the truth. That he hates you, that he never comes back . . ." The words out of my mouth were vicious, hateful. I was scared. I was mean. I needed not to be responsible for Sean Coleman's death.

Rick had been staring at his shoes, lost in his memory, and then he slowly looked up, his face transformed. "I will tell you once. One time. And then you will tell me."

I nodded slowly. This was what I had come for, after all. To tell him. To find the truth.

"My son was in the room, and my wife was dead. It was an accident. It was. I believe that. She was cleaning and he came home, not himself. He was not himself, he was not. You could see it in his eyes, he was not . . . the boy I knew. I found them like that, and he looked at me like . . . like . . ." Rick shook his head. "I told him to leave right then. I handled it all wrong. I didn't want to hear it, what he had to say. I made him leave, and he did. Nobody knows he was home when it happened. I handled it. But he didn't come back. You want to know why? He can't look at me because he's ashamed. Because we lied, but not for me. Not for me."

His eyes were swimming, staring straight at me. My own eyes were burning; I was scared to blink. Scared to look away. Scared of what to say.

"Now you," he said.

"I didn't do it," I whispered, because that was the only truth I could believe, too.

"It could've been an accident," he said. "Maybe you were protecting yourself. I'd seen you sleepwalking earlier that week. Tell me, were you sleepwalking then?"

I swallowed nothing. The truth, then, the thing he suspected but never said. The same thing Bennett suspected, that Detective Rigby must. That Calvin Royce feared. I didn't deny it; didn't lie—not to him.

He stood, took a step toward me, holding out his hands like he did that first night when he found me outside, like I was an animal that might spook. "I know it happened when you were younger. I know who you used to be."

I backed up, placed my hand on the counter. "Detective Rigby told you?" It wasn't fair, playing us against each other.

"No, no. Child, I knew when your application came through. Ran a background check with a cash offer like that." He nodded to my arm. "The scars. I know who you are."

I shook my head. "I was going to tell you," I said. "I came here to tell you."

"My wife followed your case. We remembered. She prayed, she—" He stopped abruptly, gestured for me to follow him down the hall, and I did, but still with that box cutter in my hand.

Both of us telling a story and begging the other person to believe it.

We passed the locked cabinet of guns—where one must've been used to kill his wife—down the hall, to a room I'd never been in. I didn't want to go any farther. Didn't like the narrowing of the walls, the lack of windows, the lack of exits. But then he opened the door, and it was almost unbearably bright. Blue bookshelves, painted lumber, stretching up to the ceiling. A rocking chair in the corner. A china cabinet against the far wall, filled with glass figurines. Books circling the room.

"My son, he's never coming back. Doesn't want to face himself. It was a terrible, terrible accident, but I told him we could get through it. That was the last time my son really looked at me, and then you showed up, and I needed to run a check, make sure your funds were legal. It pulled up an old name, and I remembered it. Of course I did. We both followed your story."

He limped to the far shelf and pulled down the book I hadn't seen in years. The pale pink cover, the photo on the front—of her and of me. Both of us with the long, wavy brown hair, impossible to tell where hers ended and mine began. *Finding Arden.*

"Marie, she bought your mother's book," he said. "I couldn't believe you were here, of all places, after everything." He shook his head, like he was trying to make sense of things that could not be put to words. "Like I was supposed to help you," he said, his voice barely audible. His eyes drifted to the box cutter in my hand. "To get it right this time."

"Rick," I said, begging him to understand. "I didn't." But at some point, you have to face the facts and yourself. "I would have defensive wounds, right?"

"I don't know," he said, but he gestured to my leg.

"That was after. I remember that. I fell." I held out my arms, turned them over for him to see. "There's nothing here. No marks, nothing."

"Well," he said, not conceding, not denying. "They're going to search this house or yours. Nina asked me this morning if I'd let them take a look around. I've been through this once before, and I told her not without a warrant. But it means they're going to get to one of us. They have to make a decision, though. They need probable cause, and that's no small thing. They can't just guess. But they're watching, trying to figure out which of us that stranger was here for."

I thought of Bennett and his suggestion to talk to his sister, her details sitting in my phone. "Have you talked to a lawyer, Rick?"

"No," he said. "I remember how this goes, Liv."

But he had the murder weapon in his house. If they came here with a warrant, he would be in so much trouble. And then I understood: He wasn't consulting a lawyer because he was protecting me. And I couldn't let him do it.

"That man was here for me that night," I said. "I was coming here to tell you. He left me a letter in my mailbox, and I'm going to have to tell them. That man, he was involved in my case twenty years ago. I don't know what he wanted. But his son is here now, and I have to tell them."

Rick nodded, then gestured to the box cutter. "I cleaned that, I don't think there's anything left. But I'm gonna bleach everything anyway." He paused. "Leave it."

I shook my head. "I can get rid of it," I whispered. At the hospital, there were multiple disposal containers for sharp objects, for biohazards. It could disappear without being traced to one of us. "Rick, until this is done, I don't think we should be talking."

He didn't say anything at first. And then, finally, "All right, Liv."

EVERYTHING WAS PUT ON hold after that—contacting Detective Rigby, calling Nathan.

I had to share the letter with the police, yes. But first I had to get this box cutter out of my possession before they came searching for it.

FINDING ARDEN

Excerpt, p. 19

They found her shoe the first day of
searching. This little green sneaker with a pink
flower on the side. It was stuck on the grate
that had been pried away from the drainage pipe,
wedged between two of the bars. It looked almost
gray when they showed me, and I didn't want to
believe it was hers at first.

But the ditch beyond the end of our road led
right there. The drainage pipe's cover had been
missing for who knows how long, they said.

It was the first sign of Arden.

I wanted to believe she was lost in the woods
somewhere, not washed away with the floodwaters.
But that shoe, it changed the search. It made
us realize she probably hadn't wandered very
far at all on her own before she was overcome
by the current.

Even now I don't want to imagine what that
was like. I don't want to imagine how scary and
dark and claustrophobic it must've been when
she woke. Part of me thinks it's better if she
slept through that part. That she only woke
after she was safe and could see daylight. That

she will never remember those dark, harrowing days.

But I know, realistically, she probably woke far sooner. Most likely when the water swept her off her feet. The impact must have jarred her awake.

She must have been awake when her foot got caught, when she had a chance for a moment to stay out of the pipes and then lost it. I know she was awake; it was the only way to save herself.

She doesn't like to talk about what happened in the time she was missing, what she endured. People say it's impossible that she held on for three days before she was found, but what do they know about my daughter? I don't want to imagine the alternative: that she spent hours or days in the pitch black, with nothing but water and filth, and no way to know whether it was day or night, or if she'd ever be found.

Whenever the doctors asked, she said, "I don't remember."

I thought it was cruel for them to keep pushing. Can you imagine? What that must have been like?

I don't want to think about it, either. I believe it would be a gift to forget.

CHAPTER 19

Tuesday, 10:30 a.m.

I COULD FEEL THE WEIGHT of the box cutter in my purse, wrapped up in paper towels to keep it clean of any contamination that could be traced back to me, including my fingerprints.

I'd been waiting for the right moment to dump it—the right excuse to be down the hall in a patient's room. I'd left a message asking Detective Rigby to meet me at my house after work, telling her that I'd found something. She hadn't called back, and I was full of an irrational hope that the investigation had moved away from me and Rick. Or that something else more enticing had grabbed her attention.

My office door was open so I could hear when the right moment presented itself: discussion of a nurses' meeting, maybe, when people would be off the floor except essential personnel. Worst case, I'd try to blend in during the lunch chaos and the changing of shifts.

I heard the voices as soon as the double doors at the end of the hall opened.

"Her office is right down here." A woman's voice—someone I knew? My pulse sped up, like my body could sense something instinctively before it registered.

"Thanks so much for escorting me up here. I didn't realize there was so much security on the upper floors." My back straightened, goose bumps rising on the back of my neck. That second voice I definitely knew: It belonged to Detective Nina Rigby, who was currently walking down my hall—toward my office. My purse was currently lying on top of the couch, the box cutter stuffed inside.

I stood quickly, chair pushing back, like I could stop this, catch her before she got here. But Detective Rigby was already in my doorway. "Olivia, I'm sorry, did I catch you at a bad time?"

Even though I was standing, I picked up my phone, just to have something to do with my hands. "Did we have a meeting?" I asked. "Did you call back? It's been hectic here, sorry if I missed a message."

"No, no," she said, stepping fully inside my office. She stood, feet apart, eyes skimming the room. "I did get your message, though, and I was in the area—had to talk to some folks downstairs, actually." She let that comment sit, let it fester, let my mind fill in all the gaps: People working in the morgue? Sydney Britton? Someone else?

We were both standing, my desk between us. "Can I sit?" she asked, gesturing to the couch.

"Yes, of course," I said, easing back down in my chair behind my desk.

She positioned herself less than a foot away from my purse, so close I could feel my body breaking into a cold sweat. "So, what is it that you wanted to talk to me about? You said you'd found something? The message was pretty vague."

I closed my eyes, nodded once. Wished I'd been more prepared for this moment, wished we'd done it on my terms. "I checked my mailbox this morning," I said. "I hadn't checked it since . . . before. Thursday, maybe? So the mail, it was from Friday, Saturday, Monday . . ."

She raised an eyebrow, urging me forward.

"There was a letter from him. From Sean Coleman."

And with that, the detective was already on her feet. "You got a letter from Sean Coleman? And you're just telling me this now?" She braced her hands on the edge of my desk, fingertips white from the pressure.

"I only just found it. On my way to work. I was running late, and I left you a message—"

She cursed to herself, hands now on top of her head. It was the first time I'd seen her with any show of emotion, and her reaction startled me.

Finally, she spun around again. "Is it here?" she asked, gesturing to my purse. Her hand brushing inches from the box cutter.

"No! No, I left it at home. On the entryway table."

"I thought you said you got the mail on the way to work."

"Timing-wise. Not literally on my way. I got the mail, brought it inside. Called you. Then left. Why does it matter?" I had officially crossed from omissions to lies, and I was curious, in a detached way, about how fluid that transition had been. Surprised that there had been no big step, no active decision, but a natural slide.

"It matters because it's a piece of evidence in a murder

investigation, and it's just sitting on your entryway table with the rest of your mail! What, exactly, did you do when you got it?"

I felt my stomach twisting, my fists clenching. "I opened it. I read it. I called you. It said—"

She put her hand out, cutting me off. "No, I want to read it for myself. For the first time. Hear it in his words. Let's go," she said, turning for my door.

"I'm at work," I said, and the purse was beside me, and there was no way I was bringing that box cutter back into my home, back within range of Detective Rigby.

She turned slowly, spoke each word clearly and point-edly. "And I'm a detective on a murder case. I'm sure your employer will understand."

I realized something then: Yes, she was in charge, and out of her element, and fighting for something herself. All of us were trying to prove ourselves here.

"I have a few things I need to take care of before I can leave. Five minutes," I said, scrambling. "I'll meet you downstairs."

She must've agreed, because she was already on her phone as she exited my office. I walked her to the elevator, waited until it arrived, watched the doors slide shut with her inside.

The purse was hitched on my shoulder. I had run out of time.

There weren't any windows into the exam rooms, but we left paperwork in a bin outside each occupied room, beside a whiteboard with the doctor and nurse on-call info. One of the whiteboards looked like it had recently been erased, the blue marker smudge remaining. I ran my hands inside the bin, and it was empty.

I pushed open the door, prepared to say I was looking for someone if I was wrong. But the room was empty and clean. No sign that anyone would be returning quickly.

I went straight for the sink cabinet. Inside was a red container marked *Sharps*. I quickly opened my purse, hands on the paper towels, unraveling the box cutter directly into the container. I shook the container gently, so it fell near the bottom. All the contents would have to be emptied by the end of the day. I closed the cabinet doors and backed away.

Like that, it was gone.

I took a deep breath, but my hands were shaking as I barreled out of the room into the hallway. The trick to looking like you belonged, I knew, was to act it. That was where I'd gone wrong when Bennett found me in the medicine room.

Head down, phone out, like I was busy. I didn't see anyone coming when I rounded the corner, walking straight into Bennett. He had his head down as well, nose to a chart in front of him.

His free hand went to my elbow. "Whoa, whoa," he said. "Hey." He stepped back, looking me over. "I didn't know you were back at work yet."

"I was. But I have to head out now." I hitched my purse higher, waved my phone at him.

His eyes narrowed down the hall, at door after door of patient rooms. "Were you looking for something?"

"No, I was in the hall and my phone rang, I just ducked inside an empty room for a minute."

He nodded slowly. "Everything okay? You look . . ." He let the thought trail, let me fill in the blank: panicked, frantic, guilty.

I had wanted to talk to him. But not *now*. Not standing in this hall, when he had to be wondering what I was doing here, if not looking for him.

I took a deep, steadying breath. "I was looking for you, but . . . I'm meeting the detective now. If anyone asks, I'll be back tomorrow, okay?"

"Sure, hey, I want to talk, too, but I'm in the middle of . . ." He waved his hand down the hall, and I understood. When we were on, we were on. Everyone here was practiced in compartmentalizing, and Bennett was one of the best.

"It's fine," I said, punching in the code to the double doors heading back toward my office.

"I'll call you when I'm done here," he said, just as I slipped through the doors.

No one had seen me do it. No one had stopped me. Twenty steps to the door at the other end of the hall. Thirty-two steps down the stairs. When I exited the stairwell, I could see Detective Rigby's shadow waiting just outside the elevators.

"Sorry," I called, so she would see me coming. "Ready?"

Three turns down the wide hospital hall to the lobby. The automatic doors slid open, and we were out. The box cutter was as good as gone. And it was all behind me.

I LED THE WAY home in my car as Detective Rigby followed behind. I drove awkwardly, like a kid learning to drive, the way I'd get any time I'd see a cop pull out onto the road, lowering my speed limit, using the turn signals too soon. Checking my rearview mirror continually, like I was waiting for the red and blue lights to turn on.

When we finally pulled up to my house, there were two other vehicles outside my driveway, and I could see the shape of a person inside each. They didn't step out of their vehicles until both Detective Rigby and I had turned in and parked.

The detective greeted the two men casually as they approached, and I realized she had asked them to meet us here.

This was evidence in a murder investigation, after all.

They both appeared around her age—one with red hair buzzed short, the other with dark blond hair and the start of a beard.

She conferred with them quietly while I unlocked the front door. "Please wait," she called up to me, as if I shouldn't step foot in my own house without her guidance.

The man with the red hair circled back with a camera, presumably to document where I'd found the letter. The other accompanied Detective Rigby up the porch steps. At closer look, he was even younger than she was—the facial hair covering for a baby face, with freckles and big blue eyes. I hadn't heard him speak a word, and he deferred to Detective Rigby in every movement.

"There," I said, pointing to the entryway table.

"Please don't touch it," she said, my hand hovering. I had already handled it, shuffled it around, hooked it under my arm as I carried the stack of mail inside. But I didn't argue.

Detective Rigby snapped on a pair of gloves, unfolded the letter, read it to herself. I watched as her brown eyes scanned the words line by line. Then she handed it over to the man beside her, who seemed to be in charge of storing it. He handled it like a rare, breakable thing, placing it inside a Ziploc bag. I wasn't sure they knew what they were doing, whether they'd ever done something like this before. Whether we were all out of our depths here.

"It sounds like he was trying to warn me of something," I said.

She snapped off her gloves the same way Dr. Britton had in the ER. "What makes you say that?"

His literal words had made me think that, but I felt like, with her, she was always trying to get me to admit to something. Like our interpretations of events exposed something deeper about each of us. "He asked me to contact him," I said. "He said it was important, that he'd come a long way to see me."

The other man waited stoically in the entrance. The only sign of movement was his eyes as they shifted between me and the detective.

"You can take that," she said to him.

He nodded and left, the sound of his footsteps fading away as he descended the porch stairs.

Detective Rigby paced the foyer, breathing slowly. "I've been reading a lot about what happened to you twenty years ago." She whistled through her teeth. "That was really something."

"I don't remember it," I said, my typical response. It used to stop the conversation in its tracks when I was younger, whenever adults brought it up. Made them say something like *Probably for the best*, which I guessed it was. Something we could agree on, nodding sagely together.

"I can understand why you changed your name," she said. "There sure was a lot of talk." The detective looked around my house. At the open arches, the light-colored walls, the new sofa. "Had a bunch of money come your way after?"

I pressed my lips together and nodded. Didn't want to get into the fact that my mother had wasted a lot of it away, that it was mostly gone, that it had given me a fresh start and now even that was in jeopardy. This house was all that was left, and I was, I thought, understandably protective of it.

She pointed to the entryway table, which was now bare. "Anyone else know about this?"

"Rick," I said.

"You called him before calling me?"

"You didn't answer," I reiterated.

"Mr. Aimes—" she began, and I thought: *You don't know everything.*

"Detective Rigby," I cut in, "which street was Sean Coleman's car found on?"

She cut her eyes to me without speaking, like she wasn't sure how I'd gotten that information. She clearly didn't know I had heard about the car. She didn't know Nathan had come here on his own.

She pursed her lips, then spoke. "We found his car along the side of the road on Haymere."

"The street behind us?" I asked. So he had walked. I pictured him parking and walking. Haymere Lane diverged from the same main road cutting toward town, but it didn't seem that close. "Do you think he walked to deliver that letter?" Could that be why he was out here that night? And then—what? Someone killed him on his way back? It didn't make sense. Why not just drive by and deliver it from his car in the daylight? But I could think of no other reason for him to be out in my yard. He'd kept himself hidden, and then this letter was in my mailbox.

The detective started pacing again, and I started to see it not as a nervous tic but as a way to process her thoughts. "No, I don't think so. You said his letter was at the bottom of the pile of mail, right?"

"Yes," I said, and then I understood. He had not been there that night to deliver the letter. He already had been, *before* the mail arrived on Friday. Probably after I'd ignored him at the grocery store. He'd known I wouldn't take well to him sneaking up on me. He'd already tried that approach. So he'd left me the letter, and then he'd come back. To . . . what?

To watch me from the borders of my yard? Or did he change his mind—was he coming closer?

What had he wanted to tell me? And why had he been killed?

"Can I take a look around?" she asked, facing away. "See if there are any other signs that he might've been snooping around in here?"

She said it so nonchalantly, as if I didn't know exactly what she was after. Like Rick had warned, they were going to get a warrant to search one of our houses. Easier if we gave permission. She wouldn't find anything, anyway. But we weren't there yet.

"You already did," I said, "that first night." I'd let her in then, let her feel like I had nothing to hide.

She turned toward me, blinked slowly. "That was before I had reason to think he'd been watching you."

A chill ran up my spine. What more did they know that they weren't giving away?

"No," I said. "I had to cut my day short for this as it is. I've got to catch up."

I held the door open, gesturing her out. She paused, and for a moment I thought she wouldn't leave, that she was going to pull out a warrant right then. But she didn't.

"A word of advice, Olivia. Stop telling Mr. Aimes things related to this case."

And with that, she left.

I knew there were two basic theories if Sean Coleman had been hanging around outside our homes:

The first was that Rick had seen him watching and hurt him.

The second was that it had been me. Either in self-defense or not. But I'd given them the letter; I'd cooperated. I'd lost any hope of anonymity in the process.

There was no way to stop it now. I had to protect myself.

DISPATCH: 911, what is your emergency?

CALLER, UNIDENTIFIED FEMALE: Oh my God, it's my daughter. She's gone.

D: Ma'am? What do you mean by gone?

C: She sleepwalks, and she's not in her bed. She's nowhere. Please, please help me. Oh my God. Arden!

D: Okay, is Arden your daughter, ma'am?

C: Yes. The front door is open and she's just gone. She's gone.

D: Okay, have you checked outside yet?

C: Of course I did.

D: What is your exact address?

C: [ADDRESS REDACTED] Please help me. Oh, God, please.

CHAPTER 20

Tuesday, 2 p.m.

THAT WAS BEFORE I *had reason to think he'd been watching you.*

That was what the detective had said. Implying that Sean Coleman had possibly been out here before.

I waited until after I was sure Detective Rigby and the other police officers were gone, and then I waited some more for good measure, before stepping out the back door.

My backyard was a square of grass and packed earth without a fence line, cleared long ago when Rick must've purchased these lots. The tree line, and the start of the wooded area, was still part of my property.

I knew the perimeter because I'd walked it the first day; Rick had given me the tour himself, pointing out what was mine and what wasn't. Which was how I knew that the slope ending at the creek was the back of the property line. It wasn't much—a slow-moving stream that I could step across easily, that probably dried up whenever it hadn't rained in a few weeks.

When I reached the creek, I turned around to see how far I'd come, and was surprised that I could no longer see my house or Rick's. I was too far down the incline, and though the density of the trees wasn't that heavy, they overlapped in layers behind one another—a trick of perspective.

My stomach flipped as I imagined being disoriented, lost. I closed my eyes, imagining what that girl must've felt twenty years earlier. Waking up as the water knocked her off her feet. Grabbing for the roots or trees or grass, anything to hold her. Everything slipping through her small fingers until her foot caught on a metal grate—the tiniest moment of hope.

And then the darkness.

The girl who survived. The girl who held on. The girl who was so fucking terrified she'd buried the entire three days in the deepest recesses of her psyche.

I turned away again, stepping across the creek. I wasn't lost; I knew if I kept moving, I'd eventually come out on Haymere Lane. I followed the incline, moving quietly, knowing I was now technically trespassing on another piece of property.

The first thing I saw was the remnants of an old fence. Just the bottom wooden slats, with a few pieces missing. The first sign of a property falling to disrepair. But I couldn't find the house. There was a small structure set back from the road, a standing shed like Rick had in his yard. It was located at the end of a grassy drive, tire tracks marking the way through the weeds. The only evidence of a house was a wide slab of concrete—either a house that had been flattened or one that was in the process of being built.

Abandoned for now, either way.

Detective Rigby had told me that Sean Coleman's car had been found on Haymere. He'd parked somewhere along this road. I followed what passed as the driveway out to the pavement. From where I stood, Haymere looked a lot like my street, with no sidewalk, a low shoulder, and a sharp curve, so I couldn't see what lay beyond this property to the right.

But unlike my street, Haymere dead-ended. To my left, I could see the road stopped at something that wasn't even a cul-de-sac, just a stretch of pavement that abruptly ended at the woods. Like someone had started and abandoned the project mid-work.

I didn't think Sean would've parked along the road itself: too great a chance of him being rear-ended. Here—this driveway—this was what made sense. Tucked out of sight from any other residents nearby. Either here or where the pavement ended, to my left.

I imagined Sean Coleman standing where I now stood. Leaving his car out of sight. Trekking through the woods, where he knew he'd end at my house . . . How many nights had he done this? How many times had he been out there, watching?

I turned back for the shed, peered into the windows, but it was mostly empty space. Dirty windows and dusty floor. Had Sean Coleman been inside? Waiting for something?

If the police had been here, whatever was inside might have already been taken.

The sound of an engine cut through the quiet of the

abandoned space. I peeked around the edge of the shed before jerking back—a police cruiser.

Turn around, turn around, turn around—

The sound of tires turning off the road into gravel and grass. The engine falling to silence and then doors opening and closing.

I felt my heartbeat down to my toes and quickly risked another look. Two men were standing outside the vehicle. I didn't think I'd seen them before. I didn't know whether they were looking for something here, or whether this was how they'd been keeping an eye on me and Rick. A central hub.

My phone started ringing, and I fumbled to silence it as fast as possible: a call from Bennett. I pressed mute and listened for the voices of the men in the driveway. I didn't think they'd heard the phone; they were too far from the shed still. But their voices carried faintly in the wind.

I had to go now, before they got closer, before I was trapped. There was nowhere to hide here, just trees and open space. But they were still talking near the car. I tried to move as quietly as possible. Facing them, moving backward, stepping over the remnants of the fence, and then fading into the woods, my heart pounding, until I could tuck myself behind a tree, and then another, until finally, they disappeared entirely from my sight—and me from theirs.

MY SHOULDERS EVENTUALLY RELAXED when I reached the creek again. Knowing I was safely on my own property, not trespassing—not watching other people from a hidden location.

But then I thought: *This was what they were doing to me.*
First Sean Coleman and now the police. I hated the feeling of being watched. Of the stories they were possibly crafting. The angles they would pick. The things I could imagine them saying.

And so I was unprepared for the man in my backyard, standing on the back steps, hands cupped around his face as he peered into my kitchen window.

He must've heard me at the same time I spotted him, because he jerked back, turning around slowly. "Jesus," he said, "there you are."

"Bennett?"

He walked down the steps—out of his scrubs, in jeans and a T-shirt—and slowed as he approached, looking at the trees behind me. "I tried calling. Your car was here and you weren't answering the door, and you mentioned that detective . . ." He swallowed, ran his hand through his hair. "I was worried."

I checked my phone, saw the time, realized Bennett must've come straight from work. He'd mentioned calling me when he was free, and I'd been unreachable.

I wasn't sure what to make of him here. Once someone knew the truth, there was always some ulterior motive to interactions. And so it sat in the pit of my stomach, this gently gnawing unease.

Then I thought I wasn't being fair. This was entirely within character for Bennett. Elyse up and left, and he couldn't get ahold of me—as if he could feel the pieces spinning out of his control and was desperate to pull them back.

"I called one of Elyse's former employers," I said, changing the topic, because there was no good answer to why I was out in the woods behind my house after the detective had asked to speak to me. "There was some implication about shady inventory practices at her previous hospital."

Bennett cursed under his breath. "How did that get through the hiring process?"

"I don't think it was known at the time. But she moved around a lot. It doesn't seem like her, to be honest, but that's what they said." Elyse hadn't seemed anything like my mother had, with the sudden shift in demeanor, the unpredictability, and the money draining in inverse proportion.

But we both knew that sometimes it could be more hidden than that. Especially in the health care field. The percentage of addiction was the same as in the general population; the only difference was access. In a medical facility, things could go missing easily on their way to the intended patient. Saline substituted for morphine. We'd all heard of cases of the diversion of medicine. It was how my mother first started, I believed. The inventory at her fingertips in the homes where she worked. The easiest accessible remedy.

It was why we had a tight inventory process at the hospital. But it could be hard to catch when the medicine was supposed to be heading out and just not reaching its intended recipient.

Or when you were in a drawer for something justified and seized the opportunity.

"What were you fighting about, Bennett? That day at my house?" I wondered if he had suspected her; if he'd made some veiled accusation that had sent her running.

He sighed. "We were both emotional, and she was

running on no sleep, obviously. She was going on and on about watching out for who showed up, telling me to keep a lookout at the window, and I thought she was being ridiculous. And she started yelling, like, *There's a dead fucking body, obviously I'm not overreacting.* And I said she was in no shape to work, not even in enough shape to care for you, and to get out of there. And that's the last thing I heard from her."

I stared at him.

"I know, I know. I might've said *Get the fuck out of here.*" He closed his eyes and shook his head. It was the same thing he'd said to me when he found me in the medicine room. "Hearing it back now, it sounds worse than I thought. I told her she was in no shape for work. I told her to go, and she did. Of course, if she was an addict, the behavior would make sense, that paranoia . . ."

"She wasn't paranoid," I said. Not usually. Not that I'd noticed. She was more free-spirited than I was. She was open, and let herself be vulnerable, and flirted with bartenders. But she also came to the hospital as soon as she'd heard, kept watch over me, cooked me food, stayed while I slept. With Elyse, I'd thought I was seeing another possible path my life could've taken, but maybe I was only seeing another iteration of the same. Another girl, another story being told in the aftermath by the pieces left behind.

I walked up the back steps, and Bennett shifted out of the way so I wouldn't brush up against him. I unlocked the door: "Are you coming in?"

"Yeah." Everything was a beat too slow, just slightly forced. We'd left things awkwardly the last time he was here—coming closer and then falling apart within the space of thirty minutes.

When I poured a drink of water, I caught him staring at the scar on my arm. He was frowning, and I heard an echo of his words—*must've been incredibly painful.*

I shook the thought, turning away, and his gaze averted.

"Did you not suspect her, Bennett?"

He looked somewhere over my shoulder, out the window, into the woods. "No, I didn't."

The way he wasn't looking at me made me nervous. I wondered if, ever since he'd found me in the medicine room, he'd truly suspected me instead. If he *had* been through my things while I was unconscious. If he was checking to see what he'd found.

"Is this why you were looking for me earlier?" he asked. I nodded, and he started pacing. "Anyway, I came here to apologize for the other day. And my reaction. And"—he waved his arm around meaninglessly—"what I said."

"Okay. Forgiven. It's a lot, I get that."

"It is," he said in the faraway voice of someone who had spent his free time researching the events of twenty years earlier. He kept stealing glances at me like he was trying to reconcile the two.

It had been a lot back then, too. For the people, for the town, for everything surrounding us; 911 had been inundated with calls. People reporting me missing, as if they hadn't heard. People reporting sightings of every child playing outside. The call center had to bring in extra help just to man the lines, I'd heard.

"Everything going okay? With the detective?" he asked.

I put the glass down, couldn't tell why he was asking. Questions like this put me on edge, on the defense. I could not unravel someone's motivation without giving too much of myself away in the process. "Yes," I said.

"Did she say anything? About what they think happened?"

I shook my head slowly. Unsure if he was here for the information or for me.

"I know I reacted the wrong way, and I can't take it back. I just—wanted to see you. And tell you that."

"I'm sorry, I'm just really shaken." I took a deep breath. "I just found out that Sean Coleman sent me a letter, wanting to tell me something, before he died."

"Oh. Oh God. Do you have any idea what?"

"No, but I'm actually about to head out. Hoping I'll know more soon."

"Sure. Okay. Do you want me to come? I mean, would it help if I was there?"

Bennett probably thought I was meeting with the police again. He was holding his breath, and I could see how badly he did not want to come. How uncomfortable he was, standing there, trying to figure out the right thing to do.

"No," I said. "But thank you."

"All right," he said. "Well, you know how to reach me, Liv."

He did not want to get pulled into this mess. Maybe he'd thought he could handle it, in theory. That he was a bigger person. But there was too much chaos here; too much even for Bennett to fix. Which was ironic, since he was trained in managing crises. He was good at the surrounding organization. At creating a simplicity and an action plan. But as much as we saw human beings reduced to checklists and spreadsheets in practice, there were no such predictable outcomes outside the hospital.

And, I realized, that was probably all Bennett ever

wanted. A predictable existence that I would never give him.

AFTER BENNETT LEFT, I thought back to Sean Coleman's letter, telling me where he would be staying. That was a sure way to find out how long he'd been in town. And how long he could have been watching me.

The Highland Inn was on the outskirts of town, new but simple. It functioned less as a hub for activity related to the hospital and more as a waypoint for outdoor treks. It was the last stop before an empty stretch of road that eventually ended at the ski resorts. But there was easy access from there to tubing, rafting, and mountain biking. There was a campground a few miles away, at the head of the river, if you wanted to really rough it. Otherwise, Highland Inn was the best option.

It was dark by the time I pulled in. The lot was half-full, but there were no people in the lobby other than a single man in a suit behind the counter who pretended he didn't see me when I walked in. The glass doors slid shut silently behind me as I walked to the desk.

He finally raised his eyes when I was standing directly in front of him. "Can I help you?" he asked with an accommodating smile.

"Yes," I said, making sure my request sounded professional. "I'm looking for one of your guests." I figured I'd start small, then try to expand—to find out how long he'd been staying here.

"Name?" he asked, hands poised over his keyboard.

"Coleman," I said, "C-O—"

His hands dropped, and his smile disappeared. "Let me

stop you right there. I've already told the rest of you people this, we're not giving out any information—"

"Olivia?"

I turned around and saw Nathan Coleman walk
through the same doors I'd just passed through.

"Hi," I said, trying to catch my bearings. This receptionist had been implying that others were asking after
Sean Coleman—probably media. He would've had to
hand over any details to the police, but they'd probably
warned him not to talk to the press, as they had to me.

"Were you looking for me?" Nathan asked.

"Yes," I said. And then, turning to the receptionist,
"Looks like I found him."

The man's face fell, and for a second it seemed that
neither of us had known there was a different Coleman
currently staying at the hotel.

As I walked toward Nathan, sirens started up in the
distance, coming closer. I tensed, imagining police cars
pulling into this lot. Nathan turned, too, so we were both
looking through the glass doors as the ambulance went
by, continuing on. Toward the campgrounds and the
mountains beyond.

"I forget sometimes that there are emergencies happening every day," Nathan said. "That people everywhere
are getting the worst news of their lives. Or the best.
Makes me feel a little better to remember."

Like it was all a cycle and we were just a small part of
it. "Me, too," I said, though I'd never thought about it
that way.

"There's a café here in the hotel, just around the corner. The coffee is adequate, but the beer is better. Want
to head there?"

"Sure," I said, following him down the hall. "I wasn't sure if you would still be in town. How long are you staying?"

"As long as it takes," he said, peering back at me. Nathan had purpose, and you could see it in every movement. It made him seem older, that he knew what he wanted. And right now he wanted the person who'd killed his father to pay. He implied that he would stay until then. I had no doubt he would make that happen.

"I wasn't sure if you had people waiting for you back home," I said. I didn't notice a wedding ring on his hand, but that didn't mean there wasn't a wife, or kids, or a serious girlfriend.

He slowed as we approached the counter. "Well, my dog will be pissed about it, I'm sure." He gave me half a smile. "But my neighbor's taking care of things. Luckily, I work for myself. I'm taking some time."

I picked the same beer that Nathan ordered, not caring either way—I didn't plan on drinking it—and followed him to an empty café table in the back corner. There were a few other people scattered around the room, but no one seemed to be paying attention.

"I need to tell you something," I said as soon as we were seated. I needed to guide the conversation, control where it led. It was better to hear it from me.

"All right," he said, taking a long sip.

"I found a letter from your father in my mailbox. I didn't see it until today. I called the detective—she has it now."

He didn't answer at first, just watched me with an intensity that made me look away. "What did it say?" he finally asked.

"Just that he wanted to talk to me. I didn't know who he was until I heard his name. But when the detective shared his identity with me, I did know, Nathan. I'm sorry I didn't tell you from the start, but I wasn't sure how to bring it up. I hadn't seen him in twenty years, but he was there the night he died because of me."

Then, as he silently listened, I told him everything. About who I was and how I'd changed my name, leaving it all behind me. How I hadn't heard from Sean Coleman ever since, and hadn't recognized him when I saw him. That I didn't know why he'd come to see me after all this time.

When I finished talking, he didn't change his expression or his body language. Didn't push back or pull forward. "I remember when it happened. I was nine," he said.

I tried to picture it, his family watching at home, seeing Sean on the news, holding me up. I'd never pictured the people beyond the screen. It was an event that bonded us all together, stretching further than we could see.

"Did he ever . . . talk about me?" I asked, breaking the silence.

"No, like I said, we weren't close. It wasn't something he liked to talk about. My parents got divorced not long after, and I lived with my mom in Lexington, mostly. I didn't grow up in that area. Didn't visit much. When I did, he didn't mention it." He took another sip. "Never did like the spotlight."

The opposite of my mother, then.

Except both of us were next of kin to people we didn't have much of a connection with anymore. I felt suddenly hollow that neither Sean Coleman nor my mother had someone closer willing to claim them.

"What about your mom? Were they still in contact?"

He let out a single bite of laughter. "No. No way. My mom remarried, got herself a whole new life, and never looked back. I've got three younger half siblings now, all in high school."

"Must be nice," I said. Even though he was estranged from his father, at least he had them close by.

"They're all right," he said with a grin. "Listen, I'm supposed to meet up with Detective Rigby soon. She called, said she'd be stopping by later. I wonder if this is what it's about."

"Probably," I said, relieved that I'd run into him. Relieved that I could tell him first. "I should probably leave you be, then." I stood, even though I'd barely touched the drink.

He stood, too, holding out his hand. Almost like he was offering to shake my hand, but instead he just clasped it in his grip. "Thank you," he said. "Thank you for telling me."

Of all the things people said when the truth of my past came out, this was the first time someone had reacted that way.

TRANSCRIPT OF 911 CALL FOR SERVICE

DATE: OCTOBER 17, 2000

TIME STAMP: 5:52 A.M.

DISPATCH: 911. What's your emergency?

CALLER, UNKNOWN MALE: Uh, I think something's happening next door.

D: Sir? What's happening next door?

C: I don't know. My neighbor is screaming. She's screaming for her little girl. I think she's missing. I don't know, I was outside getting ready for work and she just came running out, screaming.

D: Can I get your name, please?

C: Stuart. Stuart Goss.

D: Mr. Goss, what is your location?

C: [ADDRESS REDACTED] I'm heading over there now. Laurel? Laurel, what's going on? What happened?

CHAPTER 21

Wednesday, 4 a.m.

THE RINGING PHONE JARRED me from sleep, and my heart was racing in a panic—like I might find myself outside again, hearing a phone, standing over a body in the grass. I sat upright as it rang once more, the shadows of my bedroom furniture orienting me. The stuffy room; the door closed with a lock up high; the window latched shut. It was still so dark, no sign of morning.

A third ring, and I reached for it on my bedside table, my vision too blurry to read the name.

"Hello?" I answered.

"Liv, sorry to wake you like this."

"Bennett?" It was his voice, but it sounded quiet and clipped.

"I knew you'd want to hear it from me," he continued.

"What? Hear what?" I was trying to ground myself, while Bennett talked in circles, like I had missed half the conversation.

He drew in a slow breath, mouth pressed close to the phone. "It's Elyse."

I didn't respond, too confused to know where to start. Elyse *what*—

"They found her yesterday. At the campgrounds." A pause as I tried to process what he was getting at. "She overdosed."

My breath escaped in a rush, like someone had knocked me back.

The sirens I'd heard last night with Nathan, the ambulance rushing by the hotel. Had it been for her? How many hours earlier had this happened?

How long had people known, the truth circulating through their group texts, until Bennett was eventually contacted? He was the only one who would call me directly.

"Is she okay?" I asked, even though I knew the answer. Heard it in his voice as soon as he spoke. A call in the middle of the night, the clipped words—he was trying to break the news to me softly, but it was only delaying the inevitable.

"No, she's not." His voice broke, and he cleared his throat, continued on. "She was crashing in one of the cabins. Hadn't paid or anything. They found her yesterday evening when a new couple was checking in. It had been too long, Liv. I'm sorry."

But I was caught in the details. She was staying at the campgrounds? I didn't understand. She'd quit; she'd moved out—"Why? Why was she there?" As if this were the detail that mattered, that could unravel all the other things he'd said, changing the outcome. As if, after the illogic had been pointed out, the rest would fall apart.

"I don't know. Her car was nearby, full of her things." And then, "Are you okay?"

"What? I don't know." I was stuck in this persisting shock. Like maybe this wasn't real. Like I was talking, dreaming, while half-awake. I stood from my bed and tried the door, but it was still latched with the hook-and-eye lock. I felt trapped, couldn't breathe.

"I have to go," I said, dragging the ladder out of the closet. I knew it was real, from the metal legs scratching against the wood floor. The cold of the steps on my bare feet. The latch, just barely in reach. A noise in my throat like my windpipe would seize up if I didn't get to the open air soon.

Panic. I knew it was panic, but I couldn't stop it.

Finally, I threw open the bedroom door and stumbled out into the dark hallway. My hands traced the wall as I followed the hall into the living room, out the front door, until I was standing on the porch with my hands on top of my head, taking big gulps of the night air, thinking, *Panic, this is panic, slow down and breathe*—until I realized I was just crying.

IT WAS WHEN I went back inside, moments later, that I thought I heard something—a rattle of silverware in the kitchen, something that happened whenever I closed the back door. I flipped on each light as I went, thinking, *Elyse, playing some shitty joke.* But when I made it there, the lock was secure.

I flashed back to the handle in my office, faintly turning.

Maybe someone had been trying to get in, shaking the

doorframe. I turned on the outside porch light, but it had burned out. Bennett had fixed the front light, but now the back was gone, too.

I wasn't keeping on top of things, instead patching mistakes as they came up. I'd been too late for everything. Too comfortable in this new place, in my new life. Not looking for the danger coming. Ignoring it, even, when it started to emerge, hoping it would fade back into the woodwork.

I'd stopped looking for Elyse after calling her previous employer. I'd trusted Bennett instead of my gut. He had talked me down from panicking, but he was wrong. I shouldn't have listened to him, shouldn't have called him first. I knew something was wrong, the same way I could sense it in my mother, and I'd done nothing.

I should've called her again. I should've texted. I should've driven around and asked all her friends— someone had mentioned an Erin, and I'd never followed up. And now she was dead. Had died all alone in a cabin. Four walls closing in, the cold and dark night, believing there was no other way out.

I KEPT SEEING THE shadow of her in my house: beside my bed, watching out the window; at the kitchen counter, cooking eggs. I closed my eyes and heard the echo of her voice: *This is scary, Liv.* I kept searching for more—the last words she'd spoken to me, standing beside my bed. But everything had slipped from me, the medicine turning my head hazy, so that our last moment together became just one more memory forever lost to me.

I wanted to go back in time. Make a different decision.

Call the police and say, *She's gone, and it's not like her, and I'm worried.* Cross that divide and give her the other side of the friendship she deserved.

THERE WAS NOTHING TO be gained by staying home. Nothing to memorialize her, or grieve, other than by reliving my own shortcomings.

I moved by muscle memory, getting dressed, packing my bag, doing my hair. It wasn't that much different from sleepwalking. I'd heard you could go through the motions, perform tasks you'd performed before, your body remembering. You could get dressed, tie your shoes, walk out the door and into the street. You could grab your keys and get in the car. You could open a drawer and pick up a box cutter.

You could.

AT THE HOSPITAL, A fog of depression had settled over the floor. Every one of us going through the motions on autopilot. I worried about the other nurses; I worried about their patients. But everything felt disconnected and slow. I couldn't have helped if I'd wanted to.

By the time I scrolled through my email at lunch, I wasn't quite focused enough to understand what I was seeing. And even after I'd read it twice, the information registering, I knew it wasn't resonating as it should.

A reporter, asking me to fact-check a few claims: if I was the Olivia Meyer who lived on Old Heart Lane; if I could confirm my college dates of attendance; what my current job title was . . . and more. Asking me to follow up before noon. It was currently 12:03.

I felt nothing.

My cell phone rang, jarring me: Detective Rigby's number, which I had added into my phone. At least she hadn't stopped by unannounced this time.

"I wanted to give you the heads-up," she said by way of greeting. "I had a reporter call this morning, looking for a quote."

"I just saw an email," I said. "I don't understand. Is it about Sean Coleman?" The questions in my email all seemed like items they could've pulled from public records, not relevant to the events of Friday night.

"I didn't comment, Olivia, but they have a lot. They used it to try to get more from us. It's going to come out, and I can't stop it. I tried, I promise."

Part of me didn't believe her; part of me thought this would help her case against me.

"What exactly is going to come out?" I asked, elbow on my desk, forehead resting in my hand.

"From what I can gather, they've already spoken to a professor at your grad school."

"The school didn't know," I said. I'd enrolled as Olivia Meyer, no Arden tied to my name.

A pause. "They did, Olivia. They knew."

My ears started buzzing.

Jonah. It had to be Jonah. Had he known all along? Had he sought me out because of it? Not granting me special attention because of what he saw in me but because of his interest in something else. The pull of the story. Something to unravel, to be close to.

"Listen," she continued, "they were digging through some incidents in your past—things they shared with me in the hope that it would inspire a quote from us in response." Another pause. "Do you want to talk about those incidents?"

I remained silent. Felt everything tensing inside me.

When I didn't respond, she continued, "I told them I could not comment on an active investigation, but they are obviously going to be coming out with something—the connection between you and Sean Coleman is undeniable. I can only help you if you help me here."

But all I could do was imagine the people who had commented. My colleagues sharing rumors? Dr. Cal's receptionist protecting her job by providing an anonymous statement? Had Dr. Cal himself tried to spin his role into something that would make his career—as it had for others in the past? Had Bennett cracked, giving them something?

It could've been anyone. It could've been everyone. This was how it started; I felt myself shutting down. The way to handle this was by not speaking. The way to handle this was by leaving.

"I know this is a lot all at once, but you've got to say something," Detective Rigby said, her voice growing tense. "They mentioned some violent outbursts in your record?"

It was related to the PTSD, the therapist back then had said. It explained what had happened to that girl in the gym locker room. And it explained what had happened to that guy in college. I'd been trapped. That's what the detective wanted to hear. She wanted my story—but I knew better by now. I knew what could happen when you turned it over to someone else.

"My friend died last night," I said through gritted teeth. "Did you know that? Elyse Ferano, overdose. So excuse me if I'm having trouble concentrating on something that happened almost a decade ago. Excuse me for thinking it matters. This is what people do. They tell a story. It doesn't matter what happens to us after. It doesn't matter if it's even true, as long as it's a good enough story."

She waited a beat before responding. "You want to keep your past secret, I get that. Is that what happened back then?"

And there it was: a motive. Had I killed to protect my past? Subconscious or not, how badly did I want to keep that part of my life buried?

Here, right here, was where everything changed.

"I gave you everything," I said. "I told you who I was, didn't hide my connection to Sean Coleman. Doesn't that count for anything?"

"Maybe the phone isn't the best way—"

"No," I said, "it's really not." I disconnected the call before she could say anything more. I dropped my head into my hands, counted the rapid beats of my heart, waiting for it to slow.

Everyone wanted the story, and oh, this was a good one. Proof of the dark side of humanity. Of hidden pasts. Of the mysteries buried at the heart of other people.

Finally, I took out my cell, scrolling to Bennett's text. I found the information for his sister, Mackenzie Shaw.

The call rang until it went to her voicemail. "Hi, my name is Olivia Meyer, I'm a friend of Bennett's," I began. "I think I'm in trouble."

I DIDN'T LEAVE MY office again until the end of the day. Where was there left to go? I focused on my work, jumping with each ding of an email.

My stomach sank when my boss's message came through. There was a single line: *Is this true?*—with a link to some article below.

It didn't matter whether the article was true. The fact that it existed was all that really counted.

I read it despite myself. Just so I could prepare. Fight back. Because that's all that could happen from here. This was the truth that currently existed—and so anything that came after would have to chip away at all that came before.

Everyone wants to be a part of the story. Sell your words, your friends, your soul.

Watch what happens.

Be careful. There's no going back.

OBSERVER ONLINE

August 26, 2020

Posted: 3:47 P.M.

*From National Icon to Person of
Interest: The Girl from Widow Hills
Emerges Twenty Years Later at the
Center of a Murder Investigation*

By Alice Perry

She was a national icon. Twenty years ago, Arden
Olivia Maynor was rescued from the underground
drainage system that ran through the terrain of
Widow Hills, Kentucky. Her case sparked national
interest when it was reported that the six-year-old
girl had been sleepwalking and was swept away
during a flash flood. The story gripped the public
interest, until thirty-two-year-old Sean Coleman
spotted her hanging on to a drainage grate in the
middle of a wooded area, three days after she'd
gone missing.

It seemed like a happy ending, but tragedy has
struck nearly twenty years later.

In the early hours of Saturday morning, Sean
Coleman was found dead on the border of a
property in Central Valley, North Carolina. According to public records, that property is owned by

seventy-year-old Rick Aimes, and the neighboring property belongs to twenty-six-year-old Olivia Meyer.

Olivia Meyer and Arden Olivia Maynor share the same birthday, per public records.

Detectives on the case declined to comment on the connection or to confirm whether Olivia Meyer and Arden Olivia Maynor are indeed one and the same. However, several sources report that, in fact, they are.

After the ten-year anniversary, Arden Olivia Maynor ceased to exist, becoming Olivia Meyer, according to several sources. Though the name-change file was sealed, administrators at Central Carolina University had been aware of her true identity since before her enrollment.

"We were made aware. There had been some flags in her file. With the sleepwalking and a few incidents on her record, we had to be sure we weren't putting any other students at risk, especially when considering living arrangements," says Arlene Shore, director of admissions. "Though I can't say there have been any incidents in her time here. She was a good student, as far as her records indicate."

But those who had one-on-one contact with her had other things to say. A professor from her graduate program who asked to be quoted anonymously tells us, "She was a troubled young woman. Very smart. A gifted liar."

Olivia Meyer currently works in health care administration at Central Valley Hospital, where she's been for the past two years. It's not clear how much contact she and Sean Coleman have had over the years. Most colleagues declined to comment, though one agreed to be quoted anonymously: "It seems like too big a coincidence. A man killed in the middle of the night outside the home of a girl once famous for sleepwalking?"

There are far more questions than answers at this time. As of the posting of this article, Olivia Meyer could not be reached for comment.

CHAPTER 22

Wednesday, 5:45 p.m.

A TROUBLED GIRL.

I wondered how many times Jonah had tried to contact me before realizing I'd blocked his number. If he was angry at being shut out so definitively. If he was drunk when he gave that quote, as he seemed to be more and more often. Or if he was trying to spin the story his way before he got pulled into it on his own.

He wasn't dumb. He understood, just as I did, that you had to frame the story first.

I could've pulled up that photo of the two of us on my couch, captioned it: *A troubled girl and her professor.* And then blasted it across social media.

He had no idea the damage I could do.

I KNEW WHAT I could expect if I went home. Since the emails had begun, it wouldn't take long for the letters to start showing up at my house. And then reporters waiting near my home. Asking for a quote or a picture. It would only multiply as the hours turned over.

After work, I found myself driving out to the campgrounds where Elyse had been found. I wasn't sure what I was looking for. If I, like Nathan, was hoping to feel something just by mere proximity.

It was still light out, but the thick foliage on the mountain road made it seem later than it was, the path from the lot to the campground completely shaded. I stepped out of the car, and it already felt ten degrees cooler.

Right away, I could tell where she'd been found. One of the cabins had yellow tape covering the door, along with a notice to keep out. The rest of the lot was empty— her death must've scared the others away.

A sign at the welcome center cabin said: CLOSED UNTIL FURTHER NOTICE.

I didn't need to get any closer. Whatever I'd been looking for, I wasn't going to get it here. All I felt was a coldness, an emptiness. A growing guilt. A lump in my throat, and I didn't even know whom to contact to say, *Yes, she was my friend. She was good to me, and I miss her, too.*

I paced the gravel lot, then turned back toward my car. Inside, I pulled out Nathan's card and called the number he'd written on the back.

"This is Nathan," he answered. I didn't think he had my cell, so I was probably coming through as a random number.

"Hi, it's Liv," I said. And then I didn't know where to go from that. Why had I called him? As an excuse to avoid returning home?

"What happened?" he asked, like he could hear it in my voice.

"My friend died." The words tumbling out, like a confession. "I'm sorry, I don't know why I'm calling you. I was nearby, and I guess I wanted to see if you wanted to finish that beer."

A pause. "Yeah," he said. "Yeah, I do. Come on over."

HE WAS WAITING FOR me in the lobby this time. Sprawled on a double couch across from the fireplace with the television hanging above, turned to the national news. The broadcast was talking about the weather, a heat wave in the middle of the country; no murders, no breaking news.

Nathan had already grabbed two bottles of beer—the same kind as yesterday—and they sat on the coffee table in front of him. He stood when he saw me, held one of the bottles out toward me. "Thought we could take these to go," he said. "I've got a suite with a table and a sofa down the hall, if that suits you."

I nodded, following him. I liked his confidence. How he laid out all the facts at the start so I wouldn't question his motives. How he managed to ask my opinion at the same time he gave his own.

His suite was at the end of the hall, the corner room. We entered into a small open space that functioned as both living and kitchen area. "Slightly more comfortable than the café. Less so than the lobby, but at least we've got some privacy here."

The television was on the same news station as in the lobby, but the sound was low, like white noise.

"It's good," I said. "It works." I sat on one end of the pullout sofa, and he took the other, shifting slightly so he was facing me.

"So tell me. What happened with your friend?"

I took a deep pull of the beer, swallowed to force the lump down my throat. "Her name's Elyse. She overdosed." I shook my head. "I worked with her, and she was younger than me . . . I didn't know she had a problem until now."

"That's usually the way it goes, I think."

I shook my head, looking down. "Oh, I knew for sure my mom had a problem. If you'd asked me how she would go? That was where I'd have placed my bet." Maybe that was what had bothered me—that I'd been so focused on my own issues, I hadn't seen any signs. I wondered if Trevor, the bartender, was evasive because Elyse had been supplying him, too. If that was what he'd written on her hand that night in the bar.

"Mm," Nathan said, settling back into the stiff cushions. "My dad had a drinking problem when I was younger. I didn't notice until it reached a boiling point and my mom left with me. I think some people are just better at hiding it."

Maybe that was why I'd come here. Because each time I spoke to him, I felt a little lighter, alleviated of some guilt. Like I was unloading a secret.

"My mom hates to see me drink. I'm twenty-nine and can't have a beer when she's over. I told her I'm not trying to hide anything, isn't that the point?" He fought back a smile. "My youngest brother is gonna give her hell, I can tell."

"Good he has you, then," I said.

"They moved away a few years back. I don't see them as much as I'd like anymore. I set up my business where I live, though. Not so easy to remake your life again."

"No, I know." I hated the feeling that I was being pushed to start over again somehow. If I even managed to make it through this. My gaze kept drifting back to the television, on instinct. Wondering whether the news would catch up to me.

"I can turn this off if you want," he said. "I don't want your friend's death to upset you any more than it already has."

I shook my head. "It won't be in the news, even, I bet." Overdoses were unfortunately all too common. It touched every area, rural and urban alike. "Meanwhile, there's this article about me. Maybe you've already seen it."

He shook his head once, sharply.

I took a deep breath. "It doesn't matter. It's not true. People I know were quoted in it. The things they said, God."

"Did they accuse you?"

I could read between the lines what they were implying. Maybe he didn't know the case well enough. Maybe, unlike Bennett, he hadn't done a Google search the second after I'd left yesterday. Maybe he didn't put much stock in the way stories were spun.

I wrinkled my nose. "Not exactly. The article just said I was a person of interest."

"Well, you're not the only person of interest. Maybe just the most interesting one." He gave me half a smile, then tapped his finger against the side of the bottle a few times. "My father's phone, it got a few calls that night. He didn't respond. But they were from a burner phone. They can't trace it."

My back straightened. This. *This* was why I'd come to him. Because it felt like we were on the same side. That

we could uncover the truth together, from different angles. I felt myself pulling closer.

"Was there a message?" I asked.

"Nope, nothing."

I shivered. I'd heard those calls coming through as I
stood over Sean Coleman's body. The ringing of the
phone waking me. Someone had been calling him just as
I'd found him. It was probably what had dragged me back
to consciousness.

"Do you . . . When you first got here, did you ever
think it was me?" I asked. Other people must have. Detective Rigby, even Rick. Maybe that was why Nathan told
me things, to judge my reaction.

He took another drink, resettled into the cushions,
buying time.

"Well, I'm looking at you, at your arms, your neck, and
I don't see how it could be." I felt his gaze on me as he
spoke. "I can't imagine my dad went down without any
sort of fight. Not someone his size compared to your size,
unless you snuck up on him—and it seems like he was the
one sneaking around. What I'm saying is, based on logic, I
don't think so. You don't strike me as the type."

I nodded, though I was thinking: *Not unless I felt trapped,
cornered.* Then, subconsciously, and truthfully, I couldn't
say for sure what type of person I'd become.

His fingers brushed my hair, pushing it back—I wasn't
sure how he could be this close and still be sitting on the
other side of the couch. "No," he said, "I don't think it
was you."

It was the logic that I hoped others saw as well. I looked
back at him, thinking I was fortunate to have him here
now. "I can't believe, after all the press, I didn't know

Sean Coleman had a son. I never heard . . ." I trailed off, because I hadn't gone searching. The stories had always come to me, whether I wanted them or not.

"It wasn't the same for us as it was for you," he said.

"I wish I'd met you sooner." It would've been nice to connect to someone tangentially attached to the story. Who understood, like I did, how you could become a list of facts, a new persona crafted from public information. One that felt both familiar and unknowable—but one that others would view you as, all the same.

Sitting beside him now, I wanted to get lost in something, to forget, to have him tell me what he wanted from me and what to expect in return. His hand was in my hair, and I started to lean in to him, then stopped. Even now I was second-guessing myself. My motives, my intentions. I wasn't sure whether I was trying to prove something to myself and others: that if Nathan Coleman believed me, and liked me, then it could not have been me.

"I'm sorry," I said. "Can I just—have a minute? I need to wash my face or something. I feel like I'm a mess right now."

"You're not," he said with a sad smile. But he dropped his hand from the side of my face. "Bathroom's through there. Please excuse the mess." He pointed to the closed bedroom door.

I let myself in, partly closing the bedroom door behind me. The volume of the television increased, and I could hear the news anchors discussing the latest figures in the opioid epidemic.

Inside, the bed was made, and the bathroom was tucked around the corner, past the closet. There was no mess to speak of, other than the towels hanging from the shower rod and a toiletry case on the sink counter. The sink and vanity were just outside the bathroom, across from the double sliding mirrored closet doors.

I splashed water on my face, then looked for a face towel. The only ones I could see were currently hanging over the shower rod in the bathroom. I used my sleeve to dry the excess water, then turned to the closet behind me, where I'd usually find extra blankets and towels in hotel rooms everywhere.

Sliding one of the doors aside, I immediately found the towels, stacked on a high shelf. None of Nathan's clothes were hung up yet. I found this quirk endearing; you could tell a lot about someone by the state of their things kept out of sight.

His suitcase was propped open on a stand instead. He wasn't kidding about staying for a while—there appeared to be enough clothes to last more than a week. His laptop was in a case on the left, on top of a stack of folded shirts. His leather jacket lay on top of the other half of the suitcase. I ran my hand over it, wondering whether I could know enough about a person after a handful of days to trust him with the things I had told him.

My gut said yes. He was someone who could understand. But the events of the last few days had me disoriented, not sure whether I could trust even myself, let alone others. That article had sent me reeling—someone at my job had talked. Who else would be giving a statement in the coming days?

I was sure Bennett had looked around my house while organizing, and now I wasn't sure what he'd been searching for. Elyse might've, too—someone had gone through my closet, after all. I could see her finding that bracelet and sliding it onto her wrist, not knowing what it meant to me, before Bennett showed up.

I picked up the leather coat, brought it to my face: I loved the scent. It reminded me of the first time I saw him, with his sunglasses on, standing beside Detective Rigby outside my house.

Underneath the jacket, there was a manila folder, a file of papers bound up inside a rubber band. My hands started to shake. I wondered if this was information about the investigation. Things Detective Rigby had told him but not me. Details that could set me free.

I peered around the corner, could see Nathan sitting on the sofa through the crack in the door. I unwound the rubber band, gently opening the file.

The first thing I saw was that article from earlier today, the one he'd claimed he hadn't seen—but must have recently printed out.

I turned it over, and I didn't understand, my mind desperate to catch up.

It was a news transcript dated from twenty years earlier. From the day I went missing—the press conference, asking for the public's assistance.

Behind that, more transcripts: witness interviews, weather reports, information on the drainage system. My hands kept shaking as I turned page after page. Transcripts from the live reports the day I was found, and the 911 calls made by my mother—and others. Articles from the ten-year anniversary. Letters marked *Return to Sender*, with a Lexington, Kentucky, postmark.

He had lied.

Nathan had known exactly who I was from the start.

"Olivia?" he called, and I dropped the papers on the suitcase. "You all right?"

"One sec!" I called back, running the water.

Then I fumbled for my phone, took photo after photo of everything in this stack. I didn't understand why he had all of this, what it meant.

When I got to the envelopes, I looked inside, read the warnings, the threats. We had received so many after the ten-year anniversary—so many, we'd had to move. Had these bounced back after our move? They had been sent from Lexington, Kentucky. Wasn't that where he and his mother had lived?

I had made a mistake. Nathan Coleman was not at all who I thought. Behind the letters, there was even more: articles, photos of my old house, a map of Widow Hills . . . like a long-running obsession.

There I was, a story in pieces, out of context, filed in chronological order.

What the hell was he doing with this?

I wondered then whether this was what Sean Coleman had been trying to warn me about with his letter: his son.

"Do you need something?" Nathan's voice was closer, just outside the door.

I slammed the file shut, bound the rubber band around it all, and tucked it under his jacket again. I slid the closet door shut just as he pushed open the bedroom door.

"Olivia?"

"Sorry," I said, rounding the corner. I knew my cheeks were flushed, and I could feel my heartbeat in my finger-tips. His eyes drifted to my neck, where he could probably see my racing pulse. "I should probably go, though."

"You don't have to," he said, taking a step closer. "Did I say something? Because I want you to stay, Olivia."

There was one way out of this room. Through the doorway behind Nathan Coleman.

Nobody knew I was here. I had trapped myself.

"I got a text," I said, phone held awkwardly in my hand. "They need to talk to me." I swallowed nothing. Held my breath.

"Who?" He shook his head. "You can hide out here," he said, stepping in my path so that he stood directly between me and the exit.

My legs twitched with the need to run.

I tried to channel calm. Dissociate. I remembered that I had survived three days in the dark, underground. "If the detective finds me here, she won't be happy." Trying to remind him that Detective Rigby was invested, that she would be coming, that he couldn't hurt me—not now. Not when others were looking for me, too.

He smiled then. "You're not just using me for information, are you?" Something in my face must've cracked, because he put a hand on my cheek. "I'm kidding." He ran his thumb along my jawline, and my skin broke out in goose bumps. It took everything within me not to flinch. Then he dropped his hand and stepped aside so I could get to the door.

Three steps to the living room before I took a breath. Six steps to the exit. I turned the lock, begging my body not to give me away.

"See you soon," he said as I gripped the handle.

"Bye, Nathan," I said without looking over my shoulder.

————

IT TOOK ME THREE tries to buckle my seat belt, my hands were shaking so much, my eyes constantly flicking back to the hotel entrance. But Nathan hadn't followed me out.

I called Rick as I backed out of the lot.

"Everything okay?" he asked as soon as he answered.

I had told him we should keep our distance. Detective Rigby had warned me not to share intel with him, but I needed him now. "Rick, is anyone out at the house?" I needed to get home, get my things. I knew exactly what to do. My entire body was humming with it: *Go, go, go.*

"Yeah," he said. "I think someone's here, parked out by the road. Someone came to my door, but I didn't answer."

"Okay. Okay," I said. "Rick, I've got to head out of town for a bit. I just wanted you to know I'm okay, though."

Silence. I knew what he was picturing. His son leaving town.

"I'm coming back," I said. "I just have to do something first."

Finally, he replied, voice low and guarded. "Be careful," he said.

"I will," I said.

I left my car on Haymere Lane, cutting through the night on foot, without a flashlight. I wasn't afraid of this— not the dark, not the openness. But my heart beat wildly, thinking of what might be coming. Who might be watching or following. Over the creek, up onto my property, to the back steps with the burned-out porch light.

I sneaked into my own house, quietly turning the key.

And I didn't turn on any lights as I hastily grabbed a bag of clothes, the essentials, my laptop.

It was when I was halfway done, looking back at the shadows as I used the light on my phone to find my things, that I saw the chaos caused in my wake by my rush: my purse on its side, contents spilling onto the table, my bedroom drawers half-open.

A chill ran up my back, because I knew where I'd seen this before: Elyse's apartment. Even her car door hadn't been firmly shut when I'd first found it in the parking lot. Like she'd been frantic, in a rush. Sprinting from her car. Racing for her apartment.

Like she'd been running from something. Like she'd known she had to move fast.

That someone was coming for her.

EMAIL INBOX

OLIVIA.MEYER@CENTRALVALLEYHOSPITALNC.ORG

Subject: ADMIN LEAVE

Ms. Meyer: Due to the nature of the ongoing investigation and the current media attention, effective
immediately you are placed on paid leave, pending
further information. Please turn in your badge and
key at your earliest convenience.

Subject: INTERVIEW REQUEST

Ms. Meyer,

We'd love to get your side of the story. Contact us
any time at the details below. We can get something
out ASAP, a rebuttal if you'd like. Ready whenever
you are.

Subject: REQUEST FOR QUOTE

Hey Olivia,

Alice here, from the *Observer*. Wanted to circle back
to see if you had a response quote to the piece that
ran yesterday?

Subject: WTF?

I thought we were friends? How could you keep something like this a secret?

Subject: OFFERING SUPPORT

You don't know me personally, but I work in the hospital. I knew Elyse, too. If you need an ear, or just a shoulder, know that I'm here.

Subject: REMEMBER ME?

I remember you. From back in high school. I knew you were a killer the day you threw me into a wall.

Subject: HELLO FROM EMMA LYONS

Dear Olivia—I've tried contacting you in the past as part of a series of interviews relating to the coverage of your rescue in Widow Hills. We've never connected directly, but I knew your mother. I want to help. Please reach out if you need anything.

CHAPTER 23

Thursday, 6:15 a.m.

HAD ELYSE BEEN AFRAID of Nathan Coleman?

Had he already been in town long before I knew it? Maybe she had seen him outside my house or worried he might be back—and that was what she'd been warning Bennett about during their fight on my front porch.

Sean Coleman must've come here to warn me about his son.

Could Nathan have killed his father while he watched outside my house?

These were the thoughts circling all night, keeping me from sleep. Too agitated, too aware of every noise outside my room, every headlight glare on my window.

I'd had to stop last night halfway to Widow Hills. The pass through the winding mountains, the darkness—checking my rearview mirror for his car, not paying attention to the sudden curves. I'd found a motel off the road with a vacancy sign, a small enough place that, even though I had to give my name and use my credit card, I didn't think the media would be tracking me down here in the middle of the night. And neither would Nathan.

Because, I realized, that's what he was.

A stalker. A longtime obsessive stalker. Would he have killed his father to stop him from warning me? Were all parent-child relationships so sacred that I should pretend this wasn't a possibility? He'd said himself that they weren't close.

As the sun rose, I wasn't sure if this handful of hours of fitful sleep counted as rested, but at least I had calmed. I sat on the bed, opening my laptop, checking in to my work email remotely.

I knew it wasn't difficult to figure out my email address. The public email accounts for the hospital all had the same format. First name, last name, followed by our hospital domain. But I still cringed to see my inbox full of messages from addresses I knew and didn't know alike.

Despite myself, I read them all, to arm myself for what was to come.

That initial article must've been picked up for wider distribution through the night. Journalists requesting interviews and quotes, people coming out of the woodwork in a very different way this time.

I paused at the email from the girl in high school. I remembered. Well, I remembered she was the reason I got sent home from school, mandatory meetings with the therapist—twisting the story to turn herself into a victim instead of the instigator.

Victim, endurance, triumph.

Shuffle the roles, craft your own story.

Or maybe that was just what she chose to remember after all this time—that she'd once been thrown into a locker room wall. Not that she had baited me, taunting me, blocking my exit from the locker room.

The cinder-block walls and the rows of lockers, no windows, no doors. Just that thick humidity and one way out, and a cold sweat breaking out, my skin rising in goose bumps—in warning. My vision turning hazy until I remembered I wasn't a six-year-old girl stuck underground anymore, waiting to be saved. I needed to get *out* in a way that took over everything, body and mind alike. The need for an exit superseding all else, including the person blocking my way.

I hit "delete" on message after message, until I reached the note from a name I hadn't seen in a long time: Emma Lyons.

She'd been a local reporter covering the search and rescue when her timely interview with my mother had elevated her to part of the national story. It had made her career. I checked the photos on my phone of the interview transcripts Nathan had in that file: Emma had been with my mother when the news broke; Emma Lyons had been on scene as I was rescued; she had landed the single interview with Sean Coleman afterward.

Then she'd been everywhere.

The footage was linked to in every online story that followed. I watched those videos myself now, from the hotel bed:

That woman in the blue dress, walking through the brush. Crossing some barrier in that moment, poised and wild at the same time. Her heels sinking into the mud. A streak of dirt across her arm.

Afterward, Emma Lyons went on to give interviews herself, an expert on those three harrowing days. There was a soothing tone to her voice, a Southern lilt—something she never tried to hide.

There were other reporters, of course. Different programs, different stations. But she'd been the one to deliver the news to my mother; it had granted her an elevated role. She became the media face of the story—a thing played back as much as the rescue itself.

I responded to her now, thinking it was too early to call. *I do need your help. Did you ever hear about Sean Coleman's son?* I left my cell number at the bottom of the email, then returned to watching the other videos.

Her interview with Sean Coleman was so brief—he looked so young, so unsure. A deer caught in the headlights, with no idea how he'd found himself there. My heart sank, watching him then, so alive. No one asked about his life. There was no indication that there'd been a nine-year-old and wife at home.

Then I clicked over to the famous clip—the one where Emma was interviewing my mother just as the news came through. I knew the words by heart, but this time, I focused on my mother's face. Knowing, with finality, that I would never see it again.

The image was so pixelated, a video from twenty years earlier. Her hands fidgeted as she spoke, and she gripped the handles of a tan tote bag slung over her shoulder. Her body turned slightly to the left, and I froze the frame. Rewound it, watched again.

That tote—it had been part of a fund-raising effort by

the volunteer center. My school photo, with the generic blue background. The words *Have You Seen Me?* printed below, along with the tip number. She was holding it in front of her, so the camera could see.

The hairs on the back of my neck stood on end.

That tote, in the box. In my house. Old and tan, with the blue-gray smudge—in the place my photo once had been. Had she kept it all this time? Both the tote and that bracelet, the things she'd held on to above all else?

My phone rang, a call from a number I didn't recognize.

"Hello?" I said.

"My God, is it really you?" Her voice was deeper, a little raspy, but I recognized the lilt right away. I'd just been listening to her.

"I know you've tried to reach me in the past," I said. "I'm sorry for never getting back to you. But I'm willing to give you an interview in exchange for your help." I knew there was always a trade: Every story had a value.

"Honey," she said, "I don't want your story. Honestly, I was hoping I'd never hear your name again, and I could go on imagining you were off living your life somewhere, away from all of this. All of us."

"That was my hope, too," I said. "I'm sure you saw what's happening, but some things have come up . . . some things I need to ask you about."

"Of course. Arden—Olivia," she said, correcting herself. "Look, I know I emailed you, and I hope you don't take this the wrong way, but I need to do this face-to-face. I need to make sure it's really you I'm talking to. I'm not interested in providing more information to the cycle."

"I understand," I said.

"So, you're in North Carolina, is it?"

"That's where I'm living. But I'm actually . . . I'm on my way to Widow Hills. I was hoping to get some answers there."

"If you have some time to spare, I'm about two hours outside. Must be on your way. If you want to stop, maybe I can answer your questions."

THE ADDRESS EMMA LYONS gave me sent me to the outer suburbs of Lexington, an area with rolling hills, farmland, and a rich history. Her home was a white colonial with a simple stone fountain in the front and a small circular drive surrounded by tall hedges. The iron gates were open, and as I pulled into the drive, she was already stepping out the front door, barefoot, with a little white dog at her feet.

Her hair had been cut shorter, and she wore tan shorts and a pale orange blouse. She looked so different from her television personality. Her smile was the same, though.

"Well, look at you," she said as I exited the car. "I mean, I wouldn't recognize you on the street. You've gone and grown up." The twenty years had aged her, but the heart of her was the same. She was still thin, but more sculpted than soft now. Without the heavier makeup, her eyes looked smaller, the wrinkles giving her a new authenticity. She had to be in her mid-fifties. "Hate to ask, but can I see your ID before we get started?"

I handed her my driver's license, didn't blame her for asking. I'd done my best to hide Arden Maynor away.

Her eyes flicked from my photo to my face, and I pulled up my left sleeve. "Can't fake this part," I said, and she frowned at the long white scar, jagged down my shoulder.

"Come in, come in," she said, gesturing me up the steps, the little white dog following behind.

She led me to the dining room, just off the foyer. There was already a pitcher of lemonade out on the table, a tray of sandwiches: a true hostess. "Figured you might be hungry." She poured me a glass, hand faintly shaking, and I realized she was nervous.

I remained standing but took a sandwich, just to have something to do with my hands. "You heard about Sean Coleman," I said. "You saw the article?"

She nodded, standing on the other side of the table, eyes flicking periodically to the front windows. "In your email, you mentioned . . . Has his son been in contact?" she asked.

"You could say that. I think . . . I think he's obsessed. With what happened." I swallowed. "Or with me. I found this stack of papers he had with him. He's been keeping everything about the case. Everything from twenty years ago." I was trying to figure out why he'd homed in on certain details. "He had transcripts from the 911 calls, even. I don't know why."

She took a sip of her drink, ice rattling in the crystal glass. "He came to me," she said. "Around the ten-year anniversary."

"God, but I was just in high school . . . he was—"

"Nineteen," she said, nodding. "He was nineteen, and very self-righteous, and hyper-focused. I only agreed to talk to him because of his father. Because I was hoping to have you all on for a special together—your mom, Sean Coleman, you. A happy reunion."

But that had never happened. I'd refused to participate, though my mom had practically demanded it. Sean hadn't done any interviews, either, though.

"So Nathan Coleman meets with me, and he says he has a big story. That his father said something once when he was drunk. Apparently, Nathan had asked him about it, about why he didn't take more interviews." She looked away. "According to Nathan, his father claimed he'd walked that same route every day of the search, and you weren't there. Said he'd even looked inside once."

I froze, unable to move. "You didn't think that was important?" I asked.

"No, I mean no one knows what happened underground. I know your mother thought you were there all along, waiting to be found, but that was highly unlikely. More likely, you were trapped underground somewhere else and were brought to a new location, back to the surface as the waters rose. The pipes were all interconnected. We were never gonna know for sure. All his comment would do was encourage the conspiracy theories."

"What conspiracy theories?"

She laughed, then stopped. "Every story has the deniers, the skeptics. The conspiracy believers. There are dark corners of the Internet that thrive on them. You're lucky you were rescued before a lot of those sites proliferated." My mother had stressed the importance of staying offline back then. But I remembered Detective Rigby saying she understood why I had changed my name. I wondered what she had been able to find from twenty years earlier—or closer, from a decade ago.

"Truly, it doesn't matter," Emma continued. "You were lost, and then you were found, and he was a hero."

"And it made your career?"

"Well. It made all of us, wouldn't you say?"

My house, my education. But I had paid for it, hadn't I? In pieces of myself fed to others?

She glanced out the window again, took a deeper drink, seemed to be fighting off a chill. "Anyway, I did follow up. He would've gone to someone else if I'd blown him off. But when I contacted Sean Coleman directly, he denied it. Said it wasn't true. Either way, the story was dead." She shrugged. "Listen, Arden, Olivia, there's always little things that don't make sense. And some people get so caught up in those details, looking for a story, that it's impossible to see anything else. I wonder if that's what set Nathan off. He said he had a big story. But all he had was a bunch of little things, none of them corroborated, none of them amounting to anything. He couldn't see anything beyond it. And if he's talking to you now, it's just been stewing for the last ten years." She paused. "And that's never a good situation."

For a moment, I wondered how he could be caught up on something from ten years earlier, from back when he was nineteen. Except I was still trying to untangle myself from a story that had lasted two decades.

But Emma implied that there was more to it than just the fact that I hadn't been in the same spot in the days before I was found. "What things? What other little things did he have?" I asked.

"Oh, he wanted to know why you were wearing shoes if you were sleepwalking. But we'd already talked to the doctors, who explained that people often managed to do normal tasks like getting dressed, putting on shoes, even driving to work." She raised a finger, keeping track of each point before moving on to the next. "He said your mother claimed she had already called for you outside during her 911 call, but the neighbor's call of her screaming came in *after*." She rolled her eyes. "But so what? She'd probably screamed for you before, then called 911, then gone back out."

I remembered that transcript in Nathan's pile. Stuart Goss saying he was outside getting ready for work when he heard my mother.

"Maybe someone should just ask Stuart Goss," I said. Clear this whole thing up. I remembered him vaguely, the grizzled neighbor, that old car in his yard. He had a big dog that was always barking.

"Mr. Goss passed away about . . . two years after the rescue, I think. Lung cancer."

"Oh," I said. But also, she had checked. All these little things she mentioned, she had followed up. They had, indeed, caused her to wonder.

"Look, the point is, nothing could be corroborated. It was a dead end. There's no story in any of it. I assure you, we did our due diligence. No one wants to get caught reporting a lie."

"But it's a lot. A lot of little things."

"Yes, but you can find anything if you look hard enough. You can see anything if you want to. I don't think he'd believe the truth if we showed him a live video at this point."

Though I hadn't touched the sandwich, I fidgeted with the glass plate, spinning it on the surface. I almost didn't ask, but I'd come all this way. "But what do you think?" I asked.

Emma Lyons turned to the cabinet alongside the

wall, refilled her drink from a separate crystal container. Like she needed to steel herself for the truth. "Well," she said, recapping the drink, "it doesn't matter what I think, Arden. Sorry, Olivia."

"Please. It will stay between us."

She took a deep breath and a long drink before speaking. "There was only one thing that really bugged me, but we couldn't air it even if we wanted to. Protected by your medical privacy. It's what one of the doctors said . . . I was interviewing him at a bar, my own poor judgment, and his, but I wanted something we could use. Not a medical fact but a quote—about how strong you were, how you'd defied the odds. We wanted general statistics, nothing that violated your privacy."

"And?"

"And," she said, drawing out the word. "He said you weren't dehydrated enough. But so what? You were inside a storm drain. It rained. Presumably, you could drink—though I'd imagine it was not the type of water one should be drinking."

She started tapping her nails against the glass, the sound echoing through the room.

"That's it?" I asked.

"Well, no." She lowered her voice, eyes to the window again, like a nervous tic. "He said that the injury was weird." She waved one hand through the air, like she had to show how trivial such a thing might be. How she didn't quite believe it herself. "I told him, look, she was stuck in a pipe. You were swept away. Surely things could get weird, the angle you'd be stuck at. Things like that. No one knows exactly what happened while you were down there, how far you traveled. But this is the one thing that sometimes niggles at me around each anniversary. I don't know how to explain it, exactly, other than a sort of sixth sense that develops when you're on to a story and you get the feeling that—*here*, there's something here."

"What is it?" I asked. She'd spent so much time trying to downplay the story, it had only managed to do the opposite. I was riveted.

"He said it was weird, but not in the way that I meant. He said it was unusual but that he had seen it before. And it wasn't from being swept away underground." An echo of Bennett's words: *That's rare in a kid. Must've been incredibly painful.* Was that why I didn't remember? The pain causing that disconnect?

We stood in silence then, the only noise coming from the dog chewing a bone under the table.

"You didn't report any of this?" I asked in just over a whisper.

"That? I couldn't. And really, it was obvious the doctors and your mother weren't seeing eye to eye by then. She worked in health care and had her own opinions on things. They saw her as an impediment toward your treatment, so I'd take all that with a grain of salt."

"I remember. She didn't like the doctors. Said they weren't interested in fixing me."

"Your mother stopped bringing you to the follow-up appointments. And then there was some talk from other medical professionals that, to hear your mother discuss it, your history of sleepwalking didn't fit any sort of profile. That she was maybe straining the truth, whether intentional or not."

I remembered Dr. Cal saying it would've been unusual that a doctor had given me medicine to stop the episodes.

Maybe it hadn't been their idea. Maybe my mother had demanded it. She'd always believed what she needed to believe.

"Well, look," Emma continued, "it's just one thing. And that doctor was sort of a jerk. The more he drank, the more outrageous he became. At one point he said he thought you were lying, too. And that's when I decided he was an asshole. You were six years old. What child knows how to lie straight-faced to adults like that?"

"Lying about what?"

She shook her head. "That you couldn't remember anything. Not a thing, for three days, until Sean Coleman looked down into that grate and grabbed your wrist."

"I really don't," I said, and she nodded. Maybe I did back then, but there was no unearthing it now. Just the darkness and the cold, the walls, the stagnant water. I got a chill even now, and took a bite of the sandwich to chase it away.

"God, I remember that moment so well," she said. "The moment I saw your arm. Still gives me goose bumps." One more drink, the level in her cup draining rapidly. How long had this story been living inside Emma Lyons, waiting to come out? "When a story gets to be this big, people come out of the woodwork. People want to tell you things. They want to take people down with their envy. Nathan Coleman was one of them—someone jealous of the opportunities that came after, for you, for your family. Not for him. His father had no interest in the media, and the media didn't know what to do with him, either. Too quiet, too soft-spoken. He shied from it all. I think Nathan just wanted a piece of what his father declined to be part of."

But I was a commodity. Even my mother had treated me as such, wanted to seize the opportunities we had. Nathan should be glad he wasn't made into a national talking point. He had no idea what his family had avoided. The things people would say about his father. How people would treat him differently if they knew the truth.

"Other people came forward?" I asked.

"With money like that in play? Of course. A lot of people were jealous after. Saying your mother hit the lottery. Look, I think if you've been through what she had, you deserve it. Took a few years off her life, I'm guessing."

"She's dead," I said.

Emma put her glass down on the table. "I'm sorry, I didn't know. What happened?"

"Overdose."

She paced around the table, eyes narrowed at something she saw out in the road. She paused for a moment before shaking her head and continuing. "Can't say I'm surprised, unfortunately. She'd been let go of several jobs for that reason, as far as we could tell. Those were the other stories we chose not to air. Irrelevant, really. Former employers saying she'd been dismissed."

"For what?" I asked. It seemed suddenly, painfully important.

"Rumors, mostly. A prescription that had gone missing. A forged refill signature. Petty infractions that had nothing to do with you or your rescue."

I felt the immediate need to leave. She dropped these facts as afterthoughts, but they were the little things that mattered, that shifted my understanding. Not of what happened in Widow Hills but of my mother. That it wasn't the media, or even the precipitating event, that had sent my mother down the path of no return. That she had always been this person.

"She was an addict before it happened?"

"Oh, I don't know about that. Maybe. A high-functioning one, if so."

"Selling, then."

She shrugged, which was my answer. My mother had done whatever she needed to do. She'd survived. Sold a prescription, sold a book, sold my story. Sold our things when the cash ran out.

"You never dug deeper," I said. Not accusing, just stating a fact. "With all those little questions?"

"No. I saw what happened after the ten-year programming. That was bad enough. Imagine if people found out the whole thing was a fraud?"

The word hung in the air, louder than necessary. It echoed off the walls, and Emma's eyes widened, like she wanted to take it back.

It was the first time she gave voice to the thing I had feared. That this was what Nathan had believed, and the pile of documents was the evidence he'd been accumulating for years. That the story was not at all what it seemed.

"It would ruin me," I said. All the people who had watched, and prayed, and dedicated themselves to my safe return.

"It would ruin all of us, honey," she whispered.

"Do you think Nathan Coleman is going to come forward with all of this?"

"If he does, I'd do the same thing I did ten years ago and ignore it. There's nothing to corroborate it, so it doesn't matter."

I closed my eyes. "I remember," I said, and I felt everything in the room stop moving. "Not all of it. But I remember the cold and the dark. I can't stand enclosed places."

She nodded. "Of course," she said. "And you survived it. So let's let this go. There's no good that comes of it now."

"Except," I said, "Sean Coleman is dead."

She frowned, and I could see all the questions rising to the surface.

"He died outside my house. And with everything you told me, it sounds like some people might think I have a pretty good motive."

She stepped closer, so close I could smell the vodka on her breath. "Oh, honey, don't you see? If this is really what it's about, we all have a motive." Her cold hands at my elbows, fingers pressing tight. "And if it comes out, we will all fall down."

VOICEMAIL TRANSCRIPTS
AUGUST 27, 2020

NATHAN COLEMAN
9:13 A.M.

I feel we left things in a weird place. Driving by your place and would love to talk. I don't see your car. Are you at work?

BENNETT SHAW
10:03 A.M.

Hey, listen, I heard what happened with work. Really shitty, seriously. If you need a place to crash and hide out from all this, I'm here. I mean it. I've been a crappy friend, Liv. I was upset you never told me. But I get it. I really do, and I don't care what they're saying. Okay? Call me back so I know you're okay either way. I'm at work, but I've got my phone on me. I know. Don't tell.

MACKENZIE SHAW
10:45 A.M.

Hi, Olivia, Mackenzie Shaw returning your call. Sorry, just got your message. This is my cell, please call back as soon as possible.

CALVIN ROYCE
10:59 A.M.

Olivia, this is Cal Royce. You missed our appointment today. I had a call from a detective and she's coming in later. Please get back to me.

NATHAN COLEMAN
11:23 A.M.

I know you saw. I know you know. Let me explain. It's not what you think.

CHAPTER 24

Thursday, 4:30 p.m.

THE SIGN FOR WIDOW Hills came up abruptly, before I was ready for it—so unassuming at the edge of the road, blending in with the woods.

I had to drive another mile, the road slanting upward into a crest, before I saw them: the peaks of the three mountains in the distance, huddling together in a cloud of gray mist.

My stomach dropped like I was at the top of a ride, about to tumble over. The anticipation before the fall; the fear before the scream.

As the roads started veering off from the main thoroughfare, I tried to orient myself. Tried to see the little-girl version of me. But it was all imagination and conjecture. There was nothing instinctive about the sloping road into town. I hadn't been here since I was seven, and nothing looked familiar.

It had been too long, even, to feel a vague familiarity with the town itself. Even the mountains themselves in the distance, the very landmark that gave Widow Hills its name, I didn't know whether I remembered it myself or if I was just remembering a photo, a story.

I remembered newspaper photos and interviews replayed. I remembered that pale yellow house with the gingerbread trim, a photograph of my mother in front of it. The humidity of the hallway; the screen door slamming shut.

More than this place, I remembered the after.

The hook-and-eye latch; the medicine; the hot chocolate. The doctors and my mother beside the bed. I remember the operations, the pain, the exercises. The looks.

Before, there was darkness.

Before, there were only the stories—the things people told me and the things I'd read. Sometimes I felt I was nothing more than a character brought to life by my mother's book. A girl who came into this world kicking and screaming. A girl whose mother knew, before her eyes had even shot open, that her daughter was gone. A girl whose mother believed she would survive it.

She had called us both survivors.

As I turned onto the street where I'd once lived, I wondered—would I remember when I saw it? Was it possible to unearth a memory from twenty years earlier, to find out what had been worth killing for decades later?

All the documents Nathan Coleman had been accruing on me flashed in my mind. The interviews, the 911 calls, the excerpts from my mother's book that he found relevant for some reason. Like he'd spent so much time dedicated to my life, he'd seen something emerging from the background.

But those details existed in a vacuum. I needed to see it. See, most important, whether I could drag my own memories back to the surface.

There was nothing to mark the spot as a tourist attraction on a map, though I knew it. On the Internet, you could get a mapped path to the site of Arden's disappearance and the location of her rescue. For a while after the rescue, I'd heard there were even tours—the commercialization of a trauma.

Widow Hills had owned its role. Found the help they needed, rescued their own. The town was a survivor, too. It had survived the media attention and then the aftermath, when they all packed up and left. The attention shifting elsewhere as everyone scrambled for relevance.

I would not have been able to find my old house on my own, without the GPS. I barely even recognized it. Sometime in the passing years, the ranch-style house had been repainted a light gray. The grass was dead. I could hear the screen door banging shut in my memory, though there didn't seem to be one attached to the entrance anymore.

Twenty years, and I guess I should've been grateful the house was standing at all. I idled my car at the curb; there were no houses across the street, just scattered trees giving way to forest. We were on the outskirts of town. The houses on either side had no cars parked in the driveways. Someone peered out a window just as I was looking, and I kept moving toward the end of the street—the direction I'd headed that night in my sleep.

I parked my car out of sight of the homes, where the road swerved to the left. This was where I'd been swept away. Off the road, down the embankment, into the wooded area. The trees were sporadic here, not yet the dense forest of the distance. A ditch was cut into the wooded area just off the road. This was where it had happened. The water rising, and rushing, knocking me off my feet. Flowing downstream, over the grass and roots and dirt.

I'd seen the footage, the reporters walking the audience through the sequence of events, the play-by-play that had led to my disappearance.

There was a faint path that marked the way to the drainage pipe. Downtrodden by the events leading up to my rescue twenty years ago. Maintained by the curious following the trail. When I arrived at the access point, the grate was sealed up. There was nothing to mark what had once happened here—this was not where I had been found but where I'd been lost. And yet this was the site most visited. It was more iconic, the image shown over and over beside the photo of my green sneaker, stuck in the edge of the torn-away grate.

I imagined those moments of hope; hoping it held, before my foot gave way, leaving the shoe behind.

I must've been awake. The memory buried while I'd dissociated. While I'd been swept into the pipes—just small enough—lost to the darkness. The terrible horror of it.

On the news, before I was found, reporters had traced the paths I might've taken with the map of the pipe system up on the screen. Where I might've gotten air. How I might've moved from section to section.

The problem with the pipe system map, I knew from both the articles and my mother's book, was that it was incomplete. This town had been an old mining area, and a new public works system had been laid on top of a less-well-understood drainage system from the past. There were more access points than the city had record of. Of course, they checked the access points they knew of, over the first couple of days, but I hadn't been found at any of those.

After, they said I must've found footholds. I must've been buoyed by water collecting in a stagnant section. I must've found a resting spot and slept at some point.

I must've had the largest dose of luck by my side.

I must've been driven and capable and determined and brave.

I must've been a miracle.

So many things had to line up for me to survive, skirting the realm of believability. But that was what made the story.

But standing here now, I felt nothing.

The spot where I was found was closer to the river, in an unmarked access point that predated the current system. That's where my mother believed I'd held on for days, waiting to be found, until Sean Coleman reached out and grabbed my wrist. There, I hoped, was the place I might actually remember something.

I walked back to my car and looped around the outside of town, following the Internet's directions on where to park, where to walk. It was less marked but functioned as a path all the same.

I'd seen Emma Lyons do it. All the reporters, in a bustle of activity, set up with their camera gear.

Now there was nothing but crickets and birds periodically calling in the late afternoon, the wind moving through the trees, the occasional animal scurrying through the bushes.

This was the same path Sean Coleman must've been following the night he found me, heading back to his car. In that rare interview he'd given, he said he'd parked outside the town center and was making his way back from the search when he saw my hand.

I knew it as soon as I was upon it. The clearing with the grate in the middle. Tall weeds growing up and over where the old plaque must still be, beside the grate. I stood in the spot where Emma Lyons once stood, pointing out the activity in the center. Where she could see Sean Coleman holding on to me. My arm, proof of life.

During the rescue, they ended up coming at me from the side, to keep the equipment away from my face. The lid was secured and welded shut, and no one wanted to drill next to my head. They dug down beside it instead, then drilled through the concrete tubing, until they could remove me that way.

I walked to the clearing, once blocked off by the perimeter to hold back the media and onlookers.

Twenty years later, and both the grate and the hole they'd dug were resecured.

I used my sneaker to brush aside the tall weeds, a layer of dirt dulling the words of the plaque:

In honor of the good people of Widow Hills
To commemorate the rescue of Arden Maynor

I stepped closer, peering into the grate. Could hear a steady drip of water, something faintly flowing in the distance. Close enough now to feel a whoosh of chilled air, hear a hollow echo. I closed my eyes, like I could feel the precursor to panic settling in.

It was a feeling like disorientation, like staring into that empty box—like I was looking for something, desperately, that did not exist.

I knelt down, closed my hands around the grates, felt the cold biting into my palms. Staring down, I saw only darkness. I shone my phone light into the abyss so I could see the bottom. The sloped walls and the stagnant water. The ledge. The input pipe from another section. I imagined myself crawling, or forced through, emerging with a sudden burst of air. Rising up with the water and reaching out my hand.

I pressed my face closer to the grates, trying to see; breathing it in, in all its horror.

I closed my eyes, straining to remember, but there was only the emptiness. A black hole in place of a memory—but something pulling me closer, closer.

I opened my eyes to darkness—a shadow, like a cloud had moved across the sun.

All the hairs rising on the back of my neck, across my arms, my hands tightening on the grate. Grass crunching behind me.

"Don't be scared." The deep timbre of his voice, so calm and assured.

I turned slowly, making sure to stand at the same time. To reach my hand into my pocket and grip my keys.

"Are you wondering how you got in there?" he asked. He wore jeans and that bomber jacket, sunglasses on top of his head so I could see his eyes, narrowed, searching.

"What are you doing here?" Though it was obvious. How he'd followed me, found me. He'd been stalking me.

And now he had me, all alone.

Nathan stepped carefully, leaves crunching beneath his feet. "I'm trying to figure out how much you really know. I read that article that called you a gifted liar."

"I don't remember anything," I said, stepping back. Phone in my back pocket; keys in my grip. Counting my exits: path to the car or run deeper into the woods—

"How could you not remember? You were six, almost seven. Of course you'd remember. It was this huge thing. How could you not?"

"Trauma," I said, repeating what others had said after. How the mind dissociates, goes to its most primitive form, where the only goal is survival. I felt the keys in my grip, biting into my fist.

"I was going to tell you," he said. "That I knew who you were. But you confessed it first, and I didn't know what to do. I went about it all wrong, I can see that now. You saw the articles in my luggage, didn't you. And you freaked. I get it." Like he was forgiving me, instead of the other way around, when he'd been stalking me for years.

I shifted in tiny steps, so as not to make him spook. "I don't care," I said, even though that wasn't true. But all I knew right then was the thing I'd always known, that singular focus: survival.

Sean Coleman was dead. Elyse was dead. And this man, he was big enough to do it.

"You *should* care," he said. "There are so many holes in that story, it's ridiculous. And nobody else seems to notice. The 911 calls don't add up. The sleepwalking doesn't add up. The shoes."

He was unhinged—ten years, building up. Ten years, about to boil over.

I put my hand out, to stop him, to slow him down. I'd heard it all from Emma Lyons. "You're seeing what you want to see, Nathan." Trying to reason him back with me. To see the marvel of it all: that there was a literal hole in the earth here—this spot that I'd been found inside. It was miraculous, and he wanted it to be something else. "No one else backs up these claims."

His eyes darkened as if he didn't like the conclusion. Then the side of his mouth quirked. "Well, that's not true at all," he said.

I had shifted another step closer to the way I'd come, but now I froze. The desire for the truth. For my own past, for who I was—"What?" The word so quiet, I might not have spoken it at all.

"The media brushed it off, but you know who didn't?" He paused, making me wait. "Your mother."

I stepped back like he'd moved closer, which he hadn't. "You knew my mother?"

"Not in so many words. But I wrote to her, told her what I knew, told her the evidence I had. She thought I was my father, the only other person who would know the truth, right? I didn't need him to confirm it when your mother reacted the way she did." I didn't ask. Didn't want to know. But he took a step closer, and there was no escaping it now. "She thought I was Sean, and she asked me how much it would take to keep me silent, make it all go away. And then she gave it."

"*You?* You were blackmailing us?" Those letters that had been returned to sender—he'd been threatening my mother, warning her.

"Blackmail?" he spat. "Is that what you call it? She's a *liar*. That money did not belong to her. To either of you."

Everything shifted, my understanding of the past; my understanding of just how far he'd go. This was the truth, then: that Nathan Coleman had been blackmailing my mother. That our money had disappeared, not to her addiction but to him. He had taken it from us—everything she'd made from our story. She'd had to sell everything to make him stop.

"You don't know what it was like to be so close to a story, to see you on the other side of it, getting everything. That should've been ours, too. If my father would seize a fucking opportunity, do one of those talk shows, something, *anything*. If he would just *tell his story*, it wouldn't have come to that. But at the ten-year anniversary, after all that new press? Your mother sure did pay up." He licked his lips. "Are you *sure* you don't remember?"

He was so close, and I couldn't see how to get by him, get to safety, get through this moment. My skin itched, and I scratched at my neck. I couldn't breathe, like the walls were closing in. "My shoulder, my arm, they were hurt. The injuries, they were left untreated for days." Proof of what had happened. Proof that I'd survived something.

His eyes followed my hand at my neck, then drifted to my arm. "Did you ever wonder what someone might do to cover up something else?"

I shook my head. Heard Emma's words echoing, what that doctor had said: The injury was weird. And Bennett's comment—that the pain must've been terrible.

Nathan could see it in me, the doubt setting in, though I tried to fight it. "They take kids away from homes like that."

"I used to sleepwalk," I said, clinging to the facts.

He shrugged. "Then what a convenient story, right? Something to say instead? She was a nurse. She would know what to do, what to say . . ."

But I was shaking my head. Could not fathom the idea. Because *we were survivors*.

We have to seize the opportunities, she'd told me.

The 911 call, when she'd told the dispatcher that I was gone. That I would sleepwalk. That I was missing. That she'd already checked outside.

And then, minutes later, running outside and screaming for me while Stuart Goss was on his own call.

Like a cause and effect. Like she had an excuse and now had to put on a show.

"They searched for three days!" I said. "I was trapped under here. They had to drill a hole to get to me." A sharp intake of breath as I fought to keep control, but he could see it, so close to the surface, the unraveling of everything I'd known to be true.

"Sure, you were under there on day three. That doesn't mean you were there the whole time."

This was my mother's fault. Perpetuating the story of what she wanted to believe. Of course I hadn't been hanging on the whole time I was down there. I'd been trapped, and I'd made my way to the grate. It wasn't a secret. It didn't change what had happened to me.

I was shaking my head, eyes closed, clinging to the memory—of the cold and the dark, the four walls closing in.

"Listen," he said, and he was so close now there was nothing else to do but comply, his body dwarfing mine. "It's the twenty-year anniversary. Do you know how big a story this could be? All you have to do is remember. All you have to do is say you remember."

And there it was, what he wanted still. I was a commodity. Something to cash in. A piece of someone else's story to be used for their benefit.

"It could be a good story. A big story. You and me, twenty-year anniversary. Revealing the truth about what really happened. All I need is for you to say it's true."

But I would not. I could not.

"The one thing I remember is being trapped. I *remember* that." An instinct in place of a memory. The fear and the emptiness. And now it mattered. It proved my past was real.

"I'll make you a deal, Arden." He'd switched to my first name, probably how he'd thought about me for years. He looked somewhere over my head, made a noise with his tongue. "Go take a tour of your old house. Knock on the door, introduce yourself, I'm sure they'll let *you* in."

I could barely remember the house at all; even the outside was mostly unfamiliar. Had he been inside? Had he sneaked in, looked around on his own?

"And then," he said, standing closer, "take those wooden stairs into the unfinished basement. Look behind the furnace for a low hidden door. Go ahead and peek inside that cinder-block room with the dripping water pipe. And then you tell me if *that* looks familiar."

"Stop," I said. Because I could feel my hands tracing over the cold rocks, the stagnant water, the darkness and no way out.

"And if you're still sure then, I'll leave it alone. What do you say?"

My stomach plummeted, the images fracturing and shifting. "It won't. No."

"Arden, I need you to fucking remember," he said,

grabbing my wrist. The hidden anger. "And if you can't, remember something else. Something your mom said. Or did. Do you know what a talk show would pay? What a book could get us? This is the moment, Arden."

I'd heard that before, from my mother. When she'd tried to convince me of the same on the ten-year anniversary.

But look what it had gotten us. A man stalking me. Demanding money. He didn't know the type of attention we got, what he was trying to throw himself into so quickly. How they would pick apart his life, literally, piece by piece.

"It's a thing that happened *to me*, and it hasn't been a story that's belonged to me in a long time," I said.

"It happened to all of us," he hissed, hands on my upper arms. "You're just too selfish to see that. People made it happen—the search and rescue, all the money that poured into it. You owe me this." He shook me once, and I felt my bones rattle.

I raised my arms to dislodge his grip. His eyes caught on the keys in my fist. "Are you going to hurt me, Arden? With your keys?" A twinkle in his eye, and I knew right then: There would be no reasoning, no escape.

Nathan Coleman was a man who got what he wanted. I was right from the start.

"Did you kill your father?" I asked, looking at his hands gripped on my arms.

He stared at me hard. "I'm not a monster," he said. Then he released me, as if he realized his mistake. The line he'd just crossed and was in danger of plummeting over. "I wanted his help, but he didn't want to give it. I never needed him for this, though." A deep breath. "I didn't even know he was there."

But he was a liar.

"I really do like you," he said. "I didn't think I would. You surprised me."

I knew that he wanted what I represented, wanted the life I had. There was a fine line between envy and hatred, between intimidation and aggression, a line you can slide across so easily—from omissions to lies.

"I have a second story, and it's a good one, too, Arden," he said slowly. "The story of how my father came to you, wanting you to share the truth. And you killed him."

"I didn't." *Box cutter in my drawer; blood on my hands.*

"Really, now. You can tell me."

I could see then that he was not only angry but desperate. Desperate people did terrible things. I could feel myself on the verge. When I was cornered, when I felt trapped.

I closed my eyes, pictured a box cutter in my hand, the thing I could get to the quickest.

What if Sean had asked me for help; what if he'd kept talking, kept moving, and I couldn't see a way out?

What if I'd run outside and he'd chased me? What if he'd grabbed me by the wrist? What if I'd caught him off guard, in one quick motion?

"Jesus, Arden. You look like you've seen a ghost. Come on." He grabbed me by the elbow, drew me close to his side, pulling me along as we walked.

But we were walking farther into the woods. Away from civilization, away from escape. "Where—"

"The river. I'm gonna show you the other access points. I'm gonna show you what really happened to you."

I wrenched myself back, planted my feet. I could not go with him. There would be no coming back. Not from the woods, not from the river. This was how people were lost. This was how things were disappeared. "Get the fuck away from me," I said, hands held out. I didn't care if he told, if he screamed what he thought was true. If he claimed my whole life was a fraud, a lie.

He'd come this far, after watching and waiting for a decade. There would be no coming back the same after this, for either of us.

"Don't do something you'll regret," he said.

There was a noise in the distance—someone moving or an animal pouncing—and when Nathan's head turned for a fraction of a second, I ran.

I heard him cursing under his breath, his footsteps keeping time with my own. "I'm not going to chase you," he called, though he was; "I'm not going to hurt you, dammit," but he was a liar. He had to be.

I kept moving because there was something I knew that he didn't. That, for reasons beyond physics, no one could catch me. The reason I'd always been able to win when I went out fast enough: I was always running scared.

I started calculating: Time to run to my car.

Time to unlock it and start the ignition.

Time to get to safety.

But the stitches on the outside of my leg slowed my stride.

It was a good story that I told myself: that he couldn't catch me, that I'd make it out. But he caught up to me before I was even halfway back to the road. Grabbing me by the arm, jerking me back—something twisting, snapping in my shoulder. A sudden jolt of pain, and I cried out, bent over, legs giving way beneath me.

A flash of light, a jolt of pain, a dark room. *Hold on, just hold on—*

"What the *fuck*," he said, pulling me back upright. "What do you think you're *doing*?"

I was breathing into his chest, holding on to my other arm, frantic to orient myself—

And then we both heard it at the same time. "Hello?" A voice through the trees. Coming from the direction of the road and my car.

Nathan's hand went quickly to cover my mouth, stifle my noise. His other arm around my chest, holding me to him. Holding me tight, my neck tipped back.

And I could see how he did it—how he could do it. A box cutter in his grip. One quick motion of his hand across my exposed throat. Dropping me back to the ground, waiting for someone else to find me.

I could see him arguing with his father, stopping him. Begging him. And then—

"Do not make a noise," he said, whispering in my ear.

Footsteps coming closer, while Nathan held me perfectly still, his hand so tight across my mouth and nose, I felt light-headed, like I couldn't breathe.

"You don't want to do that, son." Another voice now, to our left. "Let go of the girl, keep your hands where we can see them." I strained to see the speaker, could just make out the police officer in my peripheral vision.

"Just a minute," Nathan said, but he raised his arms, and I fell forward, sucking in a huge gulp of air in the process. "We were just having a conversation here. You scared us, is all."

But I was scrambling away from him, toward the officer

on my left, who had a gun drawn and was gesturing for me with his free arm.

"This is all a misunderstanding," Nathan said. "Arden, tell them. Tell them who you are. What we're doing here."

"Hands behind your back," called the other officer, now visible, approaching him with handcuffs. He patted Nathan down, pulled something out of his pocket. "You been tracking this lady's car?" the second officer asked.

And only then did Nathan stop protesting. The officer beside me called for backup, and we all moved silently out of the woods.

I SAW MY CAR through the trees, Nathan's parked directly behind it. There was a police cruiser parked behind Nathan's car. And another pulled up just as we arrived.

I wanted to feel relief, like I'd escaped something. But I could only see Nathan, hear his words in the woods, feel his conviction in his story.

And all the while, even as they questioned him and searched through his car, he kept staring at me—like he was merely choosing not to break free of their grip on him. As if he was only doing me the favor of not taking me down with him.

I sat in the passenger seat of my car, legs out the door, and couldn't hear what any of them were saying until Nathan raised his voice. "Tell them, Arden. Tell them the truth."

The newest officer on the scene stepped in front of me, squatted down so he was on my level. "Arden?" he asked.

"Olivia," I said.

He nodded, held out a hand. "All right, Olivia. Come with me and tell us what happened."

———

IT WAS LATE BY the time they let me go, taking my statement, contacting Detective Rigby. Dusk was settling, and they offered a nearby motel. But I just wanted to get moving.

They knew who I was at the station, of course: The girl from their town. The mechanism that had put them on the map.

The officers were my age or a little older, had grown up with their own claim to the story. Their parents had searched. Their aunts and uncles had been interviewed. Their neighbors had drawn search grids. Their schools had lent lights and equipment.

They'd told the stories that only they knew, passed down from the generation before.

It was a rite of passage during high school to trek out in the night to that grate beside the plaque, find your way in the dark, make your own stories, and leave them there. Fade to black.

They remembered the name Sean Coleman. They did not remember his son.

"I'M COMING HOME," I told Detective Rigby on the phone, desperate to get as far away from Nathan Coleman, and all that had happened here, as possible.

"I'll meet you there as soon as you get back," she said. "I'll send a cruiser by your place in the meantime, just to be safe. Okay?"

I hoped that would at least scare off any of the remaining attention around my place. But the danger had followed me here.

It was time to get the past contained again, keep it where it belonged—underground, in the dark. There was no good that could come of it now.

Everyone claimed to know things here.

I knew she was gone before I woke. The first line of my mother's book.

The words seemed flat now. Deadened; wrong.

Of course she knew. She knew, because she had done it.

DISPATCH: 911. What's your emergency?

CALLER, UNKNOWN FEMALE: I'm on Devereaux Lane in Widow Hills, and I just saw a man follow a woman into the woods.

D: Can I get your name and location, please?

C: Devereaux Lane, about halfway down, you'll see the spot. There are two cars. The woman's was here first, and he just pulled in and took something from the bottom of her car.

D: What did he take?

C: I don't know. He followed her in. I wonder if he was tracking her car.

D: Is it a hiking trail?

C: It's a trail but . . . Listen, that man is going to hurt her. Sometimes you just know things.

D: Okay, we'll have an officer swing by to check it out.

C: No, not to swing by. Hurry, goddammit.

CHAPTER 25

I WAS THE GIRL WHO left. Who did not look back.

I did not knock on the door to my old home, asking to look around. I did not peer into the windows to check for a basement door. After I left the station the previous evening, I got right in my car and started driving. And I did not stop until I was well outside Widow Hills.

I would not return.

I was born with a healthy dose of self-preservation. I let it be, just like Emma Lyons told me to do.

I left it all behind, stopping at the same motel I'd stayed at the night before, then hitting the road again at the first sign of light.

MY SHOULDER WAS KILLING me. The adrenaline yesterday must've covered the pain from where Nathan had grabbed me—and pulled. Stretching my arm beyond its capabilities. I took a generic painkiller but had to drive carefully, keeping my left arm down low on the steering wheel.

I called Bennett on speaker while I drove, knowing he would be up and at work by now.

He answered right away, and I could hear the overhead announcements of the hospital in the background. "Hey," he said, "I went by your place last night. I've been worried."

"So, that's what I'm calling about. I'm on my way home, but I was in Widow Hills."

He paused for a beat. "You *what*?"

"I wanted to tell you that I'm okay." Something I should've known to do days ago. "I mean, I was almost hurt. I'm a little bit hurt. Slightly sore. It's a long story, but I'm almost home now."

He listened as I told him about finding the pile of material in Nathan's things, about going to the reporter in Kentucky, about Nathan following me. But he cut me off abruptly.

"Who's Nathan?" he asked. And I realized there were still so many things I had kept for myself.

"Sean Coleman's son. He'd been obsessed with me for years," I said.

"Jesus, Liv."

"Well, I'm okay now."

For a moment, I could hear only him breathing. "Heard you called my sister."

"Yeah, thanks for that. I think I'm good, though. Nathan's in custody."

"Do they think he killed his father?"

"I don't know. I'm meeting with the detective later today. But yeah, seems that way."

I promised to call him when I made it back. I kept moving, yearning for home. For the detective to close the investigation, and something more I'd realized on the drive: I'd longed for the permanence of the place, and this house, and these people. Something I wanted to return to.

MY STOMACH DROPPED WHEN I saw the shape of a car as I pulled into my driveway. Imagining the journalists or reporters who might be waiting around, hoping to catch a glimpse. The girl from Widow Hills, person of interest in a murder investigation. How long until their interest petered out again?

But as I drew closer, I recognized the car—and the person sitting on my porch steps, waiting for me.

Bennett stood when I exited the car. "Had to see it for myself," he said, "that you were really still in one piece."

"More or less," I said, hooking my overnight bag over my right shoulder. I looked behind me at the empty road. "Anyone else been by recently?"

"Just your neighbor, looking for you. Think he saw me sitting out here." He looked toward Rick's house, through the trees. "I filled him in. At least with the gist of it."

When I passed Bennett, I noticed the dark circles under his eyes, the tension in his shoulders. I unlocked the door and let him in, then immediately dropped my bag. His smile was subdued, and I worried it was me, that I'd missed another nuance of our relationship.

"Are we okay?" I asked.

"Yeah, sorry, Elyse's family came to the hospital this morning, I didn't get the chance to tell you earlier. Pretty somber day. I'm just trying to shake it."

"Oh, I wish I could've been there." I wanted to tell them that Elyse was my friend; that she brightened my life in the short time I'd known her; that I missed her; that I was sorry.

"She had a history of abuse, but they thought she'd kicked it. Her family had gotten her help after her previous job, and they swore she was clean . . . but, I guess . . ." A shudder, all the things we had missed under the surface of one another.

"What had she been taking?"

"From the hospital? Opioids, benzodiazepines. What you might guess. They said she'd had a problem with opioids in the past, after a car accident in her late teens." Like my mother, then. God, how had I not seen it? Elyse had even told me about her accident, her experience in the hospital that had led her to this career in the first place. She had given me enough to piece together the truth, and I'd missed it. "Best guess, she was selling the rest." I'd thought I knew her better than that. But we all had our secrets.

Bennett stretched, working out a kink in his neck. He moaned. "I got someone to cover for me now, but I have to work the evening shift."

"You okay to work?" I asked.

"Yeah, I'm gonna have to be. We had to ask the ER to lend us some help from their department to cover Elyse's position, and apparently, her replacement just quit, too. She was friends with Elyse." He sighed. "It's hitting the whole hospital hard."

"Yeah." I could feel it coming on here, too: the grief, mixed with the guilt.

He looked around the house. "Will you be okay here?"

Nathan was being held in Kentucky, and Rick was home, presumably watching. "Yes," I said.

"I'm so glad it's over," he said, voice lower. "That you're okay."

My stomach sank. "It's not over. It's going to be chaos." In a way, it was just getting started. Nathan might be gone, but people were still watching. The girl from Widow Hills was a victim, a witness—if there wasn't a deal, I might have to testify. I'd have to ask the detective about that, but one thing was certain: It was not over yet.

He frowned. "I meant the part where someone was . . . watching you. Jesus Christ, I can't believe I left you alone here."

I looked at him. "None of us knew," I said. None of us guessed at the reach of that story—across time and distance. Across a generation. Stories like this, they didn't end. They only grew.

He smiled when he left. A promise to see me this weekend, to catch up, like everything was normal now. I let him believe it. His hope was contagious.

RICK DIDN'T COME OVER after Bennett left, though I knew he'd been looking for me.

I crossed the boundary between our yards, sidestepping that black hole of gravity where Sean Coleman had waited and died. I could hear movement inside Rick's house, something dragging against the wood floor, and I knocked. "Rick? It's me. It's Liv."

"One minute," he said, before opening the front door.

He looked the same as always, but behind him, there was a duffel bag on the wood floor. His hands hovered just over my shoulders before dropping. "Been waiting on you to get back. Your friend, there, he told me what happened. Nina, too. But I wanted to hear it from you, that you're okay."

I leaned against the doorjamb, able to be honest here. "It was horrible," I said, the word scratching at my throat.

He nodded, gesturing for me to come inside. "He's locked up now, though?"

I walked across the living room and sank into his couch, staring at the bag on the floor, trying to process. "Yes. He's being held in Kentucky." I gestured to his luggage. "What's going on, Rick?"

"Well," he said, and now he was looking off to the side, out the window, his throat moving. "I thought I might try to talk to my son." He shuffled his feet. "He's in Atlanta, it's not too far."

"Now?" I asked. "Today?"

"Well," he said. "As long as you're okay. I was waiting on you."

It seemed that the events of the last few days had shaken something loose in everyone. Like we could all see the potential for harm—how the past inevitably snowballs into the present. But that this moment, in turn, would soon enough become the past, the start of a new chain of events. "No, that's good. That's a good idea."

And then he stepped forward, dropped his voice. "The weapon, is it gone?"

I nodded once, stoically.

"I'm not sure if we should've done that," he said.

I wondered then whether he was leaving right now to avoid the questions, the lingering missing pieces of the investigation that we had disrupted with our distrust for each other—and ourselves.

"It's done," I said. "It's gone." Left behind in a hospital room, scrubbed clean and disappeared. Something that I now knew could've linked Nathan to the crime instead.

"Liv, he must've been in your house."

I froze. Held my breath. Finally putting the pieces together. Rick was right—for Nathan to have used my box cutter, he must've been in my house while I slept. He worked in security. He could do it. I shuddered. That feeling of a person who had been inside when I'd returned from the hospital. The noise at the back of my house after I'd found out Elyse had died. How many times had he been in there, watching?

How close had I come to a very different type of story? Before, presumably, Sean Coleman showed up?

"He's gone now," I said. "Either way, he can't hurt me." Though that wasn't entirely true. He could try to spin his story, tell anyone who would listen. But he was obsessed. He was a killer. He was not to be trusted. And, as Emma Lyons had told me, there was nothing to corroborate his claims.

"Go ahead, Rick. Before you're stuck driving at night."

"It's just, I want to be sure. You could hurt yourself still, out in the yard . . . No one would hear you."

I hadn't had a sleepwalking incident since waking up over Sean Coleman's dead body, and I was starting to believe that I wouldn't. That I'd successfully exorcized whatever trauma had taken hold of me, whatever had been threatening to resurface. Anyway, I had that extra prescription from Dr. Cal, should I need it.

"It's under control," I said, standing from his couch.

He nodded. "All right," he said, dragging his bag out the door, locking up after I followed him outside.

I wasn't entirely sure of his reason for leaving right then. Whether it was to avoid having to lie about the box cutter, or because he couldn't stand to waste another moment. Because I also understood how the present could suddenly seem urgent. That feeling of wanting to rush straight for it. How I'd wanted to come straight home. How I'd known exactly whom to call.

Rick walked to his car, hefted his bag into the back seat. "There's a spare key in the shed, Liv. You need anything, you just help yourself."

"That's a terrible place for a key, Rick," I said.

He grinned as he climbed into the driver's seat.

"Hey, Rick, I was wondering. What was I saying the night you found me outside? You said you heard me?" I had always wondered what I had been yelling the first night Rick found me. If I was calling my mother's name, the nightmare of being trapped underground, waiting to be found, kicked close to the surface with the arrival of the box of her things.

He turned his gaze out the windshield, and I saw his throat move, the muscles in his forearms twitching as he settled his hands on the wheel. "*Get away from me*," he said, and a chill ran through me. "That's what you said."

I stepped back. A bad dream. A nightmare. Like I could see something coming for me. I ran both hands up my arms, brushing away the goose bumps.

"Drive safe, Rick," I said, and he raised his hand one last time before driving out of sight.

Chances were, it was the nightmare. Calling out into the night to no one.

But I couldn't shake the image of Nathan Coleman in my yard even then. Thursday evening, before the murder. I wondered exactly how much he knew. How much he'd be willing to say.

How much he would be believed.

OBSERVER ONLINE

August 28, 2020

Posted: 2:33 P.M.

Sean Coleman's Son Arrested in Widow Hills: New Details Emerge in Murder Investigation

By Alice Perry

OBSERVER ONLINE previously shared details about the recent case of Sean Coleman's death in Central Valley, North Carolina, just outside the property of Olivia Meyer, the woman once known in the media as Arden Maynor, the girl from Widow Hills (link: see previous article). Twenty years ago, Sean Coleman was the man who found Arden Maynor clinging to a storm grate. Arden/Olivia had been viewed as a person of interest in the case.

However, sources inside the police department are now sharing that Nathan Coleman, Sean Coleman's twenty-nine-year-old son, has been arrested for stalking and assault in Widow Hills, Kentucky. Per the incident report, charges were pressed by Olivia Meyer.

There's no word yet on how this might connect to the active investigation into the death of Sean Coleman, but sources say more charges may be forthcoming.

CHAPTER 26

Friday, 4:30 p.m.

CALLED DETECTIVE RIGBY MYSELF.

I knew she wanted to talk as soon as I was back in town, and I was eager to find out what was happening with Nathan's case. Whether there was closure in the immediate future; whether something was just about to crack open.

It felt like a delicate balance, like we were one step from everything tipping over again. There was no containing who I was any longer, but I could keep the rest from spinning out of control.

Detective Rigby's steps echoed as she walked up my porch. I was waiting for her in the open doorway, and I watched her carefully this time—watched as she took everything in, seeing everything, making assessments, while trying to give away nothing.

"How are you doing, Olivia?"

"All right," I said, holding the door open for her to step inside. "Can I get you something? Water, juice?"

"I'll take water," she said, following me into the kitchen.

"Any news on Nathan's case?" I asked. I held my breath as I pulled a glass down from the cabinet.

"Well," she said, taking a seat at the kitchen table, "he's being held in Kentucky on the assault and stalking charges. We can try to build a case in the meantime. These things take time, though."

"I thought it was pretty cut-and-dried," I said. I hoped it wasn't the lack of a murder weapon. Currently in some hospital disposal holding area.

"Main problem is he says he wasn't in town at the time of his father's death. And we can't prove he was yet."

"Isn't there a shed back there? At the edge of that property on Haymere?" I asked, gesturing toward the back of my house. "He could've been staying there, right?"

She cut her eyes to me again, in the way I'd come to understand: that I had just given something away about myself. Like she had been trying to unravel me, as I had her. Both of us trying to prove ourselves here.

I turned on the faucet with my elbow, then held the glass under the sink.

"Why are you holding your arm like that?" she asked.

"Oh." I handed her the glass. "It's been getting worse. I thought it was okay yesterday, but I can barely move it now."

"Did Nathan do that?"

I nodded. "He grabbed me when he was chasing me. I felt something snap, or pop, but it was okay until this morning."

She stood up, stepped closer. "Did you get it checked out?"

"No. I can take some pain medicine, see if that helps first."

She left her glass in the sink. "It can help the case, Olivia. If Nathan harmed you during the assault, it will help in the trial. We need to get it documented."

"Okay," I said. "I'll get it checked out."

She took her keys from the pocket of her slacks. "I can't let you drive like that. Come on, I'll take you."

THE SECOND TIME I was in Detective Rigby's car, I had a better handle on her.

She continued the conversation as we pulled out of my driveway. "If there's anything else you're not telling me, now would be the time, Olivia."

Her tone could be savage; it was growing on me. I thought we might've been friends under different circumstances. But I didn't know how much she knew, or just suspected.

"Did you find the papers in his hotel? He's been obsessed with me for years."

"We did," she said. "And like I said, the folks in Widow Hills have charged him with stalking and assault. I'm asking about anything else here."

Detective Rigby wasn't convinced yet, though it seemed she was trying. I knew how it could be, to try to shift your perspective, to allow the possibility of a different truth—and to have someone else do it for you. But I needed her to see that it was neither me nor Rick but an angry Nathan Coleman.

"I think Sean Coleman was trying to warn me that his son was coming. And that's why Nathan killed him." He had motive, he had drive, he had years of pent-up anger, revenge, desire—for himself and what he was owed.

"Sean Coleman was killed where he stood. There didn't seem to be a struggle. I think there was an element of surprise," she said.

"Look at the size of Nathan." He'd be able to over-power someone fairly easily. He'd done it to me.

"Mm," she said, looking at me briefly instead.

In my head, I could pull all the pieces together, with him at the center. But Detective Rigby was reluctant. Everything could be explained away by Nathan. He could've gotten into my house; he seemed to know the area, kept hanging around. He could've taken the box cutter, con-fronted his father, tried to frame the whole thing on me—another type of story, like he said. A different one, that set him as victim this time, that he could exploit for his benefit.

But the detective was more focused on the fragments that still remained, just like Nathan had been, from a story twenty years earlier. Hung up on the details that didn't quite fit.

"Here's where I keep getting stuck, Olivia. You said the phone woke you that night," she said. "That's how you found the body."

"Yes." I didn't like how she was circling back, just as she had done that very first day, focusing on the specifics.

"It was a call from a burner phone. Can't trace those." She repositioned her hands on the steering wheel.

"Nathan," I said.

"You think he called his father's phone so someone would find the body?" she asked.

"Yes," I said. It made sense to me, those conflicted

feelings about a parent you'd lost contact with. The guilt that could haunt you after. Maybe he thought, hopelessly, that his father could still be saved.

"I know he said they weren't close, but there were several calls from Nathan to his father in the weeks prior."

I nodded, encouraging her. Nathan had told me that he'd gone to his father, who had refused to help. That must've been when Sean decided to do something—to come here and warn me. And Nathan must've found out somehow.

She turned onto the main road, eyes narrowed, gaze out the window. "He thinks the story isn't true," she said. "About what happened twenty years ago."

So he was talking. He was telling his side, trying to shake everything loose. The story, threatening to unravel. "I know," I said. "But does it matter?"

He had killed over it, been driven by this singular focus. He had confessed to me that he had blackmailed my mother because of it—but I couldn't tell the detective that part. Not without exposing all the rest.

But maybe she knew. She must've seen those letters in Nathan's hotel room, and she knew he had been after us for something.

Your mother sure did pay up, Nathan had said. His words echoing. My mother had thought she was being contacted by Sean Coleman, the man who rescued me, and she had paid him off. Something I'd have to come face-to-face with. Except I'd thought Nathan was leading me down a path, manipulating me, until I couldn't see another possibility.

His words about the 911 calls, my mother, the injury. The underground cellar, the cinder-block walls. I shook the image. He could've been lying. Playing me.

My mother could've paid because she knew that the words, and the implication, were enough on their own to damage us both. He was creating chaos with the story even now.

But the fact remained that I was prone to sleepwalking. It was true now, so it must've been true then.

"Well, we'll get there eventually," she said. "Like I said, these things take time." But I wondered how much experience she had with cases like this in a small county. Whether the loose threads would gnaw at her, as they did Nathan, driving her to some other belief. Whether I would ever be free of this.

"I'm just glad," she said, "that someone saw him following you there and could sense it wasn't right." The sign for the hospital came up, and she took the exit, the same route I took to work every day. "You know that call was anonymous?"

"The officers there mentioned it," I said. Something surprising and not. The town of Widow Hills, protecting its people. Knowing who belonged and who didn't. It would be almost supernatural, if not for the realization that people there had come to value their privacy.

But I had a feeling that maybe it was Emma Lyons—that she'd known where I was going, and had someone watching me, keeping me safe, a true guardian angel. Maybe she was more worried about Nathan than she let on. I'd have to ask her one day, when this was all behind us.

"You can drop me here," I said, gesturing to the pull-through entrance in front of the ER. I didn't want the detective to get any ideas about accompanying me into the hospital again, accumulating information when I wasn't paying attention.

She parked the car, put a hand on my arm before I turned away. "Have the medical report sent to me, okay? We'll get it to the folks in Widow Hills. I assume you can find yourself a ride home?"

"Yes," I said, opening the passenger door.

She tipped her head as I slid out of the seat, and I smiled back. I hoped it was the last time I'd see her.

I ASKED FOR SYDNEY Britton directly, grateful to hear that she'd just come on shift.

It took longer, without the police escort, to be called back, or maybe it was because I was waiting for Dr. Britton specifically. I had my shoulder x-rayed and generally examined before being sent to the semi-private area to wait once more.

Sydney Britton stood in the curtained entrance, glasses on top of her head, mouth a straight line. "We need to stop meeting like this," she said. And then she slipped the X-ray into the slot against the wall, placed her hands on her hips. "I heard what happened. You all right?"

She looked back once, and I nodded. She did the same, and that was enough.

"No break," she said. "No dislocation." She turned back to where I sat on the exam table, tried to maneuver my arm, but stopped as I hissed in air. "Some ligament damage. There's a lot of scar tissue as it is."

I looked over at the X-ray, wondering what she could see. "Can you tell what happened when I was a kid?" I asked. This was why I'd asked for her. To ask without being documented. To know: What had happened to me twenty years earlier?

She moved my arm in another direction, gently, getting the full range of motion. "Not really. Twenty years is a long time, Liv. Your bone is much different now from when you were a kid, still growing. There's only so much I can tell from an X-ray now—only the places the damage remains. Time covers the rest."

And so I might never know.

She stepped back. "Rest and anti-inflammatories are what I'd suggest for now. But you know, there are things you can do about that. Things that could help." She pointed to the X-ray. "It can take time, but I've seen people make good progress with physical therapy alone."

My mom had stopped taking me to my follow-up appointments. And I'd been afraid to visit doctors; afraid of what they might see. I hopped off the table. "Maybe," I said.

I WAS WAITING FOR Bennett outside the hospital entrance. I'd asked if he had time to swing by to pick me up and take me home before he headed in to work, partly because I wanted to see him again, partly because I knew he'd hear about this anyway, and I wanted it to be from me.

"What's the prognosis?" he asked. He moved his messenger bag to the back seat as I let myself into his car.

"A sprain." I had the X-rays and documentation tucked under my arm to send to Detective Rigby and the Widow Hills Police Department. "Just have to take it easy."

"Well," he said, "I'm glad you called me."

As if on cue, his cell started ringing from his bag in the back. I twisted around to be able to reach it with my right arm. "It's fine, leave it," Bennett said, "probably just work."

But I was already unzipping his bag.

"Liv, stop—"

The phone was in my hand—yes, it was work. I didn't answer it. Because I had just understood the urgency in Bennett's voice. The thing he didn't want me to see. My name on a form tucked away under his phone. I pulled the paper out, and his hands tightened on the wheel.

I wished he would look at me so I would know what this meant.

"It's not important," he said as I was reading the heading. "Liv, I was bringing it out of the hospital. I was going to get rid—"

"What the hell is this?" I asked, trying to process the pieces. It was a hospital incident report. One of the things Bennett was in charge of, reporting infractions up the chain of command.

But this had my name on it.

It had a list of infractions: unauthorized access to medicine room; unauthorized access to patient room—

It had the signature of the person who had reported it: one Erin Mills.

And it had Bennett's signature and date beside it.

"What the *fuck*, Bennett?"

"I was going to get rid of it," he repeated, which sounded wholly unlike Bennett. "Look, someone reported you. Unauthorized access to medicine room. Unauthorized access to patient rooms. I didn't know what to do with it. I didn't do *anything* with it, I swear."

Someone had been watching me. Noticed what I'd been doing. I'd thought only Bennett knew. The name, though. I had never even met her. "Who the hell is Erin Mills?"

"She's a nurse in the ER, hangs out in our lounge a bunch. Older than us. She was friends with Elyse." I remembered the name now. The person who lived next door to Elyse, in 121. "She was supposed to fill in for us and then quit. That's what I'm trying to tell you. It doesn't *matter*. She quit now. So no one's gonna know. I'm the only one. I didn't escalate it. It's in my bag, I'm taking it home. I'll get rid of it there."

The opposite of how I'd disposed of the box cutter.

My hand was shaking, though. Because someone else knew I'd been inside the medicine room. And someone else knew I'd been in a patient room—did she know about the box cutter? If she had reported me to Bennett, would she have reported the rest to the police?

I could remember only one nurse in the lounge the day I'd sneaked into the medicine room. That curly auburn hair, facing away. I hadn't known her; hadn't thought she knew who I was, either. Now I was worried about what else she had seen. What else she knew.

"Liv, please. Say something."

"Why didn't you tell me?"

He moved his lower jaw, and I thought I probably already knew the answer. Because he hadn't decided what to do with it. And now the decision had been made easier for him.

"You had a lot going on," he said. "A lot to deal with already. I thought I was helping."

We pulled onto my road, but I was still working through this piece of information. Bennett had caught me in the medicine room; he'd heard everything the detective said that first day; he knew about Dr. Cal; he'd been through the things in my house while I was unconscious; he'd convinced me not to search harder for Elyse.

"Take it," he said, looking straight at me before turning in to my driveway. "Take the paper and destroy it. There's no copy."

He'd also given me the information for a lawyer; he'd also shown up any time I called. At some point, I had to choose to trust him and the things he told me. "Okay," I said.

He parked the car behind my own in the driveway, looking to the house. "Can I come in for a sec?" he asked. "Make sure everything's okay?"

I understood what he meant: make sure we're okay.

Bennett would be leaving for work. The detective was gone. I thought of Elyse all alone at the campgrounds. What might happen to any of us with no one around and no one noticing when something was wrong.

"Yeah, come on in," I said. "How long do you have?"

He checked his phone and grimaced. "Not long."

He followed me up the steps, followed me as I unlocked the front door, dropping the X-rays on the entryway table, walking straight into the kitchen.

I caught him yawning when I turned around. "You need a break," I said. We all did after this. I thought of Dr. Cal's suggestions: to take care of myself, make sure I was getting rest and putting myself first.

"I do, and I'm planning on it," he said, running his hand through his hair. "I've got so much vacation accrued, it's ridiculous. I'm really bad at taking breaks."

"I've noticed," I said, smiling.

"Well, I'm going to take some time off. Starting this

weekend. So, I'll be around." He grinned. We stood there in my kitchen in silence.

"Can I help with anything before I go?" he asked.

I took down a glass from the cabinet with my right arm. "You can open the bottle of wine in the fridge," I said. I hadn't had any since I'd finished the last bottle, the night after the bar, the night I'd found Sean Coleman. And I wanted to get back to my routine. Relax, watch TV, fall asleep, wake up tomorrow for a fresh start.

He took the fresh bottle from the inside of the fridge door. Unscrewed the top. Held the bottle to my outstretched glass, poured more than I'd typically give myself.

His mouth twitched. "I don't know how you drink this extra-sweet screw-top wine, Liv. Seriously." He took a step closer, and I raised my glass. I didn't know everything about him still, and it set my pulse thrumming.

"Dare you," I said, holding out my glass.

"I have work." But he took a tiny sip, indulging me. His nose crinkled up, tongue out to the side. "I mean, seriously. It's really bad." I laughed, and he grinned. "I really do have to go."

"Go, then," I said. "Leave me to my wine and television."

I saw him out, standing on the front porch, watching his headlights disappearing, dusk settling in. Nothing but the crickets, the fireflies. Darkness at Rick's house. The single light from down the hall in the kitchen, behind me. And I felt at home, and secure, and good.

Back inside, I took the glass of wine into the living room, settling on the couch. I turned on the television, tipping the glass back.

But I gagged at the first sip, coughing as it went down.

Bennett was right, it was horrible. But not in the way I'd thought he meant.

It had turned.

But it was a new bottle—I hadn't had any yet, had stopped my nightly routine when everything spun out of control. I didn't think I'd opened it yet, but I couldn't be sure.

I went back to the kitchen, dumped the rest of the glass into the sink, then picked up the bottle on the counter. I couldn't find any crack, any other way for the wine to turn bad.

It had definitely been opened, though—and I didn't think it was by me.

My hand started shaking.

Bennett had told me the drugs that had gone missing: opioids, yes; and benzodiazepines. I knew what those could do. They could act as sedatives to calm you. Some were used for anesthesia, to lower anxiety, so you wouldn't recall the trauma of a medical procedure. I'd had an adverse reaction to one when I was younger.

I sniffed the bottle, swirled the liquid, peering through the faintly tinted glass, wondering if this was just paranoia. I set it down carefully on the counter, took a step back, then stared out the window into the darkness.

It was possible there was nothing in my wine at all, just a bad bottle, turned on its own. Except for the timing. Each night, starting when Rick had found me. A glass of wine, the fuzzy details of the entire night, waking up outside . . . the box cutter taken.

Which meant that someone had been drugging me.

Someone had been in here.

Hand to my mouth, another step back, flipping through the possibilities:

Elyse, who had shown up at the hospital so fast I won-dered how she knew I'd been there . . . She had been here with me after, had access to the drugs. She'd been out at the bar that night, too.

But so had Bennett. Bennett, who made me coffee at work. Who brought me juice, who gave me food. Bennett was in my office all the time. He could've taken my key, made a copy—

Stop it. Not Bennett, not Bennett, it couldn't be Ben-nett.

He legitimately had not known who I was. I'd witnessed the betrayal he'd felt when he found out. Except all the questions started swirling: why he'd talked me out of look-ing for Elyse; why he'd had that paperwork in his car—

When would I stop seeing the darkness in everyone, the terrible possibilities? Would I ever look and not see the darker intentions of people surfacing?

It had to be Nathan. He could've bought the drugs from Elyse, he could've told her what to do. He could've been in here. He must've been, to take that box cutter. Maybe that was what he'd been doing in here all along.

Except someone else had tried to frame me for taking the medicine. That was what that paperwork implied. The paperwork that Bennett had signed off on, that someone else had reported to him.

Why me? What did she have against me?

Maybe it hadn't been Elyse but someone else, some-one who understood that an investigation was going to kick off—and was running.

Erin, who lived next door to Elyse in apartment 121, who hadn't answered even when I'd sworn I'd heard movement inside.

According to Bennett, she had been in our lounge, on our floor, across from the medicine room. Maybe I hadn't seen the signs in Elyse because it hadn't been her. Maybe Elyse knew and was chased—the chaos of her apartment, like she knew someone was coming for her.

And now this woman was trying to blame it on me instead.

I just had to look her up. Pass the information on to Detective Rigby—that bottle of wine could be proof, the last thing she needed to pin Nathan Coleman, and all of this would be over. If he'd been drugging me . . . it was so much worse than I'd thought. If this Erin Mills was involved, it was another angle we could take. Another person who could point the finger at Nathan Coleman.

I'd been the only one to see the state of Elyse's apartment. To believe that she was running from something, in a panic.

Get away from me—the thing I'd been calling out in the night. Had it been Nathan Coleman? Someone else?

I opened my work laptop. Searched for her name. The thumbnail photo from her badge, small and grainy, like they all were. Only the doctors had full bios and head shots. Everyone else had a small ID photo from their access badge, blurry when enlarged.

I could tell she had long, curly auburn hair—yes, the woman who had been in the lounge that day, whom I'd seen from behind. But now I could finally see the rest of her: a thin face, large glasses that distorted her face's dimensions. I leaned closer, trying to get her into focus, and something prickled. A twinge of familiarity. I might've seen her other times in the nurses' lounge, maybe. Or in the cafeteria. Downstairs near the gift shop.

But it was something more. It was her smile, the shape of it—the wideness. Goose bumps rose down my neck. I heard Bennett's words again: *older than us.*

I shook my head, to concentrate. To keep the past from rising up and overlapping with the present.

I read her employment history, but there was only one place listed before here, a few years earlier: in Ohio.

A wave of intense nausea washed over me—a darkness, settling in my limbs, before everything went numb.

My hand shook as I grabbed my phone and scrolled through my call log. I moved back in time to more than a week ago, to before the box arrived. The only number that didn't have a contact attached. That out-of-the-blue call that had caught me off guard, like whiplash: *Is this Arden Maynor, daughter of Laurel Maynor? Ms. Maynor, I'm afraid we have some bad news—*

Every nerve was firing as I called that number back now.

When that man had called, I hadn't asked for specifics, too caught by the shock of the moment. I had accepted what he said at face value: that they had taken care of everything, and all that was left were her possessions. It was part of my past, and I'd wanted to keep it there. There was nothing I could do about it now. I couldn't get off that call fast enough.

I held my breath one second, two, as the number processed. It was late; I expected the call to go to an answering service, but I needed to hear who it belonged to.

It rang once, and then I heard it: a muffled echo.

I put the phone down. Dropped it to my side. Listened, my nerves on fire, my heart in overdrive, as another phone rang, in echo—from somewhere down the hall.

I stumbled to the end of the hall, into my bedroom, looking for the source. Another ring—in the closet, on a shelf. In that box.

The phone that I'd ignored—the old flip phone, useless, presumably dead.

Someone had turned it on. The screen was lit up and ringing.

I sank to the floor, feeling four walls closing in and not caring, not caring at all. I opened the phone, checked the outgoing call log. The only thing that existed, not deleted, were calls, one right after the other, on the night of Sean Coleman's death.

Like someone had stood just outside this closet, with the window open, watching me there. Watching me and wanting me to wake—or wanting someone to find me there with the body. Calling the number until I heard it. Until I woke.

Not Nathan Coleman but a woman. A woman with long brown hair, disproportionate to her small frame, and a too-wide smile—standing there, like I'd summoned her.

The moment I had feared for years.

I wasn't sure how long I'd been sitting on the floor when I heard the footsteps.

A flurry of movement under my bedroom window.

I stood, silently walking through my bedroom, to listen but not be heard. There was movement coming from outside the house, but there were barely any lights on inside. I couldn't be seen.

And then: the creak of a wooden step out back.

I remembered waiting on Rick's couch, waiting for the police. The time stretching and contracting when he told me: *It takes so long for help to get here.*

911 DISPATCH CALL CENTER TO CENTRAL VALLEY POLICE DEPARTMENT

DATE: AUGUST 28, 2020

TIME STAMP: 9:21 P.M.

911 DISPATCHER: We've got a report of a home invasion happening at 23 Old Heart Lane. Unidentified female. The call disconnected and we can't make contact again.

POLICE DISPATCH: Copy. Is caller still inside?

911: Yes, single female inside the house. She said she was trapped.

PD: Sending units to 23 Old Heart Lane. Any further information?

911: That's all we got before the line went dead.

CHAPTER 27

Friday, 9:20 p.m.

I CLOSED THE BEDROOM DOOR, grabbed the ladder from the closet, hand on the hook-and-eye latch. Ready, waiting, ear pressed to the wooden door.

Listening for the rattle of that back door. Or the sound of breaking glass. But there was silence.

I opened the bedroom door again, slipped out into the dark hall. Other than a dim bulb left on in the corner of the kitchen, only the television glowed in flashes of light. I padded barefoot down the hall toward the entrance of the kitchen, peered around the corner, but couldn't see anything out the window, into the night—the back porch light was still out.

But I heard the moment the key slid into the lock, the latch turning, and then the creak of the back door swinging open.

I held my breath. Eight steps to the front door. Car

keys on the entryway table. Three steps across the front porch. Seventeen steps to the car.

All I could see out back was her silhouette, illuminated, until she stepped inside.

I saw her before she saw me, clinging to the corner of the hall, in the shadows. Her long hair was pulled back now, and she wasn't wearing the glasses from her photo. She was smaller than I remembered, all sharp angles. I saw her look to the counter, where the wine bottle sat, still open. She picked up the empty glass, peering inside.

"Mom?" I asked, stepping out of the shadows.

Because there was still the chance that this was the drugs and the wine; that this was the nightmare. Not that she'd sent me that box herself, setting up that call, convincing someone else to make it, convincing me that she was dead.

But then she spun around, setting down the empty glass, and there was no going back.

This was the person Rick had heard me yelling at—shouting to get away from me.

The familiar laughter I'd heard at the hospital; that voice leading the detective to my office. A moment I had been expecting, subconsciously, for years. So close and yet continually out of sight.

"Hi, baby," she said, her face splitting open in that too-wide grin.

"Mom," I said, "what did you do?" There were so many layers to that question. What had she done, to Elyse, to Sean Coleman—to me, twenty years earlier.

"I kept you safe," she said, walking toward me. "You're safe now. This can all be over. Here." She gestured toward the table, expecting me to be malleable and compliant. "Sit, sit."

She'd thought I'd finished the glass. She'd thought I was under the influence of whatever she'd been drugging me with. Watching, learning my routine. Had she sneaked into my unlocked office, copying the key to my house? It wouldn't be hard. Anyone with a badge would have access. I'd been too trusting, too complacent, in my new life, thinking myself anonymous and safe.

I stepped back instead of forward.

"Arden, come here, come sit," she said, hand at my back, guiding me to the table.

My feet started moving forward of their own volition. I sat in the chair she'd pulled out. Yes, I was malleable and compliant. She took the phone from my hand, sliding it into her back pocket.

"Mom. I thought you were dead," I said.

"Did you, now?"

"You sent me that box."

She smiled sadly. "I thought you would look for me. I thought you would speak. But you just . . . put it in the closet, went on with your life. I thought you would recognize things, and, well." She shook her head, half a smile. "You always did surprise me."

"You changed your name," I said.

"You're not the only one who can start over." Her hand ran down my hair. "You and I are survivors, baby girl."

My head was fuzzy, but I didn't think it was the medicine. It was her, and the echoes of the past—the way I couldn't differentiate between then and now.

She walked over to the counter, pulled down a mug, like she had every right to be here.

"Mom," I said again. "Mom, did you hurt them?"

"Did I what?" she asked. "Hurt who?" She filled the mug with water from the sink.

My throat was dry. I didn't know where to start. "Sean Coleman."

Her face turned hard, angry, and I remembered the mood swings, how intense she could be. "Sean Coleman had been blackmailing us for years. He was . . . a drain. A leech. Taking something that wasn't his. You know I saw him last week? Walking into the hospital lobby? He did a double take, called my name. My old name. He was coming for us, baby. You'd never be free."

She had it wrong. Sean Coleman had been looking for me because he thought his son was going to come to me, the same way he'd come to Sean. The same way he'd come after my mother ten years earlier. Sean was coming to help me, and then he saw my mother.

Was that why he'd been watching? To see what she would do?

This. *This* was what Sean Coleman had been warning me about with his letter. Not his son. But this: my mother. And now she was here.

"No," I said. "It wasn't him."

She turned, looked at me hard. "Don't be naive, honey." She turned back to the kitchen cabinets, heated up the mug of water in the microwave. "I have always, always been there to help you. Who do you think called the police when Nathan followed you?"

That anonymous call, I suddenly understood—when she said she had kept me safe. She had called it in, made sure the police came after us. And now Nathan Coleman sat in jail, the case circling around him instead of me.

"His father was blackmailing us for years. Well, like father, like son, it seems."

"It wasn't his father. All those years, the letters, the blackmail—it was the son. It was always Nathan," I said.

She stared at me blankly and then took a deep breath, her shoulders pressing back. "No, he was watching this house, Arden. He was watching you."

"No," I said, my voice rising, "he had come here to warn me. Not about his son. Not that at all. He was coming here to warn me about *you*."

I stood up too fast, the chair pushing back.

She tipped her head, momentarily confused. "Arden, calm down. You're not acting like yourself."

She was right. I needed to calm down. Couldn't let the panic settle in, rendering me useless, telling me to run.

Six steps to the back door; thirteen steps to the front door. Could I make it to Rick's house? To his shed? To his guns? With a stiff knee and one good arm?

No one was here—no one could help.

The microwave beeped, and I saw her fingers find the amber vial of my prescription from Dr. Cal in the space beside it. I saw her read the label, then quickly turn it back.

"Mom, I need to know. I need to know what happened back then."

She sighed. "Go lie down, Arden. Rest, I'm making you a hot chocolate." She pointed down the hallway, and I complied.

I started walking down the hall, then heard the gentle rattle of pills, like I had so many times in my memories. My mother, at night, making me hot chocolate—to calm me. The rattle of pills to stop me.

A chill ran down my back. Had she always been this

person—even before? Like Emma Lyons had said? Had she drugged me long ago, before the episodes? Dr. Cal had said that sleepwalking was, unfortunately, a side effect of other medications.

Whom had I been living with all those years? A monster?

I kept moving, barefoot, quietly—by the glow of the television—peering around the living room for something I could use.

"Arden," she said, voice closer. "Where are you going?" The squeak of a hinge, a click, and then the last of the lights went black.

She had just cut the electricity. And I understood: She knew exactly what she was doing. We were bathed in darkness, and then all I could feel were the walls on either side of me closing in. I couldn't run from this anymore; couldn't ever be free of it if I did.

I stood perfectly still, my eyes unaccustomed to the dark. I couldn't tell where she was—could hear only my own rapid breathing, my own heartbeat, until the shock of her cold fingers at my elbow, her grip tightening.

She jerked me toward her, and my arm pulled. I yelled out—the flash of another memory then, another time, another possibility.

"Did he hurt you?" she asked, her voice in my ear.

"Yes," I whispered, but she didn't release her grip.

"Okay," she said. "I've got something to help you. Come. Come on." And then we were moving, down the darkness of the hall, my free hand feeling for the wall.

A door opened, and I could feel the chill of cooler air escaping. "This way," she said, pushing me toward the staircase. One way up. One way out. "Don't move. I'll be right there."

And then she closed the door.

There was no light in the stairwell, just darkness. The narrowed walls, the smell of wood. My entire body began to tremble.

Like so long ago—the only clear memory. Of walls and stagnant water and no way out. I did now what I must've done back then. Not going back the way I came, but forward. I went up.

I stood in the middle of the room, in front of those glass windows: the only way out. I could feel the panic brewing. Knowing the eaves were narrowed, and the space was finite, and there was one way out of this room. I held myself very still, and I sat in the single rocking chair in the middle of the room, staring at the beveled glass windows, until my eyes adjusted to the dark.

And I waited.

Because I needed to know. I needed the truth. I needed to come face-to-face with myself, and with her.

The door opened again; the scent of hot chocolate wafted through the room. She ascended the steps and walked around the rocking chair so she was standing between me and the window, the moonlight fracturing through the glass. Like she had been here before, knew her way around. I suddenly knew she'd been the one to remove that light bulb. She'd been here all along.

"Here," she said, holding out the mug. "For the pain."

"I don't want it. I want you to tell me what happened back then."

Her mouth was a thin line before breaking into a small grin. "All right. Drink, and we'll talk."

I took the cup from her hands, and she waited until I brought it to my lips, taking a sip.

The liquid burned. A piece of me in exchange for a piece of her. How far was she going to take me? Was she feeding me this in the hope that I wouldn't remember? So I would remain compliant? Or did she want to hurt me?

"How did this happen?" I asked, gesturing to my left arm. "Back then." Bennett had an opinion, the doctors had an opinion, Nathan had an opinion. But none of them knew for sure.

She cocked her head. "You really don't remember?"

Emma Lyons had told me about that doctor—how he thought I'd been lying. Six years old and lying because my mother was in the room.

"Did you hurt me?" I asked.

She looked off to the side. "It was an accident. You had some reaction to a medication, it was making you wired . . . you were uncontrollable, Arden, truly, I had to—" Her arm flung out to the side as she spoke. "We were on the steps—I swear, you were going to take us both down, and I—it all happened so fast. I tried to pull you back, but you screamed and I let go. And you fell." She shook her head. "I was trying to keep you from getting hurt, I promise. But a child's bones are so fragile."

A flash. Someone grabbing my arm—a pop, a crack. Bracing myself and falling.

Steps. The only steps could've been to the basement.

And then—a pain so bright and intense it stole my breath.

Her face. Her voice. *Okay, okay, stay calm, take this—*

It was her. Always her.

When had my omissions turned to lies? When I was six, in the hospital, with my mother standing over me?

Had she believed even then that I understood and was complicit? A survivor, like her.

The medication must have caused the sleepwalking episodes—whatever my mother had given me at night, trying to keep me calm and complacent while she went on with her life. But children didn't react the same way adults did. They were more prone to sleepwalking, to overexcitement.

"You staged the whole thing?" The whole story. *A fraud.* She stared at my cup, waiting, and I took another sip.

"No, it all took on a life of its own. It was supposed to be just a few hours. Just a little while. Your shoe outside, to lead them to the woods, where you wandered off and could've gotten hurt all by yourself. But it all got carried away. It rained—it *poured*, and the shoe got caught on a grate, and, well." She shrugged. "It took on a life of its own, and we just had to seize it."

The cellar. The four walls. The stagnant water and the cold rocks. The unfathomable darkness and the pain—for which she must have treated me. The black hole of my memory while I'd been kept unconscious. A pain medicine she must've given me to keep me that way.

"How did I get underground?"

She waited until I took another sip, and I could see the white granules of my medicine. How much was too much? Did she know? Did she care?

"The media attention got to be so much, they were going to find you. They were coming with infrared, and I got you to an access point closer to the river." She gave a small laugh. "My God, Arden, you about gave me a heart attack. They couldn't find you. You weren't *there*. I told you to sit tight, but you didn't. You didn't."

Her reaction on the television was surprise—she hadn't been acting. I had gone missing. I had traversed the darkness on my own. I had saved myself.

"I know it must've been terrible, but you have gotten so much from it. So much. And we have another opportunity right now."

I shook my head. Hated that she was here, that she couldn't stop. That all she ever saw in me was another opportunity worth taking, another story to spin, another piece of me to give away.

"People are going to want to talk to you. To us. That boy tried to frame you, and you survived it—again."

"Mom, stop," I said, eyes closed. Because I realized something—every night, even before Sean Coleman, she had been drugging me. She had been up here, keeping me in the dark; locking me outside. Had she been trying to scare me, to make me run or call for help? Did she bring me outside, leading me into the night, for nothing more than a story? Putting my life in danger so I'd have to get help, get attention? So people would notice?

Until she saw Sean Coleman out there, and everything went horribly wrong—

I was always just a commodity to her. Something to cash in on. She hurt me. And Sean. And—

"What did you do to Elyse," I said.

"You need to relax," she said. "Drink, relax."

What was she doing to me? The same thing she'd done to Elyse?

No more. I stood, letting the mug fall to the floor, shattering into pieces, the contents splashing. She jumped away, surprised. "Did you hurt her?" I said.

She stepped back, before she regained her footing in

the conversation. "Some people are more than willing to hurt themselves," she said. "She told me the very first day we met how she was in recovery. How she'd just come from a rehab facility. You can't give away things like that about yourself. You need to be more careful."

Oh, God, it was my mother. It was no one but her. My mother had harmed her. I felt my pulse racing, the four walls closing in. "No," I said. "Please, no."

"She wasn't some innocent, love. She kept an eye on you. Helped me move things from the hospital. Was more than happy to take money to keep her hands clean of the worst of it."

Elyse had been scared that day, looking out my window. Like she knew something more than I did. And she'd tried to run. My mother had stopped her.

I had been wrong. My mother was not an opportunist but a predator. And right now I was just another part of her story. If I wasn't going to help her, what would I be this time? The poor, tragic figure who overdosed? The girl who couldn't take the police attention, the stories, the rumors?

If I wouldn't go along with her, what would she *do*?

Would she hurt her daughter for her own gain? I had no doubt. She had done it before. She would hurt anyone.

"You're horrible," I said, the word scratching against my throat.

I heard them before I saw them, the faint blare of the sirens. My mother turned to the window, frowning. "What did you do?" she asked. The lights fractured through the glass. Her hand went to her back pocket, where she'd kept my phone.

"I called 911," I said.

She closed her eyes. "Okay, okay." Hands out, like she was thinking up a story even then. A way to spin this, to come out on top. She stepped closer. "You're on something, honey," she said, like she'd arrived just in time to help me. "It's making you not yourself."

"I'm not, though," I said. "I didn't drink it."

She was so close, I felt the four walls closing in, with no way out. She grabbed me around the arm, like she was incredibly angry but wasn't sure what to do.

"This is what we're going to do," she said. And up close, I could see the cold calculation in her eyes. Tallying her own way out. I knew, of course, there was only one.

How many steps she had taken to this point. How many options remained.

I was doing the same.

The sirens were getting louder, more insistent, and in that moment, I felt it: the cold and the dark, reaching out for the cinder-block walls. Pushing back against something that was no longer there. I pushed her off me. I pushed her back with everything I had, watched her fall through the fragile window, glass shattering, glass everywhere.

She collapsed onto the decorative balcony, which was not built to hold any weight. I thought it might fall, might crumble to the earth right then. But it didn't. A scattering of glass and blood, and her, unbalanced, pushing to her feet again.

The sirens upon us now, the red and blue lights in sight, catching on a shard of glass in her hand as she stood upright. I stepped closer, and she said, "Arden," and I did not care to hear. I did not care to hear a single thing she said, ever again. She would've killed me. Still might.

The steps behind me; the window in front of me. The night air billowed in, cold, freeing. Letting me know I was no longer trapped. That there was a way out.

I focused on the glass in her hand, on what I had to do to escape her. Before she could stand, before she could lunge with the glass: one more push, and the decorative balcony rail gave way. Her eyes met mine for a fraction of a second—her hand grasping for me as I stumbled backward—and then she was gone.

The first car pulled into the drive, lighting up the night. There was glass everywhere, up here and down below. Glass and blood and my mother, at the center.

THEY TOOK THE BOTTLE of wine.

They took what was left of the fragments of the mug, sticky from the hot chocolate.

And soon enough, they took my mother—on a stretcher, under a sheet. I didn't know whether it was the multiple lacerations or the impact. But it didn't matter. I'd already come to terms with her death.

I watched with an odd detachment from that broken upstairs window.

"You shouldn't be up here. There's still glass." Detective Rigby stood behind me, peering out into the darkness. I should move. Out of this enclosed space, into the open air. But I didn't feel trapped right then.

"I've survived worse," I said. The truth: I'd survived her. Twenty years earlier, my entire life had been an escape from her control and the stories she told—until they became all I had ever been.

"You sure you're feeling okay?"

She knew about the drugs, about the pills. But I wasn't sure what she was asking. I waved her off, then turned over my hands, showed her the small cuts coating my palms. "I can't even feel this," I said.

The detective nodded slowly. "We'll be sure to get those checked out downstairs, yeah?" Then she held up my phone. "By the way, this was on her," she said. "But I recognized it. I think it's yours."

"Yes," I said, reaching for it. "She took it from me."

Detective Rigby didn't quite release her grip. "Good thing you were able to get a call for help out first."

"I remembered," I said, "how long it takes you to make it out here. I called as soon as I heard someone outside my house."

"That was smart," she said, her face giving away nothing. "You didn't know it was her?"

"I thought she was dead," I said, which wasn't a lie.

She spent a few seconds staring at me before releasing her hold on the phone, severing the connection between us.

She stood beside me, watching the ambulance drive away, lights off.

For a brief moment, I thought about telling her the truth. Saying it for once—that Nathan was right, that the story was not at all what it seemed. That my mother had always been willing to gamble my life. That she'd hurt me once and tried to cover it up, and she would easily do it again.

But that knowledge belonged just to me.

Detective Rigby stepped a little closer to the window so she could peer over the edge. She whistled through her teeth. "Scary scene," she said. "You could've fallen. You're very lucky."

"I had to do it," I said. I was trapped. Four walls and no way out.

"I know you did. I heard your 911 call," she said. Then she turned to face me. "You could tell quite a story here. About all of this."

"No, thanks." Nathan had been arrested for what he had done—I'd fight to keep him in jail, or I'd get a restraining order. Without Sean Coleman, without my mother, I was the only living witness to what had really happened twenty years ago. The story could be only mine, and I wouldn't give it away this time.

What I said in the next few days about the events surrounding tonight would be the last I ever spoke of it, if I had my way.

You become the stories you tell—I'd learned that much from my mother.

The truest type of story is the kind you tell all alone, to yourself.

TRANSCRIPT OF 911 CALL FOR SERVICE

DATE: AUGUST 28, 2020

TIME STAMP: 9:19 P.M.

DISPATCH: 911, what's your emergency?

CALLER, UNKNOWN FEMALE: Someone's in my house.

D: Ma'am, what's your exact address?

C: 23 Old Heart Lane in Central Valley. Please help.

D: Can you get out of the house?

C: No, I'm trapped. I'm hiding. The footsteps are getting closer.

D: Okay, I'm sending help your way now. Look around you for windows or doors. They might not know you're home. You need to get out.

C: She knows I'm here. There's no way out.

CALL DISCONNECTED.

TIME STAMP: 9:20 P.M.

ACKNOWLEDGMENTS

THANK YOU TO EVERYONE who helped see this book through, from idea to publication.

Sarah Davies and Jennifer Joel, for all the guidance and support along the way.

My editor, Marysue Rucci, for the brilliant insight, feedback, and support from initial idea to final draft. And the entire team at Simon & Schuster, including Richard Rhorer, Jonathan Karp, Zack Knoll, Amanda Lang, Elizabeth Breeden, Hana Park, Marie Florio, and so many others who had a hand in bringing this book into the world. Thank you also to everyone at Marysue Rucci Books. It's such a joy working with you all!

I'm very grateful to Dr. Pam Hoyt and Detective Sergeant Lee Ann Oehler for taking the time to answer my many hypothetical questions and for providing extra insight.

Thank you to my critique partners, Megan Shepherd,

Ashley Elston, and Elle Cosimano, for the check-ins, the brainstorming sessions, and the feedback on early drafts. And to Megan S., Beth Revis, Carrie Ryan, and Gwenda Bond, who listened to me talk about this idea in its earliest stages, helped brainstorm ideas, and encouraged me to write this story. I'm so grateful to all of you for the friendship and support.

Lastly, thank you, as always, to my family.

ABOUT THE AUTHOR

MEGAN MIRANDA IS THE *New York Times* bestselling author of *All the Missing Girls*; *The Perfect Stranger*; *The Last House Guest*, which was a Reese Witherspoon Book Club pick; *The Girl from Widow Hills*; *Such a Quiet Place*; *The Last to Vanish*; *The Only Survivors*; and *Daughter of Mine*. She has also written several books for young adults. She grew up in New Jersey, graduated from MIT, and lives in North Carolina with her husband and two children. Follow @MeganLMiranda on Twitter and Instagram, @AuthorMeganMiranda on Facebook, and visit MeganMiranda.com.

Read on for an excerpt from
Megan Miranda's twisty new thriller!

PROLOGUE

THE DROUGHT STARTED IN the West. We watched on the news as the waters dropped in the reservoirs and lakes, and their secrets and ghosts slowly emerged. The Great Salt Lake was suddenly in danger of disappearing, threatening to release the toxic gases hidden at the bottom. Skeletons surfaced from the edges of a shrinking Lake Mead—in barrels, in boats, bare bones scattered on a dried-out shoreline. Missing persons, finally found. Unknown crimes, suddenly uncovered.

We watched from the safety of our enclave on the East Coast, where freshwater rivers cut down the mountain, sustaining our lake, our community. We watched from our living room couches, with lush forests of trees right outside the windows, the promise of the green North Carolina landscape. We thought ourselves protected, immune.

It came here on a delay, like everything else—the latest fashions, high-speed internet.

And then slowly, the rotted wood beneath the docks became visible, soft and black. Boats were raised up into dock houses, or anchored farther out, where they drifted back and forth like ghost ships in the night.

We were told not to water the grass, not to launch a boat onto the lake from Gemma's Creek, not to worry. Even as more things slowly started appearing: branches and trunks, reaching out from the surface; sunken beer bottles wedged into the newly exposed mud.

In the West, there were the bodies. But here, we were less flashy, less prone to drama and sensation. We preferred our crimes quiet, our cases closed—that was my father's motto. He was the last of a dying breed, I thought. A detective who got no shot of adrenaline from either the chase or the justice. So very different from the craving of my youth: *Give me a wrong, so that I may punish.*

So when the drought finally arrived, I supposed it was fitting that the first thing to attract attention was not a body or a barrel or a bone. It was something quieter— something we didn't understand at first.

Quieter, but no less dangerous.

PART 1
FATHER

62 Days without Rain
Wednesday, May 15
5:30 p.m.
Precipitation: Zero

CHAPTER 1

THEY RAISED THE CAR from the lake on the same day as my father's memorial, two unrelated but equally newsworthy events: Something lost. Something found.

My father had been gone for over three weeks, and in the days since, I'd found myself measuring time differently. A recalibration. A new reality.

I listened to the weather reports each morning on the radio in Charlotte—*sixty-two days without rain*—and thought, instead, *Twenty-three days without him.*

It seemed like half the town had come out for the celebration of life—crowding the deck of his favorite restaurant, raising a glass (or two, or three) to the portrait of Detective Perry Holt—while the other half was gathered around an inlet on the opposite side of Mirror Lake, watching as the salvage company hooked a crane to the car that had been spotted below the surface a few days earlier.

All I could think was: *Of course this is happening now.*

I'd always suspected that my father alone had held things together by sheer force of will—not only in our family, but in the entire town. And without his careful gaze, his steady oversight, everything had shifted off-kilter.

Even for this, he had left us his guidance. A cremation instead of a burial. A party instead of a funeral. Food covered by the department. Drinks on him.

But the discovery of the car was big news in a small town, and no one had seemed sure what to do, with the outside world watching. It had made headlines all the way in Charlotte, even: the water level of Mirror Lake had dropped to the lowest it had been in decades, and a fisherman had practically run up on top of the sunken vehicle.

There was no evidence of a crash—no bent metal or crushed vegetation at the curve of road above the inlet— so the rumor spreading through the crowd was that the old rusted sedan must've been there for years, before the addition of the new guardrail. Apparently, a dive crew had been out to inspect the car the day it was found, but saw nothing inside.

And yet, it had the air of something I couldn't quite put my finger on: a sign of things emerging, changing.

A warning, that things were beginning here too.

There was something in the air, keeping everyone on edge: a buzzing of insects in the muddy puddles beneath the deck; the setting sun glaring sharply off the surface of the water, so we had to squint just to look at one another; leaves, dry and brittle and churned up in the wind, falling to earth at the wrong time of year.

This wasn't how things were supposed to go.

There were supposed to be stories on the mic set

up beside the bar, for anyone who felt moved to speak. We were supposed to find solace in the liquor, and the laughter—a release, an acceptance. Perry Holt was gone too soon, and it wasn't fair, but my god, what a life he had lived.

So many people here attributed their lives to him. Whether he'd pulled them out of danger, or pushed them toward the help he knew they needed—today, we were supposed to remember it all. But now news of the car was splitting everyone's attention and sense of responsibility and propriety.

For every comment of *He was such a good man, a good leader, a good role model* booming from the sound system, there was a quieter whisper, carried in the crowd around me.

It's coming up.

No license plate. No VIN.

Stolen and dumped, probably.

While the youngest Murphy girl—now a few years out of high school—told the story of how my father found her drifting in the middle of the lake as a kid, her tube cut loose from the dock, I heard the group to my side taking bets on what they'd find inside the trunk.

A body. Stolen goods. A gun.

I turned to stare, hoping to shame them into silence, but they were looking toward the entrance instead, where a group of uniformed officers had gathered in the doorway.

It didn't help that a lot of the people here were presently or formerly connected to law enforcement, either by profession or family ties. Or that men and women in uniform kept rotating in, alternating between paying their respects and relaying updates to my brothers.

Both of whom had suddenly disappeared again.

I didn't blame them.

I was pretty sure I'd find them on the long sliver of deck at the side of the building—the only reprieve from the crowd.

I saw Caden first, pacing back and forth, all frenetic energy. He paused periodically to hold his phone out over the water, trying to catch a signal. Any other day, he'd be out there himself. He'd been the very first on scene; the call about the car came in while he was working his normal shift on lake patrol.

Gage, meanwhile, remained perfectly still, arms resting on the wooden railing as he stared out at the water. From a distance, he looked so much like our father it stopped my heart: sharp nose, prominent jaw, dark cropped hair. Heavy slanted eyebrows that gave everything he said an air of gravity.

I slid up beside him, mirroring his posture. How many years had I mimicked him, idolized him, revered him as the hero of my youth? He let me follow him around far longer than most older brothers might, and I relished his praise: *Hazel can climb that tree*; and *Hazel will jump from that bridge*; and *Hazel can beat you in a race*.

All I'd had to do was show up, and prove him right. Now I tried to mirror not only his position but his emotions. *Find the balance. Rise to the moment.* Like our father, Gage was always the responsible one—and now he found himself in a new role not only in the department but in our family. Maybe that was the curse of being the oldest.

"Are we hiding out?" I asked, as Caden's footsteps retreated down the deck.

Gage tilted his head to the side, squinting. "We're hiding out."

Then I could feel Caden's footsteps getting closer again—a metronome, keeping time.

He stopped pacing behind us. "Mel's trying to send pictures. They're not coming through." I could see the pent-up energy in his stance, though his expression remained calm, controlled. The things he could hide under his cherub-shaped face, even at twenty-seven, with the dimpled cheek, and his brown hair swooped to the side, like he was still on the cusp of adulthood.

"What's going on out there?" I asked.

If anyone would be able to distinguish the facts from the rumors, it was my brothers—both of them had proudly followed our father onto the force. Though Gage would probably be the only one to tell me. Caden and I got along best when I remembered to bite my tongue, and he remembered to ignore me. Today, we were both mostly doing our part.

Gage was tall and lean-muscled, where Caden was more broad-shouldered and stocky. The only discernable features they shared were the color of their deep blue eyes and the low tenor of their voices. *The Holt voice*, my dad had called it, though his had turned more gravelly as he aged.

"Probably some insurance scam," Gage said, dark eyebrows knitted together. "The guardrail was installed fifteen years ago. The car must've been there for a while."

I knew that stretch of road, right before the narrow, single-lane bridge. "It's easy to lose control there," I said. I remembered the warning myself, from when I was learning to drive. My father's echo: *Careful. Slow it down, Hazel.*

It had always been a dangerous bend, especially in the night.

The township of Mirror Lake didn't believe in

streetlights or painted center lines or regular pothole maintenance, it seemed. It *did* believe in respecting the natural geography that had existed before, which was why the roads forked sharply, banked unevenly, rose steeply. The side roads were generally only wide enough for one vehicle at a time. Growing up here, we had learned to be both cautious and aggressive, to maneuver through tight spaces, to step on the gas before someone else did first.

So driving was a dangerous activity, especially for someone from out of town.

I imagined someone speeding around the curve, unfamiliar with the dark mountain curves, the dark mountain roads, tires losing traction—how quickly something could sink below the surface, unnoticed.

"There was no one inside the car, Hazel," Gage answered. "They checked."

"Could've escaped," I said. I closed my eyes and saw it: someone clawing their way out of the vehicle as it sank. Their head finally emerging above water—that first, primal gasp.

"Yeah, well, no one called it in, if so. And the plates were removed. Seems more likely it was dumped there on purpose. It's a convenient spot." Gage was logical, pragmatic, levelheaded. All things that made him a good detective now. It was always so easy to believe him.

It made sense: here was a place no one would go looking.

Caden glanced up briefly from his phone. "I can't believe it's been there that long. I used to jump from that spot in high school."

Gage rubbed the side of his chin. "Me too," he said.

I shuddered. We had all jumped off the rocks at the edge of that curve, when the summer sun got too hot, and we were desperate for something to happen, despite the warnings from the adults. I could still feel the cold shock of that pocket of water, always in the shade no matter the time of day, the feetfirst plunge, and how the bottom seemed so endlessly far away.

How close had we come? How many of us had brushed up against a strip of metal and thought *boulder* or *branch*. How many of us had imagined something else instead?

"Jesus," Caden said, holding his cell closer to his face. He stopped breathing for a moment, his only tell. And then his eyes narrowed. "Someone really needs to help with the crowd control over there."

I tried to peer over his shoulder at the screen, but he was already on his way. He quickly rounded the corner back toward the guests.

Apparently by *someone*, he meant himself. I couldn't believe he was leaving like this.

"Seriously?" I began. "Dad would—"

"Dad would be out there himself," Gage cut in, squinting at the water, the surrounding mountains reflecting off the hazy surface. "And you know it."

I did. Over the years, I'd watched our father leave the dinner table for a break-in; a birthday party for an overdose; a soccer game for a high-speed chase. He made no excuses or apologies. We all understood that his responsibilities stretched beyond the boundaries of our family.

"You should head home too, Hazel," Gage said, turning back to face me. "This is only going to get worse. Everyone knows you've got a long trip back."

Two hours, really. But Charlotte might as well have been a different world from Mirror Lake. I was a different person out there, without the anchor of history.

"You sure?" I asked. "I feel like I should stay to help clean up. . . ."

But Gage shook his head, releasing me. "Drive safe," he said, like my father would do. "And Hazel?" He looked at me with wide-open eyes, a wide-open expression. "Don't be a stranger, okay? He wouldn't want that."

I forced a small smile, even as a wave of panic gripped me from nowhere. I felt, then, the finality of this moment; I wasn't ready.

"You should be so lucky," I said before turning away, eyes burning.

Even as I joked, I wondered what would next bring me back. Thanksgiving? My niece's birthday in the summer, maybe, if Caden invited me? I felt untethered suddenly, ungrounded. All the emotions I'd fought to contain today suddenly fighting for the surface.

I kept my head down, weaving through the crowd, a study in evasion. Eyes forward, stride confident, hoping no one stopped me. It didn't help matters that I was the only one in black amid a sea of khakis and floral. Or that I looked like I was dressed for a business meeting— tailored A-line dress, blazer, stacked heels—while the rest of the guests had arrived in what I could only call Lake Casual.

I grabbed the bag I'd stowed behind the counter and slipped into the restroom. I wanted to change before the drive home—I had plans to swing by our latest renovation project on the way, which was still an active construction site. I needed to focus on something else, to let my work consume me again.

The bathroom was down a dimly lit, wood-paneled hall, and my vision was still adjusting to the change as I pushed through the door and nearly collided with the person on the way out.

"Oh." A hand on my shoulder, to brace herself. A whiff of coconut. A curtain of hair.

Even in the dark, I would know: Jamie.

She slowly removed her hand from the front of my shoulder, then ran it through the ends of her long, honey-colored hair, an old nervous habit. "Hazel," she said, locking eyes with mine. Her voice was like something sharp and piercing, straight to the heart. Maybe it was because my guard was already down, or my nerves too exposed, or because I was already hovering so close to the edge. Her attention shifted to the bag in my hands. "Are you leaving?"

"Yeah. Just changing first." I gestured to my outfit. "No one told me the dress code." Jamie wore a spring floral dress and beige sandals.

A twitch of her lip—an almost smile. A portal to another time, before her gaze slid away again. She stepped to the side, closer to the exit.

And then, because I didn't know where to go from here: "Is Skyler around?" My six-year-old niece was always a welcome distraction.

"She's outside with some of the department kids." She cleared her throat. "Are you coming back this weekend?"

"For what?" I asked.

She frowned, peering at the door. "Caden said they're cleaning out the house. I thought you knew."

This was what happened when you were the only one who left home. I had to hear about things secondhand, default to my brothers' preferences, concede to their decisions.

I shook my head, grief giving way to anger—a familiar and welcome slide. "When?" I asked, louder than necessary.

"Sunday."

I did my best not to look surprised. Maybe Gage forgot to tell me in the chaos of the day.

Sometimes Jamie mentioned things in a way that sounded offhand but seemed almost intentional instead. As if she was still trying to bridge the gap between me and Caden.

Or maybe I was being too generous, blinded by nostalgia and the years of friendship that had once sustained us.

Back when we were in high school, Jamie used to say I had an A-plus asshole radar—warning her of the boys who would let us down; the teacher who would not give second chances; the classmates who would take particular pleasure in our missteps. But I felt my instincts went to something deeper than that, like I could see what was underneath—less action, more intention.

Unfortunately, it never rubbed off on Jamie, considering she married my brother Caden.

"Thanks," I called as she opened the door. "I'll be there."

AFTER CHANGING, I THOUGHT about going out to find Gage, tell him I'd be back Sunday—but there was currently a straight shot to the exit, the sun was setting, and this celebration was quickly becoming something else.

I had started to get that subtle, creeping feeling—like the walls were closing in, and I needed to escape. A reminder of why I'd left in the first place.

Stay too long, and you became exactly what Mirror Lake decided you would be.

Out front, the department kids were playing a game of hide-and-seek in the trees. One of their mothers leaned against the wooden railing, keeping tabs on them, like mine had once done. I caught a flash of Skyler's blond hair rushing past, and saw, instead, a group of us racing through these woods, a generation before.

I kept moving.

How quickly the past could grasp onto you here, and pull.

THE DIRT PARKING LOT was overflowing, and several vehicles were combing the area, looking for free space. I raised a hand to the nearest car as I walked to my SUV, gestured I was heading out. I had gotten the last viable spot at the edge of the lot, half my car fully in the woods, tucked under the branches of a large oak.

The driver's side window lowered as the bright blue car slowly pulled up behind mine.

"Hi," he said. A familiar voice, a familiar face.

I froze, shoulders tensing.

Last I saw Nico Pritchard, he was driving away in a different car, and doing his best not to make eye contact.

I paused, one hand on my car door. "Hi," I repeated.

"Sorry I'm late, I got held up," he said. And then, when I didn't respond: "Been a while, Hazel."

Two years and two months, but who was counting?

"Yeah, guess it has," I said, like I hadn't just done the math. "Lucky timing on the parking spot, though."

He drummed his long fingers on the steering wheel, as if debating his next words. "Seems like I keep just missing you," he said.

I nodded. We'd been just missing each other for over two years, at holidays and family visits and birthday parties; I just wasn't sure which of us was the more active player.

It was a feat, considering he was Gage's oldest friend, and he still owned the house on the other side of the inlet from my dad.

The pattern of evasion was broken only with the message he'd sent me the night my father had died: *Hazel, I'm so sorry.*

He'd been away on vacation when it happened. Even then we'd missed each other.

There was a time that Nico was anywhere Gage went, and was nearly as much a part of my childhood. Our fathers had been partners on the force—a different type of family, I supposed.

"Well," I said, "good to finally run into you."

It was, and it wasn't.

For years growing up, I had been singularly focused on Nico Pritchard. Attuned to the careful way he did everything, from baiting a fishing line to saying my name. The way he pronounced each syllable carefully, not letting the second half get swallowed up, like everyone else. The innocent look of his wide brown eyes, like he was always trying to take everything in, quietly and carefully, to file away for later. The shape of his down-turned mouth, so that his sudden smile was both a surprise and a game changer.

My infatuation was obvious in a way that bordered on embarrassing. As we grew older, the fact that it had been reciprocated by him was not nearly as evident.

"Sorry it has to be under these circumstances," he said.

Even his words were carefully chosen. He'd managed to apologize twice in as many minutes.

"Me too," I said. I opened my car door, before it was too late.

"Hazel, hold on," he said.

I held on, hand tightening on the top of the door.

To my horror, Nico stepped out of his idling car: long, tailored pants; white button-down, tucked in; a silver watch that I knew had once belonged to his father; a flush along the top of his high cheekbones.

It didn't matter how much time had passed, or how badly we'd left things the last time—whenever I saw him, I pictured him at fifteen on our swim platform; at seventeen, leaning against my bedroom door; at twenty-one, home from college, eyes slowly scanning the room, before landing on me.

"I wanted to call," he continued, taking a step closer. "I've been meaning to. I just didn't know—"

"Nico," I said, cutting him off. "I'm sorry, but I really do need to go."

I needed to leave before he did something terrible—like resting a hand on my shoulder; placing a thumb under my chin.

I slid into the driver's seat, did my best at smiling. "If you can't find Gage, he's hiding out around the corner of the deck."

I started the car and didn't look back. I had learned long ago that this was the only way to truly leave.

SINCE MIRROR HIGHWAY WAS a loop, there were technically two ways out of town. Going to the right would be faster, but turning left would take me by the scene of the salvaged car.

Sorry, Dad. It was human instinct. I wanted to see it too.

There was a slowdown before the curve, a line of cars steadily crawling forward, inch by inch. Most of the traffic seemed to be due to the line of emergency vehicles along the side of the road, and the fact that only one lane could move at a time. I could just make out a man in the distance, directing traffic past the site.

When I finally approached, I realized that it was Caden in the road, guiding us on. He was still in his khaki pants and light-blue polo. There was mud on the side of his pant leg, like he'd been pressed up against the car, checking inside. Curiosity, before crowd control.

I paused for a beat, like all the rest before me, taking in the scene beside the lake.

The guardrail had been removed and now lay curved and crooked against the trees.

The old vehicle rested at a slight angle on the side of the road, tires flattened, rubber disintegrating. I felt myself holding my breath, like I did whenever driving past a graveyard.

The car was coated in a layer of mud, like something alive, sliding off the surface, dripping onto the asphalt. I couldn't tell the color underneath anymore, but the body was boxy and long, like something a grandparent would drive. The windows were either down or broken, and the inside was piled high with mud and grime. The trunk had been pried open, and it remained that way, like the mouth of an animal.

Goose bumps rose across my arms, the back of my neck. The car seemed like it had become something else under the surface. Something more visceral. A part of the landscape, swallowed up by it, pulsating with the place it had just been.

Caden's face didn't change as he waved me past.

But when I glanced in the rearview mirror, he had turned in my direction, watching me drive away.

MY PHONE CHIMED ONCE I had exited the town, on the weaving road toward the main highway that would bring me back to Charlotte. I thought it was probably Keira or Luke—my business partners and closest friends—checking in, updating me on the day's progress. Making sure I was doing okay.

I peered down at the phone, and saw a message from my uncle: *Did you leave?*

I ignored it, but then my phone rang, the name ROY HOLT on the display. Since I'd left Mirror Lake, he'd rarely reached out. But in the years before, he'd sometimes step in for my father when work called him away.

I answered on speaker. "Hello?" I said. A question, more than a greeting.

At first his voice was choppy, as if he was still in a dead zone himself. "Hazel?" he said, like he'd just repeated himself. "Are you still here?"

"No, I'm on the road already. I have a project I have to check in on."

If he was calling with a lecture, I wasn't interested. Though he'd often seemed proud that I'd set off on my own—building a business, charting my own course— he'd always had a closer relationship with my brothers. *Caden left already too*, was what I wanted to say.

"I was hoping to catch you before you left." A beat of silence, as he searched for what to say next. "I'm the executor of the estate, Hazel," he said, voice low, as if he was trying to find someplace quiet to have this conversation.

It made sense, since he was the only lawyer in the family. He'd begun his career as a prosecutor—he and my dad used to tell stories of the old days, when the cases would pass directly from one Holt to the next. He'd since settled into family law, so of course my father would entrust this part to him. I braced myself for whatever he was about to say.

"Look," he began, voice even lower: "There's something in the will you should know about."